Guinevere's
Gamble

Nancy McKenzie

ALFRED A. KNOPF

NEW YORK

For Elizabeth

THIS IS A BORZOI BOOK PUBLISHED BY ALFRED A. KNOPF

Published in the United States by Alfred A. Knopf, an imprint of Random House Children's Books, a division of Random House, Inc., New York.

Knopf, Borzoi Books, and the colophon are registered trademarks of Random House, Inc.

Visit us on the Web! www.randomhouse.com/teens

Educators and librarians, for a variety of teaching tools, visit us at www.randomhouse.com/teachers

Library of Congress Cataloging-in-Publication Data
McKenzie, Nancy.
Guinevere's gamble / Nancy McKenzie. — 1st ed.
    p.   cm. (The Chrysalis Queen quartet ; bk. 2)
Summary: Thirteen-year-old Guinevere learns more about her destiny when she accompanies her aunt and uncle to an important council of Welsh kings and finds that she has a powerful enemy in the High King's sister Morgan.
ISBN 978-0-375-84346-4 (trade) — ISBN 978-0-375-94346-1 (lib. bdg.) — ISBN 978-0-375-85360-9 (e-book)
1. Guenevere, Queen (Legendary character)—Childhood and youth—Juvenile fiction. [1. Guenevere, Queen (Legendary character)—Childhood and youth—Fiction.   2. Fate and fatalism—Fiction.   3. Morgan le Fay (Legendary character)—Childhood and youth—Fiction.   4. Merlin (Legendary character)—Fiction.   5. Arthur, King—Fiction.   6. Great Britain—History—Anglo-Saxon period, 449–1066—Fiction.]   I. Title.
PZ7.M198632Gam 2009
[Fic]—dc22
2008050617

The text of this book is set in 12-point Goudy.

Printed in the United States of America

June 2009

10 9 8 7 6 5 4 3 2 1

First Edition

Contents

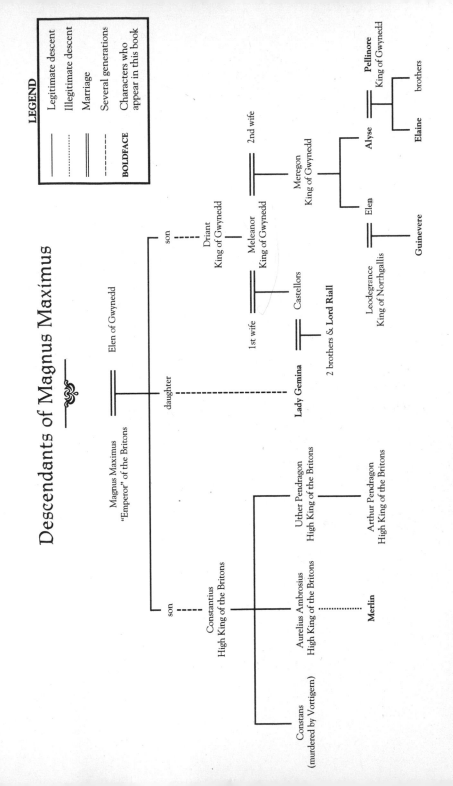

Descendants of Magnus Maximus

CHAPTER ONE

Royal Wedding

Guinevere stood at the narrow window and looked out on a bright September day. Grazing cattle dotted the fields and meadows beyond the orchard wall, and distant foothills rose dusty green to a cloudless sky. It was a warm day and still, with that special clarity of air that signaled the coming change of season. It was a perfect day for a ride.

A fresh bout of sobbing from the bed behind her made Guinevere turn around. Princess Elaine of Gwynedd lay prostrate across the fur-trimmed coverlet, her golden curls flung dramatically against the pillow, her entire body trembling with the violence of her grief.

"For pity's sake, Laine, you'll give yourself a headache."

The sobs increased in volume, and Guinevere turned back to the window. She had tried half the morning to comfort

Elaine, but Elaine did not wish to be comforted. She was determined to make the most of her sorrows. Guinevere was used to her cousin's weeping fits, as was the entire household, and usually had little patience with them. Today was different. This time Elaine's grief was unfeigned and her plight unenviable, for there was nothing on earth that could ease her distress. Arthur Pendragon, High King of the Britons, was married at last.

The event was hardly unexpected. Ever since the King's betrothal last spring, few in Gwynedd had talked of anything else. Highborn women throughout the land had spent the summer refurbishing their gowns and polishing their jewels. Queen Alyse and King Pellinore, Elaine's parents, had left three weeks ago to attend the royal wedding. Last night they had returned. And this morning Queen Alyse had gathered her household around her and told them all about it in exquisite detail.

Guinevere wondered if Elaine would have reacted less dramatically had Queen Alyse broken the news more gently. Only six months ago, before the news of his betrothal reached Gwynedd, the queen, too, had been dreaming of a marriage between Arthur and her daughter. But Queen Alyse was nothing if not practical, and unlike Elaine, she had accepted the fact of the marriage and could look beyond it. Her excitement was contagious. This was a wedding all Britons had waited four long years to see.

Since the High King Uther's death four years ago, young Arthur had led the Briton kings against the invading Saxon hordes. He had gathered around him the finest warriors in the land and built them into a formidable fighting force. Men flocked to serve him, and he found a use for every skill he was offered. In four years he had grown from youth to man, from cavalry commander to king. Arthur of Britain, they called him now, for the rival kingdoms of the Britons had begun to regard themselves as allies in a single cause, led by a single leader, in the service of a single nation.

Ever since his crowning, everyone had waited impatiently for Arthur to marry. It was the only subject more gossiped about than his victories. For four long years he had done nothing but fight, regroup, and fight again. His was a life lived in tents or on horseback, always on the move against the rising tide of Saxon invasions. Elaine's father, King Pellinore, was gone six to twelve weeks at a time to fight for Arthur and stood high in the King's graces on account of it, but at least he could come home to Gwynedd between campaigns. Arthur had no home to go to. His father's old castle in Winchester now lay too close to the Saxon border for safety, and until this summer there hadn't been time to start work on a proper fortress—a place to bring a wife to, a place to make a home. It was no surprise, really, that he hadn't married.

Now work had at last begun on the construction of a hilltop stronghold that the young High King could call his own. At the edge of the rolling hills of the Summer Country, and in sight of the Tor at Avalon, Caer Camel promised to be a fair fortress, a bulwark against the Saxon invaders, a center and a heart for the new Kingdom of the Britons. Arthur was no longer a youth of fourteen with only a splendid sword and his father's word to recommend him. He was eighteen now, a survivor of four years of constant war, an acknowledged commander and a force to be respected. The general feeling among the people was that it was high time for the King to wed.

Queen Alyse had spared no adjective in her praise of all she had seen at the royal wedding. She had held her women spellbound with her descriptions of Caerleon, the old Roman fortress town in the South Wales kingdom of Guent where the wedding had taken place. Set on a rise above a curve in the river Usk, the ruins of Roman occupation had become the focus of a small but growing town. Arthur, like a score of Briton kings before him, had patched up the barracks and rebuilt the walls. He had enlarged and refurbished the old commander's villa and made it his headquarters. With so many soldiers about, Caerleon had become a safe haven in the west country, and people came in droves to live within the safety of its walls.

Arthur had also built a Christian chapel on the site. Here, among a throng of rich and poor alike, and lit by the glow of a hundred candles, the Bishop of Caerleon had performed the rites so many Britons had waited so long to see. The crowd of guests had spilled out the chapel doors into the courtyard in a living stream of color, awash with the vibrant hues of expensive fabrics, the glitter of polished armor, the flash of jewels. Queen Alyse had counted six rubies larger than her own, but none that compared in quality to the bloodred stone in the ring of office on the High King's hand.

The bride had looked young for sixteen, the queen thought, and pale with the enormity of the event. But she had carried herself well when Cador, King of Cornwall, led her forward, and the sight of her had made the High King smile.

Arthur himself, adorned only with a slim crown of beaten gold around his brow and his magnificent sword at his hip, had dressed plainly in white. A diplomatic color, Queen Alyse implied, but one that allowed him to stand out in any crowd. It was the way he dressed for battle, the soldiers said.

The wedding feast had lasted until midnight, but the celebrations had gone on for days. Bonfires lit every village across the land. Queen Alyse had never seen so much free-flowing wine. In spite of such liberality, the High King, who was entitled to it, was never drunk. Nor were his Companions, that small cadre of young men who had first flocked to Arthur's side four years ago and had since become his friends as well as his battle captains. All of them maintained a sense of watchfulness, as if expecting a call to war at any moment. Which they might well receive, Queen Alyse allowed. All spring and summer, the barbarian Saxons had been attacking up the rivers and along the coasts. It was a minor miracle that the High King had found a space of peace in which to wed. And now, with the King married and his bride bedded, there was at least a hope of a succession of leaders as strong as Arthur and a hope of lasting peace.

Guinevere returned to Elaine's bedside and tried again to reason with her. "I know you've always admired him, Elaine, but you can't have expected to marry him. He—"

"Why not?" Elaine's head shot up and she glared at Guinevere with fierce, reddened eyes. "Why shouldn't I?"

"Well, after all, he's the High King. . . ."

"I'm not good enough; is that it?" Elaine's voice rose sharply. "Who else should Arthur Pendragon marry but the daughter of one of his chief nobles? Gwynedd is first among the Welsh kingdoms! Arthur depends on Father for influence in Wales, as well as for support in his campaigns. How many times in the last four years has Father gathered up his men and gone to answer Arthur's call? What king has done more?"

This time, Guinevere had the sense to stay silent.

"Look at the girl he wed!" Elaine stormed on. "Who is she? Guenwyvar of Ifray, for pity's sake, whom nobody's ever heard of. Her father was a minor lord who served the king of Cornwall. My father serves Arthur himself. Nobody knows who her mother was. My mother is a king's daughter and queen of Gwynedd in her own right. I outrank the girl, Gwen; even you must be able to see that."

"Of course," Guinevere said evenly. "But birth isn't everything, and she *is* sixteen."

Elaine sniffed. Her twelfth birthday was only three months behind her. "Twelve is old enough for betrothal, and thirteen for marriage. He could have waited another year. I'd have brought him more honor, more land, more power, more everything." She gulped as fresh tears spilled down her cheeks. "It's all happened too fast and too soon. He doesn't know I exist. He hasn't had time."

Privately, Guinevere agreed with her. King Pellinore had probably never mentioned his daughter to the High King while they'd been on campaign. It would not have occurred to him. On the other hand, it might have made little difference if he had. A man of eighteen looking for a bride who could give him an heir was unlikely to choose a girl of twelve. Five months ago, when the betrothal was announced, Elaine had been eleven.

Guinevere also thought, but did not say, that Arthur's bride was not a nobody. When the lord of Ifray had died in Cador of Cornwall's service, King Arthur's mother, Queen Ygraine, had, with Cador's blessing, taken the girl into her own household at Tintagel. Thus, Guenwyvar of Ifray had brought to the marriage the backing of both Arthur's mother and Cador, one of the High King's staunchest supporters and the man whose forces protected Tintagel. Guinevere could think of no stronger advocacy, except the High King's own. Perhaps the girl had had that, too. Arthur might have met her on visits to his mother. Perhaps he had chosen her himself.

"You should be glad for him, that he married a girl he knew," she ventured. "It must be awful to marry a stranger."

"Glad?" wailed Elaine. "Don't be a half-wit, Gwen. How can I be glad that he's married someone else?"

"Listen, Laine," Guinevere said, sitting down beside her and stroking damp curls away from her cousin's face. "You'd be glad for him if you really loved him. But you know you don't. How could you? You've never even seen him. You can't love a man you've never met."

"Can't I?" Elaine shook off her hand. "What do *you* know about love? You've never loved anyone but your horse and that primitive savage who follows you about—"

Guinevere rose to her feet. "Llyr is *not* a savage. He's as civilized as you are. Besides, I don't love him in the way you mean. He's a friend."

"Friend or not, he's an Old One. He's like no one else we know. He's certainly a far cry from Arthur."

Guinevere sighed wearily. "Enough about Arthur. You'll make yourself ill and over nothing. You have no idea what he's like."

"And you do?" Elaine's voice, hoarse with weeping, grew shrill. "You've always been against him. You scoff at his virtues. You belittle his prowess and jest at his victories. You do it to hurt me. I know you do."

"Oh, for heaven's sake." Guinevere turned sharply away and had to force herself to turn back. She took a deep breath and kept her voice calm. "I've never jested at his victories. He is without doubt the most successful war leader in a hundred years, since the Emperor Maximus himself. If I scoff, it's at the legends that cling to him and make him seem larger than life. You don't, you *can't* know what he's really like."

"But I do," Elaine protested. "I know everything about him—every legend, every tale, every prophecy. He's the greatest man alive. Look at all the astonishing things he's done."

"Firedrakes across the heavens? Pulling swords from stones? Bards' tales. Arthur is a war leader. He can organize men; he can lead armies; he can slay thousands. That makes him successful, but it doesn't make him the kind of man you'd want to marry."

"Of course it does," Elaine said fiercely. "A war leader as victorious as Arthur must be courageous and clearheaded, a man of intelligence, principle, strength, and skill. If he weren't, men like Father wouldn't follow him, and the Saxons would have killed him long ago."

Guinevere thought it equally likely that Arthur was simply more violent, more bloodthirsty, or luckier than other warriors, but she did not voice these doubts aloud. Instead, she merely said, "Kings like your father would follow anyone who could keep the Saxons off. I doubt it matters to fighting men what kind of person their leader is, so long as he wins."

"Nonsense!" Elaine snapped. "You ask Father about him. He admires King Arthur, and he actually knows him. You don't." She sniffed triumphantly when Guinevere did not reply. "Arthur is the greatest man of our age, and I am in love with him. Nothing you can say will ever alter that."

Guinevere went back to the window. The sky was deep blue and perfectly clear. It would be cool in the upper meadows. The grass would be fetlock-deep, and it was three days since she had given her filly a good gallop. "Then I pity you, cousin. I pity any girl who marries a man she sees only six weeks a year. Have you ever thought about what it would be like to be the High King's wife? He fights three, sometimes four campaigns a year. He's always on the move, always calling for more troops. The Saxons aren't going away. That poor girl in Caerleon left everyone she knew and the country she called home to come out of Cornwall and marry the King. She'll be sorry she did. She'll never see him."

"Sorry!" Elaine screamed. "*How do you dare?*"

A flung pillow caught Guinevere in the stomach. Elaine hurled another pillow, missed, and burst into wild sobs.

The door opened and footsteps hurried across the antechamber. Grannic, Elaine's nurse, came through the curtain at a run.

She shot Guinevere an evil look on her way to the bed. "What have you done to her?" At the bedside, she grasped Elaine forcibly in her large, strong hands and made little cooing noises. "Now, now, my lady, now, now. Come along. Come along."

Guinevere picked up the pillows and returned them to the bed. "I've been trying to comfort her."

Grannic grunted. "A sad job you've made of it. She'll be ill, she will, if this keeps on."

Another woman entered the room puffing, a plump woman with a kind, round face. Guinevere's eyes lit at the sight of her own nurse.

"Oh, Ailsa!"

"Gwen, dear, what's been going on?" She looked worriedly at the bed. "We could hear her from the workroom."

"She doesn't want to be comforted. She'd rather weep."

Ailsa cast her a knowing look. Elaine's weeping fits were a regular part of life in Gwynedd for both of them. The household routine would be disrupted for a day or more, with everyone's attention focused securely on Elaine.

Grannic scowled at them both. "Send for blankets and hot water. Be quick about it."

Ailsa pushed Guinevere ahead of her into the antechamber. "I'm sure to be busy here for the rest of the day. You'd best take yourself away somewhere until she's ready for company again. Why don't you go for a ride?"

Guinevere kissed her quickly. "You've read my mind."

"That's not hard these days." Ailsa chuckled as Guinevere flung open a trunk and reached for her tunic and leggings. "If you're not on that filly's back, you're trying to get there. Be home well before lamplighting. The queen wants both of you present at dinner. She has some sort of announcement to make."

"Do you know what it's about?"

Ailsa picked up the discarded gown and replaced it neatly in the open trunk. "A courier rode in a little while ago with a message for King Pellinore. I'll wager it has something to do with that."

Guinevere pulled on her doeskin boots. "I wish you luck with Elaine. She won't want to appear in hall with puffy eyes."

"She'll have to. We've strict orders to get her ready in time. Whatever upset her, do you know?"

Guinevere paused with her hand on the door latch. Ailsa, bless her dear and all-forgiving heart, could not keep secrets. It wasn't entirely her fault; the queen's women gossiped all day as they worked, and most of them were adept at prying information from unpolished souls like Ailsa. Elaine would not want her most private feelings made the focus of household gossip. Who would? On the other hand, Grannic and Ailsa might only make Elaine's suffering worse if they said the wrong thing.

"Try to pretend that the royal wedding never happened."

CHAPTER TWO

Stannic's Silver Coin

Elaine did not attend the feast. Despite their best efforts, Grannic and Ailsa could not coax her out of bed, much less make her presentable. Queen Alyse pursed her lips when she was told, but accepted the fact with a readiness that made Guinevere believe she had expected it all along. Grannic returned to her nursing, as did Ailsa, who knew better than to accompany her own charge to dinner when the queen's daughter was ill.

Guinevere found herself sitting between Cissa and Leonora, two of the queen's women, at the king's round table in the dining hall. Across the polished expanse of oak, Queen Alyse and King Pellinore sat side by side, with Marcus, captain of the house guard, standing at attention behind them.

Marcus winked at Guinevere as she took her seat. She flashed him a smile in return. Last spring, when King Pellinore had been away at the wars, she and Marcus had been thrown into an adventure together, and with Llyr's help had saved the kingdom of Gwynedd from a rebel's grasp. In her gratitude for his help, Queen Alyse had promoted Marcus to his present post.

The queen had shown her appreciation to her niece more subtly. No longer was Guinevere blamed for the consequences of Elaine's misbehavior. No longer was her excellence in the schoolroom ignored. No longer were the stables forbidden to her, or her riding restricted. She was more or less free to do as she pleased, provided she completed her lessons and her daily chores. For the first time since her arrival in Gwynedd five and a half years ago, Guinevere felt like one of the family.

It was a heady feeling, and she strove to be worthy of the queen's newborn respect. All summer she had tried to put duty before pleasure, to keep Elaine's love of mischief in check, and to work as hard at her lessons with the priest Father Martin as she did with the pagan tutor Iakos. Having recently been baptized a Christian, she had resolved to put the pagan gods of her childhood behind her. She was thirteen and on the verge of womanhood. It was time, she told herself, to put away old things.

A new face looked at her from across the table. In the place of honor at the king's right hand sat a fresh-faced young man with dark, unruly hair and a badge bearing the royal cipher pinned to the shoulder of his tunic. A King's messenger! This must be the courier who had come that day. Queen Alyse was paying him a compliment by inviting him to dine with the family. Usually, couriers were given supper in the kitchens and a wash, if they desired one; for, being always on the roads, they were always dirty.

This man was not dirty. He sat calmly in his place and looked about with interest. There was straightness in his carriage and directness in his gaze. When Queen Alyse spoke to him, her voice held no trace of condescension. When she introduced him, Guinevere understood why. This was no ordinary courier. This was Sir Gereint, one of King Arthur's Companions, come straight from Caerleon with a message from the High King himself. Guinevere knew by the flush of pride on the queen's cheeks that she appreciated the gesture. Arthur Pendragon had sent her no weedy youth with dusty hair and broken fingernails, but one of his own lieutenants, one of his own friends.

"Now, there's a likely young man if ever I saw one," Cissa said under the noise of general conversation. "Clean-shaven, too. What do you think of him, Nora?"

"Too young," Leonora returned. "He's barely twenty."

Cissa giggled. "I meant for Princess Elaine."

Leonora let her assessing gaze rest for a moment on the polite, self-assured countenance of Sir Gereint. "It's a pity the queen will never consider it. He might do the child a world of good."

Cissa nudged Guinevere's elbow. "You didn't hear that."

Guinevere smiled. "I never do."

"Wise child."

Throughout the meal, Guinevere glanced covertly at the only one of the High King's Companions she had ever seen. He wasn't tall and he wasn't particularly good-looking, but he had a dignity about him that commanded respect, and a gentle smile full of friendliness. She wondered how many battles he had fought and what kingdom he called home. Her pulse quickened. If he was one of the King's Companions, he must know the High King's master of horse, foremost of all the Companions—the knight with the foreign name who had bred and trained her filly. For Zephyr had come to Gwynedd straight from the High King's stables, a gift from Arthur to King Pellinore in recognition of his service on campaign, and from King Pellinore to Guinevere on her thirteenth birthday.

She looked up to find Sir Gereint's eyes on her. He was too far away for private speech, and there would be little chance to talk to him after the meal, for the men always lingered long after the women left. She would have to hope for some opportunity tomorrow.

"Well, well," Leonora murmured. "The King's Companion seems to have found something interesting at table. Keep your eyes down, girl."

Guinevere flushed and lowered her gaze. "I need to talk to him. I need to ask him a question. Do you think there will be time tonight?"

Leonora looked at her in mild surprise. "Of course not."

"If I asked Aunt Alyse to arrange it?"

Leonora coughed to cover her snort of laughter. "I should think that would make it downright impossible. If you wanted speech with him, you should have come downstairs earlier and talked to him while everyone was waiting to go into hall."

Guinevere bit her lip. She had been late coming in from her ride. She had missed that companionable gathering of the household every evening outside the closed doors of the great hall, where king, queen, family, courtiers, retainers, knights, and guests met to talk before going in to dinner. It was her own fault she had missed her chance to speak to Sir Gereint.

His eyes were still upon her when he turned to King Pellinore and asked a question. The deep rumble of the king's reply vibrated across the table. Guinevere caught the words *ward* and *Northgallis*. The queen's head turned sharply in her direction, and Guinevere, out of habit, lowered her eyes again to avoid that cold blue gaze.

"Storm clouds on the horizon," Cissa murmured into her winecup. "Take in sail."

When the meal was over, Queen Alyse rose and the hall quieted to hear her. King Arthur, she said, had called a council of all the Welsh kings to be held in three weeks' time in Deva, a village on the Rheged road just east of Wales. The High King was to escort his sister, Princess Morgan, north to marry King Urien of Rheged. He proposed to stop at Deva for a short time to allow the women time to rest and prepare for the final leg of their journey. While the women rested, the High King would help the kings of Wales work out a plan for their joint defense. The High King had cordially extended this invitation to include the wives and daughters of the Welsh kings in the hope that they might attend his royal sister during her stay. For this reason, Queen Alyse finished, she and King Pellinore would be taking Elaine and Guinevere with them when they left.

The hall resounded with cheering and applause. Shouts of "Arthur of Britain!" and "Long live King Pellinore!" rang out from every table. Sir Gereint looked pleased at this response and rose to thank everyone on his commander's behalf.

When Queen Alyse led the women out shortly afterward, she pulled Guinevere aside. "Well, Gwen, are you glad to be going on such a journey?"

"Oh, yes, Aunt Alyse. I've never seen the other side of the mountains. I've never been out of Wales."

The queen's smile was dry. "You have yourself to thank for the invitation. Until Sir Gereint saw you at table, he had no idea that Pellinore and I had young women in our care. It seems," she said, her voice growing hard, "that in all the years they've campaigned together, Pellinore never once told Arthur he had a daughter."

She turned away in an angry swirl of skirts, and Guinevere, instead of following the women to the queen's workroom to share a last cup of wine around the fire, hurried back upstairs. The bedchamber was in near darkness, with the window shuttered and a single candle burning. Ailsa and Grannic dozed in their chairs. Elaine, too, appeared to sleep. No sound came from the bed, and the mound of blankets did not move.

Guinevere tiptoed closer and knelt at the edge of the coverlet. With her face on a level with her cousin's, she touched Elaine's shoulder and whispered her name. A blue eye opened.

"Elaine, wake up and listen, for I have such news! Half your wish has been granted—we are going to see the High King!"

The blue eye gazed at her, unblinking. Slowly, Elaine raised herself on one elbow. Her lids and cheeks were puffed from weeping, her face dragged with weariness. Her voice was barely audible. "What did you say?"

Guinevere found her hand and squeezed it. "We are going on a journey, Laine. Across the mountains to the Rheged road to meet King Arthur. He's called King Pellinore to a conference, and we're going along to entertain his sister."

"Sister?" Elaine blinked. "What sister? When?"

"We leave in two weeks. You should have come down to dinner. The High King sent one of his Companions with the message. He sat at table with us."

"Really?" Elaine pushed herself to a sitting position. "What is he like?"

"He has excellent manners. He completely charmed your mother."

"He must have flattered her, then."

"I think it was Arthur who flattered her."

"Yes, of course, by sending her one of his Companions. I always said he was a clever man."

"It's a point in his favor that Sir Gereint is his friend. You must come to breakfast, Laine, and meet him."

"Try and stop me," Elaine laughed, throwing off her blankets and startling the nurses awake. She paused in mid-movement. "Or is this some extravagant ploy of Mother's to get me out of bed?"

Guinevere grinned. "Your mother's forgotten all about you. She's got a journey to plan."

"Thank God for that." Elaine jumped out of bed as Grannic came forward tentatively with a bowl of broth. "Take that tiresome soup away and get me some real food before the kitchens close. I'm hungry as a bear in springtime."

Early in the morning, before Elaine had begun to stir, Guinevere donned her tunic and leggings and hurried to the stables. There was time for a ride before breakfast if she was quick about it, and she knew there would be no time later. The rest of the day and all the coming days would be spent in frantic preparation for the journey.

She stepped into the close warmth of the stable and let its heady aroma surround her. All her life she had loved the smell of horses, hay, and oiled leather. To her, they were the scents of sanctuary.

Stannic the stablemaster greeted her with his customary cheerfulness. "Good morning, my lady. A misty morning for a ride, but it will clear. Today, for once, you're not the first one out."

Guinevere turned to him. He was holding a silver coin up to the stable lantern and squinting at it. With a sense of foreboding, she asked, "Who beat me to it?"

"The High King's man, the knight who rode in only yesterday. He has the horse for it, I'll give him that. Legs like iron bars."

"Sir Gereint is gone?" Guinevere could not keep the disappointment out of her voice, and Stannic turned to her.

"Rode out at dawn for Northgallis. And Dyfed and Powys to visit after that. Rode out on the best piece of horseflesh I've ever seen." He smiled at her expression. "Barring your filly, of course. What's the matter, lass? Did you want to see his stallion?"

Guinevere nodded. "Yes, but I wanted more to meet the knight. Elaine will be furious to have missed him."

Stannic thrust out his hand, with the silver coin lying in the middle of his palm. "Look at that. He gave it to me for taking such particular care of his horse. It's newly minted. Go on, take a good look. Hold it up to the light."

Guinevere did as he said and looked at the coin carefully.

The silver was new and shone like a polished gem. One side of the coin pictured a glowing sword; the other, a man's face in profile. It was a clean-shaven face, with a noble brow and a direct gaze that looked forward into the future. Around the edge of the face were engraved the words ARTURUS REX—KING OF THE BRITONS. Above the sword on the other side ran the phrase TO HIM UNCONQUERED.

"The first coin of a new realm," Stannic said proudly. "There'll be more, the knight said. Coins for Britons. Makes no sense to use Roman money now, does it? We're not Roman anymore."

"No indeed," Guinevere said thoughtfully. "It's a beautiful coin. It could unite us."

Stannic nodded. "That's what the knight said. A new coin for a new Kingdom of the Britons. They're minting them in copper and bronze, too. And maybe someday in gold."

Guinevere smiled at his enthusiasm. Stannic had been a warrior once. Now, like an old warhorse long put out to grass who still lifts his head at the call to battle, Stannic sensed change in the wind and longed to be part of it. Perhaps, Guinevere thought as she went to bridle her filly, Sir Gereint was bringing a larger message to the kingdoms of Wales: It was time to work together, despite border disputes and ancient rivalries, to achieve a greater good for all. It was time to unite against the pressure of invasion. It was time to form a nation.

CHAPTER THREE

Llyr's Dream

Llyr awoke as dawn broke across the meadows. He looked up at a soft pearl sky through the canopy of boughs above him and swung lightly from his hammock. Mist moved among the meadow grasses, gray-pink and tinged with light. Across the field, hardwoods crowded thick along the forest verge, looming like ghostly giants behind a veil of smoke. He pulled the stopper from his waterskin, poured a libation on the ground for the god of the place, and drank. It would not be long now.

He rinsed his face in a nearby stream to clear his head. Last night, he had dreamed of home—of rushing torrents born in the snow-clad heights; of steep paths, craggy peaks, and wise-eyed mountain goats; of Y Wyddfa, the Snow Mountain, where the gods walked. He had awakened in a sweat. Why had this dream come to him now, when he had lived two years among the Long Eyes and no longer suffered from homesickness?

In his dream, summer had gone from the mountain. He had pulled on his wolfskin cloak and begun to climb. The higher he went, the lower sank the clouds. Gray mists clogged his throat and breathed cold on the back of his neck. He stepped onto the old, familiar rock ledge and raised a hand in greeting. And stopped. The greeting ground was empty. Where the cave had been, he saw a solid wall of rock. Where the spring had been, he saw a giant fir blocking his way with spiky arms. Home had disappeared.

Llyr shook his head to clear his mind of the dream. It was not the normal sort of dream that a few moments of wakefulness dispelled. It was an omen, and he could not ignore it. But its meaning was not clear.

The sharp, staccato rap of hooves on the hard dirt of the ride brought his head up. Out of the mist and into the pale gold of early light came the dark gray filly with her dappled coat and the golden girl astride her. The last shreds of nightmare fled.

Llyr watched with leaping heart as they raced uphill the full length of the meadow, then circled back, slowing to a canter and traversing the width of the meadow again and again, back and forth, changing leads at every turn with a fluid grace delightful to observe. It looked almost like dancing. Horse and rider moved as one in a strange and beautiful rite.

The first time he had seen Guinevere ride, he had thought her possessed of magic. He could find no other explanation for the beauty of the sight, for the seamless unity between two such different beings. Now that he was learning how it was done—that it was a matter of communication between human and beast born of physical coordination and long practice, and not the casting of a spell—he admired the girl even more.

To him, it was still magic of a kind. The ability to speak to the horse through seat and legs and hands, and, once understood, to engage the animal's will, to harness his strength and speed for one's own purpose, not by force, but by securing the animal's willing cooperation—what could be more magical than that?

Guinevere reached the bottom of the meadow and turned the filly around, gathering her for another race uphill. He could see the horse's ears switch back to listen; the hind-quarters bunch, the forelegs dance in place, and the high neck curve as the filly fretted against a restraint he could not see. The girl barely moved. It was not her puny strength that kept the horse in place; it was her will. He saw her shoulders sink, and in that instant the filly exploded forward, hurling herself up the hill, the girl a mere gleam of gold clinging to the dark, whipping mane.

Llyr sighed. Many could ride, but few could ride like that. Never would he be one of them. In all his seventeen years, he had never been on a horse until last spring. He had hunted them, as the Old Ones always had, for their flesh, their skins, and the strong fibers of their manes and tails; for their hooves, their tendons, and the marrow of their bones. But he did not hunt them anymore. Now he had a pony of his own, named Thatch, living below in the valley in the king's own paddocks, right next to the king's own horses. More amazing still, for five unbelievable months Guinevere of Northgallis had been teaching him how to ride.

How much had changed in those five months! Last April, he had been living happily enough in the heights above the castle as foster son to Mapon, leader of the Long Eyes. His own father, leader of the White Foot of Snow Mountain, had charge of Mapon's son in exchange. Until last spring, the only thoughts in Llyr's head had been for hunting, pleasing Mapon, and treading lightly to avoid the notice of the One Who Hears. For a long time he had missed his family, his friends, and his dark-eyed Alia. But on the day he had first seen Guinevere, his life had changed. Nothing that had mattered to him before mattered to him after that. Meeting her had altered everything.

Since then, he had spent more time with the valley dwellers. His friendship with the girl had alarmed the Long Eyes, and they had punished him for it in the most grievous way possible: they had cast him out from the clan. But the punishment had not mattered. All that mattered was the girl's presence. Most of the Long Eyes had ridiculed him, accusing him of infatuation. The One Who Hears alone had understood. She knew, being a wisewoman, that Guinevere had changed the very composition of Llyr's world. Perhaps that was why she had appointed him the girl's guardian on behalf of all the Old Ones. What had been a joint effort among the clans for thirteen years was now a responsibility placed squarely on his own slim shoulders. Llyr no longer belonged to any clan. He belonged instead to the Goddess and to the girl he protected. His life's purpose was to keep her from harm until the great king who was her destiny came to take her away. Afterward . . . Afterward was something he did not think about.

Since he could not guard her and continue to live in the

hills among the Long Eyes, he had exchanged his pallet for a hammock and the cave for a canopy of leaves. Now he lived in the fertile lowlands among the valley dwellers, learning their customs, speaking their language, and trying to make sense of their violent and noisy society. He was making progress. Washing his face and hands on rising had already become a habit. He had a woven tunic now, and a fine pair of doeskin leggings, for the queen of Gwynedd objected to men clad only in skins and loincloths. He had made a friend of Marcus, captain of the house guard. He had met Queen Alyse and King Pellinore. He was learning the king's laws. He was learning to ride.

He watched horse and rider reach the top of the meadow and slow to a walk. The girl with hair of light dropped the reins across the filly's neck and for the first time took a good look about her. She saw him at once, which pleased him.

"Llyr!" She waved, and without a movement that he could see, without even touching the reins, she directed the filly across the field toward him.

He raised a hand in greeting. "Good morning, princess. Another beautiful day, I think." He spoke to her carefully in Welsh, proud of the new form of address he had learned only yesterday.

She slid off the filly's back and came forward to greet him. "A wonderful morning. And I have news, Llyr, very exciting news. Will you walk with me while I cool off Zephyr?"

He listened to the exuberance in her voice as she told him of the upcoming journey. She had taken only one journey in all her life: from the kingdom of Northgallis to the kingdom of Gwynedd when her father died. Then eight years old, she had traveled in a litter surrounded by guards. He doubted they would get her to ride in a litter now.

"It will be my first trip out of Wales," she said, turning to him with a wide smile and dancing dark blue eyes. "Our first stop will be at Caer Narfon. Riall, the lord of that place, is coming to Deva with us. We'll spend at least one night camped outside his walls. It's not far from Y Wyddfa, they say. You will be able to go home for a visit. You can see your family again."

His dream returned to him with sickening clarity. Again he saw the blocked path, the closed cave, and the empty greeting ground. If he went back, was this what he would find? Or was the dream simply a reminder that he no longer had a home?

"What's the matter, Llyr? Don't you want to go home? You'll see your father again, and your mother and sister and brother. Doesn't that please you?"

"Of course," he said, groping for a smile and failing to produce it. "I am very pleased."

"You don't look it."

"I am sorry. It is not completely true. I am pleased, yes, but also not pleased." He shrugged. "It is complicated."

They walked on in silence. Below, through a gap in the trees, Llyr could see the gray stone towers of the castle outlined against the sea beyond. It was an impressive building. He had been inside it twice and thought it a sensible dwelling, although far too large for the number of people it housed. It seemed to be as close as a valley dweller could come to living in a cave.

"Is it because of what happened last spring?"

Guinevere spoke hesitantly, and he appreciated her

reluctance. She had been part of a very private ceremony, held in a deep cave in the heights above the castle, which no valley dweller had ever before attended. She had sat in a circle with the elders of the Long Eyes while Mapon had summoned forth the One Who Hears. She had seen the clan's wisewoman call up a vision for all to see and give Llyr a new life. Guinevere had been part of it, but she was not one of the Old Ones, and she had no way of knowing all the ramifications of that gift.

"Yes," he said at last. "It is because of what happened last spring."

"There is something I have wanted to ask you," she said slowly, "but it is none of my business and it is . . . well, very personal."

"You may ask."

She glanced at him swiftly and looked away. "I wondered . . . do the other Old Ones, like the Red Ears of Northgallis and the White Foot of Snow Mountain, know what the One Who Hears has done?"

Llyr's mouth tightened. "News travels faster than wind among Earth's Beloved. Everyone knows."

"Then your father knows."

"Yes."

"He will be proud of you, won't he, for such an honor? I mean, even if you can't take your rightful place as his first-born son?"

Llyr sucked in his breath. This was another difference between his own people and the Others, as Earth's Beloved called the valley dwellers. The Others used language so much that they had lost the gift of divination. Among his own people, the question would not have been asked. The answer would have been already known.

Guinevere's hand touched his. "Forgive me. It was impertinent to ask. Will you come down to the castle with me? There's time for a ride along the beach before breakfast."

The filly's back was warm and alive under his seat. He wished that he could ride his pony without a saddle or pad, as Guinevere did her mare; it was a wonderful feeling. Or perhaps the wonderful feeling came from the nearness of her person, from his arms about her waist and his cheek against her long, pale hair. He shut his eyes for a moment and wished he were one of the Others—the prince of her destiny, perhaps, who could hold her in his arms forever.

He bit his lip. He could still hear the voices of the Long Eyes accusing him of falling in love with She With Hair of Light. He had thought the charge unjustified when it was made, but now he understood it. It must be true, for at the thought of another man's arms around her, a rage possessed him—a rage against his destiny and hers, a rage against the prophecy made at her birth. For the first time, he understood her struggle to deny that prophecy, her refusal to believe in its truth. For the first time, he wanted to join her in that fight.

"Gwenhwyfar," he whispered, pressing his lips against her flowing hair and falling back into the language of the Old Ones, which she did not understand. "It is too late. I am lost. That is what the dream meant."

CHAPTER FOUR

Caer Narfon

"I hope you know," Elaine said tartly, "that you're making an utter fool of yourself."

It was the morning of departure, and the courtyard bustled with last-minute activity. Unable to sleep the night before, Elaine and Guinevere had taken their places early and now had to wait for everyone else. Only half the guards had arrived. The wagons, which had been loaded during the night to save time, were now unpacked and reloaded, over and over, with items that could not be left behind. None of the rest of the family had yet come out of the castle. Servants ran hither and yon with no concern for anything but haste. Marcus shouted orders, horses stamped, men grumbled, and Guinevere had her hands full keeping the excited filly under control.

"It's all the bustle," she said breathlessly as the filly danced about in little circles. "She's not used to it. She'll be better once we're on the road."

"I'm not talking about the horse." Elaine's voice was sharp. "You look perfectly ridiculous, Gwen. People will take you for my brother. Did you even bring a gown?"

Guinevere ignored the question. Elaine knew exactly what Ailsa and Grannic had packed in the girls' trunk, which was more than two-thirds full of Elaine's clothes. But the remark about being taken for a boy stung. At twelve, Elaine had already developed a figure; at thirteen, Guinevere had not. She had grown taller by leaps and bounds—she was nearly as tall as Queen Alyse—but her body still showed no sign of any change. Since she was not interested in suitors, she lost no sleep over their absence, but the lack of a figure had begun to bother her unreasonably whenever Elaine brought the subject up.

"Your father gave me permission to ride," she countered, having brought the filly to a momentary halt. "*He* doesn't think it's ridiculous."

Elaine sniffed. "He always gives you whatever you want. And he's the last one to understand how it looks. Mother's furious. If I have to ride in her litter, I won't forgive you, Gwen. Be sensible just this once. You'll make us the jest of all Wales."

Zephyr shied as a servant darted by, and Guinevere struggled to keep the filly from wheeling. She knew why Queen Alyse was angry. King Pellinore had granted Guinevere permission to ride her filly to Deva and back without first consulting his wife. Aghast at the prospect of her niece and ward appearing before the High King clad in boots and leggings, never mind bareback astride a horse—a horse, moreover, that Arthur had given to Pellinore only five months ago and no doubt expected him to keep as a broodmare—the queen had argued long and hard against it. Highborn ladies rode in litters. To do else was to live beneath one's rank; to invite malicious comment, endless gossip, scorn, and ridicule.

King Pellinore often lost these battles of will, but this time he stood firm. In his estimation, no one cared two pins what happened in the royal family of Gwynedd; he had never heard a breath of gossip. Gossip about what, he should like to know. Moreover, he had seen Guinevere ride, which Alyse had not, and if she thought the girl was going to come off the horse and land in a ditch somewhere, she should think again. That child rode better than most of his men.

Not caring to admit that her foremost concern had not been for Guinevere's safety, Queen Alyse lifted her chin and sniffed. She finally relented when King Pellinore assured her that the High King, far from being disappointed, would be delighted to see what use had been made of his gift.

The queen might have lost the battle, but she won a final skirmish: Guinevere was permitted to ride her filly only if she used a saddle. It was bad enough, the queen said acidly, that the king and queen of Gwynedd would be thought eccentric guardians by every soul they met, but she refused to be thought negligent as well.

The saddle was part of the problem now. Zephyr hated it, even after two weeks of practice. She wanted the instant communication she was used to from her rider's seat and legs, not the rub of saddle and pad or the cinch around her belly. The horse was frightened by her own confusion, and the excitement of the crowded courtyard made her skittish. It was all Guinevere could do to keep her still for a dozen heartbeats.

"I'm sorry to be the cause of your mother's temper, but you know I loathe litters. And the ride will do Zephyr good. Besides, there's more room for the rest of you without me. Ride with Ailsa and Grannic, and leave your mother to her women. Her mood will improve once we're under way."

"It's not that." Elaine shrugged unhappily. "We'll be meeting important people, Gwen. The way you're dressed—like any stable lad—you'll ruin my chances."

"Chances for what?"

"For making a good impression. For not disgracing us all."

"Tell them it doesn't run in the family."

"That's not what I mean."

"For heaven's sake, Elaine." Guinevere leaned down across the filly's withers. "I won't embarrass you in front of King Arthur, if that's what you're afraid of. I promise it. He shall never see me astride a horse. He shall never see me at all, if I can help it."

Elaine looked up, her sky-blue eyes wide with gratitude and relief. "Really? Do you swear it?"

"On my honor."

Elaine brightened and, turning to climb into the nurses' litter, flashed Guinevere a smile. "In that case, it doesn't matter to me what anyone thinks of you."

The filly spun on her haunches as a tremor went through the crowd. The castle doors opened, and at last the king and queen appeared. Immediately, the chaos of the court-yard resolved itself into an orderly pattern of readiness. The king's groom came forward with his stallion, the queen led her women into the litters, the standard-bearers raised the banners of Gwynedd, the gates opened, the horn sounded, and the escort began to move. Zephyr's ears pricked forward, and Guinevere sighed in relief. At long last, the journey had begun.

At a trot, it was less than half a day's ride to Caer Narfon, but with wagons and litters it took until sunset. The port town, so close to Mona, the Druid's Isle, lay along the northwest coast of Gwynedd. The fertile lands behind it ran up into the foothills of Y Wyddfa, the Snow Mountain, the highest mountain in Wales.

King Pellinore's party came over the last rise above Lord Riall's stronghold as the westering sun blazed on the horizon. Torches flared beside the stronghold gates. A horn blew notice of their approach as the gates swung open to receive them. The procession passed into a courtyard paved in stone. Guinevere brought the now obedient filly to a halt beside Elaine's litter and looked anxiously about for Llyr.

She had not seen him all day. She knew he had come on the journey, for he had taken his pony from the paddock that morning. Since then, however, he seemed to have disappeared. It was just like him to evade notice and fade into the background. He preferred the forest paths to the open roads and, like all the Old Ones, had the gift of invisibility in a wood. She wished he would make an appearance before the gates shut for the night. She wanted to find out when he was going to visit his family and beg him to take her along. She scanned every face in the courtyard, but Llyr's was not among them.

King Pellinore dismounted as two people came forward from a torchlit entranceway. Elaine poked her head out from between the litter curtains, ignoring Grannic's efforts to pull her back. "Who's that?"

The taller of the two was a sharp-faced man of about thirty with thin reddish hair and a straggling mustache and beard. On his arm leaned a small, aging woman in antique garb whose gilded linen scarf hid the gray of her hair and the wrinkles about her throat. As they approached, moving stiffly, she surveyed the newcomers with fierce, unwelcoming eyes.

"Lord Riall and his mother, I think," Guinevere whispered. "Or his grandmother."

"Lady Gemina," Elaine breathed. "So that's her. Mother told me her great-great-grandfather was a Roman governor somewhere in the south, and she thinks she's someone important on account of it."

"For heaven's sake, keep your voice down. She'll hear you."

Guinevere slid off the filly's back and helped Elaine from the litter. Ahead of them, Queen Alyse went forward on King Pellinore's arm to greet their hosts. Cissa and Leonora followed, six paces behind.

Elaine shook out her gown and patted her hair in place.

"She tried to take Mother's crown, you know, years and years ago. Drove her husband, Mother's uncle, to his grave trying to make him king of Gwynedd. *And* two of her sons. They're all dead now."

"And Lord Riall?"

"The third son. The youngest. Mother's hoping Lady Gemina has finally decided to keep him at home and make him tend to his obligations."

"Does he fight for King Arthur with Pellinore?"

"No. He's never gone on campaign. Mother says that's what makes his request to accompany us to Deva so puzzling."

Guinevere gazed ahead at the regal form of Queen Alyse silhouetted against the torchlight. She did not look puzzled. She stood at King Pellinore's side, tall and elegant, her hair glinting gold in the flickering light and her head held confidently high.

Lord Riall gave both king and queen a gracious bow and words of welcome, but Lady Gemina barely bent her knee. The rigidity of her upright posture and the arrogant angle of her chin held no hint of fealty. Lord Riall shot his mother a meaning look, and with a charming smile invited his royal guests into his stronghold. Lady Gemina bent her head a mere fraction. Queen Alyse brushed past her, trailing the dirtied edge of her traveling cloak across the toes of Lady Gemina's antique slippers.

Elaine grinned. "The fat's in the fire now."

"My wager's on your mother."

The girls and their nurses followed the king and queen

into Lord Riall's stronghold, where they were duly introduced and led away to the rooms prepared for them. Elaine and Guinevere were given a set of spacious rooms with carved beds, pallets stuffed with down, and soft woolen blankets.

"Better quarters than ours at home," Elaine observed. "A silver bowl for washing, a pitcher of Samian ware, a triple-flamed lamp, and applewood in the brazier. No expense spared."

"So Lady Gemina has impressed you." Guinevere pushed open the window shutters and peered out. The view faced northeast, toward the rising ground and the famous silver mines of Y Wyddfa. Beyond the stronghold walls, she could see the king's men setting up horse lines, raising tents, lighting cooking fires, and preparing for night. She saw no sign of Llyr or his pony.

"I wonder what ancient family treasures she's put in Mother's chamber." Elaine stepped out of her traveling gown as Grannic lifted a fresh one from the trunk. "They're probably all gold and as old as Rome itself."

"Where is the postern gate, did you notice?"

Elaine looked up in surprise. "Why? Are you going some-where?"

Ailsa hurried forward with Guinevere's second-best gown held carefully across her arms. "You've no need of the postern gate, my lady. Close the shutters now, and let's get off those boots and leggings. We don't want to insult our hosts by being late for dinner."

Guinevere sighed. Whenever Ailsa called her "my lady," it

meant she saw trouble ahead and was anxious to avoid it. Reluctantly, Guinevere pulled the shutters closed and began to undress.

"Don't worry, Ailsa," she said under her breath. "I won't go far. I only want to find Llyr."

Elaine examined the embroidered belt Grannic had chosen to match her gown and tossed it aside. "I want the silver one. Didn't you bring the silver one? Look harder. It must be there."

"Llyr can take care of himself," Ailsa whispered. "The gates are shut for the night. I heard Lord Riall give the order. Please, Gwen, don't risk it."

Guinevere glanced worriedly at the shuttered window. Perhaps Ailsa was right. There would be too much attention paid to them tonight, and if she was caught, Queen Alyse would never let her live down the disgrace. Tomorrow, in the lengthy bustle of leaving, it would be easier to slip off unnoticed and find Llyr. But she would have to be up early. If he was going to visit his family on Snow Mountain, he would start at dawn.

"Very well," she agreed as Ailsa pulled the gown down over her head. "I'll go at first light. But you and Elaine will have to cover for me at breakfast."

It was still dark when Guinevere slipped unnoticed out the postern gate. Long years of practice with Elaine had made her expert at soundlessly lifting latches and sneaking past guards.

The gate gave onto a steep-sided gulley leading north along the edge of a rise. She followed the gully until she was out of sight of the guards, then circled east around the horse lines. The cooking fires were banked for the night, and no one was about except for the posted guards. They were easy to find and evade. They were all men she knew.

She found Zephyr easily enough and led her into the thin woodland behind the camp. Leaping onto the filly's back, she headed through the trees and rode east toward the mountains. As the sky began to lighten, she found the rutted track leading north to the silver mines. She followed the track deeper into the foothills, stopping only to let Zephyr drink from a mountain stream.

There was a dell here to one side of the track, a little open space carpeted in pine needles. Guinevere slid from the filly's back and prodded at the pine needles with a twig. Her heart leaped as she uncovered the hidden remains of a small fire. The earth was still warm to the touch.

An Old One had been here last night. Llyr himself had taught her how to search for the signs. The discovery of a few rope fibers caught in the bark of a maple tree and a set of pony prints, partially brushed over, near the edge of the stream convinced her that the Old One was Llyr. This was where Llyr had spent the night—in the foothills of Snow Mountain, not with King Pellinore's men. That meant he had decided to go home.

She had expected as much, but the fact that he had taken steps to go without her gave her pause. She did not want to barge into his reunion with his family without his permission.

She decided she would follow his tracks for a little while longer. The Old Ones would learn of her presence on the mountain long before she saw any signs of them, and the message would be passed along. If Llyr accepted her coming, sooner or later one of the Old Ones would show himself and lead her to him.

Guinevere remounted the filly and followed the pony tracks upstream.

CHAPTER FIVE

Y Wyddfa

Llyr climbed steadily up the mountain, following the main approach to the cave to make his intentions clear. He knew he was watched, although he never saw the watchers. He knew he had been watched all the way.

Last evening, he had ridden into the foothills of Y Wyddfa as soon as the gates of Caer Narfon had closed. With Guinevere safe inside and under guard, he had gone straight into the hills. He knew the paths, and he knew the place he sought.

When he reached the clearing on the western slope, he made an offering at the shrine in the oak tree above the spring, threw down some fodder for the pony, and slung his hammock between two maple trees. His snares yielded a rabbit, which he skinned and cooked over a small fire. By morning, word of his coming would spread throughout the clan. He had announced his presence in the traditional way by honoring the god of the spring, and in the modern way by lighting a fire. He had given the White Foot plenty of time to decide if and how they would receive him.

He rose at dawn, muzzy-headed after a fitful sleep, and knelt to drink from the spring. Rinsing his face and hands in the cool, limpid water cleared his head. Feeling airy, light, and purified for action, he covered the traces of fire and footprints and led the pony uphill. In a greenwood where grass grew in patches between the trees, he hobbled the animal as Guinevere had taught him and left him to graze.

Now he paused on an outcrop of rock and looked back the way he had come. Mists rose from the valley floor. Smoke from the breakfast fires of Caer Narfon drifted toward him on the sea breeze. A hawk floated gracefully above. No matter where he looked, everything was familiar to him and as welcome as the pure mountain air he breathed.

He had been gone only two years, but in that time his life had changed completely. Since he had last seen his family, he had suffered a great disgrace and received an undeserved but overwhelming honor. Nothing, not even home, would ever be the same again.

He still did not know what he would say to his father or to Alia. Returning to the past was impossible, and the White Foot, his own people, no longer figured in his future. What could he be to them, or they to him, but a memory? Or a nuisance. Would they think him foolish for coming back? Would they allow him past the greeting ground? Would Alia see past his mask of impassivity and discern the secret he had himself only just discovered?

A shadow touched him, and he looked up to see a speckled hawk slide by in perfect silence overhead. The sight of the great bird made him smile. He had always been at home in the heights, where the air was light and clear and eagles soared beneath his feet. He preferred the open spaces of the heights to the closed-in leafiness of the valley forests, even though the rock was jagged and the way of going never straight. It saddened him to think that he would never again live on the slopes of Y Wyddfa, but his future lay among the valley folk. He might be able to come back and visit from time to time, if they let him. . . .

Soon he would know. In the space of a dozen heartbeats he would round the last rocky outcrop and descend into a little corrie made green by its ancient spring. There, before the wide mouth of a cave, on a long, flat ledge the White Foot called the greeting ground, the judgment for or against him would be made. If the clan had decided to welcome him, he would find them waiting on the ledge. If the ledge was empty . . . Llyr swallowed, nauseated by the thought. Some disgraces could not be forgiven by Earth's Beloved. Still, whether he was rejected or received, he had been given a mission that transcended clanship. When it came to his destiny, the opinion of the White Foot did not really matter, except to him. Armored by this thought, he shut his mind against fear and went forward.

A wall of people met him on the greeting ground. His

father, Bran, was foremost, holding the leader's staff. Llyr came to a halt before him and bent his head in greeting.

"Bran of the White Foot, greetings. Llyr begs entrance."

For a moment there was no reaction from the rigid figure before him. The entire crowd of people he had grown up with and had known all his life stared at him voraciously, as they might at a stranger of whom they had heard fabulous tales . . . or an outcast condemned to be thrown off a cliff to his death.

"Which Llyr begs entrance?" In the silence, Bran's quiet voice reached every ear. "Llyr of the White Foot? Llyr of the Long Eyes? Or Llyr of Gwynedd?"

Llyr held his father's eyes. "None of those. It is Llyr who asks. Simply Llyr."

Whispers ran through the crowd, and the stiff lines around Bran's mouth relaxed. He bent his head.

"Greetings, Llyr. Welcome."

As if the leader's words were the signal they had waited for, the people called out to Llyr and pushed closer to give him their personal greetings. Eventually, he was led into the cave and given the place of honor beside his father around the communal cooking fire. The clan elders, who formed the rest of the traditional circle, gave him the choicest morsels to break his fast and milk still warm from the goat. No one bothered him with questions. No one mentioned his great disgrace or his undeserved honor. For the moment, they expressed nothing but pleasure at having him back among them.

His mother hovered behind him, touching his shoulder, caressing his hair, as if she could not quite believe her eyes.

Lydd and Leatha, his little brother and sister, stared at him from the edges of the standing throng beyond the seated circle. They were not the children he remembered. Leatha, almost nine, had discarded her child's wrap for a long tunic of soft goatskin bound with a braided thong. A necklace of shells encircled her throat in the style of the older girls. Lydd, now eleven, had grown a handspan taller. Soon he would be ready for the rites of manhood. Llyr did not think it possible he could have changed as much as they had.

After the public greeting and the meal, he was taken to his family's chamber deeper within the cave, where the real talking, if there was to be any, would take place. Mats had already been set out on the cold stone floor and, without thinking, Llyr started forward to take his accustomed place, the firstborn's place, next to his father. He stopped abruptly. Lydd had also come forward, and to the same place. The boy, uncertain, lifted his face to Llyr's. Llyr stepped back at once, color rising to his cheeks. How could he have forgotten? He had no place here now; he did not belong to the White Foot anymore. It was a knowledge his family had lived with, for Lydd had approached the seat with the assurance of the firstborn—as now he was.

Llyr swallowed. From the moment the Long Eyes had cast him out, he had ceased to exist as a member of any clan. In the eyes of Earth's Beloved, that act had robbed him of any chance to follow in his father's footsteps. He had known, in a general way, that Lydd would take his place in the family and among the White Foot. It was the custom whenever an eldest son died. But it shook him to see it.

Bran, at his elbow, gestured to the guest mat, and Llyr sat down. Kinsmen filed in through the curtained opening and stood lined up against the walls. Llyr's throat tightened. They were not treating him as the outcast he was. They were treating him as an honored guest.

Hope rose in his breast, and he braced himself against it. He had to remember that, although they knew of the prophecy made at her birth, they had never seen the girl they called She With Hair of Light. He hoped they never would. To prevent that very thing, he had kept out of her sight during the journey so that she could not ask permission to come with him. He had hurried into the hills as soon as she was safely inside the stronghold. He had erased his tracks to make it difficult for her to follow. He was afraid that if they saw her, the White Foot, like the Long Eyes, would understand all too well why he did not deserve the honor he had been given. For which among them would not doubt the motives of her guardian once they had seen the girl he guarded?

Two more people came into the chamber, and Llyr's heart began to thud. Brith and Enna were not kinsmen. They were Alia's parents. He held his breath as Alia herself followed Enna inside. For a moment, her great dark eyes met his. Llyr looked away. He could not help himself.

Bran made a short speech of welcome on behalf of all the kinsmen. He asked after Llyr's health and the health of the Long Eyes. Llyr responded formally and with equal courtesy. Bran plied him with questions about his life during the past year, especially about his degree of acquaintance with the king and queen of Gwynedd. This was not yet dangerous ground, and Llyr answered calmly. He understood their curiosity about the ways of the Others, who farmed the river valleys, built ships to sail the seas, raised horses instead of hunting them, and delighted in the killing of men.

Llyr did his best to satisfy their curiosity. They stared at him as he spoke, their eyes examining him from head to foot. His hair, unlike theirs, was cut to shoulder length and evenly trimmed. He was not dressed, as they were, in skins and furs. He wore a tunic of dyed wool woven on a loom in the queen's workroom, and beautifully stitched lightweight doeskin leggings. Guinevere herself had made his soft leather boots. He must look as strange to them as the king of Gwynedd himself.

Next it was the kinsmen's turn to ask him questions. Some, like Bran, were interested in the current political situation among the Others. They wanted to know which kings were friendly with the king of Gwynedd and which were not. Llyr told them what he knew, which was not much, but assured them he would soon find out. King Pellinore and his party were traveling east to attend a conference of kings, and the friendships and feuds between them would soon become common knowledge.

Some were more curious about how the Others lived and wanted details of daily life inside a castle. Of this, Llyr could tell them little, for he did not live on castle grounds. When he told them about the tending and guarding of the king's cattle and sheep, the Old Ones nodded in approval. When he described the stables and horse paddocks, they shook their heads and smiled. But when he revealed that King

Pellinore had given him a pony of his own and that he could ride it anywhere he chose, they stared at him in astonishment.

Lydd wanted to know if it was true that the Others raised hawks from the egg and taught them to fly on command. Llyr described how the king's falconer rescued injured birds or fledglings pushed from the nest and trained them to hunt. Likewise, the king had a stablemaster to look after his horses and a kennelmaster to raise and train his hunting dogs.

"But why don't you live on the castle grounds?" asked Leatha, who wanted to know about the women's gowns and slippers and ornaments, and whether it was true they wore colored ribbons in their hair.

Without pausing to think, Llyr replied, "I don't live in the castle because with distance comes perspective, and it is impossible to guard without perspective. Stay too close and you do not see the threat until it is upon you."

Too late, Llyr realized he had broached the subject he wanted most to avoid. He glanced quickly at Alia. Her face was stiff with the effort of control, but the fear in her eyes gave her away. Llyr paled. He had never before seen Alia frightened.

"So," Bran said quietly. "We come to She With Hair of Light. Tell us about her."

Llyr dropped his eyes to his lap but did not speak.

"You saved her life, we heard."

"Before that, she saved mine."

His father nodded. "She is your friend?"

The question hung in the air. Llyr could feel Alia's eyes on his face and strove to keep his expression neutral. "Yes."

A stocky young man standing just behind Bran said, "She saved the Long Eyes from attack, we heard."

Llyr recognized Bilis, son of Mapon, leader of the Long Eyes, who served as Bran's foster son, just as he himself had been Mapon's foster son until last spring. He bowed politely to the young man. "That is so. She With Hair of Light is very brave."

"And very strange-looking," someone else put in.

"And very tall," another added. "Especially for a female." The abnormal size of the Others was, to Earth's Beloved, one of the most fearsome things about them.

Llyr almost smiled. "To us she may seem so. It is a matter of perspective."

It did not bother Llyr that Guinevere was his own height and growing taller. It would not bother him when she outgrew him. What he admired about her was difficult to put into words, but it had nothing to do with her height, or even her appearance. It was something so grand and all-encompassing that it altered the very air he breathed. Being with her was like stepping into a new world or a new skin. He no longer cared how he lived his life, provided he could share some part of it with her.

"She is different," his father agreed. "It is said that one day she will outshine all the Others. In their eyes, at least."

"She must be very beautiful." It was Alia who spoke. She

waited, standing straight as a spear with her hands locked into fists, braced for his reply.

Llyr took a deep breath and tried to keep his voice normal. "That also is a matter of perspective," he croaked.

Alia paled. No one spoke. All eyes turned to her, as if this were a confrontation long expected. Tears brightened the girl's eyes. She faced him for a breathless moment, then turned and fled.

The curtain of skins parted to let her pass as a boy darted into the chamber. He pushed forward to the seated circle and signaled to Bran, his eyes wide with excitement.

"Mador sends a message, sir."

"Tell me."

"She With Hair of Light is on the mountain." He looked around at the wide-eyed kinsmen. "She found the spring, but took the wrong turning in the wood. She is headed toward the shrine at the crossroads. Mador wants to know what to do."

CHAPTER SIX

The Crossroads

Guinevere brought the filly to a halt where two paths crossed in a piney wood. She looked carefully about her for landmarks. She was sure they had come to this crossroads twice before. They seemed to have been traveling in circles for hours.

Unable to see the sky for the leaves overhead, she could not judge how long she had been lost. She did not like to think what would happen if she was not back by the time Queen Alyse looked for her. She might be made to ride in a litter, or worse, be sent home in disgrace. She had counted on the king's party taking half the morning to get ready, as they had at home. They might take even longer today, with Sir Riall's escort and baggage to be organized and added to the train. She had been sure that, in the resulting bustle, she would not be missed.

But now, as she looked about the wood for the third time, deep misgivings assailed her. The morning was advancing. Queen Alyse was difficult to fool and liked to keep a close check on the girls. Both Ailsa and Elaine had promised to cover for her, but Queen Alyse could always tell when Elaine was dodging the truth, and Ailsa had been caught before fibbing on Guinevere's behalf. Last night it had been easy to dismiss these doubts. Now they hovered like vultures, pressing closer with every step farther into the forest. If the queen had discovered her absence, there would be search parties out even now. If the search party should stumble across the White Foot—something she herself had been singularly unable to do— Llyr would find it hard to forgive her.

Her anxiety transmitted itself to Zephyr, who began to fidget and paw the ground. Guinevere patted the filly's neck to calm her. There was no point in envisioning disasters. She must concentrate on finding her way to the White Foot, or on getting off the mountain and back to the stronghold. It was foolish, frustrating, and an utter waste of time to be lost in a wood.

Zephyr's ears shot forward as a long cry pierced the air. A rhythmic, breaking wail came through the trees ahead. Guinevere touched the horse with her heels and chose a path.

Pine needles covered the forest floor and silenced their approach, so that they came unawares upon the wounded creature whose wail of despair had drawn them. A girl lay prostrate on the mossy ground in the center of an open space beside a mountain stream. A tangle of black hair hid her face. Nearby, an old standing stone, gray-green with lichen, cast its blurred shadow across her shaking body.

Guinevere slid off the filly and went toward her. She moved almost silently, but the girl heard her and whipped around, fast as a snake, to crouch beside the standing stone. A small, bright-pointed knife slipped into her hand. Her breath came in rasping gulps, tears slid down her muddy face, and her dark eyes glinted with malice. She crouched there, a half-feral creature, torn between fear and aggression, at the edge of desperation.

Guinevere stopped and opened her hands, palms outward, to show she carried no weapon. The effect of this on the other girl surprised her. The dark eyes widened into an incredulous stare. The knife slid to the ground. The girl straightened. Even at her full height, the top of her head came only to Guinevere's chin. Her small face, stretched for a moment in awe, now twisted in fury. She pointed a finger at Guinevere and cried out, her voice rising and falling in a rough but deliberate cadence. The words were unintelligible, but Guinevere did not doubt their meaning. She was being roundly cursed in the ancient tongue of the Old Ones.

She shivered. She had been raised in the pagan kingdom of Northgallis for the first eight years of her life, and the subsequent five years of Christian training in Gwynedd had not assuaged the ancient dread of curses. She struggled to ignore the sound and raised a hand in greeting.

"I mean you no harm," she said in Mountain Welsh. "I come in peace."

At last she had found one of the Old Ones. The girl was dressed in ill-cut animal skins, primitive ornaments, and soft leather slippers, very like Llyr's, that left no tracks on the forest floor. Llyr knew Mountain Welsh, a polyglot language—a mixture of Old Welsh and the tongue of Earth's Beloved. If this girl was an Old One, she might speak it, too.

The girl stopped her chanting and stared at Guinevere with unconcealed malevolence.

Guinevere tried again. "My name is—"

"I—know—your—name." The girl spat out the words. "She—With—Hair—of—Light."

Guinevere sighed. It was what the Old Ones called her, for reasons of their own, but it was not her name. "Gwenhwyfar," she said carefully, using Llyr's pronunciation. "My name is Gwenhwyfar. I come in peace."

The girl glared at her, defiant and unconvinced. "Where you go," she said in perfectly fluent Mountain Welsh, "there is no peace."

Guinevere stiffened. She had given the stranger the gift of her name and received only hostility in return, an insult by anyone's standards. "If that is true, it is not of my willing. I mean you no harm. I'm lost and in need of your help."

She knew from Llyr that the Old Ones were a hospitable people who, despite their aloofness from her own race of men, would not deny a direct plea for help. But this fierce girl might be the exception. She did not look at all sympathetic. Guinevere waited, keeping her expression neutral and her hands open at her sides.

"You are on Snow Mountain without permission."

"I beg forgiveness. I came to find a friend."

There was a long pause. "What friend?"

Guinevere found herself almost unwilling to tell her. "Llyr, son of Bran, leader of the White Foot of Snow Mountain."

The small face paled under its overlay of mud and tears. The girl said in a frozen voice, "You will not find him."

Guinevere shrugged. "I know. I lost my way, and now it's too late."

"The Goddess barred your path."

"Very likely." Guinevere drew a deep breath. "Could you take Llyr a message from me?"

The girl seemed to struggle against speech. Her face flushed pink. After a long and strained silence, she thrust her knife into the knotted cord around her waist and strode away.

"Wait! Oh, please wait!" Guinevere cried, but the girl ignored her. At the edge of the stream, she knelt and began to splash water over her face and hands.

Guinevere leaned against Zephyr for support. She trembled for fear the girl might vanish into the woods. This strange person, who appeared to despise her, was her only link to the White Foot. She must do nothing to anger her or frighten her into running away. Not that the girl would run away from fear—she was as fierce as a wildcat and every bit as wary.

Her ablutions finished, the girl rose and returned to the standing stone. She had a pretty, heart-shaped face and large, dark eyes brimming with suspicion. She touched the stone and raised her chin in an attitude of defiance. "What is the message?"

Guinevere exhaled in relief. She was going to help. Yet it was clear she did not want to. Despite the ingrained hospitality of her people, malice flowed from her like a blast of cold wind. Her posture was stiff, her speech clipped, and her furious eyes almost impossible to meet.

"Please tell Llyr that I am sorry I tried to follow him up the mountain. It was wrong of me to think I might be welcome. Tell him that King Pellinore's party will be leaving soon. It is time to come down. And if he . . . doesn't want to see me, I will wait for him at Deva."

There was no response from the girl. Guinevere stepped away from the filly and said, in a neutral voice, "Do you know Llyr? Are you a member of the White Foot clan yourself?"

It was as good as asking outright for her name. Again, the girl refused to answer. She looked as if she had reached the limit of what she could endure. But why should she need to endure anything? What had Guinevere done to make her so angry?

Between one heartbeat and the next, she knew. It was She With Hair of Light who had made the girl angry, not Guinevere of Northgallis. After that first fleeting moment of incredulity, She With Hair of Light had been taken for an enemy. Why should that be, when all the other Old Ones Guinevere had ever met respected, even revered, this personage they had invented? Guinevere could think of only one reason: She With Hair of Light had been indirectly responsible for Llyr's being cast out from the Long Eyes clan and, as a consequence, from all of Earth's Beloved. Because She With Hair of Light needed guarding—a need evident only to Earth's Beloved—a wisewoman among the Long Eyes had solved both problems at one stroke by appointing Llyr as her guardian. It had never before occurred to Guinevere that someone who loved Llyr might resent that. Such a person might hold She With Hair of Light responsible for cutting Llyr off from his family and friends, for stealing him away from his intended path of life. If this hot-tempered girl had been part of that intended path, her animosity was easy to understand.

Guinevere came farther into the clearing and stopped beside the standing stone. "Please don't believe what they say about me. I am not really She With Hair of Light. Not inside, anyway. I am an ordinary person. There is no need to be afraid."

The girl bristled instantly. "I am not afraid of you."

"Good. Then I will try not to be afraid of you."

The dark eyes narrowed. "You are jesting."

Guinevere swallowed. "I am not."

"What could you fear?"

The words came out in a whisper: "The future."

"*You?* But you know your future! It was prophesied for you."

Guinevere gazed at her helplessly. She could not deny it. On the night of her birth, a hill witch had told her father, King Leodegrance, that his laboring wife would bear a daughter destined to become the highest lady in the land. She would wed a great king and come to glory with him. Her name would be remembered beyond a thousand years. "I would give anything to avoid it," she said.

The girl's mouth fell open, and she shut it with a snap. "Then you are a coward and a fool."

"Why? Is it a fate you envy? I would change places with you in a heartbeat, if I could."

The girl made a sign with her fingers as she thrust her hand behind her back. Guinevere's heart sank. She knew that sign. In Northgallis, villagers had used it to ward off monsters, to defend against the unnatural, the grotesque.

The girl said in a shaking voice, "That cannot be true."

"Why not? Do you think I like having everyone expect wonders of me? How can I do what is impossible?"

"You are She—"

"Stop saying that! I am not that person. I have no magic arts. I live in Gwynedd on the sufferance of my aunt, Queen Alyse. I have no claim to land or power, nor any influence over those who have. I have no wealth, no prospects, no ambition—I have nothing to recommend me to this great king of yours. I have not the slightest chance of even attracting the notice of such a man. And yet—and yet"—her voice quavered—"that is what everyone who has ever heard that wretched prophecy expects of me."

"You—you don't believe the prophecy?" the girl whispered, paling.

Guinevere shuddered. "No. How could I? No single mortal could fulfill all those expectations. I've always believed the hill witch who made that prophecy came down to my father's castle to cadge a place by the fire. She told him exactly what he wished to hear."

The girl looked scandalized. "But the prophecy is true! It *must* be true! We have been taught—we have been taught since we were children that it is the marriage of She With

Hair of Light to the great king of her destiny that will save Earth's Beloved from annihilation by the Others."

She chanted the words as if she had known them by heart for years. Guinevere stared, frozen in horror at the enormity of such an expectation.

"Keeping you safe," the girl finished breathlessly, "is our only chance for survival."

Guinevere fought back panic. Here it was again, the nightmare terror she lived with: the hope of rescue, salvation, invincibility, and now *survival* for an entire race of people had been unfairly placed by some malignant power upon her own narrow shoulders. She seemed to be the only one who knew she was incapable of carrying such a burden.

She realized she was shaking and that she could not control it. "How can any one person do that? I can't. You must see that *I can't.*"

"But you *must!*"

"How?" Guinevere cried, flinging out her arms in desperation. *"How?"*

The girl backed a pace, frightened now at the new and terrible possibility that had arisen. "I—I don't know."

"Well, I don't know, either."

There was a long silence as each girl looked at the other. Even the birds were still. Finally, the Old One spoke.

"It is necessary to try."

With a shaking hand, Guinevere wiped her eyes. "I know. I know. Even though I don't believe the prophecy, I am bound by it. I am bound by everyone else's expectation. *That* is my fate. Do you envy it now?"

". . . No."

Guinevere turned to take up Zephyr's reins, but stopped at the touch on her arm.

"Stay," the girl said slowly. "Perhaps I have misjudged you." She gazed into Guinevere's face. "You are no coward. You accept sacrifice."

Guinevere tried to smile. "I understand why you dislike me. It's Llyr, isn't it? In your place, I would feel the same."

The girl did not smile back. "You couldn't. You don't love him."

Guinevere drew breath sharply. She reined in her first impulse to deny the accusation. It was true. She loved Llyr as she loved Elaine, as a friend and companion, but she remained a stranger to the kind of painful passion that burned behind the girl's dark eyes.

"Not as you do, perhaps," she admitted. "We are friends."

"Thank you," the girl said, and at last her expression softened, almost to a smile. She raised her hand in greeting. "This ill-mannered person is Alia, daughter of Enna of the White Foot. I beg forgiveness for my anger. . . . For so long I have wanted to hate you—have been determined to hate you. And you do not allow it."

Guinevere flushed. "I'm sure I can't prevent you. But I am glad to meet you, Alia. Thank you for sharing your name."

"I beg forgiveness for my rudeness. I should have given it to you before. But I did not want to trust you." Alia smiled bitterly. "It is still difficult."

"I mean you no harm."

Alia shrugged. "Even so, harm is done."

Guinevere frowned, not sure she understood. She made a guess. "Llyr will not be my guardian forever. One day he will return to the White Foot."

Alia laughed, a bitter sound. "It's too late for that."

"It can't be. The White Foot are his people. Snow Mountain is the only home he has."

"His place among us belongs to his brother now."

This news startled Guinevere, and she was loath to believe it, but it did explain Llyr's reluctance to visit his family and his refusal—by evasion—to take her with him. He had not been sure of his reception.

"Do you mean he would not be welcomed back?"

"To visit, yes, but not to stay. Our home is not his home any longer. And even if he could stay, he wouldn't want to."

Guinevere gaped at her. "Whyever not?"

Alia regarded her critically. "You must know. And if you do not, it is time you opened your eyes."

Guinevere paused. Alia sensed a danger to Llyr that she did not, and try as she might, she could not imagine what it was. "Does he have a rival among the White Foot? Someone who would become an enemy if he stayed?"

There was a long pause. "How old are you, Gwenhwyfar?"

"Thirteen. Why?"

"Thirteen." Alia sighed. "Forgive me, I thought you were older. My ignorance of the Others leads me into many mistakes."

"Why does my age matter?"

"I thought you were being devious or playing with me. I

see now that Llyr has behaved himself and that you have not been trying to deceive me."

Guinevere looked at her in utter astonishment, and Alia, with a wide smile free of condescension, reached out and took her hand.

"You are the reason Llyr will never return to the White Foot," she said simply. "It is best to acknowledge it. For both of us. You have his heart."

Color rose from Guinevere's throat to engulf her face. Alia squeezed her fingers. "Part of you knew already, no?"

Guinevere shook her head. "No."

"I can understand now what happened to him. I could not before. So I am glad that I met you."

"I don't see . . . What happened to him?"

Alia gazed at her until Guinevere lowered her eyes. "He met you and his world changed. The Long Eyes saw it and cast him out. The One Who Hears saw it and put it to use. All this time I have thought him ill-treated by the Long Eyes, but now I see that no one, not even Llyr, had any choice. It was the prophecy at work."

At that, Guinevere's chin lifted. "I don't believe in the prophecy."

Alia shrugged. "Nevertheless."

"We are friends, Alia," Guinevere repeated, but her voice sounded hollow even to her own ears, like a reed when the wind blows through it.

"Yes," Alia agreed. "And you are bound by the prophecy to someone else. Even so, Llyr will not come back." She squeezed

Guinevere's hand again and let it go. "So someday I will have to become a wanderer myself."

Tears filled Guinevere's eyes. "And leave your people? That is a sacrifice indeed."

Alia's lips trembled. "The gods love sacrifice, my mother says. And besides, one day you, too, will have to leave home for a foreign land." She stepped back and pointed down the path by which Guinevere had come. "Go left at the crossroads until you reach the pine tree by the stream. Take the downhill path to the mines. There's a road from there to the meadows behind the town." She paused. "Llyr is with his family now, but I will take him your message."

"Thank you, Alia."

Alia raised her hand in the gesture of farewell. "Light with thee walk, my sister."

Guinevere returned the gesture and gave the response she had learned from Llyr. "My sister, dark from thee flee."

Alia turned, stepped back into the shadow of the standing stone, and faded silently into the forest.

CHAPTER SEVEN

A Matter of Perspective

Llyr hurried downhill after Bran, his heart racing and his thoughts spinning wildly. She With Hair of Light on the mountain! She had succeeded in escaping the stronghold and following his traces. The knowledge pleased him as much as it annoyed him. She had remembered the skills he had taught her and, like any teacher, he was proud of her success. On the other hand, she should have known from the distance he had kept between them on the journey that he was not yet ready for his people to meet her.

His father must have sensed this reluctance, for he had made the excited kinsmen stay behind when the lookout brought the news. Everyone had wanted to see her, but Bran had refused to let them follow. Thankful as he was for his father's discretion, Llyr prayed silently that Guinevere might be gone by the time they reached the shrine.

He wondered what had drawn her to that particular place. It was far from the path she should have taken. He had only been to the crossroads once himself, for his manhood rites. The clearing, the stream, and the shrine were sacred to the Good Goddess, Mother of men, whose gifts were fertility, fecundity, birth, and life. The clan's women tended the shrine until they were past the age of bearing. Virgins who had reached the age of bearing, Llyr knew from Alia, went there often to pray for the attentions of the young men they admired.

Llyr knew that Guinevere would not seek the place, especially if she knew what it was, so the Goddess Herself must have led her there. The thought unsettled him. The girl was not ready for her future, and neither was he. He found himself praying to the Goddess to keep that future from her for years to come.

Bran stopped so suddenly that Llyr almost careened into him. "Listen."

Llyr trembled. He recognized the voices.

Bran moved silently across the carpet of pine needles to stand in the shadow of a great tree at the edge of the clearing. He made no attempt to hide himself, which would anger the Goddess, but the two girls in the clearing were so focused on each other that neither of them saw him. Llyr did not follow his father forward. He could not. His legs shook, and his feet were rooted to the earth.

At last the voices stopped. Alia spoke her farewell and

retreated from the clearing. She saw Bran almost at once. Making the sign of acknowledgment to the leader, she went to stand beside him. All three of them watched as Guinevere leaped onto her filly and went back the way she had come. When there was no trace left of her presence but a shimmering of sunlight in the air, Llyr began to breathe again.

Alia turned and saw him. Llyr stiffened.

"It's all right," she said to him in the voice usually reserved for endearments. "I've forgiven you."

Bran still stared at the place where She With Hair of Light had been. There was no expression at all on his face.

Alia bowed her head as she addressed him. "I beg the leader's pardon for running away. I was afraid, and I was ashamed that I could not hide my fear from the elders. Or from Llyr. I came to ask the Goddess to thwart Llyr's fate. In answer, She sent me She With Hair of Light."

Bran turned to her. His eyes asked the question.

Alia nodded. "She is the one. She thinks herself a lowly and powerless person, but she is not. She *must* be guarded, and by someone who understands. That is why Llyr was chosen."

Llyr's mouth fell open.

"*You* say so?" Bran asked. "You, who have cause to resent her?"

"She sacrifices herself to a future she dreads," said Alia. "That is enough for me."

"Even," Bran said quietly, "if it means that you must do the same?"

Alia faced him, trembling. "Even so."

Llyr cleared his throat with difficulty. "Alia . . ."

"Follow her," she said quickly, giving him no time to consider. "It is time to go. She asked me to apologize to you for following you onto the mountain. I make this apology now on her behalf."

"Alia . . ."

"It is time for you to go, for the king is leaving. If you do not wish to see her, she will wait for you at Deva."

If he did not wish to see her!

"Go with my blessing." Alia's voice faltered as her eyes grew bright. "Light with thee walk."

She turned on her heel and left him before he could reply.

Both men watched her disappear back up the hill. Bran put a hand on his son's shoulder and looked into his eyes. "Do you understand?"

Llyr shook his head.

"Alia has been touched by the hand of the Goddess. She sees what you do not: that your love for She With Hair of Light, which shines from you like the clear light from a new torch, and which you are so eager to hide from everyone, is necessary to your guardianship."

Llyr could not believe his ears.

Bran sighed. "You were chosen because you love her. Because you will, without thinking, guard her with your life. The One Who Hears was wise."

"I thought," Llyr whispered, "that you would not approve of my guardianship if you saw her."

Bran almost smiled. "You told us it was a matter of perspective. Let us say that now that I have seen her, I understand your point of view. You are lucky that the Goddess has given Alia perspective as well."

"Luckier than I deserve," Llyr mumbled.

"As you say. Now listen to Alia the Wise and go."

"But Mother, the elders, the cave—I have not said farewell."

"I will take them your farewell. Do as Alia says. Find your little horse and get off the mountain. It is time to go."

Llyr bowed his head. "Farewell, then, Father. Light with thee walk."

Bran nodded stiffly to hide his emotion. "Dark from thee always flee, my son."

CHAPTER EIGHT

Deva

Merlin the Enchanter stood alone at the edge of a wood on a low rise above the Deva road. He stood perfectly still, with less movement than the shadow of the oak beside him. People thought him old for a man of forty, for his skin was seamed like leather and his beard was flecked with gray. But it was also said that in forty years he had lived an old man's term. Nothing of importance had happened to the Britons in the last forty years without Merlin's help.

Born in the days of Vortigern the Wolf, Merlin as a boy had seen his country at its worst. Vortigern was a brutal man who had come to power by murdering the rightful King, the boy Constans, thereby earning the contempt of his people. After inviting the Saxons in to swell his forces, Vortigern found he had no power to control them. In a bid to save his

Kingship, he wed a Saxon queen and sealed his fate. For in the intervening years, the younger brothers of the murdered King had fled to Less Britain, grown to manhood, and raised an army poised for invasion. The elder of the brothers, Aurelius Ambrosius, proved to be a gifted commander. When he and his forces landed on British soil, loyal Britons everywhere flocked to him, and together they destroyed Vortigern and beat back his Saxon allies.

No one knew how much of this Merlin had seen firsthand. He grew up in Dyfed, a small seagirt kingdom in South Wales, where his mother was said to be a king's daughter and his father a demon of the night. All his life this superstition clung to him, and he was everywhere regarded as no man's child and a wizard of profound power.

While still a youth, he had crossed the Narrow Sea to Less Britain and offered service to Ambrosius. He returned to his homeland with Ambrosius's invading army and stayed at the great commander's side until his death. In the space of two years, Merlin saw Vortigern killed, two Saxon hosts defeated, and Ambrosius crowned High King of the Britons. Five years later, when Ambrosius died, Merlin had him buried in the center of the great henge called the Giants' Dance, whose fallen stones he had raised by magic arts to honor the great commander.

Afterward, Merlin served Uther Pendragon, the younger of Constans's brothers. As political advisor, he helped King Uther keep the kingdoms in rough alliance for fifteen years. By this time, his powers of foreseeing and mastery of the magic arts had won him widespread acclaim throughout the land. Yet his finest achievement had yet to be accomplished. For it was Merlin the Enchanter who had brought Arthur into being.

All Britons knew the tale. At Uther's crowning, with all his nobles in attendance, the new High King had developed a violent passion for Ygraine, the young wife of Gorlois, the old king of Cornwall, his most powerful ally. And Ygraine, a girl of twenty on her first trip out of Cornwall, had responded to his attentions like a flower awakening to the sun. Although she shunned his advances like a proper wife and spoke not a word to him alone, Uther saw the truth of her passion in her eyes. The fragile alliance of kingdoms that Ambrosius had so carefully stitched together seemed ready to split apart. On Merlin's advice, Uther had curbed his desires and permitted Gorlois and his wife to return to Cornwall at the end of the festivities. But after a week spent in an agony of body and spirit, Uther stormed after him.

While the High King's forces faced the king's on a Cornish battlefield, Merlin changed Uther by magic arts into the very likeness of Gorlois, and helped him sneak into the fortress of Tintagel to lie undetected with the waiting Ygraine and beget Arthur. For this had always been Merlin's goal: to bring into being Arthur Pendragon, the man the gods had chosen to stem the Saxon tide and bind the kingdoms of the Britons into a single, lasting Kingdom of Britain.

For this he had sacrificed everything else dear to him. He had worked, fought, and schemed with a dedicated ruthlessness to fulfill the prophecy of Arthur's coming, to raise the boy away from court, to give him the kind of education he would need to be the King the prophecies foretold.

It had not been easy. People agreed it was enough to age

any man. Yet Merlin's powers—spiritual, intellectual, political, and magical—remained undiminished. Rumor and speculation continued to follow him wherever he went, and superstition hugged him like a robe. Most men feared him, and even the very few who knew him regarded him with awe. In all the world, only one man loved him.

On this hot afternoon in early October, Merlin the Enchanter turned his fathomless eyes on the faint cloud of dust in the distance, the telltale "road smoke" that betokened the presence of men and horses. The jingle and scuff of a rider behind him alerted him to the approach of Sir Bedwyr of Brydwell, and he waited without moving while the knight dismounted and came up, light-footed, to his side. For a moment they stood in silence together, watching.

"There can't be any danger," Sir Bedwyr suggested, glancing at the enchanter's face in the futile hope of reading something there. "Pellinore's an ally."

Merlin did not reply. He kept his gaze on the dust cloud and his thoughts on what it might contain.

"He has Lord Riall with him, of course," Sir Bedwyr murmured. "That's probably why they're late. But Riall's nothing to worry about, is he, my lord? He's little more than his mother's pawn."

Receiving no reply, Sir Bedwyr glanced back down the hill to where he had left his men. His lieutenant signaled that it was time to move if they were to greet the approaching travelers. Sir Bedwyr acknowledged the signal and turned again to Merlin. The man was so still, the air around him seemed to tremble.

"If Riall's no threat, who else could be?" Again there was

no response. Sir Bedwyr frowned. If there was no threat at all in King Pellinore's party, why had Merlin the Enchanter come alone to this hilltop to wait for the first sight of them?

"My lord," he pressed, "I'm the commander. I need to know if there is danger coming."

Not a leaf moved. The air hung heavy and breathless around the stillness of the man. Sir Bedwyr backed off a pace, hairs rising on the back of his neck as a sense of foreboding struck him. "Sir," he breathed. "I must have an answer. Is there an enemy among them?"

The dust cloud grew larger. Light flashed from speartips held aloft. Banners began to show their colors through the smoke. Merlin's black eyes bored into the dust, picking up the gleam of helmets, bearded faces, sweating horses, and a train of men, wagons, and litters. He focused on the foremost litter and caught a gleam of gold, a whiff of scent, and the whisper of women's voices—

"Please, my lord!" Sir Bedwyr touched his sleeve. "I must go down to greet them. Tell me what you see. Is there danger there or not?"

At the touch, the vision shattered, turning the world into a visual maelstrom and thrusting the enchanter back against the oak tree. He gasped once and held his hands to his temples to contain the agony.

Sir Bedwyr fell to one knee. "A thousand pardons, my lord. But I need to know *now*."

Merlin's lids closed over blinded eyes. It was a moment before he could speak.

"There is no danger yet."

"Then why——?"

The enchanter drew a long, shuddering breath. "There is someone in the party I wish to see."

"Tell me who, my lord, and I'll have him escorted to your tent as soon as you've recovered. Surely, there is no need for . . . this." Sir Bedwyr gestured helplessly at the bent body, rigid with pain.

Very slowly, Merlin straightened, withdrew his hands from his head, and looked at Sir Bedwyr with clouded eyes. His lips twisted. "Let me be the judge of need." He gestured toward the road. "Go. Make them welcome. You have nothing to fear from them."

Sir Bedwyr knew better than to ask more questions. He thanked the enchanter for the information and hurried back to his horse. If Merlin said there was no danger, there was no danger, and he could reassure the escort. But if Merlin said there was no danger *yet*, that meant that danger was sure to come. This did not worry Sir Bedwyr overmuch. Considering the work Arthur and his Companions were about, it was no very difficult prediction.

But as he returned downhill to his men, Sir Bedwyr was seized by a new and acute interest in the arrival of King Pellinore's party. Whom among them, he wondered, did the most powerful enchanter alive risk such agony to see?

Guinevere breathed in a mouthful of dust and coughed. Elaine poked her head out between the litter's curtains. "What is it, Gwen? Is he there? Can you see him?"

Guinevere coughed again. "Not yet. There's a group of men ahead, on horseback. They're probably a greeting party."

"Look for a bay mare," Elaine urged. "Father said the High King rides a bay mare when he's not at war."

"I'll look. I promise."

Elaine retreated behind the curtains, and Guinevere waved dust away from her face. A formation of men and horses blocked the road. The leader, astride a flashy chestnut stallion, raised his hand in greeting. The procession lurched to a halt. King Pellinore rode forward amid his standard-bearers as the dust began to settle.

"Well?" Elaine looked out anxiously. "What's happening now?"

"They're greeting your father. There's no bay mare. The knight who leads them wears the same device as the others. A red dragon, I think, on a field of gold. The High King's badge. But no one is wearing a crown."

Elaine's face fell in disappointment, then brightened. "The High King has sent his second-in-command to greet us, that's all. Of course he would. He's waiting until we've had a chance to settle in before he formally receives us. That gives me time to change into a fresh gown and wash this dust off." She grinned up at Guinevere. "You, too."

Guinevere looked down at the film of dust on her tunic. She could feel the fine grit on her skin, even taste it in her mouth. It would take a month of combing to get it all out of her hair. Zephyr shook her head and sneezed. Dust flew from her mane and set Guinevere coughing again. She hoped that

Elaine was right and that they would get the chance to wash before they met anyone Queen Alyse thought important.

She was not in the queen's good graces at the moment. Yesterday, the queen had been magnanimously silent after Guinevere's return to Caer Narfon only moments before the party was ready to set off. To Llyr, who had returned soon afterward, she had nodded a frosty acknowledgment that kept him at a distance. Guinevere had expected chastisement, which she knew she deserved, but Queen Alyse said nothing. This was so unlike her, it made Guinevere wonder for a passing moment if the queen was ill. But there was no way to know. Once the procession started moving, the curtains of the queen's litter closed and she disappeared from view.

Llyr took his place in the procession as if he had been there all along. When they camped last night in the eastern foothills, he stayed within sight and slung his hammock in a nearby wood. Although she hadn't had a chance to speak with him yet—which, in light of Alia's revelations, she was growing reluctant to do—she knew that once they got to Deva, he would be there when she looked for him. His avoidance of her had come to an end on Y Wyddfa.

The procession began to move again. Peering ahead, Guinevere saw the knight on the chestnut stallion riding at King Pellinore's side, pointing out the way. His men stationed themselves along the sides of the road, saluting the newcomers as they passed by. Guinevere straightened and collected the filly into a dignified walk, but she could not keep from staring at the escort's horses. These were not the crossbred animals King

Pellinore kept in his stables—part mountain pony, part plow horse. These were creatures of speed and spirit, long-legged and swift, with fine, dry faces and widely spaced, intelligent eyes.

She shivered in excitement. They looked like Zephyr. They must be the High King's horses, as Zephyr had once been. She had never seen another horse that looked like Zephyr, and here were twenty of them, each with that wise eye and innate dignity of carriage that made her own filly so dear to her. Had they all been raised and trained by the High King's master of horse, that knight with the foreign name she could never remember? She decided to seek out the rider of the chestnut stallion at some convenient time and ask him. Perhaps he would agree to take her message of thanks back to Caerleon and the foreign knight himself.

Up ahead, the trees fell back from the roadside and the procession turned into a wide field. Guinevere could see dozens of tents staked out in clusters, with one large tent—surely four or five tents strung together—in the center. Horse lines had been set out at the edges of the field, and beyond, a sinuous line of gold-green willows marked the course of a river. She could see no signs of a town. All she could see was tents and people emerging from them to stare at the long train of newcomers.

As King Pellinore's party passed into the field to their appointed place, Guinevere saw the knight on the chestnut stallion waiting to one side, watching them ride in. He sat the big horse with ease, although the animal was restive, while he carefully examined the new arrivals. Without knowing why, Guinevere tightened her grip on the filly's reins. Zephyr danced a little, but settled down again once they had ridden by. The knight's searching gaze slid past her, and Guinevere relaxed. She had promised Elaine that King Arthur should never see her in boots and leggings, and here she was, riding within feet of his second-in-command. But he hadn't noticed her. She grimaced to herself. He had probably taken her for a boy under all this dust. Everyone always did.

King Pellinore's party was given a place of honor near the big tent in the center of the field. It took the king's men until dusk to set up the four Gwynedd tents: one for the king and his servants, one for the queen and her women, one for the girls and their nurses, and the last for the men themselves. The horse lines were set out behind the tents, not far from the edge of the woods. Guards were posted around the perimeter of the cluster, and the banner of Gwynedd, a gray wolf on a field of blue, fluttered in the evening breeze above the entrance to King Pellinore's tent.

As soon as their own tent was ready, Ailsa and Grannic shooed the girls away and began the laborious process of turning the makeshift dwelling into an acceptable living space for the two or three weeks of their projected stay. Elaine tiptoed away to get as close as she dared to the High King's tent, and Guinevere took Zephyr to the horse lines. She groomed the filly, removing the hated saddle and rubbing her coat to a smooth sheen. The horse was tired from the long day's journey and content to be among the animals she knew. When the king's grooms came by with armfuls of hay and skins of water hauled from the river, Guinevere gave her a last affectionate pat and headed into the woods to look for Llyr.

CHAPTER NINE

Trevor of Powys

Llyr sat on the low limb of a beech tree and waited for her. He knew she would look for him after she had seen to her horse. She would want to collect his pony, Thatch, and put him with the king's horses, where he could be better fed and tended. To that end, he had hobbled the pony and left him to graze in a green patch not far from the beech. But she would also want to talk about her visit to Y Wyddfa, and he could no longer avoid her.

Llyr did not understand the urgent need of the Others to talk about everything all the time. His own race of men spoke only when necessary, for they were fluent in the language of posture and stance, expression and gesture, indicating by swift, subtle, and silent means most of what needed to be known. But the Others—Llyr shook his head at the wonder of it—the Others seemed blind and dumb when it came to body language. They used words, floods of words, for everything. Only when they were hunting did they keep their voices down and communicate by gesture—large, obvious pointings and wavings that no alert prey could fail to miss. It was thanks to the speed of their horses, the power of their weapons, and the strength of their nets that they captured anything at all.

Not for the first time, Llyr wondered if his growing association with the Others was making him more like them. In some ways it already had, but even though he was learning their language, he doubted very much that he could ever accustom himself to using it as they did. This made it doubly difficult to sit and wait for Guinevere. He knew she would have questions to ask him—questions about Alia—that he did not want to answer.

He still could not believe that the two girls had met and talked. Whatever they had said to each other had changed Alia forever. Soon he would know if it had changed Guinevere, too.

She came toward him through the trees, her pale hair clearly visible in the fading light. He slid to the ground and waited.

"There you are," she said. "I've been looking for you. I've . . . I've come for Thatch. There's a place for him in the horse lines next to Zephyr."

He nodded. She did not come up to him as she usually did, but stopped ten paces away and lowered her eyes.

"I . . . I know you went home to see your family. Did they receive you? Did they honor you as you deserve?"

There was an unaccustomed shyness in her voice that Llyr found mystifying. He nodded. "More than I deserve."

"And your father?"

"He approves."

She looked up and smiled. "I am so glad." She gestured to the woods around them. "Are you—are you going to stay here?"

"Sometimes here. Sometimes there." He pointed to the woods across the field. "There are guards enough around the tents. I will do better at a distance, and it is possible that I may learn something useful."

"As a spy?" She grinned. "That's a great idea. I've been wondering how I shall occupy myself if I can't go riding all day. Queen Alyse has made it plain that when I am in public, I must wear a gown."

Llyr was relieved to find her more like herself. She had always hated wearing gowns.

"How shall I know how to meet you?"

Llyr patted the smooth bark of the beech. "Come to this place at lamplighting. I will wait in the tree. You can call me down with a whistle or a song." He smiled. "I prefer a song."

It was a mistake. She withdrew into a formal stiffness and, unless he imagined it, blushed. She released the pony from his hobbles and climbed onto his back. "What about food? Will you come eat with us? The queen won't mind."

He shook his head. "I can feed myself. It is better if I am not part of . . . all this." He gestured toward the field—its tents, its people, its bustle.

"All right." She met his eyes with a reluctance he had never seen in her before. "It is good to see you, Llyr."

He acknowledged this with a nod. "And you, princess."

He watched with misgiving as she rode the pony to the

horse lines. She *had* changed. She had not asked the questions he had expected her to ask. She had not told him about her meeting with Alia. She had been distant and shy, which was unlike her. The diffidence in her manner reminded him of their first meeting in the hills above the castle last spring. But they were old friends now. Why should she suddenly treat him like a stranger?

After leaving Thatch with the other horses, Guinevere took a shortcut through the clustered tents from the horse lines. She misjudged her way, arriving at the High King's tent instead of at her own. Hurrying past the royal guards, she ran toward the banners of Gwynedd. She was almost there when she heard someone behind her call her name.

She whirled, recognizing her cousin's voice, and was astonished to see Elaine walking toward her at the side of a laughing young man. He was a big-boned youth still growing into his strength, with large hands and feet, red hair, and a square, freckled face designed for cheerfulness. Elaine grinned at his laughter and waved to Guinevere.

"Gwen! There you are! I have someone I want you to meet."

Guinevere had hoped to meet no one of importance before she had time to change into a gown, but the meeting was unavoidable now. She waited.

"Who's that?" she heard the young man ask Elaine. "Your brother?"

Guinevere stiffened as color rushed to her face.

"No, no," Elaine giggled. "You've got it wrong again. She's my cousin."

"*She?*" The young man had the grace to color himself as he met Guinevere's eyes.

"Gwen," Elaine said, "meet Trevor, Prince of Powys. He's here with his mother, Queen Esdora. His father, the king, is too ill to travel. Trevor, this is the daughter of my mother's sister, my cousin Guinevere of Northgallis, who lives with us."

Trevor of Powys bowed politely. "I am honored to meet you, Guinevere."

"She's a king's daughter," Elaine whispered belatedly.

Trevor's blush deepened until his face was nearly as red as his hair. "I beg your pardon, princess," he said. "I meant no discourtesy."

Guinevere made him a reverence as best she could in boots and leggings. "The discourtesy was not yours, my lord," she said evenly. "And the honor is mine."

She turned to enter the tent, but Elaine stopped her. "We have been watching the High King's men build a bonfire," she said eagerly. "Trevor says we shall meet everyone tonight. We are the last to arrive, and also the most important, so the greeting ceremony will be formal." She giggled. "You'll have to wear a gown."

"I intend to."

"Tell us, my lord," Elaine continued in a jaunty voice, "what you and your mother wore when you were presented to the High King. Was it so very formal? Were you dripping with jewels and weighted with gold?"

Trevor smiled. "I'm afraid that Powys is not as rich as Gwynedd. We have too few jewels to drip and too little gold to cause discomfort. But of course you must do your best for Princess Morgan. As a woman, she will appreciate your efforts." He added, as an afterthought, "The High King, as you know, is not here."

The joy drained from Elaine's face. "Not here? What do you mean, *not here?*"

Trevor looked from Elaine to Guinevere and back again, perplexed. "I beg your pardon, but I thought you knew. The High King was called away on the eve of his departure by news of a Saxon invasion in the east. Sir Bedwyr leads the escort in his stead. And the council." He bowed politely. "Forgive me for bearing such ill tidings."

Angry tears sprang to Elaine's eyes. "Not here! We've come all this way, and he's *not here!*" She tore aside the curtain and bolted into the tent, leaving Guinevere and Trevor standing awkwardly outside to listen to her sobs.

"Forgive me," Trevor murmured. "I didn't know you didn't know."

"It's not your fault, my lord. It's not anyone's fault. But it's the only reason Elaine wanted to come."

Trevor shrugged and said, with a little smile, "One of those, eh? The land is littered with them, I hear. But I'm afraid she's a little late to the, er, race."

Guinevere smiled. "We did hear about his marriage. Gwynedd is isolated, but not quite that isolated."

"I'm glad to hear it. Do forgive me, princess, won't you, for my mistaking you before? In Powys, we knew about the

queen's daughter—indeed, that's another reason I accompanied my mother—but not about you."

"That's all right," Guinevere replied, charmed by his frank-
ness. "It's an easy mistake to make. I dress like a boy when I
ride—it's the only way—but I can't expect everyone outside
Gwynedd to know that."

"You didn't arrive in a litter, then?"

"Goodness, no. I loathe litters."

Trevor smiled, a spark of interest lighting his eyes. "And
you have a fine horse, I suppose?"

"The best in all the kingdoms."

"Is he fast?"

"She is. Very fast."

"How fast?"

"I don't know. I've had no one to test her against."

Trevor's eyebrows rose. "A test can certainly be arranged.
Does King Pellinore know you have the best horse in the
kingdoms?"

Guinevere's eyes danced. "He should, my lord. He gave
her to me."

Trevor laughed. "Well, then, I think we must settle the
matter sometime. Are you game for a race?"

"If the ground is good."

"It's settled, then."

He extended his hand like any man making a wager. Guinevere hesitated only a moment before taking it firmly in reply.

CHAPTER TEN

The Presentation

It was well past lamplighting when a royal page came to summon King Pellinore and his family to meet Princess Morgan. The family, with Lord Riall, had gathered in Queen Alyse's tent. Guinevere was relieved to see the queen looking healthy and regal in a rose-colored gown and a fox-trimmed cloak. Her face was a little thinner than usual, but her eyes were alive with excitement as she surveyed the girls and commended their nurses for having them ready on time.

Elaine, whose eyes were still pink from weeping, had begged her mother to excuse her from the ordeal of presentation. It would be long and tedious, she was certain, and since the High King would not be there, it held no interest for her. Queen Alyse had met this request with indignation, telling her daughter sharply to stop living in a world of dreams and dry her eyes.

"I will not be disgraced by my own daughter on such a significant occasion," she had said. "Princess Morgan is the daughter of Ygraine of Cornwall, who was High Queen not so long ago and is still the most powerful woman in the land—in spite of turning into a recluse since Uther's death. Morgan is also Arthur's sister, his full, legitimate sister and his only trueborn sibling. The man she is going north to marry rules a kingdom twice the size of Gwynedd. She has influence, and influence is power. For political reasons alone I prefer to be in her good graces. So you will behave yourself tonight."

Elaine had turned her head away, too miserable to object. Queen Alyse had grabbed her chin and forced her daughter to meet her eyes.

"If you are ever to be a queen, Elaine, you must learn how to comport yourself in all circumstances, even uncongenial ones. You set an example by your behavior. You will smile even when you are unhappy, you will show interest even when you are bored, and you will attend even when you are sick. Do you understand me?"

Ailsa's eyes had fastened on the queen as she spoke the word *sick*, and for a moment Guinevere had wondered if her earlier guess that the queen might be ill had been correct. But Ailsa had denied it when directly asked, and now, standing dressed and ready in the queen's tent, Guinevere could see for herself that there was nothing much amiss with Queen Alyse. She looked beautiful, composed, and in full control of her considerable authority.

Elaine stood sullenly at her mother's side. Cold compresses had taken the puffiness from her cheeks and most of the redness from her eyes, but nothing could erase the impression of recent tears. Guinevere thought she looked lovely in spite of herself, with her golden hair held in place by a double string of river pearls and her costly gown the same vivid blue as her eyes. No wonder Trevor of Powys had been walking at her side.

Guinevere fidgeted with the sleeves of her own gown, which barely hid her wrists, as she and Elaine followed the king and queen past rigid sentries and stands of flaming torches to the entrance of the High King's tent. The gown was her newest and best, a soft green the color of oak buds. Six months ago it had fit her straight frame perfectly, but now she was dismayed to find it tight in places and already a little short. Ailsa had added a dark green border to extend the hem, but there hadn't been fabric enough to alter the sleeves. Queen Alyse did not seem to notice this deficiency, however, and Guinevere sincerely hoped Princess Morgan would not, either.

Sir Bedwyr met them at the entrance and welcomed them formally on behalf of the High King, cordially expressing Arthur's regret that he was unable to greet them in person. His gaze lingered for a moment on the two girls before he swept aside the entrance curtain and led them all inside.

Warmth and light greeted them, and the subdued hum of voices. The interior of the tent was filled with people dressed in finery, who turned as one as they approached. Faces stared and voices died away as they passed through the crowd in Sir Bedwyr's wake. At the far end of the tent, amid a cluster of bronze oil lamps emitting scents of cedar and lemon, a slender girl sat alone on a great carved chair.

"My lady Princess Morgan," Sir Bedwyr said with a sweep

of his arm and a formal bow, "I present to you the High King's loyal subjects King Pellinore and Queen Alyse of Gwynedd, Princess Elaine of Gwynedd, Princess Guinevere of Northgallis, and Lord Riall of Caer Narfon, a kinsman. My lords, my ladies, Princess Morgan, daughter of Ygraine of Cornwall and Uther Pendragon, and sister to the High King Arthur."

As they made their reverences to the girl in the chair, Guinevere thought what a pleasant voice Sir Bedwyr had, and how he had gotten all their names right, even though he was not a Welshman. And how surprising it was to find Princess Morgan so plain when her mother was a beauty of such renown. She had an elegant figure, to be sure, and beautiful dark brown hair combed to a sheen and bound with a triple strand of garnets around her brow. Her hands, long-fingered and slim, were adorned with rings, and her heavy gown, dyed a rich Pendragon red, was exquisitely cut to accent her figure. Her cloak was edged with ermine and matched her slippers. Proud and regal down to her fingertips, Princess Morgan ought to have been beautiful. But she was not. Her features were too strong, and her amber eyes too light for a girl with such dark hair.

This discordance between expectation and appearance disconcerted Guinevere. It was the way she felt whenever she and Elaine sneaked into Queen Alyse's chamber to look at themselves in her mirror of polished bronze. Too well did she recall staring with rising dismay at the reality of her own image, which seemed to belong to a stranger, so little did it reflect the way she felt about herself. She wondered if Princess Morgan had ever been thrown off balance by the sight of her own reflection. Did she recognize the face that stared back at her? Or did her inner eye provide her with a more satisfactory vision?

Pleased by the discovery of a possible bond between them, Guinevere glanced at Morgan as she rose from her reverence. For a moment, she shared a sense of sisterhood with the older girl. She, too, was the only daughter of a woman renowned for beauty, and she, too, had always fallen short of everyone's expectations. But if Princess Morgan sensed this bond, she gave no sign of it. King Arthur's sister sat stiffly in her brother's great chair and looked down at them all with chill dislike.

"I am honored to make your acquaintance." She spoke in a voice almost casually cool. "My lords, my ladies, please make welcome the royal family of Gwynedd, their kinsman, Lord Riall, and . . ." She turned to Guinevere and said with unapologetic abruptness, "I'm afraid I've forgotten your name."

Guinevere sank into another reverence as color rushed to her face. Sir Bedwyr spoke quickly over her head. "Guinevere of Northgallis, my lady. Daughter of King Leodegrance, who was a great ally of your father's, and Elen of Gwynedd, sister to Queen Alyse."

Princess Morgan ran her cool gaze over Guinevere's flaming face. "Another Guenwyvar? A name I cannot escape wherever I go, it seems. You are cousin to Princess Elaine?"

"Yes, my lady," Guinevere breathed, unable to hide her surprise that Princess Morgan would refer to her brother's wife with such disdain.

"And you live not in Northgallis but in Gwynedd? Under the protection of your aunt and uncle?"

"Yes, my lady. It was my father's dying wish."

Morgan's laugh was sharp. "Foresighted man. No doubt he had ambitions for you. But it is dangerous for dependents to harbor ambition. You'd best keep yours in check. Unlike your namesake."

The princess turned her attention to Elaine, leaving Guinevere frozen in place, trembling with anger and trying to pull her wits together. Princess Morgan had deliberately chosen to slight her before all these people, as if it mattered that she had the same name as King Arthur's bride. But why? She was nothing to a woman of Morgan's rank—less than nothing. There was no conceivable reason for the princess to take against her, and yet she had.

Already the people around her were looking at her askance and whispering to one another, all except one stocky, dark-bearded man who glared at Princess Morgan with outrage on his face. Guinevere smiled at the sight of him. Her half brother, Gwarthgydd of Northgallis, was her father's eldest son by his first wife. From Guinevere's earliest years, he had been a rough but adoring uncle-like figure in her life, a powerful ally, and the father of Gwillim, her dearest childhood friend. At their father's death, Gwarth had become king of Northgallis and Gwillim his heir. She had seen little of them since her move to Gwynedd until last spring, when Gwarth had brought Gwillim to King Pellinore's stronghold to have a look at Elaine.

Gwarth turned and met her eyes, and by the brisk nod of his head gave her to know that an insult to her was an insult to him, and that he was ready to fight in her defense. Quick tears of gratitude rose to Guinevere's eyes. She had forgotten what it was like to have Gwarth on one's side.

Servants brought in the wedding gifts the family had carried from Gwynedd and laid them carefully at Princess Morgan's feet. Queen Alyse had done the best she could on such short notice, especially since most of the king's personal treasures had been lost in a fire last spring. The gifts were few in number but of very high quality: a pair of silver goblets rescued from the fire and polished until they blazed; a set of fine linen bedsheets and four thick blankets of good Welsh wool, banded—in the last two weeks—by wide borders dyed Pendragon red; a small dagger, taken in a chance encounter with a Gaelic raiding party, made for a woman's hand, with a hilt of entwined serpents and a pretty enameled sheath; and an old, probably Roman brooch of silverwork chased in gold that had been in Queen Alyse's mother's family for generations.

Princess Morgan gazed politely at these gifts and praised them mildly, which produced a certain stiffening in Queen Alyse. The only gift that caught Morgan's attention was a coverlet of imported white silk backed with bleached Welsh lambswool. In the center, embroidered colts and fillies kicked up their heels in a meadow of wildflowers. Princess Morgan rose from her chair and came forward to touch the coverlet, to run her hand over the smooth fabric and the stitched horses at play.

"I like this," she said in some surprise, lifting it to the lamp to see it better. "The stitching is amazingly fine, and the little horses look almost real. I congratulate you, Queen Alyse. It is quite original. I have never seen anything like it."

Queen Alyse nodded briefly. "Thank you, my lady. You are very kind, but I cannot take the credit. That coverlet was designed and stitched by my ward and niece, Guinevere of

Northgallis." She gestured toward Guinevere, the tiniest of smiles on her lips.

Guinevere fell into an immediate curtsy, but no words of thanks or commendation came from Princess Morgan, only silence, a thick, tense silence that grew and spread until it filled every corner of the tent. No one moved. Everyone waited with held breath for the spell to break.

At last, Princess Morgan spoke. "How very fortunate you are to have such a gifted seamstress among your dependents, my lady queen. I almost wish I could take her with me. I could use her."

Guinevere's eyes flew up at that.

"I regret," Queen Alyse responded coolly, "that such a gift must be denied you. Lady Guinevere, as Sir Bedwyr has already told you, is my sister's daughter and a most trusted and beloved member of our family. No one in Gwynedd regards her as a dependent."

"No, nor in Northgallis, either," boomed Gwarth's deep voice from the crowd behind.

"Nor in all of Wales, I'm sure." Princess Morgan's smile was condescendingly kind, leaving them all to wonder if this was a slight directed at Wales itself.

"Ladies, if I may have your attention for a moment . . . ," Sir Bedwyr intervened, bowing low to a space between them. "The High King has charged me with the task of . . ."

Guinevere did not hear him finish, for when she looked up, her gaze was caught by a man standing motionless in the shadow of Morgan's chair, a man hitherto unnoticed in all the hubbub, a tall specter of a man wrapped in a black cloak from chin to heel. He captured her gaze the instant she raised her head, and he looked into her eyes as if the distance between them did not exist. She trembled as she sensed a foreign presence enter her mind and search among her thoughts, her memories, her plans and dreams, with the precision of a disemboweling knife. She wanted to cry out in protest, she wanted to flee, but she seemed to have lost command of her body. A bubble of stillness surrounded her and held her motionless, deaf and blind to the outer world.

Desperate for some way to defend herself, Guinevere stared back at the forbidding figure and tried to funnel her rising resentment into some sort of resistance against this unpardonable intrusion. At once the intrusion ceased. There was surprise, regret, a touch of respect, and even apology as the other mind withdrew and released her. The bubble dissipated into the lamplit air, and the noises, smells, and vivid colors of the common world returned.

Shaking, Guinevere turned away. She was astonished to find that time had passed and that no one had noticed anything amiss. King Pellinore and Queen Alyse were busy greeting the royalty of Wales. Trevor of Powys was chatting again with Elaine, and Gwarth was bearing down on her with arms outstretched.

"Why, Gwen, just look at you! You've grown another handspan since spring, I'll wager. And still as light as a reed." His great arms engulfed her in a bear hug and swung her from the ground. "Pay no mind to that mealymouthed wench in the scarlet clothes. Royal is as royal does, I always say. She's no likeness of her brother, may the gods be thanked." Gwarth's voice, even when he whispered, could be heard across a room.

"Shhh. She'll hear you." Guinevere kissed his rough cheek and hugged him.

"Don't care if she does." Gwarth grinned. "Besides, she's gone. Sir Bedwyr took her out." He chuckled. "There's a man who earns his salt. Turned a catfight into an administrative meeting right under the princess's nose. More than I could've done."

Guinevere stared at him blankly. She had heard nothing of Sir Bedwyr's administrative meeting.

He ran his eye over her in evident satisfaction. "You're looking fine, Gwen—you look more like your mother every time I see you. The fairest woman any of us in Northgallis ever saw."

Guinevere grabbed his sleeve. "I need your help, Gwarth. Who is that man behind Princess Morgan's chair? No, don't stare, just take a quick look and tell me."

"What man? There's no one behind the chair."

Guinevere whirled around. It was true. The shadows behind Princess Morgan's chair were empty. "But there was a man there! All during the presentation. Didn't you see him?"

Gwarth's eyebrows rose and he shook his head. Guinevere fought down rising panic. Had she dreamed it? Or had the villain sneaked out while her back was turned?

"I'll find him, if you like," Gwarth offered, watching her. "What did he look like?"

She shivered. "A vulture. But never mind. . . . Where's Gwillim?"

"Left him home to run the kingdom." Gwarth grinned. "I hope it's still there when I get back. . . . Are you all right, Gwen? You look pale."

"It's only a headache."

"Too much stink from those lamps. Let's go outside."

"That sounds wonderful."

"I'll tell the queen I'm walking you back to your tent."

Guinevere let him take over with gratitude. She was suddenly so tired, she didn't think she could move without help. A calamitous thunder roared inside her head, and she longed for sleep. Her visit to Deva was off to an unlucky start. Without willing it, she had somehow made an enemy of Princess Morgan—and after she had imagined a kinship of spirit between them! Even if she could avoid the princess for the rest of her stay, which seemed unlikely in so small an encampment, would she be able to avoid the sinister specter that dogged her?

She shivered as Gwarth took her arm and led her out into the cool of the evening, but not with cold.

CHAPTER ELEVEN

The Black Bowl

In the morning, Princess Morgan sent for Elaine and Guinevere.

Leonora, Queen Alyse's woman, delivered the summons. "You're both to attend her this morning—the queen's orders. And you, Guinevere, you'll have to change your clothes."

Guinevere, who was half dressed in tunic and leggings for a visit to the horse lines, put down her boots with obvious reluctance. "Both of us? Are you certain?"

Leonora ignored the question. "The queen thinks your blue gown would serve best. Not the gray. On no account the gray. Elaine will wear yellow. Lady Elaine, your mother reminds you to behave yourself and to remember, when you open your mouth, that the honor of Gwynedd is at stake."

Both girls smiled to hear Queen Alyse's words so exactly

reproduced, even down to the crisp arrogance of her voice. But Guinevere's smile faded. If Queen Alyse placed enough importance on this meeting to direct what they were to wear, there was no possibility of avoiding it. She would have to face Princess Morgan again, and in her blue gown, too, which Queen Alyse did not like her to wear in company because it matched the color of her eyes and made her too noticeable.

Today she wanted nothing more than to fade into the background. But today Queen Alyse apparently intended that she, Guinevere, should stand out and that Elaine, mono-chrome in a gown that matched her yellow hair, should stay in the background. It was a reversal of the natural order of things, and Guinevere wondered why.

She supposed the queen must have some plan afoot, or perhaps she was ill, seriously and secretly ill. At dawn that morning, Guinevere had awakened to the muffled sound of vomiting from the direction of the queen's tent. She had heard the sound several times before. If Queen Alyse was ill, she might not be thinking straight or be in full command of her wits. She had seemed well enough last night, except at odd moments when the lamplight caught her face just so and revealed hollows below her cheekbones that had not been there before.

This thought made Guinevere so uneasy that she tried to cajole information out of Ailsa as she peeled off her tunic and leggings. "Ailsa, what's the matter with Aunt Alyse? Something is, and don't tell me you don't know, because I see that you do."

But Ailsa refused to be drawn. "Never you mind," she said,

refolding the discarded clothes and replacing them in the trunk. "If the queen wanted you to know, she'd tell you. Let be. Look, here's your lovely blue gown, which always makes you look so like your mother, and which the queen hardly ever lets you wear. . . ."

The change of subject confirmed Guinevere's suspicions. Something *was* wrong with Queen Alyse. She asked no more questions, but stood quietly while Ailsa finished dressing her and combing out her hair. Elaine was ready first and danced impatiently about the crowded space, jubilant in her excitement.

"It's such an *honor*, Gwen. Aren't you thrilled? I mean, that's why we're here, Mother says—to entertain King Arthur's sister, and now she's sent for us. She's taken notice. We must have made a good impression—or I did, at any rate. So stop looking so glum."

She twirled around in place, the skirts of her gown swirling above her ankles and showing off her yellow slippers. "Maybe she's invited us to give you a chance to apologize."

Guinevere's head came up. "Apologize for what?"

"For whatever you did last night to annoy her."

"For the thousandth time, I did *nothing* to annoy her. You know that. You were standing right beside me."

"Well, you must have done *something* to make her take against you."

"When you've figured out what it is, I hope you'll tell me."

The arrival of the princess's page put an end to argument. He led them outside into a fine autumn morning, cool and sunny, with a breeze that sent clouds flying across the sky. A perfect day, Guinevere thought, for riding out. As they passed by the sentries posted outside the High King's great tent, they could hear the grumble of men's voices from within. The council of kings had begun.

The page led them halfway across the meadow to Princess Morgan's compound. The royal tent was foremost among a group of three clustered at a distance from all the others. There were twice as many guards posted here as around any other tent, and as soon as they entered, Guinevere understood why.

It was lavishly appointed, with polished tables and cushioned chairs, hanging tapestries, oil lamps of bronze and silver, fine ceramic bowls and platters, and exquisite jewelry all laid out for anyone to see. These, Guinevere guessed, must be Morgan's wedding gifts, or perhaps part of the dowry her brother had provided. Of their own gifts, the silver goblets, the brooch, the blankets, and the dagger were already on display. The white silk coverlet with its dancing horses was nowhere to be seen.

Elaine looked wide-eyed at all the gathered wealth while Guinevere scanned the shadowed corners for any signs of the cloaked figure she dreaded seeing. When Princess Morgan entered through a side curtain, both girls fell into nervous curtsies. The princess wore a plain day gown of dark red and had bound her hair into a long braid down her back. Her hands, her throat, and her brow were free of ornaments. Only a pair of tiny garnet earrings graced her ears. To Guinevere, she looked a hundred times more regal than she had last night.

"Good morning," Princess Morgan said with a light smile. "Princess Elaine, isn't it? And Princess Guinevere? Thank you for coming so promptly." She indicated a low cushioned couch. "Sit down."

The girls obeyed. "First," said Princess Morgan, "I must apologize for my rudeness of last night. I understand that I gave offense to Queen Alyse, which was never my intention. But I am shy of crowds. I become stiff and formal and apt to say things which I do not mean." She smiled charmingly. "I hope you can forgive me."

"Of course we can," said Elaine. "Think nothing of it. But why should a small group like that make you shy? I should think you would be used to it by now."

Princess Morgan lowered her eyes for a moment. "I should be, I suppose, had my father lived a little longer, for I grew up at court. But he died just before I turned twelve, and since then my mother and I have lived at Tintagel."

She looked up into two uncomprehending faces. "Tintagel is a great fortress on the Cornwall coast. It is built on an island of rock inaccessible by sea and connected to the mainland by a single narrow causeway. All the kings of Cornwall are born there because it is so easy to defend. My brother was born there, and so was I."

Elaine straightened, eyes wide at the reference to Arthur.

"It's all very well as a nursery, for the place is impregnable. But it's a prison for a girl of marriageable age. It sits on a sweep of rugged coastline, all alone. No one lives anywhere near it but shepherds and peat diggers. The nearest fishing village is ten leagues south—more if you go by the coast road. No one comes to visit. Life there is extraordinarily dull. Mother likes the isolation, but then she's withdrawn from life. She mourns my father still and won't set foot outside the walls. She waits for death." She paused. "And I've been cooped up there for the last four years."

Guinevere heard echoes of anger and resentment in her voice and wondered if she blamed her mother or her brother for this imprisonment. Her mother's plight was unenviable, but probably beyond her power to control. As for her brother, where else was he to keep her? He and his men were always on the move, fighting Saxons, Gaels, Angles, and anyone else who coveted Briton lands. His court at Caerleon was more a fighting fortress than a home. Tintagel was safe.

Princess Morgan must have heard the echoes, too, for she said more mildly, "I'm only explaining why I am unused to speaking in a public forum. At Tintagel, there was only Mother, my nurse, my tutor, the household, and me."

"Then how did you meet your husband?" asked Elaine. "Did he visit Tintagel and fall in love with you there?"

Princess Morgan laughed. "Hardly. I've never met him." She smiled at Elaine's confusion. "Mine is a political marriage, arranged by Arthur. Rheged is a large kingdom, and Arthur needs King Urien as an ally. You needn't look so sorry for me. I agreed to it. I will have power in Rheged." Her face changed subtly, hardening around the mouth and eyes. "And power is something I've never had."

Elaine shivered. "I should hate to marry a man I didn't

love. Mother has promised me that I shall not have to marry anyone I don't want to."

"Indeed? And you a king's daughter? How very indulgent of Queen Alyse. I wouldn't have expected it of her."

"It's the same promise her mother made to her," Elaine explained, glossing over the implied insult in Morgan's words. "I shall make it to my own daughter, when I have one."

Princess Morgan's smile grew gently condescending. "And you, Guinevere? Has Queen Alyse made the same promise to you?"

Guinevere raised her eyes only briefly. "No, my lady. Not yet."

"She will, Gwen," Elaine said. "Of course she will. She believes in marrying for love. It's just that you're not, well . . . ready for courting yet, so the subject hasn't come up."

Guinevere bowed her head to hide the flush of color that rose to her cheeks, but Princess Morgan, to her great relief, showed no interest in her lack of readiness for courting. She turned back to Elaine and said demurely, "Prince Trevor of Powys has taken an interest in you, I understand. Perhaps you will fall in love with him."

"Never. There is only one man I could ever—" Elaine stopped, having seen the pitfall too late, and gulped. "I mean . . . I couldn't love Trevor of Powys. I just couldn't."

"Because you are already in love with someone else?"

Elaine blushed.

"May I ask who he is?"

Elaine's color deepened. "I wish you wouldn't."

Princess Morgan laughed in genuine amusement. "Very well, I won't. I don't need to. And I see it would do no good to warn you off. But I am sorry for you." She turned to Guinevere. Her words, although casually spoken, carried an intensity that made them sharp. "And you, Guinevere? Have you not yet lost your heart?"

"No, my lady."

"I have heard something about you, I think. Aren't you the one who is called the Lark of Gwynedd?"

Guinevere's eyes widened in surprise. She had thought that an epithet known only in Gwynedd. Four years ago, after the bloody battle against the Saxons that had won Arthur his crown and cost Uther his life, Queen Alyse had asked the girls to help out in the hospital tents erected on the castle grounds to house the returning wounded. Unable to abide the sights and smells within the tents, Guinevere had been made to sit on a stool outside and sing to the suffering men. Those who had lived had given her the epithet in appreciation.

"Yes, she is," Elaine supplied. "Because she sang to all the wounded men who made it home after the battle of Caer Eden, and they all said that the sound of her voice eased their pain. Didn't they, Gwen?"

Guinevere flushed and shot Elaine a meaning look.

Princess Morgan turned her stony gaze on Guinevere. "Singing after the battle of Caer Eden? When the rest of us were in mourning?"

"Mourning for what?" Elaine cried, heedless of Guinevere's

warning elbow in her ribs. "That was the day King Arthur came to power and beat the Saxons back!"

Princess Morgan seemed to freeze in place. "It was also the day my father died."

Too late, Elaine stuttered an apology.

Princess Morgan rose. "Come with me." She walked to the side entrance and beckoned them to follow.

The chamber beyond was Princess Morgan's bedchamber, regally furnished with a carved fruitwood bed hung with scarlet hangings. A thin middle-aged woman sat in a corner and stitched by the light of a candle. Morgan did not introduce her, and Guinevere guessed that she must be the princess's nurse. The woman watched, frowning, as Morgan crossed the chamber to another entranceway on the far side of the tent.

"Go on in," Princess Morgan said, holding back the entrance flap. "It's dark, but I'll bring a candle. Marcia, give me yours." The nurse yielded the candle, and Morgan followed Elaine and Guinevere inside.

It was very dark, even by candlelight. Herbscent and earth smells filled the air, and something acrid, like ashes from a fire. As their eyes grew accustomed to the dimness, they could see a shelf or tabletop before them, and a brazier to one side, unlit now but reeking of recent use. On the shelf stood a myriad of objects: bowls, spoons, jars, and cloth bags tied with ribbon.

"This is my secret," Princess Morgan said softly. "This is how I occupied all those dull hours at Tintagel."

"But what is it?" Elaine wondered aloud. "And why is it so dark?"

"It's a stillroom. There are herbs in those bags, and oils and other things in the jars. And this bowl . . ." She set down her candle next to a large black stone with a concave surface. Her fingers caressed it. "This is the source of my secret knowledge."

Guinevere and Elaine looked at each other. This place was nothing like the stillroom at home, which was right off the kitchen garden and filled with light. Cissa, who gathered herbs from the garden and bark from the woods, brewed teas, and mixed medicinal potions for the family, considered bright light essential for her work. Guinevere knew at once that what took place in this small, suffocating space was something very different.

"I have made a study of the magic arts," Princess Morgan said, pulling the stoppers from two of the jars and pouring oil and water into the black bowl. "But not everyone has the gift of Sight. Would you like to see if you do?"

"I—I thought you were Christian," Elaine stammered. "Mother told me so."

"So I am," the princess said smoothly, "when I need to be. But Christ is a man's god. His disciples were all men, and so are his priests. Women are nothing but obedient servants to him. There are other gods, older gods, who offer power to a woman courageous enough to grasp it. Come closer now, and look into the bowl while I stir in these herbs. I saw the Lark of Gwynedd in the bowl last night, before the presentation, but I was not certain which of you it was. A pair of swans you are, among so many Welsh geese. Perhaps we shall see something new today."

While Elaine and Guinevere edged fearfully closer and peered into the oily reflective surface of the liquid, Morgan took a small knife from her pouch and cut off two strands of hair from their heads. Making no apology for the liberty, she dropped the hairs into the liquid, added three pinches of silvery powder, murmured something unintelligible, and stared into the swirling liquid with intense concentration.

Guinevere stepped back a pace. Morgan's hand shot out and grabbed her wrist. "Look," she commanded. "Tell me what you see."

Guinevere obeyed, but all she saw was a glimmer of her own reflection. "I don't see anything."

"Concentrate. Empty your mind and concentrate."

Guinevere shook off the restraining hand and backed away. This was foolishness. If her mind was empty, there would be nothing to concentrate upon. "I see nothing."

"You don't try." Morgan glanced at Elaine. "Have you more courage than your cousin? Look. Wait. What do you see?"

Elaine approached the bowl resolutely, eager to see a vision. She waited, stared, and squinted. "There's nothing there but oil and water and hair and herbs. I have a headache. I want to leave."

But Princess Morgan did not reply. She bent over the black bowl, gripping its sides as if it held her swirling soul. With a little gasp, she pulled away. In the utter silence of the dark they seemed to hear the pounding of her heart.

"It has begun," she whispered. "The wheel of time is turning. I feel its pull."

"Come away, come away," Guinevere breathed, tugging at Elaine's hand.

"She's on the verge of prophecy!"

"She doesn't know anything. Come away."

Morgan shut her eyes and began to sway back and forth. In the shivering candlelight she looked inhuman. Terrible shadows raked her face, turning it into an old woman's visage. Elaine whimpered and retreated. Guinevere placed herself between the witch and Elaine, and pushed Elaine toward the door. So it was that she, and not her cousin, heard the grievous words Morgan uttered: "The Queen shall die of what she carries in her, and another shall be appointed in her place."

Guinevere grabbed Elaine's hand, pushed open the door flap, and led her away—past Marcia, sitting silently on her stool, past the regal bed decked in the color of blood, past the collected treasures of a witch, and out into the breezy, sunlit air.

CHAPTER TWELVE

Morgan's Plight

Marcia rose to her feet as Princess Morgan came through the curtain. "You ought to be ashamed of yourself, frightening those girls like that. Your mother would have your hide. You know better."

"It amused me."

"Morgan!"

"I didn't harm them. I wanted to get to know them. I need to learn their . . . talents and interests."

Marcia scowled. "Their strengths and weaknesses, you mean. Don't you lie to *me*, Mistress Morgan. I changed your swaddling clothes."

Princess Morgan threw up her hands in exasperation and sank to the bed. "What do you want of me, Marcia? What is it you and Mother expect? I'm marrying him, am I not?"

"You needn't. You know your mother has reservations. He's old enough to be your grandfather, and he's got grown sons living. It's not too late to change your mind."

Morgan covered her face with her elegant, long-fingered hands. "Not too late? I'd laugh, but I'd be sick. It was too late a long time ago. It was too late the day my father died and Arthur's ambition was let loose upon the land."

"Tsk, Morgan, hush."

"It's the truth."

"You had a choice."

The hands came down and Morgan's eyes blazed. "You think so, do you? You think I could have refused my brother? He only asked because he knew he could make me do it."

"Morgan, that isn't true."

"Oh, for pity's sake. You and Mother are just alike. You've always doted on him. No, not on him, but on the *idea* of him: the lost son, given away at birth and raised by strangers far from home in ignorance of his parentage. Missed. Longed for. Dreamed of. Out of nowhere he returns—a young Hercules, a hero—just in time to snatch victory from defeat and make himself a name." Her voice held more sadness than bitterness, despite the words. When she paused, her amber eyes glittered with tears. "Everyone forgets that Uther Pendragon died in that battle. Everyone marks the day and celebrates it yearly. It—it infuriates me. No one grieves for him."

Marcia came to the bed and sat down beside her. "Ygraine does," she said, slipping her arm around Morgan's shoulders. "Your mother has grieved for him every day and every night for four long years. He was the only man she ever loved."

"Besides Arthur." Morgan shrugged off the arm and rose. "There wasn't any choice, and there isn't anything I can do about it now. Once I'm queen of Rheged—" She paused and changed what she had been about to say. "Until I'm queen of Rheged, I'm a pawn in my dear brother's hands."

"Now, Morgan—"

"Don't scold me, Marcia. I've accepted it. I'm sixteen, after all. It's time I wed. And Urien's the most powerful king in Britain, after Lot. I shall have power in Rheged. At long last, I—" Again she broke off and changed her words. "I will achieve some influence over my life."

"My dear," Marcia said, rising quickly. "You're shaking." She wrapped her own shawl around Morgan's shoulders. "It's only natural to be afraid when you leave home for the first time. But the strangeness will soon pass. Rheged will become your home."

Morgan shivered. "That's not what I fear—leaving home, remaking my life in a new land. That I welcome. But . . ." She twisted the ends of the shawl around her fingers and stared off into space.

Marcia edged closer to her. In all the years she had served Queen Ygraine, she had never seen Morgan afraid. "What is it, my dear?"

Morgan forced a laugh. "I have been so little in company since Father died, and I was barely twelve then." She turned to look Marcia full in the face. "I fear men. I know so little about them. We were a community of women at Tintagel. Men were guards or servants. One gave them orders, and they obeyed. But what of the men I face now, men of my own rank? I don't know how to flirt with them or how to please them. I don't know what they think about or what they fear. Yet in a few short weeks I will have to know how to deal with a great many different men. It will be important to handle this right. If Urien's sons resent the match, my very life may depend upon it. Did you and Mother never think of that?"

Marcia smiled at her proudly and kissed her cheek. "Your mother and I gave you credit for the wits you possess. You'll land on your feet. You always do." She squeezed Morgan's arm. "Besides, no woman can teach another about men. You learn as you go."

Morgan's lips twisted. "It would help to be beautiful. Mistakes might be forgiven."

"Heavens, no, child. Never think so. There's nothing more troublesome than beauty. Ask your mother. A beautiful woman brings out the very worst in men . . . and in women, too, come to that."

Morgan looked at her sharply. Had Marcia guessed her reaction to those two golden girls? But Marcia was straightening the coverlet on the bed, and her face was hidden from view.

"You're awfully full of sage advice today."

"And you're full of emotion. It's unlike you."

Morgan turned away, letting the shawl slip from her shoulders to the ground, where Marcia dutifully bent to retrieve it.

"That's perceptive of you. I must have let that girl get under my skin."

"Which girl?"

"You're right, I shouldn't have frightened them. I suppose I shall have to pay Queen Alyse a visit and try to remedy the situation."

"My dear, I think that's very wise." Marcia folded the shawl with care, keeping her eyes down. "Did one of those girls upset you? They looked an innocent pair to me."

Morgan hesitated. "Elaine of Gwynedd. The pretty one. I shall have to make a friend of her, I think."

Marcia looked at her doubtfully. "You didn't think the other one was rather, er, startling?"

"The scarecrow? No. Certainly not."

Marcia's eyebrow rose, but she said mildly, "Well, by all means visit the queen of Gwynedd and befriend her daughter. She's a powerful woman in the prime of life, and her influence is growing. It can only help you to know her. She has a reputation for intelligence—you might even enjoy her company."

Morgan walked to the door of the tent and stood between the poles, looking out. The Sight did not come to her often, nor did it come on command, but when it came, it came clearly. Over and over again, in her bowl, in her crystal, in the dark pool below Tintagel, she had seen the same truth, sharp as a cutting blade. One of those girls in Queen Alyse's care posed a danger to her—and to her plans for her much too popular brother.

Last night, when she had been seized by such an immediate dislike for Guinevere of Northgallis, she thought she had found her enemy. But after meeting both girls today, she was less sure. They were much alike, after all, growing up together as the daughters of two sisters renowned even beyond Wales for their beauty. They were alike, too, in their unthinking ability to annoy her. But she would get the best of them; she would divide them. She would befriend one of them to learn about the other. She would ferret out their little vanities, their fears, and their dreams, and she would use this knowledge to divide them. Singly, they were no match for her.

This had to be done now, before Sir Bedwyr moved her party on to Rheged, for who knew when a chance like this would come again? Travel was slow and difficult for a royal personage, and even as queen of Rheged, she would not be free of fetters on her movements. This might be her only opportunity to meet her enemy face to face and take her measure. For this reason alone, she had persuaded Arthur to stop and rest at Deva and to invite the royal families of Wales to visit.

Of course, she hadn't revealed all this to Arthur. She had woven him a tale he would be more likely to believe, about the importance of meeting as many of the west county Britons as she could, getting to know the lay of the land, and making a good impression on local folk in advance of her marriage. These were arguments she knew her brother would be unable to resist. That he had turned a social visit into an excuse for a military conference had not surprised her in the least. Fighting—winning—was all he ever thought about. But she had welcomed his decision. Thanks to Arthur, the men would be out of the way, and she would be at liberty to examine the women.

No one had been better pleased than Morgan when Arthur was called away to war and Sir Bedwyr put in charge of her escort. Without Arthur, she would have a freer hand. None of the men had the rank to oppose her, and she knew they would not, simply because she was Arthur's sister.

Only Merlin the Enchanter could spoil her plans. But this was a woman's affair, and it was well known that Merlin avoided women. He would pay no attention unless he had to.

CHAPTER THIRTEEN

Lord Riall's Treasure

Guinevere and Llyr rode side by side along the grassy verge at the river's edge. It was a cool, cloudy afternoon with a rising breeze, and Zephyr danced in anticipation of a chance to run. Guinevere restrained her. She did not want to outpace Llyr, and Thatch took very short steps. This was only the second time in five days that she had managed to ride out with Llyr, and although they had met briefly each evening in the beech tree to exchange news and gossip, the reticence that had grown between them since Y Wyddfa had only partially dissolved.

This change in their friendship saddened Guinevere, but she was at a loss to know what to do. She could not forget Alia's words. She had seen the truth of them in Llyr's eyes when they had met again at Deva. Every day he seemed to grow more withdrawn and shy. He tried too hard to be natural and ended up sounding either casual or stiff. He was no longer at ease in her presence. It did not seem to matter what she said or did; he had retreated from her, and she could not draw him out again.

Unable to talk about personal subjects, they stuck to gossip. Llyr had interesting things to report from his nightly vigils in the treetops. According to the guards, who frequently discussed what they knew of matters when they went to the edge of the woods to relieve themselves, the council was not going well. Listening in the branches overhead, Llyr heard them compare the kings of Wales to an unruly wolf pack, jostling for position, attention, and dominance. Old rivalries and border disputes had surfaced. Ancient insults were recalled. They had not sunk to name-calling because of Sir Bedwyr's presence, but they seemed in no mood to negotiate a treaty for defense.

"Northgallis will keep faith with Gwynedd," Guinevere said when she heard this. "My father swore it when he married my mother, and Gwarth has promised to hold fast to that oath. He even tried to persuade Gwillim to marry Elaine." She smiled at the memory of Gwillim's visit to Gwynedd last spring. "What a mistake *that* was."

"The division, I think," said Llyr, "is between north and south. Forgive me, I don't know the names of the kingdoms."

"Northgallis and Gwynedd are in the north. Dyfed and Guent are in the south. Dyfed is next to the sea, and Guent is east of it. The king of Guent is a powerful man now that King

Arthur has made Caerleon his headquarters. Caerleon's in Guent."

"And Powys?" Llyr asked, his voice markedly casual. "I have seen the boy from Powys, the one with spots on his face."

Guinevere grinned. "They're not spots; they're freckles. And I wouldn't call Prince Trevor a boy. He's sixteen and represents his father in council."

"He is a king's son?" Llyr sounded sullen.

"Yes. Why?"

Llyr shrugged. "I saw him talking to you."

Guinevere's heart sank. If Llyr was going to resent everyone she spoke to, it was going to be a laborious friendship indeed. "You'd best get used to Trevor of Powys, because I'll be seeing more of him," she said evenly. "We're going to race our horses when we get a chance. He thinks he can beat me."

Llyr did not reply, and they rode steadily on, each staring at the path ahead. Guinevere wished fervently that he would come to his senses. She missed the Llyr who had been her companion all summer, the Llyr with the ready smile and the zest for adventure. She had taught him to ride, and together they had ridden all over the hills behind the castle. Llyr, being an Old One, was at home in the heights and knew all the animal trails. They had explored cliffs, caverns, and eagles' eyries, and hidden springs on the mountainsides.

She had learned about the ways of the Old Ones by watching Llyr set snares, follow spoor, and tease fish into his net. She had stopped at their wayside shrines and left gifts—a handful of mealcakes plump with raisins or a slice of mutton filched from the kitchens—for the gods of the place. She had grown to love Llyr almost as dearly as Elaine, and it grieved her to see his affection take a different turn. Since nothing could be done about it, it must be endured, and the easiest way to endure it was to ignore it.

She drew breath, clucked to Zephyr, and reminded herself what a pleasure it was to be out riding. It might even turn into an adventure, for Llyr had found something in the forest south of Deva that he wanted her to see, something he could not describe and was afraid to remove from its setting. More interesting still, it was something that Lord Riall was hiding.

She was curious to see it, since it might explain why Lord Riall had come to Deva. According to Queen Alyse, he had not been invited by the High King, but since Lord Riall's father had been Queen Alyse's uncle, he had presumed upon his family connections to join King Pellinore's party. Thus far, he had been at loose ends in Deva, being the only lord not in council. The only attention anyone paid him was to wonder why he was there.

In the five days since their arrival, life had settled into a busy routine that left little time for leisure. Sir Bedwyr called the council to order every morning after breakfast, and sometimes again in the afternoons after a break for the midday meal, which, like breakfast, was cooked over each kingdom's communal fire. Dinner, however, was prepared by the High King's men over a central bonfire and was eaten together by the entire camp.

The task of supplying food was shared among all. Whenever they were not in council, the men went hunting. The grooms, who were always up at dawn, fished the river as soon as the horses were fed, and anyone not on duty was expected to set rabbit snares or hunt the flocks of waterfowl gathering in the marshy inlets on their annual flight south.

With so many servants busy hunting, the women had to perform the servants' tasks. Water had to be brought from the river for washing, cooking, and drinking. Firewood had to be gathered to supply all the cooking fires, and wastepots had to be emptied into the trench the High King's men had dug at one end of the field. All of Queen Alyse's women were pressed into service. Elaine and Guinevere, too, were given daily chores.

Guinevere usually did Elaine's chores as well as her own, since Elaine now spent her days with Princess Morgan. Every day after breakfast, the princess sent her page to the girls' tent to lead Elaine away. To Guinevere's astonishment, Queen Alyse approved this arrangement. Cissa said the queen had received a very pretty apology from Princess Morgan, so perhaps she had thought twice about offending a woman whose brother was not only High King of all the Britons but also King Pellinore's commander.

Elaine was thrilled to dance attendance on Princess Morgan. She was flattered to be so singled out, and when she returned to her parents every evening at the bonfire, she sang Princess Morgan's praises. Queen Alyse made no response to this, but Guinevere, who watched her aunt carefully these days, could sense her annoyance. She suspected that Queen Alyse distrusted Princess Morgan despite her apology, and the queen's social instincts seldom led her astray.

Guinevere certainly did not trust the princess. She was sure Morgan had befriended Elaine to serve her own ends, and not from any natural liking for the younger girl. It was of course impossible to say this to Elaine. She would not hear a word said against her new friend. For the moment, Princess Morgan could do no wrong in Elaine's eyes, and nothing would change her mind. At least it was not likely to be a friendship of long standing. Soon Sir Bedwyr would lead Princess Morgan north to Rheged, and King Pellinore would take his family home.

Elaine's daily absences gave Guinevere time to visit with Gwarth and reminisce about the old days, time to ride her filly, and time to spend with Llyr. But as the days passed, Guinevere grew increasingly worried about Queen Alyse. The queen kept to her tent all day and only appeared in the evenings for the communal feast around the bonfire, where she ate little and drank less. Her gowns had to be taken in almost daily, but her increasing emaciation only accentuated the fine bones of her face and lent her an ethereal beauty that, in the flickering light of the bonfire, hid her illness from other eyes.

Guinevere wondered if she was in pain, but the queen's women denied it, and King Pellinore did not seem concerned. On the other hand, none of them had stood captive in the darkness and heard Princess Morgan utter, in a voice eerily unlike her own, *The Queen shall die of what she carries* . . .

Guinevere pushed this fear away by reminding herself that there was no reason to think that Morgan's prophecy applied to Queen Alyse; there were plenty of other queens among the Britons, and even more, no doubt, elsewhere in the world. Besides, she was loath to believe that Morgan's "seeing" was real. She preferred to believe that it was a pretense staged to impress and frighten her and Elaine. And yet she had sensed a presence in that small, dark space, an ominous and other-worldly presence that had drifted in unseen with Morgan's candle. Since that morning, she had been unable to rid herself of the feeling that something was very wrong.

"Here is the turning," Llyr said, dragging her abruptly from her thoughts.

Llyr pushed Thatch into a trot and headed for the trees at the forest verge. The forest was thin here, for the old Roman road lay nearby, and the Romans had cut down every tree and bush for a hundred paces on either side. They had also thinned the woods between the road and the river, as had each generation after them. The Romans had not trusted the river, and they had been wise.

It was an excellent place for hunting deer, for the brush was low and afforded a good chase. Guinevere was not sur-prised to find signs of the recent passage of horses. Llyr ob-served the marks but did not pause to examine them. All his concentration was on finding the way to Lord Riall's hiding place.

They rode into the cool and windy woods in single file. After a series of turns between the trees, Llyr slid off his pony's back and led the animal toward a dip in the forest floor, a hol-low where an old oak tree grew inside a blackthorn ring. Guinevere dismounted and followed him to the thicket's edge. He pointed to the tree. "That is the place."

She eyed the blackthorn dubiously. "Is there a way through?"

"Watch." Llyr reached into the hedge with both hands and carefully pulled aside a large section of the dense, spiky growth. A narrow path had been cut into the hedge beyond, and it led straight to the base of the grandfather oak.

"Did he do all this himself?" Guinevere breathed. "Just one man?"

Llyr nodded. "He made the way. I saw him."

"But the thorn—this brake was here."

"Yes," Llyr said, struggling to pull the section of twisted branches back in place. "This thorn is old. As old as the tree, perhaps. I think this used to be a sacred place."

Guinevere shivered. Oaks were sacred to Druids, those select and clever pagan priests who still worshipped the Goddess in ways long proscribed in civilized kingdoms. There were few of them about anymore, and for this she was thankful. One did not cross a Druid; his curse could follow a man for years before striking at the least expected hour. Druids' memories, it was said, went back at least a thousand years.

"Not recently, I hope," she said aloud to still her trembling. "If there had been a way through the blackthorn, Lord Riall wouldn't have had to cut one."

Llyr gave her a reassuring smile. "This space has not been used for a very long time. The oak is dying."

He had finished pulling the movable section back into place. The solid circle of blackthorn around the tree seemed to seal the two of them off from the outside world. The hedge was tall enough that they could not be seen if they squatted down, and this gave them a sense of privacy.

Llyr approached the ancient tree, gnarled with age, and began to climb. At twice his height a dark gash cut partway through the trunk. Here, ages ago, a lightning strike had pierced the rugged bark, making an entrance for decay. Llyr swarmed up, threw a leg over the lowest branch, and, hanging upside down, stretched his hand into the open wound.

Carefully, he withdrew a long, flat package wrapped in canvas and tied with twine. He wedged it firmly under his arm and jumped to the ground.

They bent over it together. "What is it?" Guinevere asked. "Open it. Hurry."

Llyr took his time undoing the knots. "Be patient," he murmured. "This must be tied up again exactly the same way so that he does not know we have found it."

"But what is it? You've seen it, haven't you?"

Llyr nodded. "But not up close. And not in daylight."

Beneath the canvas and twine was an inner wrapping of leather bound with thongs. Again, Llyr untied the knotted thongs with consummate care. Inside the leather lay an oiled cloth wrapped around something thick at one end, flat and slender at the other. Gently, Llyr pulled back the final fold.

Around them the forest grew strangely still.

The sheath of a dagger gleamed with the dull luster of old gold and gems deep-set in the Roman style. Silver chasing ran along its edges, fine, threadlike work that spoke of superb craftsmanship and long-lost skills. The hilt was a masterpiece of the goldsmith's art, and Guinevere uttered a soft cry as her hand reached out to touch it.

Llyr watched her anxiously.

Her palm closed on the grip, worn smooth with use, and pulled the weapon free. It had a long steel blade, forged by an expert hand, with honed edges and perfectly balanced weight.

Heavy as it was, Guinevere found it enticingly easy to hold. She had never been one to worship weapons, but the sight of it in her hand produced a heady rush of exhilaration.

"Oh, Llyr," she breathed. "It's magnificent!"

He edged closer. "Whose do you think it is?"

"I don't know. But it has power. I can feel it."

"Put it down, Gwenhwyfar. It could be cursed."

She almost laughed. "Oh no, not cursed. Not when it makes me feel like this!" The dagger's grip seemed made for her hand, so close was the meeting of metal and flesh. She could not tell where one ended and the other began. Cool power flowed from the blade into her wrist and arm, and then into her body, making her heart pound and her breath come fast and light.

When Llyr held out his hand for the weapon, Guinevere almost recoiled. The fear in Llyr's eyes brought her to her senses. It was not her dagger, and it never would be. Reluctantly, she let it go.

"A weapon that makes you feel like that is dangerous," Llyr said gravely as he returned the dagger to its exquisite sheath. "It is better out of sight."

He wrapped it up in the oiled cloth, and as it disappeared from view, the forest came alive with sound—not only of wind and whipping leaves, but of the thudding hoofbeats of a horse coming fast in their direction.

"Zephyr! Thatch!" Guinevere gasped. "We left them outside—they'll be seen!"

Llyr jumped to his feet and struggled to push the movable section of blackthorn out of the way. "Send the pony home and ride south as fast as you can."

"But—"

"Whoever it is, lead him away from here. You must. Or I cannot put this back unseen."

Obediently, Guinevere squeezed through the thorny hedge.

"Head for the road," Llyr urged. "The High King's men will come that way after hunting. You will be safe."

Guinevere did as he asked. She loosed Thatch and slapped him on the rump, sending him off to find his own way home. Someone shouted from the woods behind her as she leaped on Zephyr's back. A glance over her shoulder showed Guinevere a tall man on a dark horse thundering toward her, his cloak flaring about him like wings. She swung Zephyr around and put her heels to the filly's side.

CHAPTER FOURTEEN

The Race

Zephyr bolted. Guinevere buried her fists in the filly's mane and hung on. They flew through the forest, whipped by wind and branches, while behind them the relentless pounding of other hooves still came on. Guinevere lightened her grip on Zephyr's reins while she talked to the mare, keeping her voice low and neutral. Zephyr's ears flicked back to her, but the horse heard the thunder of her pursuer and would not be calmed.

Guinevere kept talking to the filly, keeping her legs steady against the animal's slippery sides and varying her pressure on the reins to distract Zephyr from her fear. Here in the woods there wasn't enough open space to turn a runaway horse; her only hope was to reach Zephyr's panicked mind and calm her down before they tripped and fell or became thoroughly lost. They galloped another hundred paces before Zephyr began to listen, and as the horse slowed, Guinevere realized that the sound of pursuit had ceased.

She brought Zephyr back to a walk and stroked her lathered neck. There was no one following any longer. There was no one else in sight. If they had galloped more or less south, the old Roman road was still somewhere off to her right. She turned the now pliant filly and headed west.

Zephyr picked her way delicately through underbrush and up a gentle slope into a piney wood. There, Guinevere found a path leading northwest, which was exactly the direction she wished to go. But sixty paces down that path a hand reached out from behind a tree and grabbed Zephyr's bridle. The filly wheeled, held fast in the expert grip of a broad-shouldered young man with a sword at his belt.

"What the devil do you mean by stealing the High King's horse, eh?" he cried. "And why did you run from me when I called out in the High King's name? A Saxon, are you? Or just a lowborn thief? Get off this mare before I knock you off!"

Guinevere looked down in astonishment at the angry, upturned face of Trevor of Powys.

"Prince Trevor!"

Too late, she remembered that she had tucked her hair beneath her mantle when she had first set out. Her hair was the only way anyone at a distance could tell her from a boy. Loosening the throat of her mantle, she extracted the long braid of white-gold and let it fall down her back. She smiled apologetically. "It's me—Guinevere. I'm sorry I ran when I heard you shout. But I didn't know who you were."

Trevor's jaw dropped. "Guinevere of Northgallis?" He released the filly's bridle and stared at girl and horse in disbelief. "*This* is your horse?"

Guinevere grinned. "Is she not what you were expecting?"

Trevor shook his head. "She's a beauty. Still a youngster, isn't she? But, my heaven, she can run!"

"She's two and a half," Guinevere said, patting Zephyr's neck. "And running is what she does best. I'm glad you were the one chasing us. I just wish I'd known."

Trevor patted the filly's neck, too. "I apologize if I frightened you. I thought you were up to no good."

"How did you know I would come this way?"

"It's the quickest way back, if you're headed to Deva." He looked up and hesitated. "May I accompany you?"

"Please do. Queen Alyse would be furious to think I'd been out without an escort."

Trevor turned aside into a thicket and emerged leading a big liver chestnut with a face and carriage much like Zephyr's, but with a heftier build. He mounted the stallion and rode up beside Guinevere.

"But I saw you with an escort," he said. "Or I thought I did. Little fellow, black-haired, moves like a fox." He looked at her questioningly. "Or wasn't he with you?"

Guinevere wavered only a moment. "You saw Llyr. He's a friend of mine."

"But not an escort?"

"No."

One sandy eyebrow rose, but Guinevere did not elaborate. Trevor clucked to his horse and headed down the path.

There was no one on the Roman road when they reached it. The afternoon had darkened under a thickening canopy of clouds, and the wind, which had grown fitful, announced itself in abrupt, unsettling gusts, making the horses uneasy.

Trevor laughed as his own mount skittered sideways. "I call him Dancer. He hates wind."

"My filly is named after the wind, the west wind."

"Is she really from the High King's stables? I didn't think they ever let go of the mares."

"King Arthur gave her to King Pellinore last spring for his service against the Saxons, and King Pellinore gave her to me for my birthday."

Trevor whistled. "That's quite a gift. She's young to be so fast."

Guinevere smiled. "You owe me a race, my lord."

"So I do. But not here. Too many of the paving stones are broken. Wait until we get nearer Deva. There's a stretch of good ground there." He patted his horse's shoulder. "Poor old half-breed Dancer. I already know he can't catch her. We were going full tilt before I stopped him, and you were pulling away with every stride."

Guinevere laughed. "Well, if you are willing to forfeit, my lord . . ."

"Don't know the meaning of the word."

Trevor waited until they had rounded a turn in the road before saying, in a casual voice, "Your friend Llyr is an Old One, isn't he?" When Guinevere did not reply, he continued in the same light tone. "Powys is a land of hills and valleys just like Northgallis, but less rugged. We have lots of hillmen.

They call themselves the Wise Ones. What clan is Llyr from?"

Again Guinevere wavered. She knew that many of her own people—the Others, as Llyr called them—distrusted the Old Ones and despised their way of life. She feared that if Llyr's presence became widely known, it might cause trouble for him. But Trevor's freckled face had an honest look, and his brown eyes a steadfast gaze.

"He's the firstborn son of the leader of the White Foot of Snow Mountain."

Trevor's eyebrows rose. "A man of standing, then. He's a long way from home. Is it permitted to ask what he is doing here?"

Guinevere drew a deep breath. "The Old Ones appointed him my guardian. He protects me." She resolved to say nothing more. If he had heard of the prophecy, he would understand. If he hadn't, she would like him all the better for his ignorance.

"I have accompanied my mother to Deva in the hope of meeting Elaine," Trevor said, honoring her gift of confidence with one of his own. "When Sir Gereint brought the High King's summons to Powys, he told us that Queen Alyse planned to take her daughter and her ward to Deva. We had long known, of course, that Alyse of Gwynedd had a likely daughter, and Mother saw her chance. Now that I've met your cousin, I've agreed to the match."

Guinevere pulled Zephyr to a halt. "You want to marry Elaine?"

"I'm about to begin negotiations for her hand. Are there any objections I should know about?"

"Not from me!" Guinevere cried. "I think it's a wonderful idea. But . . . have you spoken to Queen Alyse?"

He laughed. "Not yet. That's my mother's task."

He nodded toward the stretch of road ahead, broad and smooth and well maintained. "What do you say? It's less than a league to camp."

Buoyant with joy, Guinevere took hold of Zephyr's mane and grinned at Trevor. "On the count of three . . ."

The filly nearly shot out from under her as the stallion leaped forward. Guinevere crouched over the horse's withers, trying in vain to see the road ahead. Zephyr's whipping mane stung her eyes to tears, and all she could make out was the broad swath of road and the dark approach of the forest on either side. She could see nothing of the footing. She would have to trust Zephyr for that.

The stallion jumped out to an early lead, but Guinevere held the filly back. She knew Zephyr's speed. There was time to make up ground. It was more important to keep the filly calm and relaxed. She did not want to repeat that panicked gallop through the woods. In her terror, the filly had flung herself forward, careless of where she put her feet. It was sheer luck the pursuit had ended before they fell or ran into a tree. Now she had to make Zephyr *want* to catch the stallion, to beat him, to prove herself the best. She stayed calm on the horse's back, in firm touch with her mouth through the straining reins, and stared at the chestnut's bouncing rump with eagerness in every fiber of her body.

Zephyr responded by lengthening her stride, lowering her neck, and increasing her speed. The stallion flicked his tail as the filly came aside of him, and Trevor glanced over in surprise. He grinned at Guinevere and slapped the stallion's side. The race was on.

Again the stallion surged ahead, and again Zephyr caught him. The filly was gaining confidence and beginning to enjoy herself. Side by side and arrow-straight, they flew together down the Roman road, the filly's long legs keeping pace with the stallion's powerful strides.

Guinevere urged Zephyr forward gradually, and the horse eagerly obeyed. She sped over the ground, hardly feeling the pace. The stallion thundered at her flank, fighting to keep up. Slowly, easily, Zephyr pulled ahead by one length, two lengths, three. She was moving as Guinevere had never felt her move before—loosely, freely, with joy and confidence in her own liberating speed. There was no question of catching her now. Like Alexander of Macedon's great Bucephalos, a stallion descended from the winged Pegasus, Zephyr was in a class by herself.

A shout rang in the air. Guinevere looked back over her shoulder and fought to pull Zephyr up. Fifty paces back, the liver chestnut stood trembling with lowered head at the edge of the road. There was no sign of Trevor of Powys.

CHAPTER FIFTEEN

The Accident

"Trevor! Prince Trevor! Are you hurt?"

Guinevere rode back as fast as she dared. One glance at Dancer, who held one foreleg off the ground, told her that he would not be running off any time soon. She slid off the filly's back and left the two horses together while she began to search for Trevor.

She found him facedown in a shallow ditch, senseless but breathing. She checked as best she could for broken bones, remembering Stannic's gentle examinations of injured horses, but could find nothing obvious. Nothing she did or said made him stir.

She rose and looked up and down the road. Nothing moved; no hoofbeats sounded in the distance. If only Llyr were there. . . . She needed to summon Sir Bedwyr. But

Llyr was far away and on foot, probably headed back to camp. Would he find her before dark? It was nearly dark now, with the clouds pressing down low and the surrounding forest thick with gloom. The skittish wind had died, leaving the air still and oppressive.

She looked down helplessly at Trevor. She dared not leave him. In his senseless state he could not protect himself from predators or robbers. A shiver ran up her spine, and she scolded herself for foolishness as she glanced around at the looming darkness of the forest.

If there was no one to help, she would have to get Trevor back to camp herself. She might drag him on a sled, if she could construct one from branches and boughs. The only tool she had was a small bronze dagger designed for polite use at table, but it would have to serve. Once she had made the sled, she would find a way to maneuver Trevor onto it. The horses' reins might be fashioned into a kind of rope, which might then be attached to Zephyr's saddle . . . except that she had ridden out today without a saddle. She shut her eyes in exasperation. She hadn't meant to defy Queen Alyse's orders; she had simply forgotten to fetch it when she went to the horse lines. In any case, it was too late now. She would use Trevor's saddle and hope that the queen did not witness her return to camp.

It was not a wonderful plan, but she could think of no other, and it was better than spending the night alone on the Roman road without warmth or light, waiting for rescue. Tucking her cloak around Trevor, who looked ominously pale in the deepening dusk, she headed into the forest with her dagger in her hand.

It seemed like hours before she stopped to rest. A small rain began to fall as she sank down again at Trevor's side, exhausted, her arms and hands scratched and bleeding from her efforts. The branches she had gathered were woefully inadequate for her purpose, and she had lost her dagger in the first half hour. One jerk too many had separated the blade from the hilt, and the blade itself had disappeared into the undergrowth on the forest floor. After that, collecting branches was a matter of yanking, pulling, and twisting with bare hands.

"Trevor," she said softly, bending over the silent body. "Trevor, it's Guinevere. Can you hear me?"

She managed to shift his shoulders so that his face no longer touched the dirt, and she freed enough of his cloak from beneath him to make a pillow for his head. "Trevor, please wake up. It's getting dark and cold. I don't know if I can make a sled. I need your help. You have to wake up."

She brushed the dirt from his face as tears rose to her eyes. "Dancer's lame. He's bowed a tendon and bruised a knee. You'll not be able to ride him for a while. He must have fallen on the stone . . . as you did, I fear. Oh, Trevor, please wake up!"

She took one of his big, calloused hands and squeezed it hard. There was no answering movement in his fingers. But his flesh, although cool, was not yet cold, and his chest still rose and fell in a steady rhythm. She closed her eyes and uttered a fervent prayer to the Christian God, the *Kyrios Christos*, that Trevor might recover. And then, because her

Christianity was new and old habits were difficult to shed, she prayed to the Good Goddess as well. She had no libation to pour upon the ground, but hoped that her tears would serve.

When she finished, she dried her eyes, tucked her cloak tighter around Trevor's body, and rose. She had begun to shiver, but work would warm her up again.

"Is he dead?"

She jumped at the sound of a voice behind her. Llyr stood ten paces away, an arrow notched to the bow he held at his side. She stared at him a moment, unbelieving, afraid he was a vision that might shatter if she spoke. Then she saw his pony tethered to a sapling at the forest verge.

"Llyr! Oh, thank God you've come!"

Llyr glanced at the two horses standing together on the road in silent companionship. "He fell? He was not attacked?"

"Yes, he fell. The horse must have tripped. I've got to get him back as fast as I can, but I'm not sure I can do it alone. No one's come by. The hunting party must have returned by a different route. I've got to get word to Sir Bedwyr. Will you go for me? Sir Bedwyr can send his men back with a litter. I can't leave Trevor. He's cold, and he's senseless."

Llyr unstrung his bow and came closer. "You're bleeding."

Guinevere looked down at her hands and shrugged. "Scratches. I've been trying to build a sled, but my dagger broke. I need an ax to do it properly. Will you go for me, Llyr?"

"Of course." He came closer and examined her, as if to satisfy himself that underneath the dirt, blood, and tears there lurked no serious injury. "You raced your horse against the boy with spots?"

"Yes, but what does it matter now?" she asked, impatient to have him gone now that he had finally arrived.

Llyr pointed to the forest. "Lead the horses to the wood and tie them. You must get them off the road. Anyone can see them."

"All right. But I will need your help to move Trevor."

But Llyr did not want Trevor moved. It was not wise to move a senseless man, he told her. If he had knocked his head on the paving stones, moving him might bring death. He advised her to stay hidden with the horses, even if she heard travelers on the road. Finally, he gave her his dagger for protection, mounted his pony, and rode back into the woods.

Filled with both hope and misgiving, Guinevere watched him go. She hadn't asked him why he didn't take the road back. Perhaps his people distrusted roads; perhaps he was more at home in a forest; perhaps he knew something about the use of roads at night that she did not. She fingered the dagger, which was wickedly sharp, and thrust it into her belt. She would lead the horses under the trees and tie them, but she was not going to stay with them and leave Trevor out alone in the rain. She would wait at his side until help came. She was his friend, after all, and if he married Elaine, he would be her brother, too. The hope was a comforting one, and she clung to it while the day darkened and the cold mist strengthened to a drizzle.

CHAPTER SIXTEEN

A Letter to Arthur

Sir Bedwyr sat on a stool before the flare of the oil lamp and peered at the scroll in his hands. He was in his own tent, which opened off the High King's great tent and which held, among its normal furnishings, a lightweight writing desk. Here he had been hard at work with Arthur's scribe for most of the afternoon. It had not improved his temper. Like Arthur, he found administrative work tiresome. He had been happy to have this drudgery interrupted by other business, although the other business had proved troublesome enough.

The scroll was a letter to King Arthur, written in a barely decipherable spidery scrawl, but in perfect Latin. Sir Bedwyr deduced an educated mind but not an educated hand. Below the letter, the same hand had drawn a dagger, rather cramped in style, but with every unusual feature of this very remarkable weapon clearly delineated. The signature was that of one Gemina Honoria Lucasta, and below it a lengthy genealogy traced that lady's ancestors back over a hundred years, on her mother's side, to no less a personage than Magnus Maximus himself.

"It's genuine, then?" he asked, lifting the parchment to the light and flicking it between his fingers.

The tall figure of Merlin the Enchanter detached itself from the shadows and approached the lamp.

"I see no reason to doubt that Lady Gemina wrote it. Her mother believed in educating women."

Sir Bedwyr grunted. "That's not what I meant, my lord, as I think you know."

Merlin smiled. It made him look twenty years younger. "Do you ask me to pass judgment on the truth of the contents? All I can say with certainty is that Lady Gemina wishes us to believe the tale." He shrugged. "We can know nothing about the dagger until we see it. As you yourself have already concluded."

Sir Bedwyr had the grace to look abashed. It was true he had not been asking for Merlin's opinion as a man of intelligence, or even as Arthur's political advisor; he had asked for the certainty of knowledge from a mage. He had asked for Merlin's power. This was something Arthur had warned him and all the other Companions never to do. For Merlin's power of foreseeing came from his god and was not at any mortal's beck and call, not even his own.

Sir Bedwyr dipped his head to acknowledge his trespass. Merlin's chastisement had been extraordinarily gentle, but then, he was used to such appeals. Everyone, including Arthur, found it hard to believe that the wizard did not know everything.

"Well, you know Riall's terms, my lord. I can't accede to them."

"No."

Merlin took the scroll from Sir Bedwyr's hand and scanned the genealogy once more.

"Even if all that's true," Sir Bedwyr said, "I'm not about to hand over the kingdom of Gwynedd. Arthur wouldn't do it. Pellinore's earned the right to it twice over, even if his wife didn't have the better claim."

Merlin looked up from his reading and met the warrior's eyes. "Tell me how this came into your hands."

Sir Bedwyr shrugged. "Lord Riall brought it. After everyone left for the hunt, I sent for the scribe to consolidate the notes from this morning's meeting. We had got only halfway through when Lord Riall begged entrance and would not be put off. He's been loitering about for days, waiting to see me when I've been at leisure. As you know, there hasn't been any leisure. I confess I was curious about his business here, so when he finally asked for a hearing, I gave it to him. He had a long list of grievances about his father's treatment at the hands of Alyse and Pellinore, but as they dated to a time before his birth, I took them to be his mother's complaints."

He paused, but there was no response from Merlin, not even a breath of movement. Sir Bedwyr reminded himself that complete and utter stillness was Merlin's gift. It marked him more surely than any speech or gesture. His stillness went deeper than flesh, deeper than spirit, down to the unfath-omable wellspring of being itself. It became a force of its own and propelled Sir Bedwyr to further speech.

"Then he told me about the dagger: its accidental find-ing in the floor of the tomb Lady Gemina is preparing for her-self, its inscriptions, its significance to Arthur. He made it sound like something necessary, even essential, to Arthur's future . . . to his legend, if you will. Last, of course, he told me his terms."

Sir Bedwyr rose and began to pace, hunching his broad swordsman's shoulders as if the available space could not con-tain him.

"I'm not fool enough to suppose that Arthur would even consider making Riall king of Gwynedd to secure a dagger, whatever its importance. I suppose, sir, I'm asking whether Arthur needs this weapon. Is it part of his . . ."—he shied away from the word *destiny*, although somehow it did not seem out of place to speak of destiny when Merlin was in the room—". . . his future? Perhaps he should see it, make the choice himself. He wouldn't stoop to such means to get it, but I can stoop and get it for him."

He stopped pacing and looked anxiously at Merlin.

The enchanter's eyes were grave. "Thank you," he said. "That's a testament to your loyalty."

"Sir, it's an offer."

Merlin drew on his cloak. "It's a courageous offer. Arthur would not accept it, but I might." He paused and said, in a low voice that for all its gravity held a note of amusement, "Whatever this dagger is, it is not one of the Things of

Power that the god has vouchsafed to Arthur for his reign. His destiny is secure. If that is what worries you, be at peace."

Sir Bedwyr swallowed. He was used to having his mind read, but never before had Merlin the Enchanter taken him into his confidence. "I shall get the dagger, my lord. I'll steal it if I can't force it from him."

Merlin shook his head. "Wait. It may not be necessary."

"And in the meantime?"

"Patience. I believe Lord Riall wants very badly to show us his hidden treasure. Why else is he here?"

He bowed politely and took his leave. But he stopped short of the tent flap. "A visitor," he murmured, and with an apologetic glance at Sir Bedwyr, dissolved once more into the shadows of the tent.

A moment later, a clamor arose outside. A sentry shouted; a sword whined free of its scabbard, followed by the sounds of a scuffle, a cry, and a smothered curse. Sir Bedwyr raised a hand to shade his eyes from the lamp's glare as the tent flap trembled and something—a shadow, a wraith, he couldn't quite see what—slipped inside.

Heavy footsteps approached, and the flap was thrown aside. A sentry appeared, breathing hard, his sword drawn.

"Begging your pardon, sir, but did he come in here, the little savage?"

Sir Bedwyr opened his mouth to say, *I think so, Bevan. Check in the corners,* when he heard himself already speaking. "I've seen no one. Take your search outside. I am in conference."

The sentry cast a frightened glance into the shadows and

backed out hastily. "Yes, sir. Very sorry, sir. Don't worry, we'll get him."

Sir Bedwyr waited until the flap closed before turning to Merlin. He was not surprised to find that the enchanter had stepped just far enough into the light to make visible the outline of his face. "Well?" He spoke more sharply than he intended, but he resented lying to his own man, even though, strictly speaking, he had not said anything untrue. "Where is he?"

The lamp flared at his elbow, and Sir Bedwyr saw a dark form crouched at Merlin's feet, forehead to the ground.

"What on earth?"

Merlin spoke half under his breath in a rough, guttural tongue and the form rose and became a slender young man, gracile as a deer, with very black hair and dark eyes that blazed in the lamplight. Doeskin boots adorned his feet, and a necklace of wolf's teeth encircled his neck. Had he been clothed in wolfskins as well, Sir Bedwyr might have placed him as one of the Old Ones, but the young man's clothes were modern and beautifully made. They were the clothes of a wealthy man.

Sir Bedwyr frowned. "Who is he?"

"His name is Llyr, son of Bran, leader of the White Foot of Snow Mountain. He brings you a message of importance. Listen to him."

Sir Bedwyr's confusion deepened. "White Foot? But he can't be an Old One. Look at him."

The young man stood defiantly before Sir Bedwyr, wary, poised for flight, but waiting. His head was not bowed in submission; his gaze was not lowered in respect. He had been chased into the tent, but he had not run out when the sentry left.

"Why are the guards after him? What has he done?"

"Ask him yourself," said Merlin. "He speaks Welsh."

Sir Bedwyr addressed Llyr sharply. "Why are my men after you?"

Llyr bowed stiffly. "I came to see Sir Bed-i-vere." He struggled with the strangeness of the name while Sir Bedwyr struggled with the thickness of his accent. "The large man tried to stop me. He drew his sword, so I knocked it from his hand. He called the guards, so I ran in here. Please, lord, I must speak to Sir Bed-i-vere. It is a matter of urgency."

Sir Bedwyr regarded him skeptically. "You knocked it out of his hand? How? He's twice your size."

Llyr shrugged at the irrelevance of the question. "I struck his wrist. The sword fell." He stepped closer, full in the light, and raised beseeching eyes to Sir Bedwyr. "Lord, Gwenhwyfar of Northgallis needs your help."

Sir Bedwyr's surprise showed in his face. "Guinevere of Northgallis? King Pellinore's ward?" He recollected the bright-haired child Princess Morgan had sought to humiliate for some reason known only to herself. He also recollected the girl astride a dappled gray filly, riding like a boy, with an ease and grace even Lancelot might have envied. His interest in the young man sharpened.

"Yes," Llyr said tautly. "King Pellinore's ward. There has been an accident to Trevor-of-Powys." Again, he stumbled over the foreign name. "The boy with spots. He fell from his horse and does not wake. The horse, too, is hurt. Gwenhwyfar sent me to beg for help."

"Where is she? Is she injured?"

Llyr stiffened at the suggestion that he could have left her if she had been hurt, and Sir Bedwyr took note of this reaction.

"She is not hurt. She stayed by Trevor-of-Powys. She would not leave."

Sir Bedwyr spun on his heel and whistled sharply for the sentry. "Are they alone, then? Where?"

"On the road south, lord."

The sentry poked his head in, saw Llyr, and opened his mouth to protest, but Sir Bedwyr cut him off. "Bevan, find Sir Lyell. Have him meet me at the horse lines with six men, a litter, blankets, and lanterns. At once."

"Yes, sir." Bevan looked askance at Llyr. "Sir! That's the man we've been looking for."

"Is it?" Sir Bedwyr snapped. "You surprise me. I should have thought it took a larger man than this to part one of the King's sentries from his sword."

Bevan's face flamed. "But, sir—"

"Go!" cried Sir Bedwyr. "For pity's sake, man, lives may be at stake. Find Lyell!"

Bevan went. Sir Bedwyr turned to Llyr.

"You will lead me to the place of the accident. Have you a horse?"

"Yes, lord. A pony."

"That will do. Follow me to the horse lines." He reached for his sword belt and looked irritably about him. The lamp was smoking now, shedding very little light. "Where's Merlin?"

Llyr did not have to peer into the shadows to know what answer was required. "Lord, the Master is gone."

Sir Bedwyr shrugged and strapped on his sword. "He would be. Never mind, let's get going." He grabbed his cloak and settled it about his shoulders. "Just pray I can get the girl back unharmed before Pellinore's home from the hunt."

In the stillness that followed their departure, Merlin the Enchanter stepped forth from the shadows and blew out the smoking lamp. He stood alone in the darkness and considered what he had seen and heard. Every instinct warned him that there was something of importance here. It might be the dagger, if it was genuine, or it might be the girl. He found it interesting that Bedwyr's response to the news of an accident to Trevor of Powys—the future king of Powys—was to rush off to rescue the girl. This was the same child whose surprising resistance had foiled his attempt to search her mind on the night of her presentation to Princess Morgan.

It was a small coincidence, but he knew better than to discount it. Sometimes the gods blared their intent across the heavens, and sometimes they spoke in whispers. One had to keep one's ear attuned to trivialities to hear the whisper of a god.

CHAPTER SEVENTEEN

True Aim

Morgan sat on her gilded stool while Marcia dressed her hair for dinner. They would be eating inside the great tent tonight, since it was still raining, and the more formal setting allowed for finery.

She glanced over at Elaine, curled on the bed—on Morgan's own bed—amid a pile of furs and cushions. What had been granted as a privilege a week ago was taken for granted now. "Shouldn't you be dressing, too? You don't want to be late."

"There's plenty of time. It takes Mother *ages* to get ready."

Morgan watched in her mirror of polished bronze as Marcia placed a triple string of garnets across her brow. She had always looked her best in red. Everyone said so. "Stay, then. You can be of use to me."

"Tsk, Morgan. Manners," clucked Marcia under her breath, and received a sharp glance in the mirror for her pains.

Elaine slid off the bed, dislodging the crimson coverlet, and came closer. "That's very pretty. Are those rubies?"

"Hardly. Arthur has rubies. I have garnets."

"Mistress Morgan." Marcia's voice was sharp.

Morgan turned on her stool. "You are dismissed."

Marcia put down the comb, curtsied, and withdrew, flicking the bedcover back into place as she went.

Morgan reached for her garnet earrings. "I heard something today I am hoping you can explain," she said, returning her gaze to the mirror. "It concerns your cousin."

"Gwen? What did you hear?"

"Apparently, a stranger came into camp last night, attacked one of the guards outside the great tent, and ran straight into Sir Bedwyr's quarters. Uninvited. I find it very odd that he was not instantly arrested. Odder still that he should have been sent there by your cousin."

"Oh, you mean Llyr. He's not a stranger; he's a friend of Gwen's."

"A friend! Oh, no, it can't have been anyone you know."

"Don't believe me, then," Elaine sniffed, retreating to the bed and reinstalling herself among the cushions, "but that's who it was. Gwen sent him to Sir Bedwyr for help when Trevor fell."

Morgan's eyes widened. "He was described to me as a very primitive, savage sort of person. More beast than human. Surely you don't call such a creature a friend."

"Hogwash. Llyr's not a beast; he's a prince among the Old

Ones. He came with us from Gwynedd as part of our escort. He has Father's permission to be here, and probably Sir Bedwyr's, too, by now."

Morgan swung around on the stool to stare at her. "A *hillman*? Don't jest with me, Elaine. This is not a laughing matter."

"I'm *not* jesting."

"Your father would never travel with a hillman!"

"Why not? He did."

"Your mother would never allow it!"

Elaine raised a shoulder and let it fall. "She'd forgive Llyr anything. He saved my life." Her sky-blue eyes, so frankly innocent, dared Morgan to disbelieve. "He killed a man who was going to kill me."

"Indeed?" Morgan lowered her eyes to hide her incredulity. "How very frightening for you. Who was the man he killed?"

"A traitor. An evil, foul-smelling, wicked traitor."

"Another hillman, was it? . . . Or one of us?"

Elaine hesitated, and Morgan immediately turned back to her mirror, cursing herself for impatience. She had let Elaine see that the answer mattered to her. Now she must change course and hope that she could find out through other sources whom the little savage had killed.

"Never mind. Whoever he was, if he threatened your life, he deserved to die. The important thing is that this Llyr fellow saved you. I trust he was handsomely rewarded for the deed?"

"He was publicly honored, along with the others. The whole clan helped."

"The . . . *whole clan?*"

"The Long Eyes. Llyr's clan. Well, actually, the Long Eyes are Mapon's clan. Llyr's clan is the—"

"Do you mean you *know* these creatures?"

"Well, we know some of them."

"And they're *in camp?*"

"Oh, no. Only Llyr came with us, and he doesn't stay in camp. He stays in the woods and keeps watch."

Morgan blinked. "For what?"

"Gwen, of course. He wouldn't be much of a guardian if he stayed in Gwynedd while she's in Deva."

"*Guardian?*" Morgan's eyes narrowed into points of bronze. "You are not," she said evenly, "attempting to imply that this . . . this hillman is hiding out in the woods at the edge of camp and spying on us all, giving as his excuse that he is guarding your *cousin?* From what, may I ask?"

"It's not an excuse. He's Gwen's guardian. The Old Ones appointed him so themselves."

Morgan looked at her blankly.

Patiently, Elaine began to explain what had taken place in Gwynedd last spring. Morgan listened in a daze of disbelief. That a rebel lord should abduct Elaine in a bid to seize her father's throne was credible enough. There were ambitious rogues in every kingdom. But that the hillmen had rescued the girl defied belief. Nor could she accept that the royal house of Gwynedd dealt in friendship with this savage race of men and accepted their protection. What did they mean by such behavior? Hillmen preyed on travelers and stole from outlying farms and villages. In her father's reign, they had been hunted nearly to extinction.

"The Old Ones have always guarded Gwen on account of the prophecy," Elaine continued, dimpling at Morgan's confusion. "Only she didn't know it until last spring, when Llyr told her. That's when the Old Ones appointed him as her guardian in their place. It was *their* prophecy, you see."

Breathless, Morgan stared at Elaine and struggled to make sense of her words. The girl seemed to be speaking in an alien tongue. *"Prophecy?"*

"It's not a *real* prophecy, of course," Elaine said soothingly. "Not like King Arthur's. No one believes it except the Old Ones. It was made in Northgallis when Gwen's father was king by a hill witch who begged shelter from a storm. Gwen's got sense enough to know it isn't true. But the Old Ones have to believe it because it was made by one of their own people. They have to keep Gwen safe until it comes to pass. Now they've given that job to Llyr."

"Elaine!" Morgan breathed, digging her nails into her palms to still her trembling. "You go too fast. *What* did the prophecy foretell?"

Elaine heaved an exaggerated sigh. "That Gwen should wed a great king and come to glory with him, and be the highest lady in the land, and have her name remembered beyond a thousand years," Elaine rattled off as if it were a chant she had memorized long ago.

Morgan swallowed in a dry throat. "Who . . . is this great king supposed to be?"

Elaine shrugged. "Nobody knows. It might be one of the Old Ones, since it's their prophecy, but the Old Ones don't call their leaders kings. Anyway, that's the prophecy—or the part of it we know."

"There's more?"

"Yes, but I don't know it. Neither does Gwen. Her father refused to tell her. He said she was better off not knowing."

Morgan pressed her fingertips to her throbbing temples. Last night, amid all the clamor and excitement of Prince Trevor's accident, she had gone into her stillroom to sacrifice to the Goddess. She had asked for only one thing: to know her enemy's name. Today the name of Guinevere of Northgallis had been thrust before her in a way that demanded her attention. Was this the Goddess's answer? Or a mere coincidence? Or a ploy by Elaine to mislead her? If the tale of a prophecy was true, why had she seen nothing—absolutely *nothing*—in her black bowl?

For years, she had toiled in the dank depths of Tintagel, that citadel of rock off the Cornish coast that had been her home, studying the black arts, slaving over preparations of herbs and potions, memorizing spells and incantations, learning from a local soothsayer how to read the portents of the future in a bowl of black water. It had cost her much to attain such precious knowledge. She had gone without sleep, meals, sunlight, and fresh air; she had devoted herself mind and soul to the achievement of power.

And, to a degree, she had achieved it. She could not read minds, as Merlin could, but she was adept at bending the wills of others to her own. She could not create fire or storm with the flick of a finger, but she could sniff out weakness in any man. She could see things in her black bowl that no one else could see.

The great events of history—the rise and fall of empires, the births and deaths of kings—threw shadows before them that skilled seers could discern. Arthur's birth had been fore-shadowed by prophecies in every corner of the known world, so Merlin had once told Ygraine. Morgan had herself foreseen events—like her marriage to Urien—that concerned her future and her brother's. Yet if Elaine was telling her the truth, the wretched hillmen had made a prophecy about Guinevere of Northgallis that fairly froze the marrow in Morgan's bones—and she had seen nothing of it in her black bowl!

It could not be true.

It was not that Elaine was lying. Morgan had become adept at reading Elaine's moods, and the girl's voice carried both conviction and the surreptitious excitement of revealing a secret she had promised not to tell. But the hillmen of Gwynedd might be lying, or themselves deceived by one of their own. It was easy to imagine how such a prophecy might, like any exciting rumor, spread among the ignorant, backward hill dwellers until it was universally believed.

It had to be false. She had seen nothing in her black bowl because there was nothing of significance to see. The birth of Guinevere of Northgallis could not be an event of importance in the tide of human history. She was only a backwoods or-phan without power or rank beyond the borders of her father's tiny kingdom, and would likely spend her life buried in the dark Welsh mountains, wed to some inconsequential lord of

Queen Alyse's choosing. A girl of such unimportant birth could never be a threat to the only legitimate daughter of Uther Pendragon. The idea was laughable.

And yet . . . the bowl had warned her again and again of a terrible danger coming out of the west, a nemesis with feminine graces who could touch even Arthur's power . . . and it was certainly not the shy, wide-eyed Cornish girl he had married.

Elaine was the more logical one to suspect. Her father was a favorite of Arthur's; her mother's lineage was impeccable by anyone's standards; the girl herself was pretty, lively, blooming with health, and blessed with a figure beyond her years. Elaine of Gwynedd was a girl poised on the edge of a glorious future. If the prophecy had been made for Elaine, Morgan would have no trouble believing it.

And yet she had found nothing to fear in Elaine. A spoiled, selfish child, Elaine had no outstanding traits of character that Morgan could discern, and no talents beyond the common scope. Her chief assets, beauty and birth, were gifts of fortune for which the girl could take no credit. As a threat to herself or to Arthur, Morgan did not think Elaine could qualify.

Guinevere was another matter. The girl was still a mystery to her. If this tale about a prophecy was true, then she had found her enemy, improbable or not. That a landless orphan should be so singled out by fate for a destiny of power and greatness seemed to Morgan unfair as well as unlikely, but the gods were well known to be fickle. Even the Christian deity her mother worshipped had chosen a lowly carpenter to bear His name.

Morgan gazed at her image in the mirror. She saw a regal woman, born of the blood of kings, with a crown of jewels across her brow. A woman worthy of power and ready to rule. A woman prepared for battle.

With steady fingers, Morgan raised a garnet earring from the table and carefully hooked it in her ear. *First, know the lay of the land* was one of Arthur's battle-tested maxims.

"Your cousin must think she's someone special. Not everyone has a personal guardian, never mind a prophecy."

"Gwen?" Elaine's laugh was dismissive. "Gwen's the *last* one who'd ever believe the prophecy. She'd rather pretend it never happened. She never speaks of it."

Morgan paused, the second earring in her hand. What kind of girl would shrink from a prophecy that foretold a glory lasting past a thousand years? A weak girl? A shy girl? A skeptic? A fool?

"You could not be such a half-wit," she said sharply. "Not a girl of your breeding. Open your eyes, Elaine. Of course she believes it. What girl wouldn't? Apparently, she's been clever enough to hide it from you all these years."

Morgan looked into Elaine's blue, self-confident gaze and smiled to herself. *Divide and conquer.* It was time to separate the cousins. "I must say, I hadn't given her credit for brains as well as beauty."

Elaine blinked at her. "Beauty!"

"Indeed. A gift that runs in your family, as anyone can see.

A gift that can raise the lowliest girl to exalted station. Surely you know its value. Your mother, like mine, is known far and wide for beauty. And your mother's sister, I am told, was in a different class altogether."

"Gwen's not like her!" Elaine burst out. "You can see that for yourself! Why, she gets taken for a boy whenever she ties up her hair!"

Morgan smiled coolly at the flush on Elaine's cheeks. "That won't be true a year from now. The signs are already there. If you don't believe me, watch the guards' eyes as she passes by. Listen to their whispers. Not everyone regards her as a boy."

"That's not true!" Elaine's protest had lost some of its fervor, and her cheeks had drained of color. Her eyes had a stunned look, and behind them a spark of fear.

"You haven't watched her as I have," Morgan continued evenly. "And you see her too often to notice change."

"She *hasn't* changed. She's *always* been skinny and plain." Elaine clutched a scarlet pillow and squeezed it convulsively.

"And she always will be? Have it your own way. But at least be vigilant. Remember, no one ever actually sees a bud blossom, but all at once the bloom is there."

Elaine rose to her knees. "Stop it. Stop it now. It doesn't matter anyway what Gwen looks like. Her future's in my mother's hands, no one else's. Certainly not the Old Ones'!"

Amusement crept into Morgan's amber eyes. It was child's play to divide the cousins. The suspicions she had planted in Elaine's mind would take root and grow, feeding off jealousy and fear. As for Guinevere, she would be easy to wound through that fellow Llyr. And how fitting that Elaine herself had handed Morgan the weapon . . .

"Your mother is honor-bound to marry you off first and best, is that it?"

"Of course," Elaine said with a lift of her chin. "I'm her daughter."

"Suppose my wayward brother were to see your cousin and want her? Would your mother have the courage—forgive me, I mean the gall—to refuse him? Perhaps you haven't noticed, but no one opposes Arthur for very long."

Elaine grew pale and then flushed. She slid off the bed, making sure the bedclothes followed. "In case you hadn't noticed, your brother's married."

Morgan's eyes glittered. "Since when has that ever kept a man from a woman he wanted?"

"Arthur wouldn't!" Elaine cried.

Morgan laughed. "Like father, like son."

Too late, Elaine remembered that Morgan's mother, Ygraine, had been married to Gorlois on the night Uther Pendragon had breached the defenses of Tintagel to lie with her.

"That was ordained by God."

"Adultery?"

"It wasn't—the king lay dead on the field of battle before the High King—"

"How do you know? Were you there?" Morgan's voice was cold. "Merlin put that tale about to protect Arthur's claim to legitimacy. Who knows at what hour Gorlois died? The point is, Uther certainly did not."

"*Claim* to legitimacy?" Elaine bristled, color flooding her face. "You can't mean—"

"It might not have made any difference," Morgan continued smoothly. "Bastards have inherited kingdoms before this."

Elaine turned almost purple. "*How do you dare?* King Arthur—"

"Is a bastard bred, if not a bastard born," Morgan said fiercely. "*I'm* the only child of that union conceived in the marriage bed."

Elaine glared at her, too furious for speech. She whirled away from Morgan and strode to the tent door, chin held high. With one hand on the tent flap, she turned.

"You're not at all like him, you know," she said. "Everyone loves him better than you. But you know that. You've grown up knowing that. That's why you're jealous of him."

Morgan froze. The tent flap slapped closed. Elaine was gone.

In the shadows of the inner doorway, Marcia crossed herself. "Beware a child's wrath," she breathed. "Her arrows are dangerous, for her aim is true."

CHAPTER EIGHTEEN

The Dagger

Sir Bedwyr sighed with pleasure as his servant eased him out of his leather tunic and leggings, heavy and clinging with two days' damp, and into his woolen night-robe. He shifted his shoulders, enjoying the freedom of movement. Mithras be praised, the long day had finally come to an end.

He dismissed his servant and blew out the lamp himself, taking a candle to his camp bed. Although it was getting on toward the middle of the night, he did not immediately turn in. He had things to think about, and the day's events to sort, before he could compose his mind for sleep. Unlike Arthur, who paced about like a young lion when he had a problem to solve, Bedwyr preferred stillness, calm, and the uninterrupted silence of the night.

His first problem was time. It was time to make a progress

report to Arthur, and he had no progress to report. Not only had the council of kings not ratified the plan of defensive communications that Arthur had in mind for them, but they had resisted all of Bedwyr's attempts to nudge them toward it.

"Steer them if you can," Arthur had told him on the eve of his departure, "but don't force it on them. They must each play a part in the solution or they won't regard it as their own. I'd prefer you come home empty-handed than with a treaty none of them intend to honor."

Bedwyr was determined not to go home empty-handed, but at this pace it would take years. And he had to get Morgan to Rheged in three weeks' time or risk King Urien's wrath. Urien was king of a vast land and a leader among the northern lords. Arthur had been after his support for years. He had finally secured it by promising Urien his sister. Morgan's marriage, if Bedwyr got her there in time, would cement the longed-for alliance with Rheged. Treaty or no treaty, he had to head north soon.

Bedwyr shook his head wearily. He had never met men as stubborn as these Welshmen, men so determined to argue over every blessed thing. As today's council had demonstrated, without Trevor of Powys, the lines of division between them quickly deepened into fractures. The South Welsh, Dynas of Dyfed and Mardoc of Guent, immediately opposed any idea put forward by the North Welsh, and vice versa. As a result, the council had rapidly deteriorated into a shouting match, and then into a drinking party. Since the heavy rain ruled out hunting and Arthur's requirement that no weapons be allowed in the council chamber ruled out brawling, the drinking was still going on.

The kings had drunk their way through the evening meal, much to the ladies' disgust. All the women had retired early; Bedwyr let them go. The kings were friendly enough in their cups, and their boisterous drinking and astonishing gift for song had done much to enliven the cold, wet evening. But Bedwyr knew well that come morning and another council meeting, they'd be at each other's throats again.

Trevor of Powys was his second problem. The prince still lay prostrate and senseless, even with the physician in constant attendance. Queen Esdora had asked Bedwyr that very afternoon if Merlin would see the boy. He had hemmed and hawed at first, for asking anything of Merlin was not a task he relished, but he could not refuse her plea. He had sent a man to find the enchanter, but Merlin was not in camp. No one knew where he had gone; no one had seen him go. Since Merlin was known for his habit of disappearing, Bedwyr was not overly concerned. He had posted lookouts and was content to wait.

If the boy should die, Arthur would have another problem on his hands. The king of Powys was ill, and there were no other sons. Leaderless kingdoms always meant war. Already Bedwyr fancied he could see a calculating look in King Mardoc's eye whenever Powys was mentioned. It would be best for everyone if Trevor recovered. Perhaps Queen Esdora had done him a favor in requesting the enchanter's aid.

His third problem was Lord Riall. Once the drinking had begun in earnest and Bedwyr had retired to his tent, Lord Riall had come to see him. He was now prepared, he said, to grant Sir Bedwyr the privilege of viewing the dagger, provided the knight promised to return the weapon to him and keep its existence secret from everyone else in camp. Bedwyr had agreed to this with a certain thinness of patience and had informed Sir Riall that his opportunities for dagger viewing were limited, as there was so much else to do.

Lord Riall had retreated, but promised to bring him the precious object that very night once everyone else was asleep. At the rate the men were going—the rich wail of drunken voices raised in song sailed clearly through the tent cloth—they would likely make a night of it. That suited Bedwyr fine. By morning, Merlin might be back in camp, and he wanted Merlin with him when Lady Gemina's precious bribe was finally presented.

He yawned, exhausted, and stretched out on his canvas bed. The next thing he knew, Bevan was poking his shoulder and calling him awake. Bleary-eyed, he pushed himself upright. It seemed only moments since he had lain down, but the candle was guttering in its holder, and the only sounds coming from the great tent next door were snores.

"What is it?" he grumbled.

"Sir, Lord Riall is without. He says you are expecting him."

Bedwyr grunted and reached for his mantle. "Who's in the King's tent?"

"About twenty men, sir. Rufus and me, we got the kings to their beds a while back when the wine ran out, but we left the others to sleep it off."

"Bring Lord Riall in the back way, then, not through the tent."

"Yes, sir."

"Wait, Bevan. Is Merlin the Enchanter in camp?"

"I don't know, sir. Shall I send for him?"

Bedwyr smiled. "*Send* for him? I shouldn't dare. Never mind. If the lookouts haven't come to report, then he isn't back yet." He sighed, rose, and straightened his robes around him. "Show Lord Riall in."

By the time Bevan ushered Lord Riall to the tent's private entrance, Bedwyr had replaced the candle and relit the lamp, waked his servant to make tea, and positioned the lamp so that its light shone on the bare surface of the writing desk. Lord Riall entered nervously. He glanced suspiciously about him but, seeing no one else, came forward politely enough.

"I beg pardon for the lateness of the hour," he said, bowing, and glanced sourly at the door flap to the great tent. "I thought they would never stop."

"Counseling is thirsty work," Bedwyr replied, his eyes on the canvas-wrapped package Lord Riall held tightly under his arm. "And they are men of appetites."

"Aye," Lord Riall agreed. "And not all worthy of their crowns."

"Show me the dagger," said Bedwyr testily. "After that, you can tell me why you think it's so important."

He watched with a fascination he could not help as Lord Riall placed his package on the desk and began to unwrap it. Layer after layer of protective cloth was carefully removed until at last the dagger lay revealed. Bedwyr almost gasped.

"Go ahead," Lord Riall breathed. "Touch it. Draw the blade."

Bedwyr was annoyed to find himself trembling as he took the sheath in his left hand and reached for the hilt with his right. The blade pulled free with a whisper of sound. Like a sigh of release, Bedwyr thought, dazzled by the beauty of the weapon. The steel blade was long and slender, well balanced and honed to killing sharpness—the work of a master smith. Couched in its sheath of beaten red-gold, set with gems and chased with silver, it was the most beautiful weapon, after Excalibur, that he had ever seen.

Watching him closely with a mixture of fear and satisfaction, Lord Riall held out his hand for the weapon. Bedwyr gave it up with great reluctance. Lord Riall smiled and held the dagger closer to the light.

"See where it is written, Sir Bedwyr, here on the blade itself: TO MY COMMANDER . . . MAGNUS MAXIMUS, EMPEROR OF THE BRITONS. We think it was a gift of his lieutenant, his second-in-command."

Bedwyr peered at the Latin lettering. The etching was clear enough to have been made yesterday. Had this lovely weapon never been used? Bedwyr picked up the sheath and examined it closely. It appeared to be old Roman work, the gems deep-set and clear, the chasing exquisitely applied. He had never seen anything like it. The sheath was strictly ornamental, the kind of gift given to one king from another as a matter of diplomacy. Yet the words TO MY COMMANDER implied that the giver had been subordinate to the Emperor Maximus. If the sheath was ornamental, the weapon itself was not. Despite the goldwork on the hilt, it was a deadly weapon—a man's weapon; a king's.

The servant came in with two bowls of bark tea, and the men sat down together on camp stools to begin negotiations.

"My mother found it when she was having her tomb dug,"

Lord Riall said. "She was quite excited. The Emperor Magnus Maximus is, as you know, our ancestor."

Bedwyr sipped the hot brew gratefully and nodded. "Yes. So she said in the letter."

"It didn't look like this when it was found, of course. It was tarnished and dirty, and two of the gems had fallen out. She took it to a goldsmith who put the gems back in, polished it and cleaned it, and fixed up a segment of silver chasing that had rotted away. It was then that she realized the value of the piece. The goldsmith offered her a good price for it, but she refused to sell."

"And told no one about it?"

Lord Riall shrugged. "She didn't want our carrion cousins to learn of it. They'd have taken it from her."

Carrion cousins! Bedwyr grunted, surprised at the venom in Riall's voice, and gave the man his opening. "What makes you think so? Alyse and Pellinore aren't thieves."

"They robbed me of my birthright!" Lord Riall cried. "My father, Castellors, should have been king of Gwynedd, and my mother queen. The genealogy makes that clear. Instead, my uncle Meregon, the second-born, was chosen. My grandfather Meleanor broke the pattern. He himself was the first-born son of King Driant, who descended in the male line straight from the Emperor Magnus Maximus."

"I've no doubt your blood is royal, my lord," Bedwyr murmured into his tea. "Why did your grandfather choose your uncle instead of your father?"

Lord Riall's face twisted. "When Meleanor's first wife died—Castellors's mother, that was—he remarried a girl straight from the mountains with not a drop of royal blood. She *said* she was descended from Elen of Gwynedd, Maximus's wife, but of course she could never prove it. My grandfather was in his dotage then, and besotted with the girl."

Lord Riall trembled with emotion. Bedwyr sipped his tea and said thoughtfully, "Was she a fair-haired girl?"

Lord Riall glanced at him sharply. "How did you know?"

"A guess, merely. There's a strain of fair-haired beauty that runs in that family still, a strain that began, they say, with the wife of the Emperor Maximus."

Lord Riall snorted. "Someone's been telling you tales. The girl my grandfather married was a witch. She ensnared him. But the marriage didn't last long. She bore him a son and died. And for the rest of his life, Meleanor loved that witch's son more than my father, Castellors—even though Castellors was fifteen by then and had already proved himself a worthy heir—"

He stopped himself, then burst out, "You can see the justice of my case, can't you? Because, by God, if you can't, I'll find someone else who can. The dagger must go to King Arthur. *He'll* understand."

"I see the justice of your case," Bedwyr said gravely. "I will put it to Arthur, if you like, exactly as you have put it to me. Will that content you?"

Lord Riall frowned. "I'm not parting with the dagger on those terms, if that's what you mean. I accompany the weapon, and Mother does not want it taken beyond Deva." He lowered his voice and glanced furtively about him. "You have felt the dagger's power, and you are not even its master. It was made for an emperor's hand—and for Arthur's, if he's to reach greatness. It was made for *the once and future king*."

He waited breathlessly for Bedwyr's reply.

"Then give it to him."

"Not without his promise to make me king of Gwynedd!"

Bedwyr slowly shook his head. "I cannot make that promise, my lord, and I am obliged to tell you that I think it unlikely the High King will make it, either. Pellinore has proved himself a good ruler and a reliable ally. One doesn't throw such men away."

"He married into the family!" Lord Riall cried, reddening. "All his power comes from his wife, Queen Alyse—a *woman*! And she should never have inherited. Meregon had no sons— the crown should have come to my brothers and me, not to his daughter Alyse. It is mine by right of birth twice over!"

Bedwyr watched a flush of anger stain Lord Riall's face. "It seems to me," he said at last, "that you have a low opinion of women. But the High King does not, I assure you. I advise you to reconsider."

Lord Riall rose. "Never. I'll take the dagger back, and Arthur can go to his fate—and you'll be to blame."

"*Sit down.*"

The voice came from behind them, and both men turned. Merlin stood just inside the door to the great tent, his dark cloak glistening with rain.

CHAPTER NINETEEN

A King's Gamble

Merlin moved swiftly into the light, where Lord Riall could see him.

"Sit down," he said again. Lord Riall sat. Bedwyr moved between Lord Riall and the door.

Merlin strode to the writing desk and gazed down at the dagger in its jeweled sheath. Like Bedwyr before him, he reached, unthinking, for the hilt and drew the blade. He studied the bared weapon intently, raised it to the light, twirled it gently between his fingers, and put the blade into the flame until it dazzled the eyes. Then he lowered the weapon carefully into its wrappings.

"My congratulations, Lord Riall," he said cordially, "to you and your lady mother on the value of her find. The dagger is genuine. However, it is of no interest to Arthur at the present time. You may return it to Lady Gemina with my thanks. It has been most instructive to see it."

Lord Riall paled as he rose to his feet. "I beg your pardon, my lord Merlin, but the High King must see it. It is essential to his future."

Merlin stepped away from the desk. "Then take it to him."

"Not until my crown has been restored!"

"It is not your crown. It never was."

"It *is*," the man insisted. "I've explained it all to Sir Bedwyr. My grandfather chose—"

"Your grandfather chose to gamble with his sons. Your father lost."

Lord Riall began to tremble. He opened his mouth and shut it again.

"Your father was man enough to accept it," Merlin said evenly. "Go home and persuade your lady mother to do the same."

Lord Riall walked stiffly to the desk. Bedwyr watched with a pang of the heart as he rewrapped the dagger and tucked it securely under his arm. White-faced, Lord Riall bowed curtly to Merlin, brushed past Bedwyr, and stalked out of the tent.

Bedwyr had half a mind to stop him, but the enchanter shook his head.

"Let him go."

Bedwyr swallowed. "What was that about a gamble? It stopped him in his tracks, all right. I was getting nowhere with him."

Merlin smiled. "What reason did he give for his grandfather's disinheriting his father?"

"An unfair preference for a second and younger wife."

"He said nothing about his father's service in the wars?"

"Only that Castellors fought for the High King."

"He did. When Vortigern the Wolf was High King."

"Vortigern! No wonder he kept that dark."

"Meleanor supported Vortigern for years, even after the murder of Prince Constans, because Vortigern was the only leader strong enough to stand against the Picts. But when Vortigern invited the Saxons in, gave them land, and sealed the bargain by taking a Saxon wife, Meleanor left his service and retreated to Gwynedd."

"And Castellors did not?"

Merlin shrugged and extinguished one of the lamp flames between his fingers. The room darkened a little.. From the shadows, he told Bedwyr the story of Castellors.

"On his father's orders, Castellors kept faith with the Wolf. His younger brother, Meregon, was growing up to be a likely warrior by that time, and their father, Meleanor, who feared being caught on the losing side, sent young Meregon south with a troop of men to join Ambrosius's invasion from Less Britain. The brothers fought against each other in the war that followed. Whoever won, Meleanor stood to gain—at the cost of a son. Castellors was lucky enough to survive the massacre of Vortigern's forces, and he went home, disgraced but alive. Meregon distinguished himself in the deciding battle against the Saxons and became an honored member of Ambrosius's inner circle. Of course Meleanor made him his heir. He had no choice."

Bedwyr shook his head. "I'd no idea. I don't blame Lord

Riall for his disappointment. Or Lady Gemina for hers. No doubt she expected to be queen of Gwynedd when she married Castellors. But it's long in the past, all of it. They can't seriously hope to reverse that turn of fortune."

Merlin put out the second lamp flame. Now the tent was dark except for the dancing flicker of Bedwyr's candle. Bedwyr watched in secret wonder. Merlin was the only good man he had ever known who felt more comfortable in shadow than in light.

"Lady Gemina's dream is at the root of all this trouble," said Merlin. "No doubt the dagger was her idea."

"Then the dagger isn't genuine after all?"

"The dagger is perfectly genuine. The sheath is not."

Bedwyr wondered at his certainty. "It looked like first-rate Roman craftsmanship to me."

"It is," Merlin agreed. "But it was made for a shorter blade. Someone, probably Lady Gemina, had the sheath enlarged to fit that dagger. All that silver chasing hides the signs of recent work."

"Lord Riall said she took it to a goldsmith for repairs."

"Not only for repairs."

"Is the dagger not Roman-made as well?"

"No," Merlin said quietly. "The dagger is Briton work. Forged in the hills of Gwynedd and cooled in the swift-flowing streams of Y Wyddfa." He paused and added, "Magnus Maximus had the dagger made as a wedding gift for his Welsh bride, Elen of Gwynedd. There are bards' tales about that gift . . . but no one sings them now."

"It *was* his dagger, then? The inscription is genuine?"

"It's partly genuine. The dagger was a gift *from* Maximus, not *to* him. The wording has been changed to suit."

"*To my commander*," Bedwyr quoted. "That didn't mean Maximus?"

"A romantic reference to his wife. The feminine has been changed to the masculine. You can see the erasures if you look. It was very cleverly done. I bow to Lady Gemina's ingenuity." Merlin's dark eyes met Bedwyr's. "But the runes revealed the truth."

"Runes?" Bedwyr breathed. He had seen no runes.

"Down the shaft of the blade, underneath the Latin letters. Put the blade to the flame and they appear, red as fire. It's an old art, lost now except in a few dark mountain haunts. The man who made that blade was a master."

Bedwyr cleared his throat nervously. "What, er, do the runes say?"

"That the blade was made for her who is first and best. Translated: for the Queen of the Britons."

"But, my lord, in that case . . ."

"You think I should have sent it straight to Arthur."

Bedwyr nodded. It was the obvious move. Arthur was King of the Britons, and now he had a wife.

Merlin shook his head. "Be easy, Bedwyr. It will go to Arthur. But not yet." His voice sank. "Before we leave this camp, the dagger will be in our hands. You will take it to Arthur. Legitimately. Not as the result of any bribe."

Bedwyr's look lightened. "Then it *is* important, after all, that Arthur have it?"

"His having it is not important. His giving it away will be."

Confused, Bedwyr opened his mouth to ask another question, but the enchanter cut him off.

"Don't ask me for more. Further than that I have not seen. Arthur will possess it, and the woman he gives it to will come to glory with him. She will be Queen of all the Britons."

"But," Bedwyr breathed, "he is already wed. He has a wife. It has all taken place, and without the dagger."

Merlin turned away, hunching his shoulders as against a cold breeze. "I have told you what I know. What must happen will not happen without the dagger. Good night, Sir Bedwyr. I can find my own way to Queen Esdora's tent."

It was not until the enchanter had gone out into the night that Bedwyr realized he had said nothing at all to Merlin about Queen Esdora.

CHAPTER TWENTY

Queen Esdora

Guinevere slipped silently out of the tent in the middle of the night. She had gone two days without news and could not bear the ignorance forced upon her any longer. She had to know how Trevor was doing. He might be dead; he might be alive but unable to wake or speak; he might be permanently maimed. She had seen such things four years ago when the wounded of Gwynedd came home after the battle at Caer Eden. Even those who recovered were not the same as they had been before. Long illness, like the loss of a limb, changed a person's life forever. She could not sit passively by while Trevor lay facing such possible futures and do nothing to help. It was her fault that he lay there at all.

What would she do if Trevor died? She had been able to

think of little else since Sir Bedwyr's men had lifted Trevor's inert body onto the litter and taken him away. Sir Bedwyr had been kindness itself, wrapping her in his own cloak, riding by her side all the way back to camp, and personally escorting her to Queen Alyse's tent even before he went to prepare Queen Esdora for her son's arrival. But nothing he said could assuage her remorse. Her responsibility was real and her guilt clear.

For the first time, she understood the burden borne by warriors and their commanders. A decision she had freely made might end in another's death. That Trevor was her friend and not her enemy made her misery ten times worse. There was no way to repair the damage she had done, no apology she could make to Queen Esdora that would ease that lady's pain.

Again and again she had begged for an audience with Queen Alyse, just to ask permission to call on Queen Esdora. But her aunt, busy with other matters, had not had time to see her. Grannic and Ailsa claimed to have heard no news of Trevor, and Ailsa tried to reassure her that no news meant his condition had not worsened. But this was a guess, at best, and of little comfort. She had tried to ask Elaine, who always knew the latest gossip, but Elaine was sunk in a black mood and would not speak to her.

As the second dark day slid into night, Guinevere decided that she could not wait any longer. She would go straight to the source and ask Queen Esdora how Trevor fared.

With infinite care in the darkness of the tent, she tiptoed around Ailsa's sleeping place, opened the traveling trunk, and drew out the topmost gown. She struggled into it, noting a new tightness across the shoulders, and laced it up. From the feel of the fabric, she guessed it must be her old gray gown, a plain and unflattering hand-me-down of Cissa's that had been altered for her only last spring. She grimaced in the dark. Another growth spurt! At this rate, she would be as tall as Queen Alyse by Christmas, an affront her aunt was unlikely to overlook. She thrust her feet into the first shoes she came to, combed her fingers through her hair and braided it swiftly behind her back, grabbed her cloak, and slipped noiselessly out of the tent.

The camp lay still as a deathwatch under a starless sky. The rain had stopped, but clouds still hugged the treetops. Torches shed small halos of light on the muddy ground, illuminating the night guards but little else. Keeping the hood of her cloak well forward and moving carefully over the trampled meadow grasses, Guinevere made her way to the Powys encampment unseen.

She paused outside the reach of the torchlight and gazed at the entrance to the royal tent. Two men armed with swords stood before the door, one young and the other old enough to be his father. She hadn't expected a double guard, but it couldn't be allowed to matter. A way must be found around them.

"Christ, I'm tired." The young guard yawned.

Guinevere started at the nearness of his voice. Some trick of the dark or the damp made him sound as if he spoke at her shoulder.

"Serves you right," the elder grunted. "Next time, drink less at dinner the night you're standing watch."

"It's not that," the young man protested. "It's Cadog, the arrogant fool. While you were out hunting, he took us five leagues north on the Deva road. Following the tracks of a hill-man he thought he'd seen around camp." He flashed a grin at his companion. "Wild-goose chase, of course. Could have told him so. Everyone knows hillmen leave no tracks."

Guinevere froze where she stood, half afraid that the night air, which carried their voices to her so clearly, might betray to them the pounding of her heart.

The veteran hawked and spat into the darkness. "Waste of time. Hillmen are best left alone."

The young guard gaped at him. "They're thieves, Derfel! They stole Cadog blind last winter. Took his stacks of peat and half his charcoal."

"That may be Cadog's story," Derfel grumbled. "But a truth-teller Cadog's not."

"But his family nearly froze to death!"

"Cadog's a reckless man. I heard he lost his stores in a wager and blamed hillmen to cover his folly."

"But—but—"

"Be still, Briant. She'll hear you. Ears like a fox, the queen has."

Forewarned, Guinevere exhaled carefully, but still Derfel's head came up. "Who goes there? Stand forth in the queen's name."

The moment to act had come. Guinevere ran into the arc of light and knelt at the veteran's feet.

"Please, sir, I have a message for Queen Esdora. From—from Queen Alyse of Gwynedd."

"At this hour?" The younger guard was openly skeptical. "Come back in the morning, maiden. The queen's abed."

Guinevere raised her eyes to the veteran's lined face. "Please, sir, I know the hour is late. But my mistress cannot rest, and I know—I *know* Queen Esdora is not asleep."

The veteran Derfel looked down at her upturned face. Briant continued to insist that the queen was not available, that she could not be waked or interrupted, and that the message must be left with them. Guinevere ignored him. She waited on her knees, her eyes pleading with Derfel, hoping he had a daughter, a sister, a niece whom he cherished, and that his affection might make him vulnerable to a girl's distress.

"Listen," said Briant, taking courage from the veteran's silence. "Leave the message with us, and we'll see the queen gets it as soon as she arises. I'll escort you back to your tent, if you like. It's not a fit night out for any maid alone."

He had reached down an arm to pull her to her feet when at last Derfel spoke.

"Leave her be." He turned to Guinevere and said, in a gentler voice, "Can't the message wait, lass?"

Guinevere shook her head. "It has waited too long already."

"For God's sake—" Briant began.

"Silence." Derfel made it a command. He sheathed his sword and nodded to Guinevere. "Come along."

"Are you mad? She'll skin you alive!" Briant's protest was no less urgent for being whispered.

Derfel paid him no heed, but pulled back the tent flap and gestured Guinevere inside. It was very dark within. To the left, a dull glow outlined a curtain separating an ancillary chamber from the central one.

"Wait here," Derfel said softly. As he pushed past the curtain, a whiff of peat smoke and herbscent escaped, followed by the murmur of voices. Guinevere deduced the location of the sickroom. Derfel reappeared, carrying a lit candle that he placed on the table in the center of the room.

"I've done what you asked, lass. I hope you know what you're about." With that, he left her and went back to his post.

As no one followed him immediately through the curtain, Guinevere had time to look about her. The interior of the tent was sparsely furnished, and rushes lay thinly on the floor. A single lamp, unlit, a small bench, and two chairs flanked a square central table. The meager furnishings were old and unmatched, but well cared for and of excellent quality. The candlestand was made of silver, and by the candle's light she could see the ivory inlay in the tabletop beneath it. There were no tapestries hung against the walls to keep out drafts; no gilded winestands, painted goblets, or cushions for the chairs. Not even a brazier to take the chill from the autumn air. Possibly the brazier in the sickroom was the only one they had brought with them. To the right, another curtain hid the entrance to a second ancillary chamber, but this was in darkness.

It seemed that the kingdom of Powys had once been wealthy but had since fallen on hard times. Guinevere wondered if that had anything to do with the illness of the present king, Trevor's father. Still, despite its paucity of possessions, the royal chamber had an air of order and elegance that she admired.

She turned at the sound of rustling behind her. A woman had come through the curtain, an extraordinarily diminutive woman, tiny and upright, whose air of assurance clothed her as neatly as her nut-brown gown.

Guinevere made her reverence. "Queen Esdora."

"That is my name." The queen's voice was firm but not unkind. "Hadn't you better tell me yours?"

Color flooded Guinevere's face and she bowed her head. "Guinevere . . . Guinevere of Northgallis, my lady."

There was a short, potent silence. "Alyse would not have sent *you* as her messenger. Why are you here?"

"I—I—" Guinevere stammered, her face hot. "I came on my own, my lady. I said whatever I thought might get me past the guard."

Queen Esdora's hard expression softened, but her voice remained firm. "I expected you before this, Guinevere of Northgallis."

Guinevere gulped. How could she explain without blaming Queen Alyse? She wished she had thought this out beforehand. She must do nothing to prejudice the queen of Powys against Queen Alyse or she might damage the prospect of Trevor's marriage . . . if he lived.

Queen Esdora observed her struggle without compassion. "Did your aunt release you? Or did you sneak away?"

"I—I sneaked away."

"Then you could have come yesterday, last night, this morning. Is that not so?"

Guinevere hesitated. This was not the interview she had intended.

"Have you no excuse?" Queen Esdora's small brown slipper tapped impatiently among the rushes on the floor.

Guinevere sighed and shut her eyes. "No."

"Well, that's something. I despise excuses. You may rise."

Standing, Guinevere was a full head taller than Queen Esdora. She felt like an ungainly scarecrow next to the queen's petite, small-boned frame. Queen Esdora looked her up and down with an assessing gaze and smiled faintly.

Guinevere realized, flushing, that her cloak and gown were muddy from kneeling before Derfel. And her feet, she saw as she followed Queen Esdora's glance, were not wearing slippers. Beneath the muddy hem of her too-tight gown poked the toes of her riding boots. The first shoes she had come to, fumbling in the dark . . . Another fountain of color splashed her face.

"You dressed in the dark, I see. At least it lends credence to your story." Queen Esdora gestured to a chair. "Be seated."

Knees trembling, Guinevere sank onto one of the carved chairs. Queen Esdora sat opposite, across the table. She was a neat, precise little person, as exact in her movements as in her speech. Her gown was expertly cut but devoid of trimming or ornament. The only jewel she wore was an amber brooch at her throat, an amber brooch with the Black Badger of Powys enameled in the center. Her sleek dark red hair was pulled back from her face and coiled in a careful knot at the base of her neck. She had elegant features that just missed beauty, and her fine skin, unassailable poise, and natural grace of bearing marked her as a lady of distinction.

Queen Esdora spoke briskly. "Derfel admitted you for one

reason only: your certainty that I was not asleep. Explain how you knew that, please. Was it a guess?"

Guinevere looked down at her own hands, clasped tightly in her lap. "No, my lady."

"No? How then did you know?"

Guinevere shifted in her chair. "I—I know Trevor. He—he couldn't be who he is if—if you were the kind of mother who could sleep while he lay at the gates of the Otherworld." Guinevere looked up at the queen with anxious eyes. "I don't know if that makes any sense. I can't put it any better."

Queen Esdora smiled. "You have put it very well. I begin to think Alyse was right not to have you whipped."

Guinevere stared at her, openmouthed.

"It's a tender upbringing you've had, whatever you may think," Queen Esdora said. "But then, I never raised a girl." She leaned forward, her eyes intent. "I have been waiting for you to come. You are the only person who can tell me what happened to my son."

Guinevere swallowed. What a terrifyingly direct woman Trevor's mother was! She had braced herself for tears and abject apologies, and here she was instead, calmly relating the events of that windy afternoon on the Roman road. She tiptoed around the mention of Llyr and said nothing about finding Lord Riall's treasure, but in every other respect she told the queen all she could remember.

Queen Esdora sat perfectly still, her bright brown eyes focused on some invisible spot in the middle distance. From time to time her gaze traveled to Guinevere's face and lingered there, speculation clear in her expression.

"When Sir Bedwyr and his men finally came," Guinevere finished, "Trevor was thoroughly wet and cold. They wrapped him in blankets and brought him back in a litter. I rode with them and led his horse." A lump rose in her throat. "Please, my lady, please tell me how he fares. No one will tell me anything, and I want so much to know. . . ."

"Did he say nothing to you when you went back to him? Did he not wake at all, in all that time?"

Guinevere shook her head. Tears filled her eyes, and she clenched her fists to keep them from falling.

"If he was wet and cold, so must you have been," said Queen Esdora. "Sir Bedwyr told me that you covered him with your cloak."

Guinevere shrugged.

"Pull up your sleeves."

Guinevere hesitated, not sure she had heard aright. Queen Esdora leaned forward and spoke gently. "It's quite all right, my dear. I'm only testing Sir Bedwyr's truthfulness. Grown men have been known to tell tall tales when a pretty girl is involved."

Obediently, Guinevere pulled up the sleeves of her gray gown. Queen Esdora saw the red welts across her forearms, the scratches and the broken nails that made her hands look like a commoner's, and her gaze lingered on the girl's face.

"One more question. If you and my son were alone on the road, how did you send for help?"

Guinevere's head jerked up. She met Queen Esdora's steady gaze and knew instinctively that a lie would be unforgivable.

"A friend came upon us. I sent him to fetch Sir Bedwyr."

"That was opportune, surely."

". . . Yes."

"Who was this friend?"

Guinevere drew a long, slow breath. "His name is Llyr. His father is Bran, leader of the White Foot of Snow Mountain."

The brown eyes widened. "You are a brave girl to befriend one of the Old Ones. Most people fear them."

"Only because they don't know them."

"The Old Ones often have little respect for boundaries or the property of others."

"They don't steal. Their ways are different; that's all."

Queen Esdora smiled. "Llyr must be a good friend to you." She rose. "Come with me."

She drew aside the curtain and led Guinevere into the warm, smoky room beyond. Trevor lay on a pallet near the brazier. His body was covered with soft woolen blankets and only his head, buoyed on downy pillows, was visible. As she watched, his eyes flickered open and he smiled at her.

In her race to his bedside, in her release from torment, in her joy at his escape, Guinevere did not notice the tall, dark figure in the shadows behind the brazier. As she knelt beside the pallet, tears blurring her vision, Merlin's thin fingers reached out to sprinkle more medicinal water on the fire. In the fog of steam and herbscent that rose hissing to the roof, he silently slipped out.

CHAPTER TWENTY-ONE

Answered Prayers

Princess Morgan bent over her black bowl and stared into its inky depths. Her lips moved in a muttered incantation, while around her the heavy stillroom air, dark and stuffy with herb-scent, breathed on the back of her neck. Night sounds came muted through the tent walls. The dim halo of a solitary candle provided the only light.

She focused her gaze on the oily surface of the liquid and waited in utter stillness for something to appear. She counted her own heartbeats to measure time—thirty, fifty, one hundred, two hundred—but nothing came to her out of the night. All she could see in the black bowl was her own wavering reflection. For the third night in a row, the Goddess had refused to answer her summons.

"Beg pardon, my lady, but you've a visitor without."

Morgan turned hastily, startled by Marcia's voice. "Don't *ever* interrupt me in the stillroom!"

Marcia curtsied to the ground. "I beg pardon, my lady, but I am told that the matter is an urgent one."

"By whom? Who goes calling at such an hour?"

"Lord Riall of Caer Narfon, m'lady. He begs your indulgence."

She remembered Lord Riall, a thin man with untidy red-brown hair and a straggling beard, one of Queen Alyse's poor relations. He could have nothing to say that would justify the lateness of the hour, and it was on the tip of her tongue to refuse him when she recalled the black bowl and her prayers to the Goddess. Perhaps Lord Riall's call was no coincidence. . . .

"Tell Lord Riall I will be with him shortly," she said, "and shake out my crimson gown. Oh, and I'll wear the crown of pearls my brother gave me."

Marcia's eyes widened. "For Lord Riall?"

"I think so. Yes."

"But it's all packed away. For when we are presented to . . ." her voice trailed away to return on a warning note. "What are you after, Morgan?"

A half smile touched Morgan's lips. "I have a feeling about this visit. It could be important."

"I can't see how."

"No, of course you can't."

Marcia scowled. "That circlet was given to you for—"

"Precisely. It was given to me. It's *mine*, and I have decided to wear it. Do as I say, Marcia. Unpack it."

*　*　*

Princess Morgan found Lord Riall standing nervously in the greeting chamber, a flat, heavily wrapped package clutched tightly beneath his arm. He greeted her with a mixture of awe and anxiety, going down on one knee as he stared at the quadruple string of river pearls across her brow and showing his teeth in a placating smile.

"Princess Morgan, it's very good of you to see me. I know the hour is late."

"Lord Riall. Pray be seated. It is not too late for me, as you can see. I value the dark hours."

Beads of sweat appeared on his brow, and he hastened to take the chair she indicated. He reminded Morgan of a mouse, a little russet mouse, twitching with anxiety but determined, for some reason of its own, to face the cat.

She seated herself in a swirl of skirts opposite him, and haltingly he began to explain the reason he had come. His mother, Lady Gemina, had stumbled upon a treasure, an ancient royal treasure, which had once belonged to her ancestor Magnus Maximus, Emperor of the Britons. Lady Gemina wished to give this treasure to King Arthur and had sent Lord Riall to Deva to present it to the King on her behalf as a token of her great esteem for his wise rule and his reputation for justice.

On the word *justice*, Morgan heard his voice harden and saw something bleak and angry flicker behind his eyes. She suppressed a sigh. Of course. He had a grievance, and he hoped to buy the King's intervention with his treasure.

She waited impatiently as Lord Riall waded through the byways of his ancestry and lingered on every detail of the old wrong done his father. He spoke with passion, but somehow the feeling did not ring true. It was not his passion, then, but another's. It was not hard to guess whose. The old woman who spoke through her son seemed far more impatient for a crown than he did. Of course, for the old, the wheel of time turned so much faster than for the young. Lady Gemina clearly had ambitions but was running out of time.

When Lord Riall embarked for the third time on a protest against his grandfather's villainy, Morgan could endure no more.

"Lord Riall," she interrupted. "If you have come here to show me this treasure, I suggest you do it now. I tire of your grandfather."

He obeyed at once. She watched as he laid out his package on the low table between them and proceeded lovingly to unwrap it. She expected some hastily fashioned, gaudy display, and so was unprepared for the antique splendor of the weapon.

"A dagger," Lord Riall announced unnecessarily, drawing the blade from its sheath. "It belonged to the Emperor Maximus himself. Look at the inscription."

Morgan took the offered weapon in one hand and, without a glance at the inscription, slid the blade home to its sheath. It was the sheath she wanted to examine, not the dagger. The chasing was rather fine, and the gold shone with a mellow luster, but what took her breath away was the large, dark, deep-set ruby centered in the goldwork.

"Fit for an emperor, is it not?" Lord Riall prodded.

Morgan looked at him thoughtfully. "If you want it to go to Arthur, why bring it to me? Take it to Sir Bedwyr."

"Sir Bedwyr is too close to Pellinore, my lady. But you are not. You are the High King's sister. And you are rumored to have . . . powers."

Morgan sucked in her breath. It was one thing to be known as a witch—and pleasing that her reputation had spread as far as Wales—but that so lowly a lord should presume to make use of her gifts for his own purposes! The insolence of the man! Did he expect her to put the King under a spell of enchantment to make him do her bidding? Arthur had grown up under Merlin's tutelage. Anyone less vulnerable to enchantment was hard to imagine.

"I am on my way to Rheged, Lord Riall," she said stiffly. "I may not see my brother for years. I cannot—and will not—serve as your messenger."

Lord Riall heard the ice in her voice and changed course without demur. "You misunderstand, royal princess," he bleated. "I have long heard praise of your beauty, your wit, and your . . . gifts. That is why I am honored—indeed, privileged—to present this royal dagger to the most charming descendant of Maximus—to you, Princess Morgan, as a wedding gift from my mother, Lady Gemina, who wishes only that she could give it to you herself, from one queen to another . . . from the queen of Gwynedd to the queen of Rheged."

Morgan smiled. "Thank you. I accept your lady mother's gift with pleasure."

Lord Riall grinned nervously, unable to take his eyes from the sheathed dagger in her hands. "On the understanding, of course, that you will do everything within your power to see that justice is done? I have your promise, princess, to use your powers of, er, persuasion?"

"I will use my powers to the utmost, Lord Riall. Have no fear of that."

"It is an exceedingly valuable weapon."

"Indeed. And a very lovely gift." She paused as an idea occurred to her. "Have you shown this dagger to anyone else in camp?"

"No, no," he said hastily, looking about him and beginning to sweat. "I trust no one but King Arthur . . . and his sister, of course."

A silence fell between them. At last Morgan smiled. "That was wise of you. The less said about it, the better. You have my thanks, Lord Riall."

Her tone implied dismissal, but Lord Riall made no move to go. He sat and sweated and stared at the dagger in her lap. Morgan rose abruptly from her chair, forcing him to his feet, yet even this had no effect. He lingered, shuffling his feet and sweating, but unable to tear himself away from the dagger's presence. Morgan signaled to Marcia, who came forward to escort Lord Riall to the door. He cleared his throat unhappily.

"Just . . . one more thing, Lady Morgan."

She waited, cold and silent, the smile gone.

"Um, uh . . . When may we expect the . . . restoration of

our rights? My mother will ask me, you see, when I get home."

Morgan's nostrils flared. She had half a mind to slap his face for insolence, but she caught Marcia's warning glance and held hard to her self-control. After a moment, she leaned toward him and spoke softly into his ear.

"Within the year, your lady mother will see her kingdom, I have no doubt. Under one condition."

Joy and relief flooded Lord Riall's narrow face. "Anything, princess! Anything at all!"

"Tell no one that you gave this dagger to me. If you do, I shall destroy it."

"I'll say nothing—I'll be as silent as the grave! Oh, royal princess, a thousand thanks."

She extended her hand and looked away. "You may go."

He kissed her fingers obediently and finally left.

"That's a handsome dagger," said Marcia. "But how are you going to persuade King Arthur to give his mother Queen Alyse's crown?"

Morgan smiled sideways at her as she turned away. "Is that what you think I've done?"

"What else?"

"She's a Christian, isn't she, the lady Gemina? Then there is more than one kingdom that concerns her."

"The kingdom of heaven, you mean? Oh, shame, Morgan!" Marcia followed her to the stillroom. "How could you? It's a sin to wish her death upon her." She stood in the entranceway and watched as Morgan, still clothed in her gown of Pendragon red and her crown of pearls, took a knife from the shelf and bent over the dagger. "What are you doing?"

Morgan grunted, straining with effort, as she worked at something Marcia could not see. Finally, she uttered a little cry of satisfaction and turned around. In one hand she held a dark red ruby, and in the other, the mutilated sheath.

Marcia gasped. "Oh, Morgan! It was so beautiful, and you've—you've . . ."

"Prized out its heart." Morgan held the stone to the light of the single candle and watched it gleam. "This is why I took the dagger from him." She held up the weapon in its damaged sheath. "And this can be useful to me, too. I shall wound the little vixen with it. I shall tear out her heart." She smiled maliciously at Marcia. "You see what comes of my labors in the stillroom, Marcia? The Goddess has answered my prayers."

CHAPTER TWENTY-TWO

Trevor's Warning

"That's a very pretty stitch," Queen Esdora said, looking down over Guinevere's shoulder. "You've an excellent hand with a needle. If you like, I shall show you a stitch I learned from my aunt Jolie, who was born a Frank. Now, *that* was skill."

Guinevere looked up, smiling, from the work in her lap. "Thank you, my lady, I would like it very much."

"Not so formal," Trevor protested from the pallet. "Less of the *my lady* please. You're among friends." He winked up at his mother. "Nearly family."

For half a moment, Guinevere held her breath. Was it possible the thing had happened, was agreed upon and decided with King Pellinore's consent? But no—there hadn't been time. It was only six days since Trevor had regained his senses. Flat on his back and in steady pain from a broken leg and a sore head, he hadn't been able to pay much court to Elaine. Negotiations were going forward without him, however, carried on entirely between Queen Esdora and Queen Alyse. They had hardly been out of each other's company in the last six days. Elaine had come once to visit, but she hadn't stayed long. Guinevere was almost certain she knew nothing about the matchmaking being carried out on her behalf.

"Nearly, but not yet," Queen Esdora said firmly, bending down to kiss Trevor's cheek. "And be nice to Gwen. She has suffered on your behalf."

"*Gwen.* Much better. Gwen's going to be my sister if you do your job. I'm allowed to tease a sister."

Queen Esdora ruffled his hair with her tiny hand. Their affection for each other was open and unfeigned, and Guinevere envied them for it.

"Now get going," Trevor said gruffly. "You don't want to make her wait. Queen Alyse is famous for her temper."

Queen Esdora adjusted her dark green fox-trimmed cloak over her exquisite moss-green gown and sailed away like a ship to battle.

"Heavens," Guinevere said once the tent flap had closed behind the queen. "I'm sure no one else dares order her about. They're all afraid of her."

"As well they should be." Trevor smiled. "She's a single-minded woman. But *you* weren't afraid of her."

"I was. Ask Derfel. I was shaking with fear."

"You came alone, uninvited and in the dead of night. Not the act of a fearful woman."

"It wasn't courage." She looked away. "I just couldn't stand it any longer, not knowing . . ."

"Bless you for that," he said gently. "I'd be bored to death without you, Gwen. Why doesn't Elaine come to see me? We'd have a jolly time together, the three of us. Bring her next time. She makes me want to shout with joy."

"I'll try," said Guinevere doubtfully. "But she's not speaking to me at the moment. She's been in an evil mood for days and I can't get her out of it."

He grinned. "Tempestuous as ever, eh? Why?"

"I really don't know. It must have been something Princess Morgan said or did, but she won't tell me what it was."

"Bring her to me," Trevor said, wincing as pain stabbed his injured leg. "I'll flatter her into a good temper."

Guinevere reached for the bowl of medicinal gruel by the side of his bed and ladled a spoonful into his mouth. He lay back on his pillow and grimaced.

"Ugh. Disgusting. You'd think an enchanter as powerful as Merlin would be able to devise a better-tasting potion than this."

"Merlin the Enchanter? He's in *camp*?"

"Of course. Didn't you know? He's my physician now, thanks to Mother. But of course you know: you saw him at your presentation to Princess Morgan. He was standing right behind her chair."

Color drained from Guinevere's face. "That was *Merlin*?" Her head began to spin. Her specter was the second most powerful man in all the land, and she had tried to deny him! Automatically, her fingers made the ancient sign against enchantment. She caught herself, whipped her hand out of sight, and crossed herself with the other. She was a Christian now and, as Father Martin and Queen Alyse had both explained at length, no longer owed allegiance to the gods of her pagan childhood.

"Why is he here?"

"He's King Arthur's political advisor. Where else should he be when there's a treaty to be made?" Trevor frowned. "Gwen? Is something wrong? You've gone pale."

She could not keep her trembling out of her voice. "You sound as if you're on friendly terms with him."

"I am. He brought me back from darkness. We've talked about many things in the last six days. He stops by every evening before dinner to share the council's doings with me and Mother. He's my proxy until I'm on my feet again. I'm decidedly grateful to him. He keeps me informed of the council's deliberations, if one can call them that, and takes my opinions—*our* opinions—back to them. In truth, Mother's voice counts more than mine. She's the strategist in the family."

"And does he carry her opinions back to council and give them as his own?"

"As mine—yes, he does. That pleases you, I see."

"Of course it does," she said. "Women should always have a voice in council. I'm sure you agree."

He laughed. "I dare not deny it. No doubt Queen Alyse speaks her mind through King Pellinore as often as Mother does through me. My father once warned me that, despite appearances, the world is run by women."

"It used to be so, long ago," Guinevere said, remembering the old tales she had learned in Northgallis and the Great Goddess she had worshipped there. "Before the Romans came. Now even the councils of the Old Ones are run by men."

Trevor looked at her curiously. "How on earth do you know that?"

"I attended one of them. With Llyr."

"Did you? I didn't know they let in any of our kind of folk. What was it like?"

Guinevere shivered, averting her gaze. "Frightening. Amazing. I met their wisewoman, the One Who Hears. Her power was real. She . . . changed things."

"How?"

"It's hard to explain. She made me see things about myself I didn't want to—to accept. I've been different since that day. So has Llyr."

Trevor did not reply, and when she turned to him, she found him asleep. Queen Esdora had warned her he was prone to spells of weariness as a consequence of the knock to his head when he fell. Quietly, she rose from her stool, took up a glazed bowl of herbal water, and sprinkled some over the embers in the brazier. Steam hissed upward, filling the tent with the clean scents of sage, comfrey, and kingwort.

If Merlin was Trevor's physician, he had probably prepared the herbs himself. He must be the one who had straightened

Trevor's leg and bound it between two carved slats of wood. He must also be the one who had told Queen Esdora that the leg would heal straight in time, and that Trevor would be able to walk and ride again. Coming from such a man as Merlin, those were comforting words indeed. There should be nothing to fear in such a man. . . .

Trevor awoke as quickly as he had fallen asleep, and with as little warning. "I beg pardon," he said irritably, putting up a hand to shade his eyes, although the room was dim. "It comes upon me like a fainting fit. I do apologize. We were talking about your friend Llyr, weren't we? There's something I think you should know. Ever since Llyr's visit to Sir Bedwyr, talk has been going around about him. Some people think he's been spying on us from the woods; others believe the Old Ones themselves are watching us, perhaps scouting our movements, preparing to attack."

"That's ridiculous!"

"I know, Gwen; calm down. Mother and Queen Alyse and Sir Bedwyr are quashing these rumors wherever they hear them, but some of the men believe them anyway. They're starting to look for Old Ones when they ride out—"

Guinevere went cold. "They're *hunting Llyr?*"

"I'm afraid so. You'd better warn him to be careful. We don't want him to be caught."

"That's not fair! He hasn't done anything wrong!"

"I'm sure he hasn't," Trevor said gravely. "But his guilt or innocence doesn't matter to many of them. They want him because he's an Old One, and because he's *here*, where he doesn't belong."

"Doesn't *belong*? The Old Ones were here before we were!"

"Yes," said Trevor, "no doubt they were. Their lineages are ancient. But—how shall I put this?—the men are bored. They've chased away all the game into the hills and it's harder work to hunt. It's time to be packing up for home, but the council's at a stalemate and the kings are not the only ones growing restless. Tempers are short. Your friend Llyr has provided the men a diversion. Half the time they're out hunting, they're looking for him. We're afraid they might kill him if they catch him."

"*Kill* him?" Guinevere was instantly on her feet. "They can't—he hasn't done anything!" She turned for the door. "I have to find him!"

"Wait, Gwen!" He caught at her arm. "*Wait*. Not in broad daylight. You'll be followed."

She gaped at him in disbelief. "Am *I* watched, then?"

"Probably. It'd be the easiest way to find him."

Guinevere sat down heavily on the stool, her eyes wide and unfocused. "I can't warn him, can I? Not without risking his life." Her gaze sharpened as she turned to him, and her voice steadied. "But he already knows they're after him. He couldn't fail to know. If they haven't caught him yet, it's because he's gone into hiding. No one can find Llyr when he's in hiding. He's an Old One. They're invisible in a forest."

"The leaves are falling," Trevor suggested.

Guinevere shook her head. "That won't matter. They'll never catch him unless he wants to be caught."

"I'm glad to hear it," Trevor said, his voice still full of doubt. "So long as you can't think of anything—any circumstance, any predicament, any person—that might make him want to be caught?"

Her eyes darkened as she frowned.

"He's a loyal fellow, isn't he?" Trevor added gently. "Are you sure there isn't anyone he would sacrifice himself for?"

Guinevere put her hands up to cover her face. Of course Llyr would sacrifice himself for her sake; his guardianship required it of him. He would not go into hiding, for he could not guard her if he hid. He would not be safe unless he left the area, and he would not leave the area as long as she was there. He would not leave even if she ordered him to, for although she was the one he guarded, she was not the one he served. The One Who Hears had spoken with the god's voice.

"What shall I do, Trevor? The only way to make him leave is to convince him that his leaving will help me and his staying will not. I have to find him, but how can I find him without endangering him?"

"Well," said Trevor, with a gleam in his eye, "if you're willing to listen to a brother's counsel, maybe I can help. . . ."

Well after moonset, when the night was at its darkest, Guinevere donned her cloak, pulled her hood forward to hide her hair, and sneaked out of camp to the horse lines. She waited there, silent and alert among the resting animals, for a long time. The twitch of a tail or the swivel of an ear would give her instant warning of anyone's approach, but nothing happened. Nothing moved.

Silent as a wraith, she slipped into the forest, settled down behind a tree, and waited again. She heard nothing beyond the night sounds of the forest: the scuffle of creatures in the undergrowth, the whispered beat of wings in the darkness above, the rasping of crickets, the call of an owl.

She moved to another tree and waited again. A minimum of three trees, Trevor had advised. *Look sharp, move slowly, be patient.* She followed his advice. The night sounds continued unabated. Eventually, she made her way to the beech tree and, from stones collected that afternoon from the river's edge, built a small cairn between the flared roots at its base. When she had finished, she moved on to another tree, and then to another, letting time pass and the silent dark surround her. Finally, she slipped back into camp, certain that she had completed her mission unseen.

She was almost right. The forest animals had ceased to pay her any attention. Only a single pair of eyes had watched her throughout. But those eyes were human.

CHAPTER TWENTY-THREE

Confessions

Every morning and evening for three days, Guinevere strolled through the woods in sight of the beech tree. The cairn stood untouched. No hand had tumbled it and dispersed its stones. That was the sign she looked for, the sign that the message— a request for a meeting—had been received. Part of her was relieved; it meant that Llyr had gone from the surrounding woodland and might indeed be in hiding. But she also feared that there might be a more sinister reason he did not come. She took comfort in the knowledge that if Llyr had been found or captured, she would have learned of it by now through Trevor or Queen Esdora.

The mood in camp was deteriorating fast. Age-old animosities had begun to surface. The South Welsh grumbled at the North Welsh, and the North Welsh glowered at the

South. There seemed no end to the verbal sparring. Even King Pellinore, normally the most cheerful of men, began to mutter and curse at the glacial pace of negotiations. Every day, Sir Bedwyr looked more haggard and exhausted. Guinevere wondered at his patience. It was nearing the end of October, and the days were growing shorter, the weather colder, and life in camp more tiresome. Work parties had to go far afield to search for firewood, using wagons to bring back the next day's supply of fuel. This left fewer men available for hunting. Fish and waterfowl began to form a larger part of the daily diet in the absence of fresh venison. Grumbling could be heard from every tent. Surely, Guinevere thought, it was time Sir Bedwyr took Princess Morgan north to Rheged. Rumor had it that he had sent a courier to King Urien to warn him that their arrival would be delayed.

Guinevere wondered what had happened to Princess Morgan. She had seen nothing of her since Trevor's accident, excepting only her appearance at the communal evening meals, where she spoke to no one. She no longer sent for Elaine, who now resumed her place in the family. Elaine would say nothing of what had passed between them. Although the two cousins worked side by side, fetching water and kindling, tending the cooking fire, airing bedding, helping Ailsa and Grannic repair the tent cloth, and performing a dozen other chores that cropped up daily, Guinevere could not cajole Elaine into deeper confidence.

Early on the fourth day after building the cairn, Guinevere was returning from the river with a bucket of water when she saw Queen Esdora running to Queen Alyse's tent. She abandoned the bucket and fled to Trevor. He greeted her with worried eyes. Sir Bedwyr, he said, had just left their tent after bringing them distressing news. Someone—Sir Bedwyr would not say who—had reported the theft of a valuable dagger. It was now Sir Bedwyr's duty to find the thief and bring him to justice. Sir Bedwyr, he finished heavily, was organizing a search for Old Ones.

"Old Ones! Why?"

Trevor did not meet her eyes. "An Old One was seen at the site of the theft at about the right time, apparently. I'm afraid your friend Llyr is the one they seek."

"It isn't Llyr!" Guinevere cried hotly. "He hasn't been in camp! The cairn is still there!"

"Listen, Gwen, I'm telling you this to warn you. Sir Bedwyr may want your help in finding him."

"To arrest him? I shan't lift a finger to help!"

"To protect him. Against the men out looking for him now. The dagger's owner has offered a talent of silver to the man who captures Llyr . . . alive or dead."

Guinevere stared at him, aghast. "Llyr was *named?*"

"Yes. Sir Bedwyr has informed all the kings in council. Mother's gone to speak to Queen Alyse. We're all supposed to keep an eye out for him . . . for his own sake. Sir Bedwyr wants him put under guard, for his own safety, until he can get to the truth."

Guinevere paled. "The truth is plain enough already! Oh, Trevor, I must do *something* to prevent this. I've got to find him first and send him home."

Trevor gazed at her steadily. "Will he go?"

The question burned in Guinevere's mind all the way back to her tent. Would she be able to persuade Llyr to abandon her and return to the safety of his family on Y Wyddfa until the real thief should be found? She had to try. She could think of no other course.

There was no one in the tent but Elaine, still curled on her pallet beneath a fur-trimmed coverlet, putting off chores until the last possible moment.

"Where are Ailsa and Grannic?"

Elaine stared at her unblinking and refused to answer.

"Please, Elaine. Whatever I've done, can't you forgive me? This is important."

"Why?"

Guinevere threw open her trunk and began to unlace her gown. "I have to go out. I don't want anyone to know."

Elaine sat up. "Out where?"

"Where are Ailsa and Grannic?"

Elaine considered before answering. "In Mother's tent. Queen Esdora's paid us an early visit. They'll be a while."

"Thank goodness. I don't suppose you'd cover for me?"

Elaine scowled. "First, tell me what's going on."

As she undressed, Guinevere told Elaine what she had learned from Trevor. "So you see," she finished, "I *have* to find him myself before Sir Bedwyr does. He'll put Llyr under guard, and Llyr will not understand it. The Old Ones don't imprison people."

"Who accused him?"

"I wish I knew. Sir Bedwyr didn't say." Guinevere stepped out of her gown. "Everybody has a dagger. It could be anyone. . . . Why do you look at me like that? Am I coming out in spots?"

"Don't be silly," Elaine snapped. "How much is the reward?"

"A talent of silver, if you can believe it. Large enough to tempt a man to murder." Guinevere thrust the gown into the trunk and reached for her tunic and leggings. "The men are hunting Llyr, and it isn't fair. There's no reason to suspect him. Why don't they concentrate on the people who live in camp? It's bound to be one of us."

"A talent of silver is a huge reward," Elaine said slowly. "The dagger must be awfully valuable."

Guinevere knew of only one dagger that might be worth the price: the dagger Llyr had shown her in the forest and let her hold, the dagger whose cool grip her hand still remembered. But she doubted very much that Lord Riall had brought a talent of silver with him from Caer Narfon. "Who could afford to offer so much?" she wondered. "The kings, I suppose, if any of them were foolish enough to carry such a sum on this journey."

"Father didn't," Elaine said firmly. "He can't afford it. Mother's always complaining about expenses."

"Gwarth can't afford it, either. Northgallis has always been poorer than Gwynedd. And I doubt if Queen Esdora could, at present. That leaves Dyfed and Guent. And Dyfed's a small kingdom. I've heard your father say that all their energy goes into keeping the Gaels off their coasts. Guent's a possibility, I suppose. There's no one else in camp who—" She broke off and stared at Elaine. "Princess Morgan!"

"What about her?" Elaine said coldly, watching Guinevere struggle into her tunic and leggings.

"She's traveling with hundreds of wedding gifts, most of them worth their weight in silver or gold. Then there's the bridegift for King Urien. The High King would have sent her off with a sizable treasure to honor him. Yes, I think Morgan could easily afford it. She's probably the only one who could."

"She doesn't have a dagger that valuable. At least, not that *I've* seen."

Guinevere paused, boots in hand. "For heaven's sake, what's wrong? Why do you look at me like that?"

Elaine made a sour face. "You're growing out of your clothes again."

"I'm *always* growing out of my clothes. There's no need to look so upset about it."

Elaine flushed. "I'm not upset. It's just that—Morgan opened my eyes, and I hate her for it."

"Morgan? What did she say?" Guinevere waited, hoping that at last Elaine was ready to share what had happened between her and the royal princess.

Elaine looked away and then turned back. Her voice was stiff. "Your shape is changing. Didn't you even know?"

Guinevere stood very still. "What do you mean?"

"What do you think I mean?" Elaine threw off her coverlet and rose. "You're not straight up and down anymore, are you? You're growing curves."

For a moment, Guinevere's breathing stopped and her heartbeat hammered in her ears. Could it be so? What had come to Elaine so easily and quickly at eleven, she had waited for in vain for three long years. Now she was nearly as tall as Queen Alyse, and still she was taken for a boy. Even Trevor of Powys had been fooled.

"Don't be such a half-wit, Gwen. Your clothes don't fit the same, do they? You *must* have noticed."

"I've—grown taller."

Elaine went up to her and tugged at her tunic. "See how tight this is? You never used to have to struggle to pull it on, did you, like you did just now."

"It's my shoulders," Guinevere whispered. "They're always—"

"Not shoulders, oaf. Breasts. See how the lacing's stretched? If you don't believe me, ask Ailsa. I'll wager *she's* noticed."

Guinevere closed her eyes. *Dear Lord in heaven, let it be true!* Finally, in the middle of her fourteenth year, to begin to grow a shape . . . to join the world of adults and leave childhood behind . . . to become a woman. She had waited so long for this, she had almost ceased to believe it would ever happen.

"Some of the men have noticed, too," Elaine said coldly. "I've been watching the way they look at you. Morgan was right about that as well, only I didn't believe her."

Guinevere opened her eyes, suddenly cautious. "Morgan's been talking to you about me? What for?"

Elaine shrugged. "She was always asking questions about you—snooping questions, trying to find out things. She doesn't like you, Gwen. She's afraid of you, I think. God knows why. I told her you were a nobody, but she didn't seem to believe me."

"Well, thanks for trying," Guinevere said with a small smile.

Elaine's look lightened. "Maybe it's Morgan's fault the men are after Llyr. If she's the only one rich enough to offer that reward, then she must be the one who lost the dagger."

"I thought of that, but it can't be her. Sir Bedwyr told Trevor that the owner of the dagger accused Llyr by name. Princess Morgan doesn't know that Llyr exists."

She was making a mental tally of the people in camp who knew of Llyr's existence when she saw Elaine's face. Her breath caught in her throat. She grabbed her cousin's arm. "*Does she?* Tell me the truth. Did you tell her about Llyr?"

"Let go! You're hurting me!"

"Did you tell her?"

Elaine jerked her arm away. "Of course not!"

"You *did!*"

"No, I—I didn't mean to," Elaine stammered. "Honest, I didn't. It just slipped out."

"Oh, Laine, how could you!"

Elaine sat down on her pallet with a thump. "She put a spell on me—she must have—because I wouldn't tell her anything about you. She doesn't believe it, though. I told her nobody believes it—not even you. But she said of course you did. She was very cross."

Guinevere struggled for words. "You don't mean—you wouldn't—*you told her about the prophecy?*"

The truth was written plainly on Elaine's face, distorted now with fear and fury. "She tricked me into it! And what does it matter, anyway? Everyone already knows. You don't think your brother Gwarth's been keeping it a secret, do you? He's *proud* of it, for pity's sake!"

Guinevere caught her breath. What a fool she had been not to foresee it! Gwarth had always been proud of the prophecy. He thought it brought the family distinction.

"*He* didn't tell Princess Morgan. You broke your promise to me, Elaine. You *swore* you'd never tell anyone, ever. If anything happens to Llyr—"

"Nothing will happen to Llyr. He's an Old One, isn't he? They'll never find him."

Guinevere shoved her feet into her boots and reached for her cloak. "They'd better not. Trevor thinks they'll kill him if they do."

"He's exaggerating."

Guinevere shot her a fierce look. "I'm not willing to take that chance."

"How can you find him when everyone else has failed? And even if you find him, will he go? He can't leave, can he, if he's your guardian?"

"He might—if I go with him."

Elaine stared at her. "You can't. They'll send soldiers after you. They'll arrest him in Gwynedd. You'll be lucky if Mother doesn't have your head on a spike outside the gates!"

"Listen, Elaine, do me a favor—you owe it to me, after all. Go see Trevor. Tell him we suspect Princess Morgan and ask him what we can do. If it's the High King's sister we're up against, we're going to need help. Will you do that for me?"

Elaine grimaced. "All right." Reluctantly, she picked up the gown Grannic had set out. At the sound of women's voices from the queen's tent next door, she cast a sly look at Guinevere. "You know what they're planning, don't you? Mother and Queen Esdora, closeted together for days on end?"

Guinevere pulled up short halfway to the door. "Yes," she said cautiously. "I do. But I didn't know you did."

"How could I not? It's all they talk about."

"Are you pleased?"

Elaine hesitated. "Not at being kept in the dark. You should have told me."

"It wasn't my secret to tell."

"No? Whose, then?"

"Your mother should have told you."

"Mother doesn't tell me *secrets*," Elaine retorted. "*You* should have told me, Gwen. What did you think I'd do? Warn Trevor off because of the prophecy? All I want to tell him is that he couldn't have made a better match."

Guinevere bit her lip against laughter. "But, Laine, he *has* made a better match. It's not my wedding they're busy planning; it's yours."

Elaine gaped at her.

"It's true. Really. I had it from Trevor himself. He fell for you the first day he met you."

"You lie!" Elaine reddened. "Mother wouldn't do that— she *knows* who it is I love!"

"Yes, of course, we all do, but the man is married. You won't be unhappy with Trevor; really you won't. He's easy to like, and he adores you. He even likes your tempers. You can hardly ask for more."

"Can't I? Oh, can't I?" Tears of fury brightened Elaine's eyes. "I will *not* be queen of Powys! Why, it's smaller than Gwynedd! And if you think for one moment that I'm going to settle for a freckled, backwoods—"

Guinevere clapped a hand across Elaine's mouth. "Hush! Don't let Queen Esdora hear you!"

Noises came from Queen Alyse's tent next door: the chatter of women's voices, the thud of wooden buckets, and the slosh of liquid. Elaine shook off the restraining hand. "I don't care—I hope she does hear me! Mother's promised me my choice, and she ought to know I'll never choose Trevor of Powys!"

Guinevere shrugged. "Have it your own way. But that means your mother and Queen Esdora have been negotiating all this time in vain. When are you going to tell them so?"

"I'll tell them now!" Elaine cried, and ran to the door.

Guinevere stopped her. "Better dress first."

Elaine looked down at her night-robe and swore.

"Hush! Someone's coming."

Footsteps and voices approached. Elaine opened the tent flap to peek out, and her shoulders fell. "It's only Ailsa and Grannic, emptying night soil and Mother's morning bucket of sick. For a moment, I thought I heard Sir Bedwyr's voice."

Guinevere gasped. "You . . . knew your mother was ill?"

"Of course. How not?"

"Do you know what ails her? And why she's keeping it a secret? Oh, Laine, it's not a mortal illness, is it?"

"Mortal?" Elaine laughed. "Not likely. She's never had trouble before."

Guinevere looked at her blankly, and Elaine heaved an impatient sigh. "She's not dying. She's with child."

The blood drained from Guinevere's face.

Elaine caught her arm. "Easy, Gwen, you look perfectly gray."

With child! Guinevere's chest tightened until her breath came fast and shallow. Her own heartbeat thundered in her ears. Through it Morgan's cool voice echoed: *The Queen shall die of what she carries in her. . . .*

CHAPTER TWENTY-FOUR

The Body

"Help! Help!"

Through mists of shadow, Guinevere heard Elaine's voice calling.

The door to the tent flapped opened. "What's the matter?"

"It's Gwen, Mama! She's fainted, and I can't wake her up!"

Gradually, Guinevere became aware of the ground beneath her back and the useless passivity of her limbs. Her eyes fluttered open to see Queen Alyse and Queen Esdora standing above her. Ailsa's arm behind her shoulder helped her to a sitting position.

"Are you ill, Gwen?" asked Queen Alyse.

"No," she breathed, looking up into the queen's lovely gray-blue eyes. Sunlight from the open door behind her set her golden hair alight and made a radiant halo around her head. Never before had her aunt appeared so beautiful or so precious to her. Fiercely, she fought back tears. "I'll—I'll be all right in a moment."

"What happened?" Queen Alyse addressed her daughter sharply.

"Nothing, Mama. She's . . . worried about Llyr, that's all."

Guinevere pushed herself up. She was still light-headed, but at least she could stand.

"I expect she's gone without breakfast," Queen Esdora said.

Guinevere nodded as Ailsa clucked in dismay.

Queen Alyse put the subject behind her. "Guinevere, attend me. We have something to say to you, Queen Esdora and I, something of the utmost importance."

Guinevere made a nervous reverence to both women.

Queen Alyse got straight to the point. "You will go find Llyr and send him home to Gwynedd. At once. I am sorry to deprive you of your friend," she added quickly to forestall a protest that never came, "but Esdora and I have talked it over and we both agree: Llyr must be sent home. It's for his own good."

"I believe, my dear Alyse," murmured Queen Esdora, "that your ward has already come to that conclusion herself."

"Yes, my lady," Guinevere said. "I'm off to see Llyr now."

For the first time, Queen Alyse noticed Guinevere's boots and leggings. The expression on her thin face lightened. "Go, then," she said. "But go quietly and tell no one your mission. They are looking for him, and he must not be caught."

Guinevere did not need to be told twice. She ran to the

door, where she nearly collided with Sir Bedwyr, who entered unannounced, armed and ready for the road.

"Lady Guinevere, you're just the one I'm looking for. . . . Ah, Queen Alyse and Queen Esdora. I beg pardon for the intrusion. My lady queen, I beg leave to have a word with your ward."

He bowed politely, and both queens gave him a stiff nod in return.

"Not alone," said Queen Alyse. "Anything you have to say to Guinevere can be said in front of me. And Esdora."

Sir Bedwyr bowed again. His voice was gentle as he turned to Guinevere, but she heard the urgency behind it.

"Lady Guinevere, one of my men has just ridden in with a dire message. When he was out hunting, he came across a group of men in the foothills west of here." He paused. "The men had gone hunting, too, but not for deer. Can you—I beg pardon, but can you guess who they were looking for?"

Guinevere nodded. Her mouth had gone dry.

"They may have found him. I can't be certain. That's why I need your help."

Guinevere tried to draw breath and found it difficult. "What—do you want me to do?"

"I've had the body brought to my tent. I'd like you to identify him, if you think you can."

"Body!" Elaine came to Guinevere's side. "Is he dead?"

"Sir Bedwyr, you go too far," said Queen Alyse. "Gwen is too young. I shall identify the boy."

Sir Bedwyr glanced swiftly at Queen Esdora, and a warning passed between them.

"Alyse," said Queen Esdora. "I advise against it. Not in your condition. Surely there is someone else who knows this young man? King Pellinore, perhaps?"

Shaking, Guinevere stepped forward. "I know him best, my lord. Do not bother the king." She turned and planted a gentle kiss on Queen Alyse's wasted cheek. "Thank you, Aunt Alyse. But Queen Esdora's right. You are not well, and anyway, it falls to me."

Queen Esdora took Queen Alyse by the elbow and drew her away. Sir Bedwyr offered his arm to Guinevere and, with consummate gentleness, led her from the tent.

Guinevere walked beside him without knowing that she moved. Numb to feeling and to thought, she floated through a world devoid of sensation. The cool, bright afternoon, the sunlight on the tent cloth, the grass underfoot, the snap and flash of colorful banners streaming in the breeze, all passed her by unnoticed. Someone pulled back the door flap to the High King's tent. Voices murmured nearby. A light appeared. Another door flap faced her, manned by guards. Sir Bedwyr came to a stop.

"Lady Guinevere," he said. "A thousand pardons for forcing this upon you. I thought, after meeting him, I could identify him myself, but—" He shrugged. "I'm afraid the Old Ones all look alike to me."

The tent flap opened. Inside stood another guard. Sir Bedwyr led her to a corner where a small form lay still—too still— on a pile of canvas sacks. The tent was quiet. The camp outside was quiet. The whole world seemed to hold its breath as Guinevere lifted her hand from Sir Bedwyr's arm and approached the body. Three paces away, she stopped. The beating of her heart thundered in her ears. The clothes were Llyr's.

Carefully, she knelt beside the body, so small and insignificant in death. Those were the leggings she had made for Llyr with her own hands, and the tunic, ripped and stained with blood, was her handiwork as well. It was clear how the boy had died. There were stab wounds in his chest.

Her gut twisted viciously. Sir Bedwyr was at her side in an instant to help her up. He spoke words of comfort and pressed a winecup to her lips. The liquid slid down her throat and trickled away into nothingness. It had no effect on the strange, invisible shell that seemed to encase her, holding her prisoner in its trance and locking out grief.

She looked down at the pale young face, unmarked except by fear. He had seen it coming, then. She uttered a silent prayer for this stranger whose spirit was already on its journey to the Otherworld, and at last allowed Sir Bedwyr to lead her away.

He took her into the large chamber next door and gave her water to drink. She sat on a carved chair, the very chair Princess Morgan had occupied the night of the presentation. As she listened to the steady flow of Sir Bedwyr's compassion, her dazed mind began to right itself. When he fell silent for a moment, she put down the cup and turned to him.

"It's not Llyr."

Sir Bedwyr blinked. "Pardon?"

"The clothes are his. . . . I made them myself. But the slippers aren't. And . . . and no matter what his clothes, Llyr wears a double string of wolf's teeth around his neck." She shook her head as if to clear it. "He looks like Llyr, but he's someone else . . . someone I've never seen before."

She shut her eyes and bent her head against an uncontrollable stream of tears. Sir Bedwyr's arm slipped around her, and he held her quietly until at last her sobs died into hiccups and sniffles.

"That's better," he said, pulling away and giving her a cloth to wipe her face. "It's as well to let it out. I'm sorry you had to see him."

"I've drenched your tunic."

"Never mind. I've another." He smiled. "I'm glad it's not your friend, princess, but that leaves me with another problem. What shall I do with the body? Where does this boy come from? Where should I take him for burial?"

"He must go back to his clan. We can contact them through Llyr."

"Ah. Llyr. His whereabouts are another problem. The men will come looking for their talent of silver, and I can't pretend that the dead boy is Llyr. It would mean cheating the dagger's owner out of a fortune. I won't do that, princess. And when the men are refused their reward, they'll be after Llyr again. I can't protect him if I can't find him."

Guinevere looked away. A spark of anger lit within her. She welcomed it, for it drove out fear. "There's also the problem of bringing the killers to justice." She was thinking of Princess Morgan. This murder was her fault, if she was Llyr's accuser, but who would bring her to account?

"Yes," Sir Bedwyr said carefully. "I hadn't forgotten that. I've got the leaders in custody, but my power over them is limited. They're not my men."

"Whose are they?"

"Banin of Mab's Bog was the leader. He's from Guent. Cadog of Green Hill was his lieutenant. He's from—"

"Powys."

Sir Bedwyr raised an eyebrow.

"I've heard of him before."

"There are others ready to take their places," he warned, "as soon as word gets out that this isn't Llyr. It's my duty to prevent more killing, my sworn duty to Arthur, but I doubt I'll be able to do it without your help." He glanced at her cautiously, and his lips twisted in a smile. "A strange turn of events, wouldn't you say, when the High King requires a maiden's help to enforce his laws? I don't have enough men to stop them, you see. And now I must mount a guard on these two boneheaded scoundrels as well."

He paused and looked down at his hands. "I have enough men to keep order in camp, but not to secure the forest. The only way I can think of to prevent the same thing happening to Llyr is to bring him in and keep him under guard. But first he must be found. Prince Trevor tells me you're the only one who can do that."

Guinevere gazed at his bowed head. He had beautiful manners. King Arthur had sent them a diplomat—a wise move when trying to persuade five Welsh kings to agree with one another. It gave her a heady feeling to be treated with such respect by one of the High King's Companions, to be treated as someone whose intelligence and understanding could be trusted. With every passing moment she grew more disposed to please him.

"I will help if I can."

A smile warmed Sir Bedwyr's grave face. "Thank you."

"But we may not have much time. The murder has changed everything . . . if Llyr knows about it."

"You think he may not?"

"It depends on how he came to give up his clothes."

"You don't think it possible that they were taken from him?"

Guinevere shook her head. "No. Not by Old Ones. And if someone of our sort took them from him, they'd have taken him as well, and we'd know about it. He may have buried them and that poor boy in there discovered them. Or perhaps an exchange was made. Llyr might have made contact with the boy's clan—I don't know, but I know he's alive. And probably watching."

"Then how do we contact him?" Sir Bedwyr leaned forward eagerly. "Prince Trevor said you had some way of communicating with him."

"I build a cairn to signal that I want to talk to him. If he's willing, he levels the cairn and waits for me. I can't force him."

"Where will you build the cairn?"

"I built it days ago. But so far, he hasn't answered."

"Will you show me?"

Guinevere rose to her feet. "All right. But come alone, not with a troop of men."

"One guard. Just in case." Sir Bedwyr smiled and bent his head. "Thank you, Lady Guinevere."

She noted the formal address with regret and made him a reverence. "Not at all, my lord. You have made it clear that it's my duty to the High King."

She went through the door before him, and so missed the delight in his eyes.

CHAPTER TWENTY-FIVE

Secrets of the Beech Tree

A hush had descended on the camp when Guinevere stepped outside. Few people were about, and most of the tents were closed up tight against the rising wind. Gray clouds scudded across a bright sky, trailing shadows over the meadow. Sir Bedwyr nodded to one of the guards at the entrance to the High King's tent, and the man fell into step behind him. They followed Guinevere past the horse lines and into the surrounding wood.

She shifted her shoulders under her cloak. A feeling of unease pervaded the afternoon, making everything around her seem strange and unnatural. She began to have misgivings about leading Sir Bedwyr to the cairn. What if Llyr should be waiting in the beech tree? Her actions would look like betrayal. But it was too late now. She had given Sir Bedwyr her word.

She stopped beside the cairn and looked about her. Llyr was not in the beech tree. The wood was empty. The half-bare branches of the hardwoods fidgeted in the wind, and their discarded leaves rustled underfoot.

"Not here?" Sir Bedwyr came up beside her. Dillon, the guard, checked the other side of the tree as Sir Bedwyr scanned the woods.

"He hasn't been here since I built the cairn. It's still standing."

A gust of wind whipped through the trees, scattering the leaves at their feet. "Is there a backup plan?" Sir Bedwyr asked. "Did you build another cairn somewhere else?"

Guinevere shook her head. "We've never needed a backup plan before. My lord, if you would allow me to ride out alone, I might be able to find him."

She expected instant objections to this offer, but Sir Bedwyr was not Queen Alyse. He considered it. "Where would you go? Westward into the hills?"

"Yes."

He sighed. "That I can't allow. You might run right into the hunters. It's not worth the risk."

"Sir!" The guard appeared from behind the tree. "There's something buried over here."

Sir Bedwyr and Guinevere hurried to join him. The wind had blown the leaves from the base of the tree and revealed a scar in the earth, a long mound of soil, loosely packed, where something had obviously been buried inexpertly and in haste.

Sir Bedwyr looked at Guinevere. "Was this here when you built the cairn?"

She gazed at the mound with deep misgiving. "No, I don't think so. It was dark, but I walked all around the tree. I'd have noticed a mound like that. I'd have tripped over it."

Sir Bedwyr nodded to the guard. "Dig it up, Dillon."

Dillon removed his dagger from his belt and started digging. The loose dirt came up easily, and at the fourth stroke he struck something solid. Using his hands to clear away the soil, he reached down and withdrew a flattish package wrapped in canvas and bound with twine.

Sir Bedwyr stared at it, speechless, and Guinevere gasped. He turned to her. "You know what it is? You've seen it?"

Too late, she covered her mouth with her hands.

"Princess." Sir Bedwyr's voice was hard, the voice of a commander. "You've dealt honorably with me thus far. Don't now start telling me tales. Tell me what you know."

But all she could think of was Llyr: Llyr following Lord Riall in the forest, Llyr climbing the old oak and drawing the treasure out of its hiding place, Llyr unwrapping it and laying it before her like a prize. If she told these things to Sir Bedwyr, he would not look twice for a different thief.

"Unwrap it, Dillon." The command came coldly, sharp with disappointment.

She watched the guard remove the canvas wrapping, the leather wrapping, and finally, the oiled cloth. He lifted the jeweled sheath and held it across his palms with the warrior's respect for a beautiful weapon. Then he drew breath sharply.

"What is it, Dillon?"

"It's been defaced, sir. Someone has ripped out a gem. Recently. The marks are still fresh."

A sound from Guinevere made Sir Bedwyr whip around. "You've seen this before."

"Yes," she whispered.

"Where? When?"

She bowed her head to avoid his eyes.

"Lady Guinevere. Please. You owe it to the King." He waited, then said more gently, "There's no need to shield him if he didn't do it."

"No?" She darted him a fierce glance.

"Not from me!" he cried. "Don't class me with those half-witted villains, I pray you. I wish Llyr no harm. I'm trying to help him."

Still she said nothing. Sir Bedwyr took the weapon from Dillon and held it before her face. "Did Lord Riall show this to you?"

"No."

"Then how did you come to see it?"

He waited. The wind blew cold around his feet.

"*I* showed it to her."

Three heads turned toward the new voice. There, in the shadow cast by the beech tree, stood an Old One. No one had heard his approach.

Guinevere sagged against the tree. Sir Bedwyr hesitated. It took him a moment to recognize Llyr in the man he saw before him, a man clad in wolfskins, carrying a spear, with the light of battle in his angry eyes. Dillon's sword slithered from its scabbard.

"Put up, man. Put up!" Sir Bedwyr said roughly. Reluctantly, Dillon obeyed. The Old One had already hefted his spear into throwing position.

"Let the princess go."

Sir Bedwyr displayed his empty hands. "She is free to do as she wills."

"Move away from her."

Sir Bedwyr signaled Dillon and they both backed five paces into the woods. Llyr lowered his spear and approached the tree.

"Gwenhwyfar?"

"Oh, Llyr, where have you been?" She ran to him and hugged him. "Did you know they were hunting for you? Did you come back because of the boy?"

His eyes were cold pits of anger. "His name is Luath Strong-Heart. I promised his father to bury him in sacred ground."

"That can be done," she said. "I'm sure Sir Bedwyr will allow it. But it's not safe for you here." She looked at his stony face and knew at once that there was no point in speaking to him of safety. He had the look of a man determined to prevail at any cost.

Trevor had foreseen this, she realized, when he asked her if there was no person or circumstance for which Llyr would sacrifice himself. Trevor seemed to know a good bit about the Old Ones. It was clear to her now that Llyr was prepared to die for his people. He had come out of the woods to protect the Old Ones from more killing.

She took his hand between her own and squeezed it hard.

Don't do this, Llyr, she wanted to beseech him. But she could not. He was doing the right thing, the honorable thing, and next to that, her fear of losing him seemed selfish and mean-spirited.

"Come with me," she said. "Sir Bedwyr has a place prepared."

His gaze softened, and he almost smiled. "I knew you would understand. You have the courage of a man, Gwenhwyfar."

Guinevere shook her head as she led him forward. It was Llyr who had courage, the kind of courage few men possessed. She wanted to reassure him that once the hunt for him was over, he would be safe from her race of men, and that under Sir Bedwyr's protection he would have no need to sacrifice himself. But she could not speak the words. They felt too much like betrayal.

CHAPTER TWENTY-SIX

Foreign Soil

By dusk, Sir Bedwyr had installed Llyr in his own sleeping quarters and posted a heavy guard outside. He arranged for food, water, and clothes to be brought to him, but ordered that no one be allowed to see him. He had his men construct another workspace within the great tent for his private use and saw that his writing desk and his scribe were settled there. Knowing that rumors of the capture and killing of an Old One were flying around camp with abandon, growing wilder and more malicious with every retelling, Sir Bedwyr paid a formal visit to each kingdom's camp to tell them the truth of what had happened, beginning with Gwynedd and ending, shortly before the evening meal, with Powys.

Queen Esdora received him cordially, but he could tell from her grave expression that she had already heard his news.

He was thus unsurprised to find Guinevere there before him when he was shown into Trevor's chamber. She made him a pretty reverence but did not meet his eyes. He knew she was angry that he would not allow her to visit Llyr, but he could not risk it. To dispense the High King's justice, he had to remain impartial. He could not allow her to influence Llyr, at least not until he had the truth from him.

Sir Bedwyr endeavored to explain all this as he took his seat by Trevor's pallet. He told them what he had already said to everyone else: He was there by King Arthur's order as his proxy and was sworn to administer the King's justice in disputes. A dispute had now arisen that must be settled before the council of kings could be concluded. He had in custody the two men who had murdered the Old One. Their ultimate disposition depended in part upon the kings they served.

"Cadog, that mindless wretch, is in our service," Trevor said glumly. "What would you have us do?"

"If you want him freed, pay a bloodprice to the dead boy's clan and give Cadog a post that doesn't require possession of a weapon. Otherwise, I must take him back to Caerleon with me and await the King's return. Arthur will decide what to do with him."

Trevor pushed himself to a sitting position. "Mother and I have already discussed this. We don't want him back. He's been a troublemaker all his life, as his father was before him. We will send a winter's worth of wood and charcoal to the dead boy's clan, but Cadog himself had better go to Arthur. Perhaps the High King can impress him into civility."

"And Cadog's family?" Sir Bedwyr asked. "What of them?"

"I will take his wife and children into my household," said Queen Esdora. "They can earn their keep in the kitchen gardens. They'll be decently housed and fed, my lord, and treated well, which is more than Cadog ever did for them."

Satisfied, Sir Bedwyr moved on to Llyr. "He's in my custody and safe for the time being. I am to be his judge in the High King's place. But before I pass judgment, I will speak privately to each person who knows anything about the dagger or its theft. Afterward, I will hold council and try to achieve a consensus about what should be done. My judgment may depend on what the council recommends."

Trevor snorted. "My lord is an optimist if he expects a consensus from Welshmen."

Sir Bedwyr smiled. "A lesson already learned, I assure you. Nevertheless, we must try. Llyr will be present at this hearing. The High King requires that an accused man have the chance to face his accusers. I will consider all opinions, but my judgment is final." He met Guinevere's eyes. "Until his hearing, no one may visit Llyr. I want no ideas put into his head. I will question him myself tonight, while he is still in a mood to be forthcoming."

"Tell me," said Queen Esdora abruptly, "what King Mardoc has decided to do with Banin of Mab's Bog."

Sir Bedwyr frowned. "He hasn't yet decided. Apparently, Banin is a kinsman, although a distant one, which complicates matters. Mardoc wants him returned to his service without having to pay a bloodprice, but that cannot be done. We can't pretend that murder never happened."

"No doubt he does not regard it as murder at all," the

queen said dryly. "He probably applauds the act. To his mind, the fewer greedy savages about, the better."

Sir Bedwyr cast her a sharp glance. "You know your neighbor, my lady."

"Indeed I do. He likes to make noise and throw his weight about. He's also the stumbling block in council. Perhaps, now that you have something he wants, Trevor and I can persuade him to a bargain. We know his little weaknesses, you see."

"If you can, I will be in your debt." Sir Bedwyr rose. "Thank you for receiving me, my lady. I will see you, I hope, at Llyr's hearing in three days' time?"

"And me, too," put in Trevor with a grin. "Merlin brought me a pair of walking sticks. I've already practiced with them." He pointed to a pair of stout carved staffs at the foot of his bed. They had broad knobs at their tops for easy gripping and tripod feet of solid oak.

"You've seen Merlin?" Sir Bedwyr turned in surprise. "Where? When? I've been looking for him for days."

"This afternoon. About the time, I guess, that you brought in Llyr."

Sir Bedwyr grunted. "I swear, that man can disappear at will. If you see him before I do, tell him I beg a moment of his time." He turned to go.

"Sir Bedwyr!" Guinevere jumped to her feet. She could hold back no longer.

Sir Bedwyr turned back politely. "Princess?"

"Are you going to interview Princess Morgan? I—I think you should, if you're going to speak to everyone who knows about the dagger."

Sir Bedwyr paused. "Do you have reason to believe she knows anything that will help?"

"Yes, my lord, I do."

His eyes narrowed. "Go on."

"I saw your face when Dillon dug up the dagger. I saw your surprise. You've been hunting for a stolen dagger, yet you weren't expecting to find *that* one, were you?"

"No," he admitted cautiously. "I wasn't. What of it?"

"Well, my lord, I've been thinking. If you were surprised to find Lord Riall's dagger, then it can't have been Lord Riall who made the charge of theft. It must have been someone else." She waited for a response and got none. "Someone else must have reported a stolen dagger and named Llyr as thief. *And* offered a talent of silver as a reward. I asked myself who among us could afford to make that offer."

She glanced up at him almost shyly. His face remained impassive and she took a deep breath to gather her courage. "The only one I could think of was Princess Morgan. I've seen the inside of her tent, my lord. Her dowry must be worth at least triple the offer."

Sir Bedwyr frowned. "Her dowry is not hers to give away."

"I don't think she ever intended to give it away. I don't think she's even risked it."

Sir Bedwyr's frown darkened. "Suppose you tell me exactly what you mean."

"I don't think any dagger was ever stolen. I think Princess Morgan made that part up. She could accuse Llyr of theft and bury someone else's dagger as evidence against him. *And*," she added fiercely as Sir Bedwyr opened his mouth to interrupt, "if it was Princess Morgan who accused Llyr and offered the reward, then she is just as responsible as Banin or Cadog for the murder of Luath Strong-Heart!"

"Keep your voice down," Sir Bedwyr said sharply. "Tent walls are thin." He paced the length of the chamber and back again, coming to a halt before the two standing women. "I tell you this in confidence. Yes, it was Princess Morgan who laid the charge against Llyr. One of her retainers saw an Old One near their tent on the night the dagger disappeared. And yes, I will speak with her since, as the accuser, she has a direct interest in the outcome of the hearing. But I warn you, Lady Guinevere, to be careful of your tongue. Loyalty to a friend is admirable, but you go too far. You are asking me to believe that Arthur's sister deliberately lied to me about the theft in order to incriminate Llyr, a man she didn't know existed."

"But she *did* know!" Guinevere cried. "Elaine told her."

Sir Bedwyr shook his head. "Why would Morgan do such a thing? What is Llyr to her? Even if Princess Elaine told her who he was, that doesn't give her a reason to wish him harm."

Guinevere lowered her eyes and twisted her hands together. How could she tell him what motivated Morgan? How could she tell him her suspicions without sounding petty and self-centered? "I know she doesn't like me. I don't know why."

She waited for his ridicule, but it did not come. The tent was silent but for the soft lick of flames in the brazier. When at last she glanced up at him, she found him gazing at her thoughtfully. Was he recalling the night of the presentation and Princess Morgan's rudeness to her, born of spontaneous dislike? Or had he seen Morgan's cold disdain at the communal dinners: her refusal to acknowledge Guinevere by so much as a word or glance and her obvious shunning of her company? Or was he wondering if Guinevere really imagined that her personal doings could ever be of interest to the High King's sister?

Sir Bedwyr drew a long breath and shook his head. "Your argument rests on Princess Morgan's planting the dagger—not just anyone's dagger, but Lord Riall's—beneath Llyr's tree. And you have no evidence at all that she did so. How did the dagger come into her hands? You don't know that, either. If you speak of these suspicions to others, you will only add to the host of rumors flying about—rumors that have already caused the death of an innocent boy and that still threaten to subvert the High King's justice."

To his utter astonishment, Guinevere smiled. And with that smile a sudden flash of beauty, as dazzling as the first burst of sunlight from behind a passing storm cloud, struck him in the chest and stopped his breath. He looked again and saw only a slender girl in an outgrown gown gazing up at him with beseeching eyes.

"But, Sir Bedwyr, I *do* know how the dagger came into her hands. Or Llyr does. That's what I've been trying to tell you. One night in the forest, Llyr saw Lord Riall take his dagger to Princess Morgan's tent. He stayed there a long time, and when he came out again, he did not have the dagger with him. He left it with her—he gave it to her—he must have."

Sir Bedwyr's gut lurched. "Llyr told you this? When?"

"This afternoon on our way back to camp."

He remembered hearing Llyr's voice, but softly and in an unintelligible language. He had assumed that Llyr was muttering to himself.

"He spoke in Mountain Welsh."

Sir Bedwyr's face hardened. "Which you speak, too, of course?"

"Yes, my lord."

"And how, pray, did Llyr know the dagger belonged to Lord Riall?"

Guinevere colored faintly. "Because he had seen it before. We both had. When it was whole." And without further demur, she told him what he wanted to know: Llyr's watching in the wood and his leading her to the ancient oak and showing her the dagger hidden in the bole, followed by their near escape from Trevor, chasing a deer.

Sir Bedwyr turned to Trevor. "Can you confirm this?"

Trevor nodded. "I can't vouch for the part about the dagger. I never saw it. But I saw two youths—I took Gwen for a boy, I'm ashamed to say—racing away from an old oak tree in different directions. I thought they were up to no good, so I followed the nearest horse and eventually waylaid Gwen. She told me about Llyr when I asked after her companion."

Sir Bedwyr turned his level gaze on Guinevere, who flushed. "He wasn't in trouble then," she said quickly. "He wasn't being chased all over the forest by armed men twice his size. There was no reason not to tell Trevor. And . . . and anyway, I've told you now."

"Yes. Thank you, princess." Sir Bedwyr spoke heavily. "Is there anything else?"

She looked at him anxiously. "No, my lord . . . I'm sorry."

"Sorry?"

"I know she's the High King's sister. . . ."

"That's only half of it," he snapped. "In two weeks, she'll be King Urien's wife. The future of Britain depends on that—Arthur's future, my future, your future." He looked directly at each of them in turn. "You will keep this information to yourselves. All of it."

It was an order, not a request. Sir Bedwyr bowed stiffly to them all and took his leave.

He walked back to his tent with a careful step. The ground he trod was unknown to him, like foreign soil. He was responsible to Arthur for administering his justice, and he had sworn an oath to Arthur to protect his sister. May Mithras come to his aid! What if he could not do both?

CHAPTER TWENTY-SEVEN

A Dark Time Coming

Llyr sat on the camp bed that had been provided for him and waited, his head in his hands. It was cold in the tent. The autumn breeze blew in around the edges and made the lamp's flame dance. A brazier near Sir Bedwyr's pallet was as yet unlit, but Llyr would not have lit it even if he'd had the means. A great melancholy had settled on his heart. He knew he was facing death, but he had chosen it himself, and for a most honorable reason. Death was bearable. The end of his guardianship was not.

He could hardly bring himself to believe that it was over after a mere six months. Had the One Who Hears appointed him to the honor knowing he would have so little time to bear it? That wouldn't surprise him. The gods and their servants enjoyed the discomfiture of men from time to time. Still, he could not believe it.

He found it impossible to surrender his commitment to Guinevere—nor could he part from her. Death meant separation, and separation death. He would suffer both in time, but not now. It was too soon. He knew this in his bones. There were years to go before his guardianship should end. The great king of her destiny was not yet on the horizon. His guardianship would end when the king arrived to claim her, and not before.

Llyr shivered inside his wolfskin. The garment did not fit him well enough for warmth. The Strong Hearts were a shorter, thicker folk than the White Foot, and the borrowed clothing did not reach his knees. He had refused Sir Bedwyr's offer of a cloak. What was the point of comfort? Cold, like the emptiness inside him, could be endured. After all, it would not last long.

He remembered the dream he'd had the night before Guinevere told him about the journey to Deva. At the time, he had thought it meant that he could not go home again. And that was true, in a way. His people had welcomed him warmly enough, but he and they knew he would never be part of their lives again.

Now he saw a larger meaning in the dream. He saw a warning from the gods that the wheel of time was turning, that the journey was the first step toward fulfillment of the prophecy, and that the past would soon be irretrievable. At the time, he had not recognized the warning. Thus he had come upon the end of his relationship with Guinevere unprepared.

Every fiber of his being revolted at the thought. He loved her; he knew that now. He could accept that love, with all its impossible ramifications, because he had nothing else left. He was one of Earth's Beloved, and such a passion was forbidden, but he was powerless to expunge it from his heart. She was the sun who warmed his world, the rain who nourished, the moon who blessed. Great king or no great king, how could he accept the death of that? What would happen to Guinevere when the Others killed him? He uttered a cry of anguish, foreseeing the desperation of her grief and his utter helplessness to prevent it.

"Llyr, son of Bran, be calm," said a quiet voice from the doorway.

Llyr looked up. A tall man in a black cloak stood in the flickering shadows. Llyr knew who he was. Myrddin was his name—a god's name—but the Old Ones called him Master. He was a great wizard who could live in many worlds at once and who commanded power in all of them.

He spoke again in the ancient tongue of Earth's Beloved. "Do not grieve, for thy death is not yet come."

Llyr slid to his knees. "Master, I do not grieve for death. It is the girl I grieve for."

"Ah. The girl." The man came toward him. "Rise, Llyr, and listen. I have come to return the body of Luath Strong-Heart to his people. Let me tell thee what will happen while I am gone."

Llyr listened obediently to the Master's words. The Others

would not drag him out at dawn and kill him, as he had expected. Sir Bedwyr was a man of law, and the High King's law required a hearing. Llyr would have the chance to face his accusers and to deny the accusations against him.

For a moment, Llyr began to hope. The moment passed. Who among the Others would believe him? He had seen those wild men hunting him in the forest. They would never be swayed by denials.

"I have come to ask a favor of thee, Llyr."

Llyr nodded dumbly.

"When the time comes for thee to speak, be silent. Say nothing. Keep a dry eye and a calm heart. Let the Others come to their decision without thy help. Let the noise and tumult sweep over thee and touch thee not. Bend to the strong wind and be still standing when the storm is past."

This was an old saying among Earth's Beloved, and Llyr knew the truth of it. He also knew that bending to the strong wind could entail enormous suffering. He could endure any suffering, he thought, so long as Guinevere was not there to see it.

The Master read his thought. "Alas," he said. "The girl must be there." His voice softened. "The path to glory is never straight. Neither is it smooth. To choose this road requires courage."

Llyr squeezed his eyes shut. It was a hard god who spoke through this wizard's mouth. Must he suffer the ultimate indignity of bringing unbearable grief upon the one he loved? Must he stand there and watch it as well? It was too much to ask.

"Master," he said, opening his eyes and making the sign of submission. "Is it necessary?"

"It is necessary," came the chill reply.

Llyr drew a deep breath. "Then it will be done."

"Thanks from my heart."

"But in return, I have a favor to ask of thee."

The Master waited in perfect stillness while Llyr fought to pull the words out of himself. "I am her guardian. . . . If I am to die . . . she must not go unguarded. Would thee be her guardian in my place?"

The Master bowed. "It would be a privilege."

A great weight seemed to lift from Llyr, and his breath came more easily. "Thanks from my heart, Master."

The wizard's hand gripped his shoulder, imparting warmth. "Son of Bran, thy strength will not fail."

The tent flap opened behind them and Sir Bedwyr strode in. He stopped in his tracks when he saw them.

"Merlin! I beg your pardon, my lord—my guards sent me no word—"

The enchanter dipped his head politely. "Forgive me, Sir Bedwyr. I came to speak with you and found Llyr here alone. You have arrested him?"

Sir Bedwyr drew off his cloak. "I've taken him into my custody for his own protection. He'll get a hearing in three days' time. I hope, my lord, you will attend?"

"I came to ask your leave to take the body of Luath Strong-Heart back to his people."

"Mithras be praised. I've been looking for you to ask exactly that. What do you need? A couple of men and a litter?"

"A mule. I will go alone."

"My lord, that's not necessary. I can spare two men, and surely a litter shows more respect."

Merlin's thin lips twitched into a smile. "A litter will be misunderstood. They will think you are making a gift of what is rightly theirs."

"Oh, very well. A mule, then. I'll have Dillon show you where the body lies."

"I believe I can find it on my own."

Sir Bedwyr grinned. "Of course. *And* get past any guard unseen."

Merlin bowed.

"Will you be at the hearing?"

"Perhaps."

"I'd be most grateful for your advice."

There was no answer from Merlin. He stood as still as stone, his vacant gaze locked on something distant and unseen. Llyr knew at once that the Master had stepped from this world into another and was temporarily beyond Sir Bedwyr's reach. But Sir Bedwyr did not yet know it.

"My lord? Are you all right?"

"He is gone," Llyr said softly. "He will not hear you until he returns."

"What do you mean, gone?"

"Away. Somewhere else." Llyr waved a hand. "Not here."

Sir Bedwyr frowned. "You're blue with cold. Wrap yourself in the blanket until my servant comes to light the fire. I'm off to dinner directly, and I'll have a dish sent in to you. Eat it when it comes, Llyr. You must keep up your strength. I will need to ask you questions later, and I don't want you falling ill."

Llyr dropped his eyes unhappily. The Master had told him not to answer questions, and he had already answered one. He resolved to say no more.

"Beware a dark time coming." The words came from Merlin, but it was not his voice that spoke. "Woe betide the dragon in his lair, the mage in his conceit, and the innocent in his womb. The dark time comes."

The dire pronouncement echoed in the small room long after the voice had stopped. Merlin the Enchanter shook himself awake.

"Wine," he croaked, shutting seamed lids over blind eyes. "Wine or water. Please."

Sir Bedwyr pushed his own flask into the enchanter's hand and guided it to his lips. Merlin gulped the contents down. Eventually color returned to his face, and he looked at them both apologetically. "I beg your pardons. What did I say?"

Sir Bedwyr stared at him, but Llyr smiled. It was likewise with the One Who Hears. The very act of hearing the god's voice robbed humankind of strength and left them weak as newborn babes. It was comforting to have proof that the Master could suffer like any mortal man.

Sir Bedwyr coughed. "Something about a dark time coming. To a dragon, a mage, and an unborn babe."

Merlin scowled. "Thank you, Bedwyr. It caught me unprepared, or you should not have heard so much." He turned to Llyr. "Remember what I told thee, son of Bran. Thy end is not yet nigh. Accept the blanket and eat the food. Light with thee walk."

Llyr bowed low as the Master nodded to Sir Bedwyr and swept out of the tent. "Dark from thee flee," he murmured after the retreating figure. It was the ritual farewell among the Old Ones, but it sounded foolish now. How did one keep darkness from a wizard who had just foretold it for himself?

"By the Light!" Sir Bedwyr snapped. "I told the guards to keep *everyone* out! Did he really have time to speak with you? What did he say?"

Llyr smiled. "He told me not to answer any questions."

CHAPTER TWENTY-EIGHT

Lord Riall's Dilemma

Sir Bedwyr was in a black mood the next morning when he sent for Lord Riall after breakfast. He had not slept well. In contrast to Llyr, who had slept long and soundly, wrapped in a thick wool blanket and with a belly full of roast partridge and the King's red wine, Bedwyr had been plagued by worry and indigestion. He was also annoyed at Merlin, who had intimidated Llyr into silence and disappeared. He had no doubt that the enchanter would manage to transform what ought to be a short trip into the foothills and back—a day, at most—into a lengthy enterprise, thereby missing the hearing altogether and failing to be there when he was needed. It was an old trick of his, this disappearing when he was wanted most.

Bedwyr had made that complaint to Arthur once.

"He's testing us," Arthur had replied with a smile. "He wants to know if we can do without him."

Bedwyr hoped that Merlin was not testing him now. He had enough to do without trying to measure up to Merlin's standards. That was Arthur's burden, praise Mithras, not his.

He walked to the writing desk and looked down at the ancient dagger in its mutilated sheath. Last night he had told everyone that an Old One had been taken into custody and a hearing scheduled. He had not announced that the stolen dagger had been found. He wanted to surprise Lord Riall. The man's first reaction on seeing it would tell him much.

When at last Lord Riall was announced, Bedwyr stood in front of the desk to block his view of the weapon. "Welcome, Lord Riall. Thank you for coming so promptly."

Lord Riall muttered something civil and stared around in evident contempt at the plainness of the hastily constructed room. "Your page said it was urgent."

"It is." Bedwyr smiled. "Sit down and make yourself comfortable. I have some questions. You can answer frankly; we're quite alone. I've dismissed my scribe." He moved away from the desk.

Lord Riall was already moving toward the chair when he saw the dagger. He stopped, his jaw dropped, and color flamed into his face. "My dagger! What's it doing here?"

"Why?" Bedwyr asked smoothly. "Had you lost it?"

Lord Riall began a sharp retort and cut it off. His eyes bulged, his face turned almost purple, and his thin red hair seemed to stand on end. He began to shake. "What've you done? Oh, what've you done! You've mangled it! You've taken the stone! Where is it? I want it back; I want it the way it was!"

He reached out a hand for the dagger, but Bedwyr caught his wrist. "Did I hear you aright, Lord Riall? Are you accusing *me* of stealing the stone?"

"No, no, my lord," Lord Riall said hastily, struggling to gather his wits. "A slip of the tongue, my lord. Forgive me, but—but how did it come into your hands?"

"I found it. Buried beneath a tree."

"Liar!"

Bedwyr stiffened. Openly insulting the High King's officer was an actionable offense, but he did not reach for his sword. Instead, he said evenly, "I have witnesses. Two of them."

Lord Riall sagged and fell into the chair. His hard little eyes darted about the room, narrowing in fierce calculation, finding no answer acceptable.

Bedwyr strolled about behind him. "I will admit I was astonished to find it there. A weapon so priceless and so prized by your lady mother? Buried rather carelessly, too. Sure to be found by someone."

Lord Riall gulped and shifted in his chair. Bedwyr paused at his side. "It's lucky it was found by someone who knew what it was. I recognized it at once, of course. Even without the stone."

"Yes, yes," Lord Riall said hurriedly. "A blessing. Most grateful to you—" Then his mouth fell open and his face went white. "It was missing the stone when you found it?"

"Obviously, since it's been in my possession ever since."

Sir Riall swallowed hard. "I—I must have it back, my lord. Even mangled, it's mine. It's my dagger."

"Is it?" Bedwyr kept his voice casual. "Then how did it come to be buried in the woods?"

"I've no idea!"

"It left your possession, then, before it was buried. Not by loss, though. You're not the kind who would be careless with your mother's treasure. I'm sure you kept it safely hidden."

"Yes, my lord, I did. I did. My mother would—"

"Was it stolen from you?"

"I—I— Yes! It was stolen."

"When?"

Lord Riall glared at him. "What difference does—"

"Why didn't you report it to me?"

"Mind your own—"

"It *is* my business. I'm King Arthur's proxy. . . . Well?"

"I didn't want it known."

"I see. You thought perhaps you would be able to recover it yourself?"

Lord Riall gave a tentative nod.

Bedwyr made a show of puzzlement. "That leaves me with a very strange, almost unbelievable coincidence. Two daggers stolen from camp in the same week. You failed to report the theft of yours, and Princess Morgan failed to describe hers."

At the mention of Princess Morgan, Lord Riall went perfectly white. His pale eyes stretched wide, and in them Bedwyr recognized the numb horror, the realization of perfidy, that he had often seen on the battlefield in the eyes of dying men.

"Yes," he said into the silence. "Princess Morgan reported the theft of a precious dagger. A wedding gift, she said. Valuable enough to warrant a talent of silver for its return. But do you know what I think?" He leaned down and placed his lips beside Lord Riall's ear. "I think her stolen dagger and your stolen dagger are the same dagger."

He straightened. Lord Riall gazed at him dumbly. His face had now gone gray, and he seemed to have shrunk in size.

Bedwyr resumed his meander about the room. "If they're the same dagger, then it was clearly in Princess Morgan's possession when it was stolen. How did it come there? I can think of only three ways: either you gave it to her, or she stole it, or she found it lying about somewhere and buried it, rather poorly, to keep it safe. I find the third alternative very unlikely, since you claim that it was stolen, and since Princess Morgan has much better hiding places within her own tent. Whoever buried it, buried it so it would be found."

He paused in his meander to glance at Lord Riall's face. "Did she steal it from you? Was she the thief? And you did not come forward, not because you didn't want it known, but because you were afraid to lay a charge of theft against the High King's sister. Is that it? More believable, I think, than the tale you told me."

Lord Riall swallowed. His eyes were glazed. He did not seem capable of speech.

"But that won't serve, will it? Because you *didn't* think Princess Morgan stole your dagger. You still don't think it." Bedwyr stroked his chin thoughtfully. "You and I both know she didn't steal it. Or find it. You had it hidden too well. Your hiding place in the old oak was inaccessible to a woman of her station."

At the mention of the oak tree, Lord Riall started. A spark of incredulity flickered briefly in his despairing eyes and died. He slumped in the chair and looked away.

"So," Bedwyr concluded, "if Princess Morgan didn't find it and didn't steal it, only one possibility remains: you gave it to her."

He waited politely for a denial. None came.

"Princess Morgan claims the stolen dagger was a wedding gift. Perhaps it was. Yours." He cocked an eyebrow at Lord Riall, who recovered enough to pass a tongue over dry lips and give thought to this possibility of escape. Sir Bedwyr smiled to himself and resumed his saunter. "But this is the same dagger that you offered to me and Merlin in exchange for the crown of Gwynedd. Did you offer it to us first and, when we turned you down, give it to Princess Morgan as a wedding gift?"

A spark of hope lit Lord Riall's eye. Bedwyr shook his head. "No, no, I cannot believe you would give away for nothing what you had offered to us on such dear terms. It argues too great a disrespect for the High King. A treasonable disrespect. I'm sure you're a more loyal man than that."

Trembling now, Lord Riall summoned the strength to nod.

"But however dear its terms," Bedwyr continued, "the dagger changed hands. From your hands to Princess Morgan's. No, don't bother to deny it. I'm afraid you were seen."

Lord Riall, who had opened his mouth to protest, shut it hurriedly and retreated into silence.

"As I recall, you refused my offer to take the dagger to Arthur and lay your case before him. You wanted more. You will tell me—today, now—what Princess Morgan offered you that I could not."

Beads of cold sweat appeared on Lord Riall's brow. Bedwyr picked up the dagger and pretended to examine its sheath. "Come, Riall. It's the only way out. What were the terms?"

Lord Riall licked his lips and swallowed. Lines had appeared in his cheeks, and his flesh sagged. Bedwyr waited, but the man could not bring himself to speak.

"If you won't tell me, I'll have to guess. I can think of at least two advantages the princess has that I lack: kinship to the High King and skill in magic. Either one might tempt me, if I were in your place. Let's say you gave her the dagger because she persuaded you that, through kinship or through magic, she could exert more influence over Arthur than I can."

Bedwyr stood before Lord Riall and looked down at him. "Don't believe her, Riall. You're fooling yourself if you think she has power of any kind. She certainly has none over her brother. Why, they don't even like each other. . . . You didn't know? I thought everyone knew. Think of them as strangers born to the same parents and you'll not be off the mark."

He shoved the dagger in his belt. "As a result of Princess Morgan's accusation of theft, a manhunt took place and an innocent boy was murdered. Whoever buried that dagger intended to implicate the Old Ones, and thus bears complicity in the murder. It's your dagger, but Princess Morgan laid the charge of theft. Either you buried it or she did, or both of you together. Am I making myself clear?"

Lord Riall cleared his throat. "I didn't," he croaked.

"Didn't what?"

"Bury it."

"Good. But trading it to Morgan to use against the High King is an act of treason."

"Treason?" Lord Riall squeaked. "It was a *gift*. She's his *sister*!"

"Mmm. But not his most loyal subject. And the dagger was meant as a bribe, not a gift, or you'd have sent it through me. I didn't promise you influence. She did." He sighed. "The way I see it, you're caught between the horns of a dilemma: murder or treason. Either you helped bring about the murder of an Old One, however unknowingly, or you attempted to betray the High King's trust. Which is it to be?"

Lord Riall jumped from his chair. "Neither! You go too far—you're trying to trick me."

"How?"

"I—I—" He stood there, shaking and swallowing convulsively. "All I want are my rights."

Bedwyr frowned. "It's gone beyond that now. Someone's been killed."

"That's none of my doing!" Lord Riall cried. "I was no part of that. And that royal witch lied to me! She promised me a kingdom within a year. Give me my mother's dagger back, Sir Bedwyr, and I'll go home. All I wanted were my rights."

"Yes, that's what I would do. I would disappear, like Merlin, with no noise or fuss. Pack up and go home."

"Yes, yes!" Lord Riall cried, overwhelmed with relief and bowing gratefully. "I'll go at once. Just let me have the dagger back, my lord."

Bedwyr shook his head. "I'm afraid the dagger is needed as evidence for the hearing."

"I could wait a day or two, my lord—"

"There's no point. The dagger will go to Arthur in any case. If it belonged to Princess Morgan, whether she received it as a bribe or a wedding gift, then she relinquished possession when she buried it in the ground for anyone to find and claim. I found it. I've claimed it. But to do you justice," he finished quickly, seeing Lord Riall on the verge of panic, "I will do as I previously offered and lay your mother's case before the High King when I present the dagger to him."

Lord Riall heard the steely note in the knight's voice and choked back an angry retort. After a struggle, he blurted, "I can't go home to Mother empty-handed!"

"Tell her you bring King Arthur's thanks and his promise to consider her appeal." He clapped Lord Riall on the shoulder and escorted him to the door. "I'll have my scribe draw up a formal letter on bleached parchment in perfect Latin and deliver it to your tent," he said pleasantly. "It will be something definite you can hand her. Will that suit? Be out of camp by midday, and may Mithras light your way."

Lord Riall cast one last, anxious glance at the beautiful weapon in Sir Bedwyr's belt, and hurried out.

CHAPTER TWENTY-NINE

Royal Skirmish

"Did you hear? Lord Riall's left camp. Without us."

Elaine came through the doorway into Trevor's chamber, her cheeks pink from the chill outside. Guinevere and Queen Esdora, side by side on a bench before the glowing brazier, looked up from their needlework, but it was Trevor who spoke first.

"At last. Overdue, don't you think?" He sat in a chair beside his mother, his splinted leg resting on a stool, his head tilted to one side, smiling at Elaine.

She scowled at him. "He shouldn't have come in the first place. He's not king of anything."

"Gone! What, his men and wagons, too?" Guinevere asked. "That's sudden."

"Indeed," agreed Queen Esdora. "And significant. Elaine, my dear, is your mother free of company at the moment?"

"Yes, my lady. I was forgetting, she asks for you as soon as you're free to attend her."

Queen Esdora tucked away her needle and looked down at the strip of twice-bleached linen on which she had been working. "I'll leave this in your capable hands, if I may, Gwen, while I pay my visit to your aunt."

"She said to tell you," Elaine continued with a gleam in her eye, "that Sir Bedwyr has gone to visit Princess Morgan."

Guinevere and Queen Esdora exchanged glances.

"Well done, Gwen!" hooted Trevor. "Now the fur will fly."

Elaine frowned. "I don't see what Gwen's got to do with it."

Trevor grinned and patted the seat his mother had vacated. "Come sit beside me, fair Elaine, and let me tell you how your evil cousin arranged an uncomfortable afternoon for Princess Morgan."

"Oh, nonsense, Trevor," Guinevere said sharply.

Elaine sat down between Trevor and Guinevere. "What does he mean, Gwen? What did you do?"

"Nothing."

Elaine turned to Trevor, whose arm had gently encircled her waist. "Let go, you oaf. I'm not going to marry you, and that's that."

"So you say," Trevor agreed, giving her a light squeeze.

"I mean it."

"I know you do." He grinned. "I like a woman who knows her own mind. I'll wait."

"Time won't change anything."

"On the contrary, time changes everything."

Elaine scowled, but there was pleasure in her eyes. "You have an answer for everything."

"I do for you."

"Gwen!" cried Elaine. "Can't you make him stop?"

"Make him stop yourself."

"Kiss me," Trevor offered, "and I'll be still."

Elaine colored prettily. "I don't want you to be still. I want you to tell me what Gwen has to do with Sir Bedwyr's going to see Princess Morgan."

Trevor sighed. "I think it's time she was part of this, don't you, Gwen?"

"Now that she's free of Princess Morgan, I suppose it's safe."

"Safe for what? What are you two planning?"

"Shall you tell her, Gwen, or shall I?"

"She'd rather hear it from you."

"If only that were so." Trevor winked at her and turned to Elaine. "Little beauty, ruler of my heart, I've a tale to tell you. Sit still and listen."

"Let me go. A tale about what?"

"An old Roman dagger, a murder, and a royal witch."

Elaine's eyes widened and Trevor stifled a sigh at their blaze of blue. "A dagger!" she cried. "Whose dagger? The one worth a talent of silver? It's been found?"

"Patience, Beauty. You don't have to kiss me, but you do have to listen. We may need your help."

Guinevere watched them out of the corner of her eye as

Trevor told Elaine about Lord Riall's dagger. Elaine's interest in the story was intense, and she didn't notice Trevor's arm stealing back around her waist. Or if she did, she didn't push it away. Perhaps she secretly liked his embrace. Something in her posture, in the angle of her shoulders, in the tilt of her head, hinted at coyness. Guinevere was delighted to see it. If Elaine began to flirt with Trevor, surely friendship could not be far away. Clever Trevor, she thought, to sneak in at the postern gate while Elaine stood guard over the barricades out front.

Princess Morgan stood as still as stone before her mirror of polished bronze. Although it was not yet dusk, she was dressed for bed in a long crimson night-robe. Her day gown lay on the floor at her feet, discarded in haste the moment Sir Bedwyr's messenger had left.

A tremor ran through her and she stilled it instantly. Who did Sir Bedwyr think he was, to summon her to a conference in his tent? He was no more than one of Arthur's spaniels, as she liked to call the Companions, who licked her brother's boots and howled his praises in exchange for a dollop of power now and then. Summoned to a conference, indeed! Of course she had refused to obey. She had instructed Marcia to tell the messenger that she was sorry to disappoint so worthy a knight as Bedwyr of Brydwell, but that she was ill and could not leave her bed. And for a while, that had been that.

But the messenger had returned. In a cold voice that carried clearly through the tent cloth, he had informed Marcia that Sir Bedwyr was on his way to visit Princess Morgan. He had already left his tent. When Marcia had objected that her lady was abed and ill, the messenger had replied that Sir Bedwyr was a strong man and not fearful of infection. Morgan flushed at the memory. The arrogance of the man! How was such insolence to be endured?

She and Marcia had scrambled to be ready in time. She had exchanged her gown for her best night-robe—another of Arthur's parting gifts and, like the others, of the finest quality but plain, without trim or ornament. The great carved bed she had brought with her from Tintagel had been dressed with crimson coverlets and furs. Two silver goblets had been set out and filled with wine—to serve as temptation only, for Morgan had no intention of offering any to Sir Bedwyr. The chairs in the chamber had been removed and Marcia's low stool brought to the bedside. It was now the only place to sit, other than the bed itself, and would position Sir Bedwyr's head a handspan below the level of Morgan's.

Now Morgan stood before her mirror, still and concentrated, summoning her strength. For despite her contempt for Sir Bedwyr, she knew he had Arthur's power behind him, and she understood Arthur's power very well.

Why was Sir Bedwyr coming to see her? He had arrested Llyr—that rumor was already old. He had found the dagger. She had been back to the tree to check. What more did he need? His course was clear. Once Llyr was executed, the dagger would be returned to her, and she would take it with her to Rheged as a prize for her daring. It was sure to be more valuable than any of Urien's own. And poor little

Guinevere would weep all the way home to Gwynedd and never know why.

Why was Sir Bedwyr paying her a visit? Had that savage, Llyr, been telling him a different story? Even if he had, it did not matter. Llyr was a hillman; she was Arthur's sister. She was the one who would be believed.

No one was likely to question that the dagger was hers. It was too valuable to belong to anyone else. Certainly, no one would suspect Lord Riall of possessing such a treasure. And it was too late to ask him, for Marcia had reported that he had packed up and left camp earlier in the day. If that little mouse had lied to her and shown the dagger to someone else—the memory of his constant sweating returned to her with force, a sweating she had attributed at the time to his relinquishing his treasure to her—she had Marcia as witness that he had given it to her as a wedding gift. She was sure she would get the dagger back.

If, however, trouble should arise—it was always possible where someone as weak as Riall was concerned—and she had to sacrifice ownership of the dagger, she was prepared to do so. She'd had the forethought to remove the ruby, which she considered to be the weapon's chief value. She would let the dagger go, if she had to. She would deny any knowledge of it, and no one could prove otherwise. There was no reason for her hands to tremble so at the thought of Sir Bedwyr's coming.

"Bring me my crown of pearls," she ordered as Marcia bent to retrieve the day gown.

"Please, my lady, not again. The High King meant you to wear it at your wedding and not before."

"He thinks only of Urien. Never of me. That's why it pleases me to wear it before humbler men."

"Morgan!"

"Fetch it."

Marcia shrugged and obeyed. With her own hands, Morgan settled the circlet of precious pearls around her head and gazed again into the mirror. The face that looked back at her, pale, impassive, and majestic, was the face of a queen. She exhaled in a little sigh of satisfaction. The trembling of her hands had ceased.

Morgan's page stuck his head through the tent flap to report the approach of Sir Bedwyr with an escort of armed men. "And a standard-bearer," he added, wide-eyed. "With the dragon standard."

Morgan smiled grimly. So this was to be a formal visit. She had been right, after all, to insist upon the pearls.

She placed herself with care in the center of the bed, arranging the coverlets, cushions, and furs neatly about her to give no hint of a sickbed. She wanted Sir Bedwyr to know that she was not ill; that she had refused to see him on his terms; and that despite surrounding himself with the formal trappings of royalty, he was seeing her now on hers.

Sir Bedwyr entered the bedchamber without bravado and politely made his reverence. He had taken care, Morgan saw, to prepare himself for the interview. His cloak was brushed, his boots polished, his face washed, and his chin shaved. The royal cipher of red and gold enamel on his shoulder, which proclaimed him the representative of the High King Arthur, had been rubbed until it shone.

She asserted her rank by speaking first. "Good day, Sir Bedwyr. I hope you are well."

He bowed again. "Princess."

She gestured toward Marcia's stool. "Please, my lord, be seated."

His sharp glance took in the neatness of the bed, the silver goblets, the crown of pearls, and the wooden stool. The corner of his mouth twitched, and he bowed again. "Thank you, my lady, I will stand."

Her gaze hardened. "To what do I owe the honor of this visit?"

"I have come for information," he said evenly. "I won't take up much of your time. The question is easily answered."

"Then ask it."

"The dagger that you claim was stolen from you—what precisely did it look like?"

Morgan hesitated. She had already told him that it was a beautiful weapon housed in an exquisite sheath; that he would know it when he saw it; that it was a wedding gift and worth a fortune. She had been circumspect out of habit, and now she was glad of it. Why did he need to know more?

"*Claim?*" She raised an eyebrow. "Do you doubt my word?"

"Please, princess. A description of the weapon."

It was a trap; she sensed it. He knew something she did not. But if she denied ownership of the dagger, she would lose any claim to it. Better to stall for time until she saw what he was after.

She kept her face calm and her voice as pleasant as she

could make it. "You've found it, then, have you? I am in your debt. That was quick work."

"I found a dagger. I don't know if it's yours."

"Is it valuable?"

"Extremely."

She forced a smile. "Then it's most likely mine."

Sir Bedwyr paused. "I most sincerely hope not, my lady."

Her smile faded. "Why not?"

"Because I found it beneath a tree in the forest. Shallowly buried. Meant to be discovered."

Morgan leaned against her cushions and reached for one of the silver goblets. Her hand was perfectly steady. Sir Bedwyr's dark eyes watched her without expression.

"No thief buries a dagger so recklessly," he said.

"Unless he's in a hurry. He buried it too hastily, I presume."

"I presume nothing. Not even the existence of a thief."

She stared at him. "Be careful of your step, Sir Bedwyr. The thief was *seen*."

He met her eyes, and Morgan recognized the look. It was an echo of Arthur's direct and level gaze. How all her brother's spaniels copied his every move! Still, in her experience spaniels were often moved by greed. "I hear you've found him and taken him into custody. Have you come to claim the reward for his capture?"

He ignored her question, but his face darkened. "I took Llyr into custody for his own protection. Whether he has taken anything from anyone is a matter yet to be determined."

Her nostrils flared. "Protection from what?"

"From the men who want to kill him; the men whose greed you excited by the size of your reward; the men whose passions you deliberately aroused by your accusation against an Old One. The men who murdered the boy in their eagerness to kill Llyr, whom you accused by name."

She sniffed and raised the goblet to her lips, saw that her hand was shaking, and lowered it again to her lap. "It's not my fault the men were angry. Hillmen are a nasty breed. Skulking about in the woods and spying on us, the thieving devils. The men had every right to be annoyed."

"But not to kill."

She shrugged. It was a graceless gesture, and a drop of wine spilled from her goblet onto the crimson coverlet.

Sir Bedwyr drew a deep breath. "Princess Morgan, you laid a charge of theft against Llyr of the White Foot and offered a reward—far too large a reward—to the man who brought him in, alive or dead. As a result of that offer, an innocent boy was murdered."

She stared at him in disbelief. Was this what he had come for? To accuse her of *murder*?

"*I* didn't kill him."

"Not directly, but you inspired the men who did. For that reason, I require your attendance at a hearing the day after tomorrow at midday. Perhaps we can get to the bottom of this tangle then."

"You've found the thief!" she cried. "Everyone says so. Kill him and have done with it."

"I don't know that Llyr is the thief. He came to me of his own accord and his tale of these events differs substantially from yours. Even if he'd told me nothing, he deserves a hearing."

"He's a *hillman*. He deserves nothing but contempt." Sir Bedwyr remained impassive. Morgan shrugged. "Have your hearing, if you must, but return my dagger to me."

"Ah." Sir Bedwyr paused. "The dagger. Are you ready to describe it now?"

Morgan hesitated. She was not ready. She could not yet discern his purpose in coming. She did not believe he really meant to accuse her of murder. He seemed to want her to admit to ownership of Lord Riall's dagger and, for that reason alone, she was inclined to deny him. Yet she was loath to relinquish her claim to the dagger, even without the ruby. Of course, Sir Bedwyr had no way of knowing that the dagger he had found had once belonged to Lord Riall . . . *or had he?* She went cold at the thought. Was the little mouse a rat at heart? Had he lied to her? She needed to stall a little longer.

"You've already seen it. You know it's the only dagger in camp worth a talent of silver."

"As to that," Sir Bedwyr said easily, "I've only seen one dagger in my life that valuable, and it belongs to Lord Riall."

Morgan froze. Her heartbeat hammered in her ears. Both hands clutched the goblet in her lap. "Lord Riall?" she whispered.

Sir Bedwyr nodded. "Yes. An antique weapon with a large blade in a golden sheath set with jewels. Perfectly stunning."

That rat Riall! She cleared her throat to gain command of her voice. "I'd no idea a man like Lord Riall could possess such a weapon."

"Didn't you?"

She swallowed hard. Her throat was dry. She longed for a sip of wine but dared not raise the shaking goblet to her lips. "No. I did not." She raised her chin defiantly and added, "Did you?"

Sir Bedwyr responded with a half smile. "Not until he came to my tent and showed it to me. It was an heirloom of his mother's family. He brought it to Deva to give to Arthur."

That demented fool! He had shown it to Sir Bedwyr before he showed it to her! And he hadn't told her! She fought for control of her voice. "Poor man," she said at last, with a chilly smile. "I suppose he wouldn't give it to you, instead?"

"He offered it to me. As a bribe for influence. I turned him down."

Morgan thought furiously. The dagger was lost to her, but now something greater was at stake. Did he know that Lord Riall had offered it to her on the same terms? Of course not. He couldn't know. No one knew but Riall, Morgan herself, and Marcia. And Riall was gone. She glanced quickly at Marcia and saw only concern on her face. No, Marcia hadn't told. She was safe, then. *Safe.* Yet her hands would not cease their trembling.

Sir Bedwyr was still speaking. "It's odd that Lord Riall never claimed his dagger was stolen or even missing. And yet I found it beneath a tree in the forest."

"Perhaps he feared to tell you. Perhaps he was afraid you

had taken it yourself." Something flickered behind Sir Bedwyr's eyes and Morgan smiled to herself. Her blow had struck home. Theft was a thing he had considered. "Or perhaps he's lying low. Ask him. Force it out of him."

Sir Bedwyr shook his head slowly. "He left camp at noon today."

"Indeed?"

"But before he left, Lord Riall and I had a little conference in my tent."

Icy fingers closed around Morgan's heart.

"He admitted to me that he gave his dagger to you. As a bribe for your influence with Arthur in his mother's cause."

Her breathing stopped, and her amber eyes hardened to glossy points. "And you believed him."

"Not him alone. You were seen."

"Impossible!" She blanched and her face went rigid. "You believe these lies because you wish to!"

"No, princess, I don't wish to. But I want the truth."

"The dagger that savage stole from me was a small woman's dagger, Gaelic in design, with a handle of twisted snakes and a pretty enameled sheath. A gift from Alyse of Gwynedd. You saw it yourself at their presentation." The words came out in a rush and left her breathless.

Sir Bedwyr's eyebrows rose. "You don't expect me to believe that. That dagger's worth nowhere near a talent of silver."

"Not to you, perhaps. For me, it has sentimental value."

"Princess." His voice was openly skeptical.

"What would I care for a dagger belonging to Lord Riall or his mother? Queen Alyse is someone of importance."

Sir Bedwyr sighed. "When Lord Riall brought his dagger to us—"

"Us?" she cried, her voice shrill. "There was someone with you?"

She sensed the blow before it fell; shadows loomed and the light dimmed.

"Merlin was with me. He read the runes on the blade."

Merlin! She shut her eyes. *Merlin the Enchanter!* The chamber was spinning about her. She swayed and found no balance.

"My lady!" It was Marcia, close by, clutching her shoulder and pulling at the bedclothes. The goblet was no longer between her shaking hands. The coverlet was wet and reeked of wine.

"Princess," Sir Bedwyr said gently. "I wish no ill to anyone of Arthur's blood, but I—"

Her eyes flew open. "Serpent! Snake!" she hissed at him. "How do you dare?" She leaned forward as if poised to strike. "Did you imagine I would agree to plead his miserable suit before the King? I'm not a half-wit. And I could care less who rules in Gwynedd!"

Sir Bedwyr looked at her in silence. She caught her breath as she realized what she had revealed. Sir Bedwyr had said nothing about Lady Gemina's desire to be queen of Gwynedd.

"Who told you Lord Riall gave his dagger to me?" she croaked. "I have a right to know the name of my accuser—it's Arthur's law!"

"Llyr saw him take the dagger to your tent and leave without it."

She threw up her hands. "Llyr! The spy from the woods! You'll believe that filthy savage over *me*? No one has ever dared insult me so! You'll give him a hearing and allow him to spread his vicious lies among Arthur's allies? He's a thieving, lying, primitive savage—he does *not* deserve a hearing—he stole my dagger; he stole Lord Riall's dagger; he buried them until it was safe to dig them up—the truth is as clear as the nose on your face! Everyone sees it but you. And you are supposed to be in Arthur's service? How does this serve him? A public hearing? You must be mad!"

"Nevertheless, well or ill, I expect you to be present."

"Or else what?"

"Or I shall have to pass judgment without the benefit of your advice."

She laughed. It was a hard, joyless sound. "You daren't let him go. And you have no evidence against me." *Merlin.* What had Merlin seen? Where was he now? Was it true that he had left camp yesterday? "Even if you did, you wouldn't implicate me. Not your beloved Arthur's sister."

"I sincerely hope I shall not have to," Sir Bedwyr said wearily. He bowed again and headed for the door.

Morgan rose to her knees in her scarlet robe, stained with wine. "Arthur needs Urien of Rheged!" she shouted after him. "If you attempt to cross me, spaniel, I shall refuse to marry him!"

CHAPTER THIRTY

Striking the Head of the Snake

In the morning, Princess Morgan paid a visit to Queen Alyse. It was a damp, cold late October day, just too warm for frost. A thin mist hanging in the air carried the sound of voices easily from tent to tent. Grannic had come running in just after breakfast with news of the impending visit, and both nurses and girls huddled against the wall of their tent nearest the queen's to hear what the princess had come to say.

It started well enough, Guinevere thought, but then, like a boulder poised on the edge of a landslide, it teetered, tipped, and rolled toward disaster with ever-increasing speed. Princess Morgan wasted no time in small talk but came straight to the point. She wanted Alyse's cooperation at the hearing tomorrow. She feared that Sir Bedwyr might be reluctant to punish the thief he had caught because of the known association between this particular hillman and the House of Gwynedd. Friends of the House of Gwynedd were everywhere respected. Everyone knew of the close relationship King Pellinore enjoyed with the High King, a position he had earned for his unstinting service in the Saxon wars. It was perfectly understandable that Sir Bedwyr would shy from taking any action that might offend such a loyal ally. But was it fair to rap the thief on the knuckles and let him go, just to please a friend? This was not justice, and she, like her brother, was committed to seeing justice done. She was certain that once Queen Alyse had had a chance to think it over, she would acknowledge her duty to urge Sir Bedwyr toward the right course.

Morgan paused for a response from Queen Alyse, but none came. She continued in a harder voice: What kind of precedent would it set to release the thief who stole a precious and valuable object—a weapon, no less—from the sister of the High King? What message would that send to the other savage tribes? And to lowborn folk everywhere? If Sir Bedwyr did not make an example of Llyr, what license might be taken, what chaos might arise, when people of every station found they could disregard the law with impunity? It did not bear consideration.

Another pause followed. This time, Queen Alyse replied. She knew nothing about the theft or the capture of a suspect beyond what Sir Bedwyr had told the entire camp. She would wait until after the hearing to form an opinion. She was sure that Sir Bedwyr honored justice as much as the High King did, and that his judgment would be fair. For Princess Morgan's sake, she hoped that the suspect was not the same young man who had saved her daughter's life six months ago, for if he was, she would be absolutely unable to ally herself to Morgan's cause. He had saved Elaine; for that, she would forgive him anything. *Even the theft of a royal dagger.* The words went unspoken, but not unheard, in the chilly silence.

Guinevere squeezed Elaine's arm. Queen Alyse was a woman of strong opinions and difficult to intimidate. Guinevere, who had often been on the wrong side of her wrath, had never been so thankful for it.

"I advise you to reconsider, Alyse. I would hate to see your reputation damaged and your husband's friendship with my brother placed in jeopardy. Especially as the building on Caer Camel has begun and Arthur is gathering about him the makings of a most illustrious court."

A chill ran up Guinevere's spine. This was a threat with teeth. Little was dearer to her aunt than Pellinore's friendship with King Arthur.

"Do you imply," Queen Alyse retorted, in a voice every bit as cold as Morgan's, "that you have the power to damage us? King Arthur is known for not believing lies."

"I will tell him none," Morgan snapped. "I will tell him the plain truth."

"As will Sir Bedwyr."

"I am his flesh and blood. He will believe me."

"You seem certain that your truth and Sir Bedwyr's differ." Fabric rustled as someone rose. "I do not yield to threats," said Queen Alyse. "Not even from the High King's flesh and blood. Go pour your poison into other ears, Lady Morgan. I will listen to no more."

Elaine giggled and Guinevere clapped a hand over her cousin's mouth.

"Your reputation for brittleness is well deserved," Morgan shot back acidly. "And sentimentality is a mistake. When I am queen of Rheged, we shall speak of this again."

"You may. I certainly will not."

With a jingle of jewelry and a rustle of stiffened silk, Princess Morgan stalked out.

Elaine pushed away Guinevere's hand. "Hurrah for Mother! That's telling her!"

Grannic caught Elaine's arm in an iron grip and held her still. "You two better get back to your chores. Ailsa and I have all this bedding to air, and we can't do that with you about. And here's the morning already half gone."

Fetching water from the river and kindling from the woods took the girls the rest of the morning. When they returned to their tent at midday, Elaine collapsed on her pallet, tired and out of temper, but Guinevere threw open her trunk and began to change her clothes.

"Where are you going *now?*" Elaine complained. "Not out riding."

"No, not out riding." Guinevere slipped into a cleaner gown and rebraided her hair in a long plait down her back. She knew it was not as neat as Ailsa would have done it, but Ailsa was not there. Her slippers were lamentable, but that could not be helped. Her only other shoes were riding boots.

"Then where?"

"To see Sir Bedwyr. I've got to talk with Llyr."

"But no one's allowed to talk with Llyr."

"He's had time to question him; he shouldn't mind."

But Sir Bedwyr did mind. He was apologetic, but firm. She could not see Llyr. No one could.

"But you've had plenty of time to talk to him," Guinevere pleaded. "You said you wanted to get the truth from him first, and you have. What's the harm in my talking to him now?"

Bedwyr grunted. "I haven't got anything from him. He refuses to answer questions."

"He . . . what?"

"He's said nothing. He's safe, warm, and well fed, but he's decided not to speak." He rubbed his forehead wearily. "Merlin talked him into it, I think. I can't guess why."

There was a moment's silence. "Merlin the Enchanter spoke with Llyr?"

"Yes, and I've no idea what they said. I wasn't there."

"You allowed Merlin to see him but no one else?"

Bedwyr shook his head. "I didn't allow it. I left the guards with standing orders to keep everyone out, and when I returned I found the enchanter in my chamber, talking to Llyr. It's a trick of his, you know, invisibility. My guards saw nothing."

"Oh, *please*, Sir Bedwyr, let me see Llyr. I can get him to talk. He might be afraid of you, but he's not afraid of me."

Bedwyr smiled gently. "No, princess, it's not fear he feels for you. But it will be harder for him to see you than to be left alone."

Guinevere colored brightly and Bedwyr sighed. "Don't

worry. He's an Old One. He'll endure. Everyone tells me that's their greatest strength."

She didn't argue. She thanked Sir Bedwyr for his patience and sped away to see her brother Gwarth.

The king of Northgallis was just returning from a hunt among the marshes. "Why, Gwen!" he called, leaving his men and their nets of waterfowl. "A pleasure to see you. Did you come to visit?"

She hugged him and kissed his hairy cheek. "Yes, Gwarth, I did. I need your help."

"Oh, aye, that's likely," he chuckled. "But I'm glad to be of service. Come along inside and share a skin of wine."

She waited, masking her impatience, while he disappeared into his chamber to change out of his wet clothes. A servant brought her warmed wine, which she couldn't drink, and a plate of mealcakes, which she didn't eat. Waiting gave her time to think. Why had Princess Morgan come to see Queen Alyse that morning? Not for her support at the hearing, as she claimed. She must have known from the outset that Queen Alyse and King Pellinore were Llyr's foremost allies, and therefore her chief opponents. Had she come to put Queen Alyse on notice that battle was joined? Or to deliver a blow that might make battle unnecessary? Guinevere remembered something her father used to say about going to war: *Strike at the head of the snake or not at all.*

Princess Morgan had struck at Queen Alyse and failed to intimidate her. What would she do next? A small sweat broke on Guinevere's brow. If she were in Morgan's place, she would gather her allies, like any good general, and prepare for the next attack.

Gwarth emerged from his chamber in the old brown robe he had always favored after hunting. To Guinevere, he looked just the same as he always had. He was still the Gwarth of her childhood, a stocky, solidly built, black-bearded man with a rough tongue and a kind heart. He was more uncle than brother to her—a strong man who could be relied upon.

"Geese for dinner," he said, sitting gingerly beside her and pouring himself a cup of wine. "We had a good catch, even if I did get bitten once or twice on the hindquarters. There'll be enough for everyone. I've let Sir Bedwyr know." He emptied the cup down his throat and poured himself more wine. "Well, lass, let's hear what's troubling you."

She told him about Llyr's predicament. "He didn't steal anything, Gwarth. He came into camp of his own accord to keep us from killing any more Old Ones." Mindful of Sir Bedwyr's orders not to mention the involvement of Princess Morgan, she finished lamely, "I need your help against someone in camp who is his enemy, someone who is determined to destroy him at any cost. Someone who's trying to manipulate the outcome of the hearing."

"Ah." Gwarth cocked an eyebrow at her. He looked worried. "That wouldn't be the High King's sister, would it?"

She gaped at him. "How did you know?"

"Because she's been to see me."

"*Already?*"

"Aye, as I was leaving for the hunt."

"What did she want?"

"I guess you know. Wanted me to stand with her against Sir Bedwyr if he sided with King Pellinore. Said she already had the allegiance of Guent and Dyfed, and could get Powys, too, before the night was out—"

"She didn't! She can't! That isn't true!"

Gwarth's smile gleamed in the black expanse of his beard. "Sure of yourself, aren't you, Gwennie? Think that young scamp from Powys would never choose a raven-haired witch over you?"

Guinevere was taken aback. "Trevor? Is that who you mean?"

"Who else? *Is* there anyone else?"

"Oh, for Lugh's sake!" she cried, reverting in her frustration to the pagan habits of childhood. "It's not *me* he wants, you oaf, it's Elaine. He came here to meet her because the match meant so much to his mother. He loves her now. Ask him yourself, if you doubt me. I dare you to ask him."

Gwarth yielded. "Never mind, then. I'll apologize. You sounded so sure of his loyalty, is all."

"I *am* sure of his loyalty! He's my friend. We talk together every day." Gwarth winked, and she threw up her hands in exasperation. *"Friends."*

"Whatever you say."

"Listen, Gwarth, because this is true: Princess Morgan doesn't have the allegiance of Powys, and she'll never be able to get it."

"Well, I didn't know that, did I? I told her if she already had three kingdoms out of five, she didn't need my help. I suppose once she finds out she'll never get Powys, she'll be back."

"She probably doesn't have Dyfed and Guent, either."

Gwarth looked thoughtful. "I wouldn't wager against it. She's been flitting around Mardoc's tent for the last week or so, and where Mardoc leads, Dynas is sure to follow."

"But that's only two kingdoms out of five."

"It's all of South Wales. Arthur depends on South Wales. His headquarters are in Guent."

"But Powys sides with Gwynedd, and if Northgallis stands firm . . ." She looked at his worried face and swallowed. "Gwarth?"

He shrugged. "How do I know until I've heard the lad's side of it? Now don't worry, Gwennie. The princess tells a pitiful story, but I don't know that it's true. I'll hear the tale from his own lips before I judge the boy."

Guinevere froze. Bedwyr's words rang in her head like a clamoring bell: *He's decided not to speak. Merlin talked him into it. . . .*

She clasped her hands together to keep them from shaking. "But, Gwarth, you can't imagine he really took the dagger? Any dagger? The Old Ones don't steal."

Gwarth grunted. "Who told you that? An Old One? They're no different from other folk, when all's said and done. They lie and cheat and steal when it suits them, just like us. Some of them, the renegades, they've come down out of the hills to steal our stores, and they've killed those who've tried to stop them."

Vaguely, Guinevere recalled stories from Northgallis. "But those men were outcasts, Gwarth! Desperate men who—" Too late, she saw the pitfall.

"Outcasts. Yes, that's what they're called. And I heard," Gwarth said cautiously, "that your friend Llyr's an outcast. Born into one clan and adopted by another, but cast out from both. He has no clan at all."

Guinevere squeezed her eyes shut to keep nausea at bay. A great fear gripped her entire body and locked every limb in place. She saw in a flash what Morgan meant to do. And Llyr had no defense against the charge, for it was true. He *was* outcast. Because he had spoken to her. "That was on my account," she whispered. "You can't blame Llyr for that."

"I don't. I blame it on the prophecy."

She opened her eyes to meet his apologetic gaze. "Yes, the prophecy. That's another thing. You've got to stop telling people about it. I don't want anyone to know. Really, Gwarth. I want to ignore it for as long as I can."

"Nonsense, Gwennie. You should be proud."

"Why? It's nothing *I've* done. Suppose some mad hill witch had told Father on the eve of your birth that you'd one day be the strongest man in all the world. How would that feel, always having people's eyes on you as you grew up? Knowing that they expected something miraculous from you that you couldn't give them? Hearing their whispers; seeing the disappointment in their eyes? Would you like it much?"

Gwarth frowned. "Not if you put it like that. Is that how it feels to you?"

"That's exactly how it feels."

"All right, then," he said, giving her shoulders a squeeze. "I'll say no more. I didn't know."

"Thank you, Gwarth. Now see if you can solve Llyr's problem as easily."

Gwarth sobered at once and shook his head. "I know he's your guardian, Gwen. The Old Ones have always looked after you, one way or another, and rightly so. They took that on when they made the prophecy. But choosing Llyr . . . I don't know, perhaps they should have chosen someone else. Let me hear what he has to say, and I'll know what to think."

"And . . . if he doesn't speak?"

Gwarth frowned. "Why wouldn't he? They'll kill him if he doesn't. No, no, he'll speak. If he did the deed or not, he'll deny it. I just want to see his face when he does."

Guinevere bit her lip. A tear rolled down her cheek, and she wiped it away before Gwarth could see it. But another followed, and another, as she envisioned what lay ahead for Llyr, who, trusting in Merlin's word, would not answer any questions tomorrow.

"Come, come, Gwennie," Gwarth said softly, lifting a grimy finger to catch a tear. "In the end, it's Sir Bedwyr's decision, not mine or anyone else's. And if he asks for my opinion, I'll stand by King Pellinore. Our father swore him an oath of allegiance, and so have I."

"Oh, Gwarth!" She hugged him, spilling tears of gratitude on his old brown robe. "Don't let him die! Please don't let him die."

CHAPTER THIRTY-ONE

Second Thoughts

On the day of the hearing, Guinevere and Elaine rose at dawn. They swallowed the hot willow tea their nurses brought them and submitted to a slow and determined dressing, despite the frosty air. Guinevere could not eat the mealcake Ailsa pressed into her hand. Fear made it impossible to swallow food. Her struggle against her fear took all her energy and concentration. It took effort to force her sluggish body into motion and follow Elaine into the queen's tent. King Pellinore was already there, fiddling with his swordbelt and adjusting his fur-trimmed mantle while he waited for the women. Cissa and Leonora hovered about Queen Alyse, applying the finishing touches to her hair and gown.

The queen looked magnificent. The sight of her standing there, tall, lovely, and self-possessed amid the bustle of her women, filled Guinevere with hope. She was still too thin, but the sunken look had gone from her eyes, and a flush of healthy color sprang from beneath her skin. She no longer looked like a woman under the curse of death, but more like a patient recovering from illness. Leonora settled the queen's fox-trimmed cloak across her shoulders, adjusted the jeweled netting over her wheat-gold hair, and nodded. King Pellinore gave the word and out they marched into the still brightness of a cool October morning.

Because the day promised fair, Sir Bedwyr had chosen to hold the hearing outdoors in the broad, flat space around the bonfire pit, where benches and stools were already in place. Beside the pit itself, a rough dais had been constructed during the night. Sir Bedwyr stood by the King's carved chair in the center of the dais, deep in conversation with a handful of guards. On his right, his scribe sat behind a writing desk. On his left, a smaller carved chair, regally draped in cloth of Pendragon red, awaited its royal occupant. The fourth chair, at a little distance from this threesome, was empty.

The kings and their families sat on benches arranged, kingdom by kingdom, in a rough half circle facing the dais. Their household retainers jostled for position behind them, and their men-at-arms stood at the outer edges of the arc. Guinevere, Elaine, and their nurses took their places on the bench behind Queen Alyse and King Pellinore, where they had an excellent view of the dais and of the front rows of the other benches.

With a cold pit in her stomach, Guinevere waited anxiously for Llyr to appear. Last night, the fear that he would say nothing in his own defense had made sleep impossible. All night she had lain awake trying to figure out what she could do to save him. Growing desperate as dawn approached, she had formed a last-ditch plan, but it was an exceedingly risky gamble. It very likely would not work, and if it failed or her part in it was discovered, she would bring disgrace upon the royal family of Gwynedd. She would have to stand up to Princess Morgan to be successful, and she did not know if she possessed that kind of courage. All in all, it was a gamble she would rather not take.

Perhaps it would not be necessary. Everything depended upon how the hearing went. Perhaps when Llyr saw the size of the crowd and felt the glare of so many hostile eyes, he would speak up and tell what he knew. He risked death if he did not defend himself. Gwarth had made that plain enough. And if he chose not to speak, someone else—King Pellinore? Queen Alyse?—would have to speak for him. But what could they say to convince everyone of his innocence? The only way to prove that Llyr had not stolen the dagger was to prove that someone else had, or that the dagger had not been stolen at all but had remained in Princess Morgan's possession. Guinevere did not believe the dagger had been stolen, but proving that Princess Morgan had had possession of it was going to be difficult. It might be possible if her plan worked, but it meant public humiliation for King Arthur's sister. In the dark hours of the morning, such an outcome had seemed only fair for someone who had intentionally placed Llyr's life in jeopardy, but now she was having second thoughts.

She knew that Sir Bedwyr was determined to keep Morgan's name clean at any cost. He had said as much that night in Trevor's chamber. Protecting her was his sworn duty to Arthur.

And political policy required that Morgan's marriage to Urien take place. Rheged's alliance was necessary to King Arthur's plans to unite all the Briton kingdoms into a single Kingdom of Britain, whose strength would deter challengers and whose sovereignty was beyond question. All their futures depended on it.

Guinevere could appreciate this warrior's dream and understand Sir Bedwyr's allegiance to it. But she could not understand why he feared that the marriage might be jeopardized by Morgan's deceptions becoming known. Was Urien so sensitive to the moral character of his wife? Most princes, according to Queen Alyse, didn't care what their wives wore, said, or did, as long as it didn't interfere with the steady production of legitimate male heirs. It was possible, of course, that Urien of Rheged was that rare and unusual prince who *did* care what kind of woman he wed, but it seemed unlikely. He had consented to the match without having once set eyes on his bride.

It seemed much more likely that Sir Bedwyr needed secrecy not for Urien's sake, but for Morgan's. Perhaps it was Morgan, not Urien, who might reject the match. Sir Bedwyr was not a timorous man. Why would he fear this unless Morgan herself had threatened to do just that? Guinevere thought this threat precisely the kind of weapon Morgan would not hesitate to use.

She looked up as a murmur swept through the crowd. Princess Morgan had arrived, gowned in scarlet and crowned by a shining diadem of pearls. Sir Bedwyr came down from the dais to escort the princess to her chair amid a rising hum of voices.

Guinevere watched him anxiously. She liked and trusted Sir Bedwyr. She had disappointed him by withholding information about Llyr, and she had forced him to suspect Princess Morgan without any proof beyond a belief in Llyr's truthfulness. She did not want to disappoint him again. He had dealt with her fairly and treated her like an adult. She would do almost anything not to lose his respect.

She knew that he was willing to put the good of the nascent Kingdom of Britain above the rights of one poor, insignificant Old One. He had already made it clear to her that she ought to do the same. But she did not think she could. It wasn't fair that Morgan should escape justice simply because she was Arthur's sister and her marriage was of importance. Her actions had to have consequences. She should not be able to do what she wanted with impunity. No one should, not even Arthur himself.

Was this the kind of Kingdom Arthur wanted to build? A land where the rich and powerful did as they pleased and the common people suffered without redress? She had heard differently of Arthur, and she wanted to believe he was a different kind of leader, but all she knew of him for certain was his ability to inspire men and lead them to their deaths in battle without losing their love. If he were here himself, what would he do? Sir Bedwyr, as his representative, had decided to protect Arthur's sister. It was hard to imagine that the King himself might prefer a different course.

And yet he might. So much depended on the kind of man he was. A strong kingdom led by a good king was a boon to everyone. In union lay strength, and in strength, safety. Hadn't she made that very argument six months ago to Liam, a poor man of peasant stock, when she needed his help in

Gwynedd's defense? Sir Bedwyr had asked her for no more than the same allegiance, for the good of all Britons. How was such a request to be denied?

She bowed her head to hide her dismay. Her arguments ran in circles within circles until they made her dizzy. Still, one thought lingered at their center like bedrock in a storm. It was not right that the Kingdom should matter more than the lives of its people. She did not want to live in a kingdom, however united or strong, that countenanced the murder of innocent men.

The crowd quieted as Sir Bedwyr strode to the front of the dais and addressed them. He began by explaining that this hearing was modeled on those the High King held when disputes were brought to him for judgment. First, the complaint of injustice would be heard. Next, the person accused of committing the injustice would be allowed to speak to the complaint. Afterward, anyone who had anything relevant to say would also be heard. Sir Bedwyr, acting as King Arthur's proxy and taking into consideration the counsel of the gathered kings, would make the final decision as to guilt and punishment. He impressed upon them the need for civil behavior. Anyone behaving in an unruly fashion would be taken into custody. Anyone objecting to Sir Bedwyr's decision had the right to appeal to the High King, but must in the meantime let Sir Bedwyr's decision stand.

Guinevere wished she could trust Sir Bedwyr to exonerate Llyr, but she didn't know him well enough. Queen Esdora knew him better, but there hadn't been time for Guinevere to share her dilemma with the queen. Looking around, she saw that Queen Esdora was not sitting with Trevor on the Powys benches, but instead sat right next to King Mardoc of Guent. Last evening, Trevor and his mother had gone quietly to visit Mardoc to negotiate some sort of bargain. There was no way to tell from the queen's politely neutral features and precise, erect posture whether or not they had succeeded.

A hum of anticipation swept the crowd. Guinevere turned back to the dais and saw Llyr led forward between two guards to the last empty chair. As Sir Bedwyr had promised, he looked well cared for. Someone had found him new clothes that almost fit him, and his black hair, shaggy and uncut, had been combed and bound by a thong behind his neck to keep it out of his face. Despite these efforts to make him look like everyone else, his essential foreignness was still apparent in the stillness of his gaze and the wariness of his posture.

He did not look for her. She stared at him until she was sure he must feel the pressure of her gaze, but he gave no indication of knowing she was there. Instead, his eyes looked straight ahead at something no one else could see. With sinking heart, Guinevere realized that he had prepared himself for this ordeal by walling himself off from human interaction and waiting patiently for his fate. He was not going to speak. He was not going to participate. He no longer shared the space they shared or breathed the air they breathed. He had already distanced himself from this world and was, in spirit, halfway to the next.

CHAPTER THIRTY-TWO

The Hearing

Catcalls erupted from the crowd. "Thief!" "Spy!" "Heathen outlaw!" "This is your last day, you dirty savage!"

Sir Bedwyr raised his arms for silence. The shouts faded to a low background grumble, and the entire camp simmered in expectation. Guinevere found herself clutching Ailsa's hand, and Ailsa clutched hers in return. Only Princess Morgan seemed unmoved. She sat placidly in her chair, her eyes downcast, the very picture of regal righteousness. Guinevere waited for her to rise and bring her complaint before the people, but she did not stir. Instead, it was Sir Bedwyr who, after a solemn glance around the gathered company, cleared his throat and began to relate the series of events that had led them to this hearing.

Princess Morgan had reported the theft of a valuable

dagger from her tent. Her serving woman had seen someone near the tent at about the time the dagger disappeared, and had the impression that the thief was an Old One. A few days later, Sir Bedwyr had found a dagger shallowly buried beneath a tree at the edge of the forest—a tree that an Old One in King Pellinore's service was known to occupy from time to time.

A wave of angry mutters swept the gathering. Shouts of "Thieving hillman!" and "Heathen savage!" resounded from the outer edges of the crowd. Guinevere bit her lip. The proximity of the dagger to the tree seemed enough to convict Llyr in the eyes of many.

Sir Bedwyr brought forth Lord Riall's dagger and showed it to them, pulling the weapon free of its sheath so that the size and beauty of the blade could be admired by the men while the flash of jewels and silver chasing on the damaged sheath raised eyebrows among the women. *A unique and valuable weapon*, the gesture proclaimed. *Worthy of royalty.*

Guinevere frowned. Sir Bedwyr did not actually say that this was the dagger Princess Morgan had reported stolen, but he certainly implied it. She wondered why. Had he come to agree with her that Princess Morgan had received it from Lord Riall and buried it herself, but could not say so because he was presenting Princess Morgan's version of events?

It was clever of Princess Morgan to make Sir Bedwyr do her persuading for her. When the High King's proxy accused Llyr of theft, the charge achieved legitimacy. Guinevere's throat went dry at the sudden thought that Sir Bedwyr might have changed his mind. Perhaps he had come to believe that

Llyr had stolen the dagger! She shook her head sharply to dismiss the thought. He was too good an advocate for Princess Morgan, that was all. That had to be all.

When she returned her attention to the dais, Sir Bedwyr was talking about the hunt for Old Ones by certain men who were supposed to be hunting deer. Now an innocent boy lay dead. He looked out over the crowd and let the words hang in the air. His contempt for the killing was clear in his face. The men responsible, he said, had confessed to the deed. They and the kings they served had agreed to make reparation to the dead boy's clan, as justice demanded.

A grumble of discontent ran through the gathering. Here and there, shouts rang out. "Justice!" someone snarled. "Wasted on savages!"

Guinevere turned in her seat to see who had objected, but Ailsa stopped her with a firm grip on her arm. "No, Gwen."

"But—"

"Shh." Ailsa nodded pointedly toward the front row, where King Pellinore had started to rise. But Queen Alyse caught his sleeve, and he sat back down. Guinevere stared at them. Were they going to say nothing? Did this mean they would not defend Llyr when it came his turn to speak? All because of Morgan's threat to rob Queen Alyse of her husband's precedence with Arthur? Then they were cowards, both of them. *Llyr had saved Elaine's life!*

Elaine squeezed Guinevere's arm. "Wait," she breathed.

Sir Bedwyr resumed his narrative. He pointed out that Llyr had come willingly into custody in order to prevent more slaughter among his people, but that because Llyr's name had been mentioned in connection with the theft of the dagger, Sir Bedwyr had thought it best to hold a hearing to determine the truth of the matter.

Mentioned in connection with the theft! Guinevere glared at Sir Bedwyr. He knew perfectly well that Llyr had been accused outright by Princess Morgan. But he would not say so in public.

Sir Bedwyr turned toward Llyr. "Llyr, son of Bran, leader of the White Foot of Snow Mountain," he said gravely. "Can you defend yourself against this charge of theft?"

Llyr gazed out at the crowd with blank, unseeing eyes. His stillness was so complete that he might have been carved of granite. People began to jeer and shout as his silence continued. They called him names, insulted his ancestry and his clan, belittled his appearance, and vowed revenge. Llyr did not stir. He remained as he had from the beginning: his body sitting obediently in the chair, his spirit already somewhere else.

Sir Bedwyr looked directly at the Gwynedd contingent before turning to the entire company. "Is there no one here who can speak for Llyr?"

Ailsa clamped a hand on Guinevere, and a moment later King Pellinore rose to his feet. "I will speak," he said, turning to face the crowd. He was a big, gruff man, well known for his courage, and the people quieted to hear him.

"I have dealt with the Old Ones in my hills for many years," he said. "They are an honorable folk who do not steal or lie. We have made treaties together, and they have always kept their word. This young man here performed a most valuable service to me last spring. He helped save my daughter's life."

Queen Alyse trembled at this public exposure of family matters, but she did not stop him.

"I tell you frankly," the king said earnestly, "that I'd trust Llyr over most men I know. He never stole that dagger. I'd lay my crown on it."

He resumed his seat, and Queen Alyse took his hand. Guinevere stared at the backs of their heads in horrified dismay. *That* was all he was going to say? He had refuted nothing! The crowd had already begun to grumble again.

Sir Bedwyr's gaze swept over the gathering once more, and this time came to rest on her own face. His eyes met hers. "Anyone else?"

This time, no hand upon her sleeve could stop her. Guinevere rose.

"Oh, Gwennie!" cried Ailsa.

Guinevere stepped up onto the bench so she could be seen by all and made a quick reverence to Sir Bedwyr. "I will speak, my lord."

Was it her imagination, or did Sir Bedwyr smile?

"Guinevere of Northgallis," he announced in a carrying voice. "Silence, please, everyone. Go ahead, my lady."

Guinevere turned to face a startled, hostile throng, but it was too late now for a case of nerves. "People of Wales," she addressed them in a shaking voice. "I beg you not to allow this terrible injustice. Llyr is no hill bandit who lives outside the law. He is a prince among his own people. A man nobly born and raised to be a leader—"

"Aye!" shouted someone from the fringes of the crowd. "And don't he look it, too!" Laughter followed from a small group of comrades.

"And do you judge a man solely by his looks?" Guinevere shot back, too angry to give thought to consequences. "Or by his actions? This man saved my cousin's life. He risked his own to do it. For how many people have *you* done that lately?"

"Guinevere!" gasped Queen Alyse. But the crowd laughed.

"Well, it was under his tree, wasn't it, that the dagger was found?" called out another voice. "If he didn't put it there, mistress, who did?"

"I don't know," Guinevere said evenly. "I don't even want to guess. Someone who intended that Llyr should be blamed for its theft. It's clear that Llyr has enemies in camp." She let her gaze wander among the crowd before she turned to Sir Bedwyr. "Isn't it true, Sir Bedwyr, that the rumors about Old Ones spying on us from the woods went around camp well before Princess Morgan reported her dagger stolen?"

Princess Morgan's eyes lifted from her lap and fixed on the back of Sir Bedwyr's head.

Guinevere said quickly, "How do you suppose those rumors arose, Sir Bedwyr?"

"Well," he said carefully, "I believe they began shortly after Prince Trevor's accident, when you sent Llyr to me asking for help. That was the only time he came into camp. He was noticed, of course. Old beliefs die hard. I suspect that for some of us, his presence was best explained by the rumors about spies."

"He tried to take Bevan's sword!" cried a voice from the back. "Tried to kill him with it!"

Sir Bedwyr shook his head. "The guard outside my tent tried to stop him from entering. Llyr knocked the sword from his hand, but made no attempt to take it. I have this from two other men who saw it happen. He carried no weapon when he came into my chamber."

"I think," Guinevere resumed, "that the rumors of Old Ones spying on us prompted someone to try to get rid of Llyr, to make an example of him."

Princess Morgan's icy gaze fixed itself on Guinevere, who pressed hastily on. "When the theft of the dagger was reported, some people assumed that Llyr was the thief and started hunting him. He left camp to avoid them—as anyone would. I know that because when I went to the beech tree to warn him, he was already gone, and there was nothing buried there then."

She looked around at all the faces turned to hers—puzzled faces, skeptical faces, contemptuous faces—and prayed to whichever god was listening that they might believe her. "Llyr's time can be accounted for. He made contact with the Strong Hearts in the foothills west of here, and they gave him shelter. At their suggestion, he traded clothes with the boy nearest to him in size. That boy, Luath, was killed by the men who were hunting Llyr. After the murder, and after Sir Bedwyr found the dagger, Llyr returned to camp." Her voice began to quaver. "He was certain we would kill him, but he came in anyway. He had to stop the hunt. He was ready to give his life to prevent more killing of his people. If that isn't nobility of soul, I don't know what is."

A small silence followed. Princess Morgan stirred in her chair and looked pointedly at Sir Bedwyr.

Sir Bedwyr cleared his throat. "It's odd, though, that the dagger was found buried beneath the very tree Llyr used as his—well, his temporary home."

"Damned odd!" cried a voice. "Suspicious!" shouted another. "Left it there for safekeeping when he ran away!" called out a third.

Guinevere turned her back to the dais and faced the hostile voices. "Safekeeping? It was buried in a shallow hole with just enough dirt mounded over the top to cover it. Sir Bedwyr found it at once when he went to the tree. Is that where *you* would hide a precious object for safekeeping? Why, I can think of a hundred better hiding places: under a bush; in the bole of a tree; in a bedroll, a saddle pack, a streambed; under a rock; in a haystack. In the soft soil near the riverbank, where tree roots don't get in the way. Safer still to carry it secretly on one's person and hide it far from camp."

She paused for breath. "The dagger was not put beneath the beech tree for safekeeping. It was put there so it would be found and its theft attributed to Llyr."

"Why?"

The question came from behind her, and Guinevere turned. Princess Morgan sat forward in her chair, the anger in her eyes, which the people could not see, belying the smile on her lips, which they could.

"I—I beg your pardon?" Guinevere stammered.

Princess Morgan half turned toward the sea of faces and said, in a reasonable voice, "You are asking us to believe that someone deliberately tried to blame the hillman for the theft. Why would anyone bother, unless he was guilty?"

Guinevere swallowed hard. Princess Morgan was daring her to make an accusation openly before all these people. She could feel Sir Bedwyr's gaze upon her as he waited to hear what she would say. Someone tittered in the silence and was quickly hushed. Guinevere's chest tightened until it was diffi-cult to breathe.

"Llyr has enemies," she croaked. "People who fear the Old Ones and want to destroy them. A real thief wouldn't have buried the dagger—not like that, not near the place he lived. He would hide it better or take it out of camp. It was easily vis-ible. It was meant to be found."

"And your hillman blamed?" Princess Morgan rose from her chair and faced the crowd. "Lady Guinevere seems to find the idea of blaming a hillman for theft outlandish. That argues a degree of attachment to him, I think. To most of us, he appears as the most likely suspect by far. After all," she said reasonably, "it isn't as if he's sworn to obey King Arthur or King Pellinore or any authority at all. He's an outcast. He isn't even a member of a clan any longer. He lives by no rules at all. Calling him a prim-itive savage is saying no more than the obvious truth."

The crowd grumbled. Some cheered; others hushed them. Princess Morgan moved closer to the edge of the dais. "We are all familiar with the vicious acts such men commit— untethered men, lawless men, outcasts. They steal our sheep and our cattle; they plunder unguarded stores; they hide in the hills and attack passing travelers for what they carry. They are thieves and cutthroats who live outside the bounds of civilized society. And this man is one of them."

Shouts of approval rang out, and several of the men began to sing a victory paean.

"That's not fair!" Guinevere cried. "Llyr has never done such things! And you've no grounds to believe he has!"

Sir Bedwyr raised a hand, and gradually the people hushed.

"On the contrary," Princess Morgan said with a knowing smile. "I have it on good authority that six months ago Llyr killed a man in your own kingdom of Gwynedd. Not an Old One, but one of our race. Not in self-defense, either, but in a straightforward, vicious attack."

Guinevere frowned. "That's not true."

"Isn't it? He didn't kill a man named Drako with an arrow to the heart? I spoke to someone who was there and saw it all."

A whimper escaped Elaine, and Guinevere turned to see her shrink against Grannic, as if for protection. Guinevere gaped at her. Was there *anything* she had not blabbed to Princess Morgan?

She turned back to the dais. "You are referring to a villain who held my cousin Elaine prisoner and threatened to kill her. In Gwynedd, we regard Llyr's deadly arrow as an act of heroism."

Shouts of laughter, approval, and protest rose from the crowd.

"You can't deny he's an outcast!" Morgan cried. "Even the Old Ones won't have him among them any longer!"

"It's true that Llyr was cast out from his clan," Guinevere said evenly when the noise had abated. "Because he talked to me. But that was my doing as much as his. And the clan who cast him out took him back again and dedicated him to the service of their goddess. Now he has a status among the Old Ones higher than the leader of any clan. Why do you think the Strong Hearts went to such lengths to protect him, even risking one of their own by having him changing clothes with Llyr? Because he has been singled out for a unique honor. He serves the divine."

She looked toward the back of the crowd, where the fighting men stood. "In a way, it's much like serving a king. Do you not swear allegiance to your king? And through him, to the High King Arthur? And does that allegiance not take precedence over all other allegiances? Isn't that why you leave home to fight for your king when he calls upon you? Isn't that why your king leaves home to fight for the High King Arthur?"

She had their attention now. She could feel it. No one was watching Princess Morgan any longer. "Llyr has sworn allegiance, too, but to a god. He has had to give up his home and his family for a greater cause. His obedience has required him to travel far from his birthplace, learn new languages, wear strange clothes, and accept the customs of a society very different from his own. If he were a lawless outcast, he could do as he wished. Instead, he finds himself here, accused of something he did not do—would not do—and ready to give his life to prevent more bloodshed among his people." She looked fiercely at the men on the fringes of the crowd. "Which of you can claim so much?"

No one spoke. Even the men at the back of the crowd were silent.

Princess Morgan broke the spell. "A very impassioned defense," she said with a condescending smile. "I do believe I was right about your attachment to the creature. Poor deluded girl," she said, turning to face the people. "She is in love with him."

"I am *not*!" Guinevere cried, her face coloring at the sound of malicious laughter. "Llyr is my friend—he saved Elaine's life—he has been part of the family all summer—he is like a brother to me. Besides," she added with an innocence impossible to feign, "Queen Alyse does not allow me suitors yet."

Laughter swept the crowd, but it was gentle laughter now, a kind and comprehending laughter, and Sir Bedwyr gazed at her with open gratitude.

Guinevere waited impatiently for the amusement to subside. "It doesn't take a sage to see the cause of all this trouble. Too many people distrust the Old Ones. When Llyr came into camp, it was instantly assumed that he was there for no good purpose. If a stranger from Cornwall or Rheged or York had ventured into camp, no such judgment would have been made."

"He's a hillman!" someone shouted. "Not one of us!"

Guinevere turned toward the voice. "Yes," she agreed. "He's not one of us. But why should he be? His people have lived in this land for generations, not just in the hills, but in the valleys, too. *Our* ancestors are the ones who drove them out. *We* forced Llyr's people out of the fertile valleys and into the hills and wastelands, into any land we did not covet for ourselves. We did to the Old Ones what the Saxons are trying to do to *us*."

She paused to let the thought take hold. "Why do we despise the Old Ones? It's an ungenerous way to treat a people on whose lands we live, I think. Does not the *Kyrios Christos* call us to turn the other cheek? To treat others as we would want to be treated if we were they? If the Saxons succeed," she said, crossing herself quickly with one hand and making the sign of propitiation to older gods behind her back with the other, "I pray they will treat us with more respect than we give the Old Ones."

"Dear God," breathed Queen Alyse.

A chorus of male voices protested. Most denied the possibility that King Arthur could lose to the Saxons. Some believed the Lord required charity only to other Christians. A few refused to believe the Old Ones counted as men at all, but were animals, like the thieving vermin who robbed hardworking folk of their stores every winter.

"Are the Saxons men?" Guinevere shot back, hands clenched to hold in check her indignation. "Are the Romans?"

"Aye, but—"

"The Gaels? The Franks? The Picts?"

"Yes, but—"

"Persians? Egyptians?" she cried, dredging up the civilizations she had learned about in Iakos's schoolroom. "Greeks?

Sarmatians? Huns? Nubians? Iberians? Hebrews? Canaanites? Carthaginians? Macedonians? Phoenicians?"

Confused grumbling followed this outburst, and Queen Alyse laughed under her breath. "At least the child was paying attention."

"This is beside the point," Princess Morgan interjected. "We are not here for a history lesson. This Old One is a murderer. You have all heard the ward of Gwynedd confess it. Not only have the king and queen of Gwynedd *not* punished him for this egregious act, they have actually rewarded him for it! They have taken him into their service. It's an outrage!"

Shouts of approval rang out above a hum of mutters.

Queen Alyse rose from her bench. "Guinevere, my dear, your courage is commendable, but it is my turn now. Ailsa, help her down."

Guinevere looked at her anxiously. "But—"

"Yes, I know," the queen said softly. "The battle is not yet won. You have done marvelously. You have driven a wedge into their flank, but it needs a more experienced hand to lead home the charge. Let me speak to them."

Guinevere stepped down from the bench and sagged into Ailsa's arms. All at once, she was more tired than she had ever been in her life.

"Besides," added Queen Alyse, "Morgan has publicly attacked me, and I should like to have my revenge."

"How?" Guinevere whispered.

"You have given them the generalities; I shall give them the particulars. They shall hear exactly how Llyr saved Elaine's life, and how the Long Eyes helped me save Gwynedd." She turned to her daughter. "Elaine, my dear, go back to the tent with Grannic, Ailsa, and Gwen. It will be easier for you not to hear the rest. I shall summon a guard to escort you."

"Send Prince Trevor," Guinevere suggested, meeting the queen's eye.

Queen Alyse smiled. "An excellent idea." She signaled Trevor, who rose and made his way toward them with the help of Merlin's walking sticks.

Guinevere watched him come. In spite of the queen's reassurance, she was worried. Her aunt might be able to win over the crowd, but words alone could not defeat Princess Morgan. And it was Princess Morgan who posed the greatest threat. If she failed to have Llyr convicted at the hearing, she would try more subtle means to destroy him. Something must be done to stop her.

Guinevere could think of only one thing to do. While Princess Morgan was trapped at the hearing, she must put her desperate plan into action. Trevor would keep Elaine occupied, and Ailsa and Grannic would obey orders. When she took the biggest gamble of her life, she would have to do it alone.

CHAPTER THIRTY-THREE

Trespass

Guinevere made for the woods behind the horse lines. She had changed into her riding clothes and tucked her braided hair under Trevor's borrowed cap. She hoped to pass for one of the young men trudging home late from the marshes, a dead goose slung over his shoulder. She had taken one of Gwarth's leftovers from yesterday's catch for the purpose.

It had not been easy to keep Trevor and Elaine from coming with her, but Trevor was hampered by his need for walking sticks, and common courtesy demanded that Elaine stay with him. Ailsa, pale with anxiety, had known from the beginning that it was useless to argue. "Wherever you're going, don't take needless chances," she had begged.

Once in the woods, Guinevere made her way to the little coppice of rowan trees behind Princess Morgan's tent. She paused beside the largest trunk to look around. There was no one in sight. Those few guards not at the hearing had taken up stations at the front of their respective tents in order to hear as much as they could of the big event. This left the perimeter of the encampment unguarded. The kings would be furious if they knew, but it was a lucky chance for her. No one stood between her and the back entrance to Princess Morgan's tent.

She lowered the goose to the ground and pulled her cloak tighter around her. She was about to break a law. Once she crossed the threshold of that tent, she would be guilty of trespass. If she was caught, there could be no going back. Uttering silent prayers to every god she knew, she walked out of the woods across open ground, unfastened the ties that bound the tent flaps closed, and slipped inside.

Dark encased her. She knew from the dank, earthy odor that this was Morgan's stillroom, a place of gloom and mysteries; a place, she was sure, that never knew a fire or a larger light than the flame of a single candle. There was not even candlelight now. She waited in perfect silence for her eyes to adjust to the impenetrable dark. No sounds came through the heavy cloth covering the doorway, no mutter of voices, no shuffle of feet, no swish of skirts. The small, close chamber seemed a world unto itself, cut off from normality of every kind.

A deep fear rose within Guinevere, less a fear of being caught than a rising terror of the place itself. She could barely control the urge to flee. Clenching her fists, she forced herself to concentrate on the lesser fear, the sane fear. Where was Marcia? She had not seen her at the hearing. Had she been left behind to guard the wedding gifts? She might be resting . . . or on patrol. If she heard anything in the still-room, would she come in herself, or would she call the guards?

Days seemed to pass and still Guinevere could see nothing. The darkness around her refused to let her through. Tentatively, she put out a hand and was reassured to feel the hard edge of a table beside her. The darkness might not be a normal darkness, but the table was real enough. Was it the table that held the witch's black bowl? It was. Her hands slid lightly across the tabletop and met a round obstacle of hard, cold stone. Recoiling, she searched the shelf above, moving her fingers slowly and carefully among the little bags and jars she remembered seeing there. The bags contained the expected herbs and powders and were soft to the touch, and the jars, when shaken exceedingly gently, sloshed a bit but did not rattle.

She turned to the next shelf, but not slowly enough. Her elbow bumped something solid, and a moment later something thudded to the earthen floor. It was not a loud sound, but after the stillroom silence it was deafening. Guinevere froze, holding her breath. Nothing happened. No one came to investigate. In the grip of stillness, black terror began to rise again inside her. Resolutely, she bent to the floor and felt for the fallen object. A brass candlestick with the nub of a candle still in place! Her longing for light was terrible, but she dared not risk the noise of a flint strike even if she could find the flint. She replaced the candlestick carefully on the table and returned to the second shelf.

There were no containers on this shelf, only various kinds of objects. She was reminded of the blindfold game she and Elaine used to play, touch-and-guess, where one girl would blindfold the other and then place an object in her hand. The blindfolded girl had to guess by touch alone what the object was before her opponent could count to fifty. They had not been kind to each other. Guinevere remembered holding all sorts of loathsome creatures and things—slimes, spiderwebs, and other revolting oddities—but she never remembered such a horror of anticipation as this.

With a racing heart, she fingered the unknowns waiting on the shelf. In each one she imagined a poisoned barb; a slithering skin; a prickling of tiny, running legs or a pair of multifaceted eyes that were not as blind to her as she was to them. When the curtain moved behind her and light stabbed into the room, she jumped and screamed.

"Who's there!" a sharp voice demanded. "Come out at once!"

Guinevere clapped a hand to her mouth and backed against the table.

Marcia pulled the curtain open and thrust her candle forward. "Who in heaven's name are you, and what do you want? Are you ill, boy? You look pale enough. Who sent you?"

Tears sprang to Guinevere's eyes. "No one sent me. I—I came on my own."

"What for?"

"Oh, Marcia, I meant no harm, you must believe me!"

"You know my name, do you? I don't know yours."

Trembling, Guinevere pulled off Trevor's cap.

"Well, I never . . . You came here once with Elaine of Gwynedd, didn't you? Aren't you Queen Alyse's ward?"

Guinevere bowed her head. "Guincvere of Northgallis."

"Why are you here? Is the hearing over?"

"No, I . . . just came away."

Marcia darted a hasty glance about the stillroom as if she half expected to see monsters in the shadows. She shuddered, beckoning Guinevere forward. "Come out of this nasty place and follow me."

Obediently, Guincvere trailed behind her into a small space partially set off from Morgan's bedchamber. It held a stool, a pallet, and an old oak chest. The small brazier in the corner warmed the tiny space and gave it a cozy feel. Marcia placed her candle on the chest and pointed to the stool. Guinevere sat down. Her knees shook, and her cloak seemed to hold no warmth at all.

"Shouldn't wonder if you were frightened half to death," Marcia muttered, stirring the coals to life. "Not even my lady goes into that stillroom without a light." She pushed a cup of warmed wine into Guinevere's hand. "Drink what's left. It will help."

"Thank you," Guinevere whispered, wiping her eyes with her sleeve. "You're very kind."

Beside the candle Guinevere saw folded needlework, hastily set aside. This was where Marcia must have been sitting and working moments before. No wonder she had heard the small sound of the candlestick falling. She had been only an arm's length away, on the other side of the tent cloth.

Gradually, as the wine warmed her from within, Guinevere's shaking ceased and she was able to meet Marcia's eyes. "Are you going to tell Princess Morgan that you found me in her stillroom?"

"Of course. It's my duty. What were you looking for? The truth, now."

Guinevere gazed down at her lap. "I came to steal a red stone, a jewel that Princess Morgan took from the sheath of Lord Riall's dagger. I need it to save the life of my friend."

Marcia sucked in her breath and, as Guinevere looked up, made the sign against enchantment. "How—how—?"

"You've seen it?" Guinevere breathed. "Is it here? Oh, please, God, let it be here!"

Marcia's lips moved stiffly. "How can you—how can you possibly know? Are you a witch, too? Is that why she's taken against you?"

Guinevere swallowed in a dry throat. So Elaine had been right about Princess Morgan's animosity. "No, I'm not a witch. I saw the dagger before Lord Riall gave it to Princess Morgan, and it had its jewel then. I saw it next when Sir Bedwyr dug it up, and the jewel was gone."

Marcia looked puzzled. "Dug it up?"

"Didn't you know Sir Bedwyr found it buried in the forest?"

Marcia shook her head. "Lord Riall's dagger? Such an unusual weapon. The creature must have buried it to hide it."

Guinevere stiffened. "He isn't a creature. Llyr is my friend. And he doesn't steal."

Marcia's eyes widened. "The hillman who's been spying on us all is your friend? How could he be?"

Briefly, Guinevere explained to Marcia what she hoped Queen Alyse was at that moment explaining to the gathering in more detail: how she had met Llyr and the crucial role he had played in all their lives last spring. Marcia's astonishment was unfeigned.

"But if he is such a valued member of King Pellinore's household, why is he living in the woods? Do the other men not want him in their tent?"

"It has nothing to do with the other men. Llyr is not a member of the household. He's free to go where he wills. But Old Ones don't like living so close to us. If they can't live in a cave in the hills, they prefer the forest. They're skilled at moving about unseen in the forest. A canopy of leaves is all the protection they need."

"It's difficult to credit," Marcia said. "My lady has such a horror of Old Ones, as you call them. I assumed they were all of them rogues."

"Are there no Old Ones in Cornwall, then?"

Marcia shook her head. "There are some strange creatures still surviving in the forest of Morois. We call them ogres. There are plenty of tales about them, but I don't know anyone who's actually seen one."

Guinevere hesitated. "You've never seen one yourself? Or an Old One, either?"

"Oh, no."

"At the hearing, Sir Bedwyr told everyone that you were the one who saw the supposed thief and identified him as an Old One. He could have heard that only from Princess Morgan. That's why she accused Llyr by name. That's why I'm here."

CHAPTER THIRTY-FOUR

A Kind Heart

Marcia blanched. She rose from the chest and, turning her back, began to stoke the fire. "I never was very good at deception."

"Do you mean that you *didn't* see an Old One? Or that you didn't see a thief?"

Marcia sighed and put down the poker. Her thin, anxious face was seamed with tiny lines, and her eyes were dark with sadness. "Both. You see, my lady told me that the dagger had been stolen and that she had seen the thief, but that Sir Bedwyr would not believe her. She begged for my help. I agreed to say that I had also seen him. She was so sure, you see, and I was afraid of hillmen."

"Why did she think Sir Bedwyr would not believe her?"

Marcia smiled bitterly. "Because he's such a good friend of

King Arthur's. Don't look so surprised, my dear. It's not new. Morgan has always resented Arthur. For being male, for being firstborn, for being someone singled out by prophecy for greatness. For being who he is. I'm afraid she can't help it. Sometimes I think if they had been raised together, like normal children, she might like him better now. She grew up as the only royal child, you see. She knew she had a brother, but he wasn't there, and you know what they say: out of sight, out of mind. Ygraine rarely spoke of him, and never before Morgan. We didn't know where he was or what he was doing, only that he was alive and safe. Ygraine did not see him again until King Uther's funeral. Morgan can't be blamed for thinking he didn't count. That was a mistake we all made, until Caer Eden." Light appeared through the tent cloth from Princess Morgan's bedchamber, and Marcia jumped to her feet. Signaling Guinevere to stay silent, she hurried away. Guinevere heard voices in low conversation, but could not distinguish what they said.

"That was only Ralf, her page," said Marcia upon her return. "Lighting the lamps. It will be dusk soon."

"The hearing will be over," Guinevere said, rising quickly.

Marcia waved her back to her seat. "Ralf will give us warning of Morgan's coming. He says no one has yet returned. It must still be going on." She settled herself on the chest. "Now, where was I?"

Guinevere sank reluctantly to the stool. It crossed her mind that Marcia was trying to keep her there, but she couldn't guess why. Perhaps it was a ploy to make her face

Morgan's wrath on her own ground. Or to distract Guinevere from the ruby she had come to steal. She could not leave without it, and she dared not force the issue. All Marcia had to do to ensure her disgrace was to call a guard.

"At the battle of Caer Eden."

Marcia sighed, her gaze far away. "Ah, yes. I remember. When Uther died and Arthur appeared from nowhere to take up his mantle. He was only fourteen, but no longer a boy. How long ago it seems now, when the children were born. I was the one who carried the infant Arthur from my lady's bed, three days old, and gave him to Merlin the Enchanter. How I hated to do it! How my lady wept!"

"Then it's true she gave him up?" Against her will, Guinevere found herself fascinated by this insight into the tales that clung to Arthur, tales that grew more fabulous every year until they verged on legend. But Marcia had been there. She had seen it happen.

"Uther persuaded her. She could never deny him anything. Those two shared a passion like none other I've ever seen. For Uther, my lady Ygraine relinquished her firstborn son."

"Why didn't King Uther want him?"

Marcia's lips tightened. "King Uther had a guilty conscience. At his crowning, with all his nobles and their wives in attendance, Uther fell headlong in love with my lady Ygraine, who had then been married about eighteen months to old Gorlois of Cornwall. Old he might have been, but he wasn't blind. As soon as the ceremonies were over, he whisked Ygraine back to Tintagel and waited five leagues north with an armed force for the King's approach. For he knew Uther would come for her. It was only the fear of open scandal that had held him in check at court."

Marcia paused, eyes shining. "He was a man of rare passion, was Uther Pendragon. And Ygraine shared it. . . . Had it been otherwise, the nascent kingdom Ambrosius had fought for might well have split apart. As it was, the rift with Cornwall posed a danger Uther could not ignore. With Gorlois's troops blocking the road to Tintagel, Uther's men took up their battle stations late one afternoon and prepared to fight their way through, come morning. But the High King left his troops that night and, with Merlin's help, sneaked into Tintagel disguised as Gorlois. I let him in myself at the postern gate and ushered him past the guards. I took him up the back way and into my lady's chamber."

Again she paused, amusement lighting her face. "Let it not be said that Ygraine, too, was deceived. Before the king took her to Uther's crowning, she had never been out of Cornwall. She lost her heart to Uther the moment he smiled at her." She laughed lightly. "She welcomed him with outstretched arms that night in Tintagel, and showered me with gifts and kisses the next day, she was so happy—until a messenger arrived with the news that the king, her husband, was dead. He had attacked the King's forces at midnight and been slain in the skirmish. When King Uther married my lady three months later—after the shortest possible mourning—she was three months gone with the King's child. Tongues began to wag. It mattered nothing to her, but King Uther was uneasy about the talk. He was afraid that if the child was a boy, he would never be accepted as a legitimate heir. He might even be taken for old Gorlois's son. Yes, Uther's conscience bothered him, as well it should, seeing that the king had been among his staunchest allies.

"Come Christmas, when the child was ready to be born, Uther persuaded Ygraine that a son begotten before their marriage could never be accepted as King. He would give her other sons, he promised, whose birth no one would question. He told her to give the babe to Merlin for safekeeping, if it was a boy. And my lady obeyed." She shook her head. "It cost her much, but Uther was her heart, her breath, her soul. She let the child go."

Silence fell between them until at last Guinevere ventured, "Why Merlin?"

Marcia looked at her in some surprise. "Who else? He was the child's closest male kinsman and a wise, well-traveled man whom no one would dare attack. He could keep the boy safe until Uther decided on his future. No one's ever doubted Merlin's powers of protection. . . . My lady wept for six weeks and mourned for years, until Morgan came along. Then she shut that grief away and gave herself to raising her daughter. . . . But in all the years of their marriage, they never had another son."

Guinevere heard only the first part of what she said. She waited until Marcia finished speaking and then blurted, "Merlin is King Arthur's *kinsman?*"

Marcia looked at her curiously. "Why, they are cousins, like you and Princess Elaine, only with twenty years between them. Perhaps it isn't as widely known as it ought to be. No doubt Merlin keeps it dark. He's a man who hates attention.

In truth, Merlin is the natural son of Aurelius Ambrosius, Uther's elder brother, who won our lands back from Vortigern the Wolf and began putting the Saxons to flight. If he'd been a warrior, he might have been High King instead of Uther, for Ambrosius acknowledged him. But he was blessed with different gifts."

Marcia wiped her eyes. "My, my, how I do go on. You're a good listener, young Guinevere. You're like my lady Ygraine in that."

Footsteps approached and a youngster in a page's tunic peeked into Marcia's chamber. "The hearing's over, mistress. The men are back."

Marcia rose. "And my lady?"

"Damon said the princess went to Sir Bedwyr's tent." He grinned mischievously. "In a temper, he said."

"That will do, Ralf."

Guinevere rose as the page departed. "I don't want her to find me here."

Marcia gave her a considering look. "Leaving without the ruby? Suppose you tell me first why you think that stone can save your friend."

"It will prove to Sir Bedwyr that Princess Morgan had possession of the dagger. That means she could have buried it herself. I think she did. To make trouble for Llyr. Showing him the ruby will make Llyr's innocence seem at least possible."

Marcia frowned, and Guinevere's heart sank. "Stay here," Marcia said, and disappeared into Morgan's bedchamber. Guinevere returned to her stool and thought about what she had heard.

Merlin a kinsman of the High King Arthur! She could not quite believe it. Yet Queen Ygraine's inexplicable behavior in giving up her firstborn son made more sense if she had given him into the arms of a trusted kinsman. Merlin a royal kins- man! That was a disturbing thought. The memory of her own audacity in trying to refuse his power at the presentation set her trembling. If she had known at the time who he was, would she have dared?

Her opinion of Morgan had subtly changed as well. She could easily imagine what a terrible blow it must have been to Morgan when her long-absent brother finally reappeared, fol- lowed shortly by her father's death and Arthur's ascendance to power. She couldn't be blamed for mistrust and bitterness, could she? That cataclysm in Morgan's life was only four years old: not time enough, perhaps, for so deep a wound to heal. For twelve years she had been her mother's only child—pampered and beloved, no doubt—only to be eclipsed in everyone's eyes when Arthur had burst onto the scene in a shower of glory, taking the sword that fell from his father's hand, winning the battle for him, driving the Saxons back, and earning his elec- tion to Kingship by Uther's nobles. It would be a difficult dis- placement for someone with Princess Morgan's pride to accept.

Marcia returned abruptly. Opening her fist, she dropped a dark red jewel the size of a thrush's egg into Guinevere's lap. "Take it to Sir Bedwyr."

Guinevere stared at her. "Marcia!"

"Take it. My lady did you a wrong, and it must be made right."

Rising, Guinevere made her a reverence to the ground.

"Enough of that," said Marcia, flushing. "But it's nearly dark, and the King's men have lit the bonfire. It's time to go."

Guinevere shot her a quick look. "If you weren't going to make me face Princess Morgan, you could have let me go before. Why did you keep me here so long?"

Marcia met her eyes. "To spare my lady. Taking this stone to Sir Bedwyr in the privacy of his own tent is one thing. Displaying it before all those unruly Welshmen is quite another." She took up her shawl. "Now we'd best get going."

"We?" Guinevere gulped. "You can't come with me—you mustn't! Princess Morgan will be so—so—"

"Furious?" Marcia supplied with a wry smile. "All the more reason for me to be there. This will be a difficult trial for her."

Impulsively, Guinevere embraced her and kissed her cheek. "You have courage, Marcia, and a kind heart. I honor you for them."

Marcia colored. "Don't speak to me of courage. You took quite a chance coming here alone to steal back that ruby. I might have called the guard and made no end of trouble for you."

"I know, but I had to risk it. It was your kind heart that saved me."

"Kind heart indeed," Marcia murmured as she shooed Guinevere outside before her. "We'll see how kind Mistress Morgan thinks it in an hour's time."

CHAPTER THIRTY-FIVE

The Bonfire

A great bonfire snapped and roared in the last of the evening breeze, shedding sparks into the sky. Scents of roasting goose and duckling filled the air, and the babble of three hundred voices raised in talk and laughter made public speech impossible.

Sir Bedwyr was thankful for it. All his problems had been miraculously resolved, and he could sit on a bench to eat, drink, and make merry like anyone else. It was a pleasure to shed the cloak of leadership, if only for an evening. When the skin of neat wine the men were passing among themselves came round to him, he took a deep and thankful draft. Strong and sour, the wine lit a fire in his belly that warmed his heart and made him feel like singing.

What a tale he would have to tell to Arthur! Failure in

council, the murder of an Old One, the prospect of public de-
nunciation of the High King's sister, and the execution of a
blameless man—all of it rescued at the last moment by the actions of four brave women. He shook his head at the wonder
of it.

Queen Esdora and Queen Alyse had solved the council
impasse by persuading Mardoc of Guent to accept a bargain.
In exchange for Mardoc's ceding to the kingdom of Powys a
bald hill called the Giant's Seat, which lay on the border between Powys and Guent, the queens undertook to pay Banin's
compensation to the Strong Hearts for the death of Luath.
Banin was a blood relative of King Mardoc's and, like the
king, steadfastly refused to recognize the Old Ones as worthy
of a bloodprice. So great was his loathing of hillmen, Mardoc
preferred to cede territory to Powys than to pay them a bloodprice. Since Gwynedd was a wealthier kingdom than Powys,
and since the two queens had become fast friends—and would
soon be related by marriage, if camp gossip could be trusted—
Queen Alyse had agreed to pay half of Banin's bloodprice on
Powys's behalf.

That was impressive diplomacy, Sir Bedwyr thought, receiving the wineskin a second time and taking another long
swallow. In the aftermath of the hearing, the Welsh kings had
quickly agreed to Arthur's plan. With the placement of a signal tower on the Giant's Seat, the network of defensive communications was complete. No matter where the Saxons
landed, the signal could be sent from promontory to hilltop to
mountaintop throughout Wales in the time it took to eat a

meal. Now Welshmen knew that when a fire was lit on a hilltop, help would come. King Arthur would be pleased.

More amazing still was the turn of events at the hearing. Never would Bedwyr forget the sight of Guinevere of Northgallis leaping upon the bench to fly to the defense of her friend. Even in her desperation, she had remembered his plea and had not openly accused Princess Morgan. He would always remember her standing valiantly against a sea of hostile faces and giving it her best. Arthur should have seen it. It would have warmed his heart.

And who would have thought that Queen Alyse would be so eloquent an orator? She had laid bare her family's debt to Llyr in no uncertain terms; she had moved the women to tears and made the men still calling for bloodshed ashamed of themselves. She had made it possible for Sir Bedwyr to let Llyr go. But the mystery of the dagger remained. The people had left the hearing dissatisfied. Was there a thief or not? If yes, who was it? If no, how had the dagger come to be buried where Sir Bedwyr found it?

When Bedwyr returned to his tent after releasing Llyr into the custody of the Strong Hearts, questions about the dagger still weighed heavily on his mind. He was dismayed to find Princess Morgan waiting for him in the great tent, livid with fury and demanding to know what he meant by releasing the thief without punishment. She accused him of rank injustice and threatened again to refuse to marry Urien as long as Llyr went free. He argued and even pleaded with her, but it was like shooting arrows at a wall. She was impervious to reason.

It was Guinevere of Northgallis who had rescued him from this dilemma. The moment she had appeared with the ruby in her hand and Morgan's own woman in tow—another brave woman—the princess had retreated into frosty silence. The ruby, which fit perfectly into the damaged sheath, and Marcia's admission that Lord Riall had, in her own presence, given Morgan his dagger as a wedding gift, along with Marcia's confession that she had never seen an Old One near their tent, had put an end to Morgan's power over him. Bedwyr knew that Morgan knew that he would tell Arthur the entire tale if she refused to marry Urien. Arthur controlled her future. He had the power to prevent her marriage to anyone of importance and consign her to a future of anonymity. Bedwyr had not the slightest doubt now that Morgan would behave. He had seen her defeat in her eyes.

To his surprise, Guinevere suggested that since people had seen the sheath only without the gem, the stone ought not to be put back. Surely, she said, Arthur would value his ancestor's dagger with or without the sheath, and no doubt he had rubies enough. The gem itself—of Pendragon red—might be trusted to Princess Morgan to give to King Urien of Rheged, who might even gift it back to his bride of Pendragon blood.

Sir Bedwyr grinned as he recalled the frozen look on Morgan's face. To accept this gift from a girl she despised was an insult she could barely support. But she had said nothing. She wanted the ruby more.

Marcia had solved the problem of what to tell the people about the dagger. She had volunteered to act as scapegoat. Like Sir Bedwyr, she had said in front of Morgan, she found it unthinkable that King Arthur's sister should be publicly portrayed as a liar or a thief. She would prefer to be blamed for the theft herself.

Over Guinevere's wild objections, Marcia had explained. Having served Queen Ygraine from girlhood, she had grown up in the presence of beautiful objects and had developed an appreciation for them. Morgan's mutilation of the dagger had shocked her deeply. She despised Lord Riall for using the dagger as a bribe and calling it a gift, just as she despised Morgan for making a promise to him, and through him to his mother, that she had no intention of keeping. Learning from Guinevere that the Old Ones could make friendships "just like real people," she had thought it manifestly unfair that Llyr should be blamed for theft because the dagger had been found beneath the beech tree.

Marcia suggested that Sir Bedwyr blame her for the dagger's theft. After all, she was the one who was supposed to have seen the Old One near Morgan's tent. While in reality she had seen nothing, the people would believe that she had lied to cover her tracks, and they would accept her story. Folk were much more apt to believe a servant guilty of theft than someone of high, let alone royal, birth.

Guinevere had objected that Marcia had no reason for burying the dagger, and also that she had no way of knowing that the beech tree was frequented by Llyr. That she would unknowingly choose the very tree he often inhabited was too much of a coincidence for anyone to believe.

Marcia had calmly replied that once Morgan had reported the dagger stolen, any servant of hers might have expected that their quarters would be searched by Sir Bedwyr's men. She would naturally look for some place outside their tents to hide the dagger. Why not bury it in the forest near a tree that was easy to find when the search was over and she wanted to dig it up? Guinevere herself had shown her the beech tree and the cairn beneath it that very evening, as they hurried from Morgan's tent to Sir Bedwyr's. Had she spent more time walking about the encampment and its environs, she might have noticed the cairn herself. A beech tree of that size, with its pale, distinctive bark, was noticeable enough, but a beech tree with a cairn beneath it would be easy to find again. Given those circumstances, Marcia reasoned, the coincidence was not so difficult to believe. She might have done a poor job of burying the dagger, but that could be attributed to inexperience. She was a queen's handmaiden, not a gardener, and she was unused to digging in soil.

Bedwyr had been satisfied, but Guinevere had objected. Would anyone, she said with a worried glance at the frozen figure of Morgan in a corner of the tent, believe that Princess Morgan's own serving woman would betray her? And if they believed it, wouldn't they expect Princess Morgan to dismiss Marcia from her service? What excuse could be given for Marcia's continuing on to Rheged in Princess Morgan's train?

Marcia had smiled at Guinevere's innocence. Life was full of such betrayals, she had told the girl in a gentle voice, especially where money or objects of value were involved. Sir Bedwyr might as well tell the people the truth: Marcia served Queen Ygraine, not Princess Morgan, and Queen Ygraine had asked her to accompany Morgan to Rheged and stay with her until her marriage. Ygraine had also asked Marcia to keep an eye out for trouble and do what she could to protect her daughter from it. Thus, Marcia's interference with the dagger could be construed as obedience to Queen Ygraine.

Finally, Marcia had pointed out that as soon as they left for Rheged, it was very unlikely that anyone now present in Deva would ever lay eyes on her again. She would soon be forgotten, and the entire incident would be forgotten with her.

When Guinevere had objected that Marcia was risking too much, that she might expose herself to criticism and perhaps even violence by accepting the blame for Morgan's acts, Marcia had smiled and replied, "I am risking too much? My risk is nothing beside yours. My future, you see, is secured by Queen Ygraine. By taking the blame for Morgan's misdeeds I am only obeying my lady's orders. *Your* future, I'm afraid, is in the hands of Queen Alyse. A most capable woman, to be sure, but not a merciful one, by all accounts. I shudder to think what she might have done had you been caught stealing Mistress Morgan's ruby."

"But I *was* caught," the girl had objected. "You caught me."

Marcia smiled. "You hadn't come near the ruby, my dear. And you told me outright why you had come when I asked you. I saw at once that you were no thief. But, my dear, you took a monstrous risk. You gambled the reputation of Gwynedd, the honor of King Pellinore, his close alliance to King Arthur, any chance for you or your cousin to make an honorable marriage, and your own condition in life, all for the chance to save your friend. I've never seen such courage in a grown woman, never mind a child your age. I risk a beating, perhaps; you risked everything."

Marcia had made the girl a reverence, and so had Bedwyr. Princess Morgan had stalked out.

Now Bedwyr took another gulp as the wineskin came round again. Things could not have worked out better. The people had accepted Marcia's tale readily enough when he told them at the lighting of the bonfire. Morgan had retired to her tent to sulk, taking Marcia with her. If he saw bruises on that brave woman tomorrow, he would not be surprised.

He was beginning to think that Guinevere of Northgallis was quite an unusual girl—brave, intelligent, loyal to a fault, and a very good friend to have, especially in a tight spot. If she were a boy, he'd speak to her parents about sending her to Arthur for warrior training. She had the makings of a first-rate Companion. He wondered what Queen Alyse had in mind for her future.

The girl was certainly popular with the crowd around the bonfire tonight. They had greeted her with shouts of appreciation when she reappeared at dinner, and later, when the singing started—the Welsh were always singing; even the most stonehearted among them were blessed with voices—they had persuaded her to join them. Sir Bedwyr had never heard singing that pleased him more. She was better than good—even the men quieted to hear her.

"Haven't you heard the Lark of Gwynedd before?" he had overheard one man ask his neighbor. "Why, she sang for me when I got back from the battle of Caer Eden with my leg still festering. Cured me, she did, in a single day, just by the sound of her voice." The battle of Caer Eden had been fought four years ago. And still that Welshman remembered her.

"Sir Bedwyr."

A hand came down on Sir Bedwyr's shoulder and he jumped. "My lord Merlin! You're back."

"Apparently," said the wizard. "I beg pardon for intruding on the celebrations, but I must speak to you a moment."

Sir Bedwyr waved an arm. "At your service, m'lord. Where've you been?"

"With the Old Ones. Has the council concluded?"

"All wrapped up. Everything agreed upon. I've got everyone's mark to prove it. We break camp tomorrow," he added with satisfaction. "In three days we'll be in Rheged."

"Good man. That's excellent news."

"Got the dagger, too, just as you predicted. Do you want to take it to Arthur, m'lord, or shall I?"

A shadow passed across Merlin's face. "You take it to him."

"Be a pleasure." Sir Bedwyr nodded. "I've a lot to tell him. No, not about Morgan. I believe I'll let that be. She's Urien's headache now." He smiled and jerked his head toward a group of Welshmen gathered in song. Above their rich voices floated a lyrical soprano that lifted Sir Bedwyr's heart. "But I know he'd like to hear about *that*."

Merlin touched a hand to his forehead as if it ached. "Bedwyr, I have a favor to ask. The Old Ones have come to pay their respects to the girl and join the celebration. With your permission."

Wide-eyed and suddenly sober, Sir Bedwyr rose to his feet. "They're here now?"

"In the woods beyond." Merlin paused. "It's Samhain Eve. You lit a bonfire."

Sir Bedwyr, who like his Roman ancestors worshipped Mithras, a god of light born in the civilized East, recalled the ancient practices of the older, native race of Britons. The feast of Samhain marked the completion of the harvest, the end of the growing season, and the beginning of the dark half of the year. A bonfire was lit as a symbol of community, and singing, dancing, and wilder revelries took place around the sacred fire as people joined together to prepare for winter.

Sir Bedwyr gulped. "The men have their weapons on them. It's the last night and I thought—I didn't ban them. It's not a council meeting."

The enchanter shrugged. "Lack of weapons never stopped a fight. But the Old Ones come in peace, and your men are singing. There will be no trouble."

Sir Bedwyr did not know whether Merlin spoke from fore-knowledge or considered opinion, but his intention was clear. With an effort, the sobered knight drew the cloak of leadership across his shoulders once again. "I'll come with you to welcome them."

"We'll be under the beech tree," Merlin said. "Bring her with you."

Sir Bedwyr noticed with a lack of surprise that neither of them had referred to Guinevere by name. There had been no need; they each knew, and knew that the other knew, who she was.

*   *   *

Guinevere followed Sir Bedwyr into the woods. It was dark out of reach of the bonfire, but the moon was full, and it was easy enough to find the way. She walked eagerly beside him, matching her stride to his. She was going to see Llyr. He had returned, Sir Bedwyr said, and he had brought his friends with him to celebrate around the Samhain fire.

She wanted to make sure that Llyr had recovered from his ordeal. She had hoped to see him when she and Marcia hurried to Bedwyr's tent after the hearing, but Sir Bedwyr had already released him. She hoped he would understand her speaking out in his defense, and that it was his own silence that had made it necessary.

Sir Bedwyr came to a halt before the beech tree. The woods around them, starkly shadowed in black and white, looked empty.

Sir Bedwyr bowed. "Prince Merlin."

Even after he spoke the name, it was moments before Guinevere could distinguish a face above what she had taken for a shadow.

"Sir Bedwyr. I have the honor to present to you Bran, leader of the White Foot of Snow Mountain."

Figures took shape in the moonlight and moved forward: Bran, Alia, and behind them a host of Strong Hearts. Guinevere's eyes searched for Llyr but could not find him.

"Princess," Sir Bedwyr said, "these folk would like to meet you. They have been hearing much about you."

She curtsied politely. "I would be honored to meet them."

The Strong Hearts came forward one by one, giving her their names and their descent, until they were all gathered about her. She understood that they had come to see She With Hair of Light, and she bore their stares with patience. Tonight, the prophecy mattered less than ever. *But where was Llyr?*

Finally, Bran and Alia came up to her. Bran looked so much like an older version of Llyr that Guinevere warmed to him instantly.

"Thank you, Gwenhwyfar, for your patience with our people," he said in Mountain Welsh. "I know you do not like being She With Hair of Light."

"I don't mind, for the sake of the Strong Hearts. I owe them a debt of gratitude. They sacrificed one of their own to protect Llyr."

"For this I, too, owe them a great debt. And to you, for preserving Llyr from harm. My son has many protections, but yours means most to him."

Guinevere colored and dipped her knee. "I am very glad to meet Llyr's honored father," she said. "And I apologize for the wrongs my people have done to yours. There should be no need for protections between us."

Alia smiled at Guinevere as Bran withdrew to join Bedwyr and Merlin. "I also thank you, Gwenhwyfar. For Llyr's life. I warned our leader, Bran, that you possessed such power, but I am not certain he believed me."

"Alia," Guinevere said in an urgent whisper, "where is he?"

Alia's smile faded. "He could not come."

"Why not? Is he hurt? Has he not returned from the Otherworld?"

Alia sucked in her breath. "So. You knew he had begun the journey."

"*Where is he?*"

"In the woods. Alone. It is his choice." Alia paused. "In a person's life there are many small moments, and a few very big moments that one remembers always."

Guinevere nodded. "Yes."

"There have been many big moments for Llyr in a very short time," she said, carefully choosing her words. "His journey away from you, away from us, was the biggest moment of all. It takes time to recover from such a journey."

"I understand. But we break camp tomorrow and leave for home. Will he not be coming with us?"

Alia gazed up at her with a worried frown. "Gwenhwyfar, I do not know. He speaks to no one but the Master."

"The Master? Who's that?"

Alia nodded toward Merlin and Bedwyr. "The seer."

"Merlin?" gasped Guinevere. "Merlin is the one who risked Llyr's life in the first place by forbidding him to speak in his own defense!"

"Yes," agreed Alia. "The Master sent him on the journey, and the Master is the only one who can help him back."

"He had no right to take that risk. It could have meant Llyr's life!"

Alia smiled. "That was the point, I think."

"*What?*"

"The Master needed to see what you would do."

Guinevere stared at Alia. "What *I* would do?"

Alia raised her shoulders and let them fall. "He was seeking for something he had to know."

Guinevere recoiled, and Alia reached out to touch her arm. "Let it be, Gwenhwyfar. He knows who you are. Trust him; his powers are great. He will bring Llyr back, in time."

When Sir Bedwyr led the Old Ones to the bonfire, Guinevere withdrew to her tent. Her celebratory mood had vanished. *He was seeking for something he had to know.* She recalled only too well the power of the man who had searched her mind a month ago. *He knows who you are.* Did Merlin the Enchanter want to know something about *her*? Something he had tried and failed to find once before, at the presentation? Something worth Llyr's life to him? Would he try again?

He knows who you are. The very idea chilled her to the bone.

To Sir Bedwyr's relief, no trouble arose when the Old Ones joined the crowd around the bonfire. They shared their skins of fermented honey with the men, who accepted this offering readily enough and in return shared their roast fowl and wine. Even without a common language, the Old Ones joined in the music-making and exchanged favorite songs with their enemies of the afternoon.

The Welsh kings led the celebrations. They excelled at drinking and feasting. Their queens did not retire early, as was the custom, but appeared as ready as the men to carouse until dawn. Queen Alyse and Queen Esdora rejoiced together, and

Prince Trevor, his arm firmly about young Elaine of Gwynedd, appeared the merriest of them all.

Just on midnight, a lookout came running to Sir Bedwyr and reported a rider coming fast along the Roman road. Sir Bedwyr signaled to two of his men to follow and hurried after the scout to the meadow's entrance. A single rider on the road at night meant a courier, and a courier coming at speed meant dire news. The thunder of galloping hooves drew closer, and a dark shape flew out of the darkness at them. Moonlight struck Sir Bedwyr's raised sword, and the rider pulled up sharply.

"Ho!" the courier cried. "I'm a King's man. I seek Sir Bedwyr of Brydwell!"

"Sagramor? It's Bedwyr. What news, man?"

Sagramor slipped from his stallion's back and held the blowing horse on a loose rein. "Sir Bedwyr." He bent his knee and delivered his message with shining eyes. "My lord, I bring the best news in the world. My lord, the High Queen is with child!"

The words took a moment to sink in. With a whoop of joy, Sir Bedwyr yanked the messenger to his feet and grabbed him in a bear hug. "Is it true? Is it known for certain?"

"Aye," laughed Sagramor. "So the physicians say."

"Does Arthur know?"

"Not yet. How could he? He's still in York." Sagramor grinned. "I'm sent to bid you light a bonfire for the High King's heir, but I see you are before me."

Bedwyr slung his arm around the youth's shoulders. "We are indeed. Come join us. You'll find a strange gathering around this Samhain blaze, but I'll wager all of them will be glad to hear your news!"

But Bedwyr was mistaken. There was one person in that crowd who did not raise a cheer at the joyful announcement. Elaine of Gwynedd shrugged off Trevor's embrace and ran from the fire into the cloaking darkness of the woods. There, Princess Morgan found her an hour later, still awash in tears and desperate sorrow.

CHAPTER THIRTY-SIX

Morgan's Revenge

The tent flap opened, and Ailsa slipped inside. "Gwen. Gwen, sit up, child. I've been looking for you everywhere. There's news."

Obediently, Guinevere dragged her aching head from her pillow and sat up. Ailsa sank to her knees beside her. "Gwen, is anything wrong? Why are you in here all alone? I thought you were with Sir Bedwyr."

"I was. Never mind. What's happened?"

"Elaine and Prince Trevor are betrothed. It was concluded at the bonfire."

Guinevere smiled, although her head was pounding. "At last. I'm so glad. Elaine gave her consent, then? When is the wedding?"

"Not for a year or two. Elaine gave in with an ill grace, but she gave in. Queen Alyse and Queen Esdora have some plan afoot for an alliance between their two kingdoms and North-gallis. Queen Alyse made it plain to Elaine that it was in Gwynedd's best interest for her to consent. Between you and me, I think Elaine actually likes Prince Trevor. She put up a show of tears, but in the end she agreed to it."

"And Prince Trevor?"

"All smiles. Says as soon as he can ride, he'll come to Gwynedd and sweep her off her feet." Ailsa laughed. "He's a fine talker, that one. They say he'll be king before long. Even the Old Ones like him. I saw him talking to them for quite a spell. But the *best* news, Gwen, came with a courier straight from the royal quarters in Caerleon. The High Queen is with child! King Arthur will have an heir next summer, God willing, and secure his line. We are bidden to feast and make merry." She paused. "The Old Ones are celebrating with us."

"Are they? I'm glad."

"Can't you join us, dear? What's the matter?"

Guinevere smiled halfheartedly. "It's only a black mood, Ailsa. It will pass. But in the meantime, I'm best alone."

Ailsa took the hint and withdrew to her pallet in a corner. She had celebrated more than she was used to and was soon asleep. Guinevere lay on her back, holding her hands to her head and looking up at the ceiling of tent cloth. Even without a lamp, it was not dark. The moonlight was bright enough to cast shadows, and every torch in camp had been lit in celebration. The sounds of song and laughter from the bonfire drifted by on the night wind and dulled fear into weariness. She waited, yearning for the oblivion of sleep.

Guinevere jerked awake as the tent flap opened. Someone stood, hesitating, just inside the tent. It wasn't Llyr, nor was it a tall man in a dark cloak. It was Elaine.

Guinevere sat up. "Elaine?" she whispered. "Come in, come in. I'm awake."

She did not know why she felt compelled to whisper. Ailsa was asleep, snoring softly, and would not be easily disturbed. The bonfire still roared and snapped, the singing still went on, and the hum of voices continued unabated. But it was darker now. The moon had sunk below the trees, and some of the torches had gone out. It felt like the middle of the night.

Elaine moved soundlessly toward her and sank down on her pallet. "I was hoping you were asleep." She whispered the words as if she, too, were afraid to speak.

"Why?"

Elaine shrugged. She looked pale and unhappy, but it was difficult to gauge her mood in the dimness of the tent.

"I heard about your betrothal to Trevor. Aren't you happy about it, Laine?"

Elaine looked away. "Trevor's all right," she said. "But I'm not going to marry him."

"Do you mean you're *not* betrothed?"

Elaine sighed wearily. "I am. Mother insisted on it. But Morgan says not to worry: the marriage won't take place."

Guinevere gaped at her. "*Morgan?* You're listening to Morgan again?"

"I've been to her tent."

A thrill of warning ran up Guinevere's spine. "Why?"

Elaine shrugged. "I ran away from Trevor when the courier

came—I was weeping, and Morgan found me. She said not to worry; I wouldn't have to marry Trevor. She said she had looked in her black bowl after the hearing and seen a greater future for me."

"And you believed her?"

"Well," Elaine said defensively, "I wanted sympathy. You had disappeared and, well, Morgan was there."

"And what future did she see for you?"

"She said the wheel of time was turning, and those who were not ready for their futures could be destroyed by them. She said it was always best to be prepared."

"Morgan said that? It sounds remarkably like sense."

"Listen, Gwen." Elaine turned to her with sudden intensity and held both of Guinevere's hands tight in her own. "Morgan was in a foul mood tonight. I shouldn't have gone to her tent; I shouldn't have followed her into the stillroom. But I couldn't stop myself. Something drew me in, something unseen and powerful. You have to believe that. I was frightened, and I was trapped."

Guinevere nodded, remembering the menacing darkness in Morgan's stillroom. "I understand."

"Do you?" Elaine gulped. "I had to listen as she looked into her bowl and told me things I didn't want to hear. I couldn't turn away. I couldn't move. She had seen our fates, she said, and was bound by the Goddess to warn us of them. She called herself Cassandra." Elaine paused. "I don't know why."

"Remember Iakos teaching us about the Trojan War? Cassandra was the daughter of the King of Troy who warned her people not to trust Greeks bearing gifts. She foresaw the

Trojan Horse, but no one believed her. That was her fate, to be a prophet of doom whom nobody ever believed."

Elaine shivered, and Guinevere squeezed her hand. "Tell me, Laine. Was Morgan a prophet of doom? What did she say?"

"I—I am to marry a great king, too—greater than Trevor, but not so great as Arthur. I will bear him a son whose name will be long remembered, and—and"—her voice caught on a stifled sob—"I will die in a foreign land."

Guinevere saw the shine of tears on her face and hugged her close, stroking her hair. "You're twelve years old," she whispered, "and death is a long way off. Besides, consider the source. Morgan is nothing if not a liar."

Elaine shook her head. "She saw the truth. I know she did. Because of—"

"Because of what?"

"Something else she saw that I know is true."

"What was that?"

"Never mind."

"Something about me? I'm not surprised. Tell me."

"I don't want to. And you don't want to know."

Guinevere managed a smile. "That's probably true. But you'll never sleep without telling me, so you might as well begin."

Elaine hesitated. "If you're sure."

Guinevere shivered and pulled the blanket more tightly around her. "Go ahead. I'm ready."

One night, Elaine said, an old woman dressed in rags came down from the hills in a fierce spring storm and begged entrance into the castle of a king. The guard at the door thought she wanted shelter and, as the king's hospitality to the old and infirm was well known, he let her in and directed her to the kitchens. But the old woman went instead to the king's hall, where the king was gathered with his men before a roaring fire. They were celebrating the impending birth of the king's child, for his young queen was laboring upstairs and from time to time the midwife sent him news of her progress.

Guinevere hugged her knees to stop her shaking. So this was the true tale that had convinced Elaine of Morgan's fidelity as a seer. She knew it well. It had been told to her often enough throughout her childhood. The king in the hall was Leodegrance of Northgallis, her father, and his young queen upstairs was Elen of Gwynedd, her mother.

The old woman approached the king, Elaine continued in a whisper so soft it was barely audible, and made him a prophecy in return for a place at his fire: *This night shall be born a daughter who shall rule the mightiest in the land. She will be the fairest beauty the world has known and the highest lady in all the kingdoms of Britain. Her name will live on in the minds of men for beyond a thousand years. Through her will you reach glory.*

"Yes," croaked Guinevere. "I've heard it before. So have you. So has Morgan, obviously. What of it?"

Elaine looked away. "There's more."

The breath left Guinevere's body. She knew there was more to the prophecy, but no one, not even Ailsa, had ever told her what it was. Now, like a fool, she had asked for it. Squeezing her eyes shut, she bowed her head against her updrawn knees and braced herself.

But she will bring you pain, King, before ever she brings you joy. Beloved of kings, she shall betray her king and be herself betrayed. Hers will be a fate no one will envy. She will be the white shadow over the brightest glory of Britain.

Silence fell in the tent, but the words rang loud in Guinevere's head. *White shadow. Gwenhwyfar.* A dark spot on a bright glory. "Oh no," she breathed, helpless against tears. "O dear God in heaven, help me!"

"For shame!" Ailsa cried, rising from her pallet. "Whatever possessed you, Lady Elaine?"

Elaine sobbed. "I had to tell her. Morgan said it was a fate she could avoid if she learned it in time."

"Princess Morgan!" Ailsa crossed herself. "What do you want to be listening to her for? Hasn't she caused enough trouble?" Ailsa took Guinevere in her arms and rocked with her, back and forth. "There, there," she crooned. "There, there."

Guinevere barely heard her. The whole world had withdrawn from her, leaving her in solitude. As her tutor, Iakos, had once said, whenever the gods granted a human being a great gift—such as power, fame, wisdom, or beauty—they also implanted in that person a great flaw, to ensure against hubris. All these years, the people who loved her had protected her from knowledge of her own flaw.

That it was the worst flaw she could imagine only made it more likely to be true. It made her words in Llyr's defense— her appeal to reason, her provoking other people's consciences to action—seem like the ultimate in hypocrisy. Who was she to admonish them, she who would one day betray her king? Who was she to rescue the Old Ones from annihilation, she who must one day be a traitor to their cause? She shut her eyes tight against the horror of it.

She told herself that Morgan had invented the tale to hurt her and that Morgan was nothing if not false. Yet all her life, Guinevere had known that there were others who knew the full extent of the prophecy. She had felt the weight of their pity like a cloak of shame.

Last spring, in the presence of the One Who Hears, she had accepted the first part of the prophecy. To deny it meant denying all the efforts of the Old Ones to protect her. But how was it possible to accept the second part? To accept that she would grow up to be false, like Morgan? Could a person really change so much? Could she grow up to be the kind of woman she now despised? It was a terrifying thought. If her name was to be remembered, would it be as a betrayer? Was her path through the coming years to be a lonely one, without friends or trusted companions? Her head ached, her mind spun, and she clung to Ailsa for strength.

Time passed. Grannic came in and made tea that no one drank. Elaine went to bed and cried herself quietly to sleep. Gradually, the camp fell silent. The bonfire died to embers. The moon sank out of sight. The stars dimmed. And still Guinevere huddled in Ailsa's arms, her knees tucked against her chest, her head bent, staring open-eyed at a future she abhorred.

CHAPTER THIRTY-SEVEN

Partings

Before dawn, Guinevere finally arose, dressed in her riding clothes, and went to the horse lines. Zephyr was already tense and excited. Although it was early, camp was bustling. Servants stoked breakfast fires to life from last night's embers, and Sir Bedwyr's men worked to dismantle the High King's tent. Guinevere approached the filly with a handful of grain swiped from the grooms' stores and stroked Zephyr's neck while the horse lipped the offering from her palm.

"Good morning, my sweet girl," she crooned, scratching the filly's ears. "It's damp and misty now, but I'm sure it will clear. We're heading home today, Zephyr. Back to your stable, back to Stannic, back to the hills we love. Perhaps forever."

The filly nickered. Dawn broke lavender-pink across the

misty meadow, and birdsong filled the air. Nearby, a voice said softly, "Blessed be the dawning, Gwenhwyfar."

She whipped around to see Llyr standing with Thatch's reins in his hand. He looked different to her now: older, thinner, and without the eagerness in his eyes she was used to seeing.

"Blessed be the dawning, Llyr. I'm glad to see you. Have you broken your fast?"

He smiled, and at once looked more like himself. "I will break my fast with the Strong Hearts. They camped yonder in the woods." He paused. "Something is the matter, Gwenhwyfar? You are not the same today as yesterday."

"No," she said roughly. "I am not the same."

He waited, patient and silent, for the confidence he expected from her. She must have changed, she thought, for she did not want to tell him. But his worried eyes persuaded her to answer.

"Last night, I learned the second part of the prophecy."

His gaze sharpened, and she saw that he understood. He, too, had protected her. "How?"

"Princess Morgan told Elaine, and Elaine told me."

"Morgan le Fey," he muttered, and made the sign against evil. "A wicked woman."

"Probably," she said wearily.

Llyr walked up to her and placed his hand over hers on the filly's neck. "Gwenhwyfar, prophecies are made by gods, but they are given to men to put into words. They are not always the right words. They do not always mean what you think they mean."

"What else can betrayal mean but going back on one's promise?"

He had no answer, and she continued bitterly, "The One Who Hears showed me that I must accept the prophecy for good or ill. If I have accepted the first part, I must accept the last part, also. Someday . . . I will betray my king." She choked on the words.

Llyr's soft brown eyes, as large and beautiful as a deer's, were full of compassion. "A prophecy is like a coin. It has two sides. Up and down. Yes and no. The god smiles while he strikes. The goddess cries while she gives birth. The One Who Hears asked you to accept your destiny, whatever it is. But because you have heard the prophecy from a person's mouth does not mean that you understand it. Only the gods know what is to come."

Guinevere tried for a smile and failed. "Then I'm still in the dark? Is that meant as comfort?"

"You cannot stop being yourself because you fear the future. If you do, you are vanquished already."

"What should I do, then? Ignore it? That's impossible."

"Put it in its place. It has no power over you but what you give it."

She looked at him curiously. The One Who Hears had given her the same advice.

"Be who you are," said Llyr. "Not who you think you must be. If you do that, no prophecy can force you to do what it is not in you to do."

Her heart lightened. "Do you mean I can make the prophecy false?"

He shook his head. "Prophecies are not false, but the way a person interprets them may be. If you continue to be who you are, you will not betray. At least not in the way which frightens you so."

"In—in some other way, then?"

He shrugged. "In some way, perhaps, that you and the ones you love do not see as betrayal, but that others do. There is always another way of looking at a prophecy."

She leaned forward and kissed his cheek. "Thank you, Llyr. I hadn't thought of that."

He winked at her. "There is still a use for your guardian, yes?"

"Yes. Definitely yes."

He gazed at her with a host of emotions in his eyes. "Gwenhwyfar, I must speak from my heart. I was—I have made many mistakes. About you. About me."

"Llyr, please—"

"I dreamed I could . . . I am one of Earth's Beloved, and you are Other. I forgot that. I must ask your pardon."

Guinevere lowered her eyes. "Of course you have my pardon. If I have yours for speaking out at your hearing without your permission?"

He smiled. "I am glad you did. The Master was pleased, but not as pleased as I was."

As he started to turn away, she said quickly, "Don't leave yet. Aren't you coming home with us?"

"Of course I am," he said gently.

"Then where are you going now?"

"To win a wager," he said with a sly grin. "The Strong

Hearts do not believe that one of Earth's Beloved can ride a pony."

Guinevere laughed. It seemed like the first time in years. "Showing off, are you? Just remember that if the Strong Hearts haven't broken their fast yet, they'll be hungry. Don't let them eat him."

Llyr pretended to scowl. "Primitive savages! I will show them a better use for ponies." He raised a hand in parting. "Light with thee walk, Gwenhwyfar."

She returned his salute. "Dark from thee flee, Llyr, son of Bran."

She watched him disappear into the woods, then slid her arms around her filly's neck and rested her cheek against the warm, smooth coat. Llyr was back—all the way back—and their friendship had somehow miraculously returned to what it had been all summer. It was amazing what comfort that brought her. She could even begin to regard the wretched prophecy with a sense of balance. The future would unfold as it would. That was beyond her control. But she could control her actions in the meantime. She could be who she was and let the future take care of itself. It did not seem quite so dreadful when put like that.

She gave Zephyr a last pat and was turning to leave when someone called her name.

"Lady Guinevere."

Merlin the Enchanter stood at the edge of the wood, watching.

Her arm slipped back around the filly's neck. She wondered how long he had been standing there.

"Prince Merlin. Good morning." She dipped him a curtsy.

He bowed and came toward her. As he neared, the noises of the morning faded into silence. When he halted an arm's length away, all she could hear was the fearful thudding of her heart.

"Lady Guinevere, I have come to beg your pardon."

His eyes were so dark they were almost black, and she had heard it said that no man could read them.

"F-for what, my lord?"

"For my presumption. After our first meeting, which I am ashamed to recall, I have avoided your company. I apologize for this."

"There's no need to apologize," she said swiftly. "I didn't seek you out, either."

Amusement warmed his features, taking years off his age. For an instant she saw in his face the comely youth he might once have been.

"That's not quite what I meant," he said, "but it's close enough. I avoided you because there was something I needed to know that only you could tell me, and I realized, after that first mistake, that I would need your permission to seek it. That is the second thing I have come for. I ask it now."

She stared at him, unbelieving. He could not possibly mean what she thought he meant. "My permission? To do what, my lord?"

"To find out what I failed to discover at the presentation."

She swallowed. "And by the same means?"

"With your permission."

His request was brutally forthright. The filly tensed, flicking back an ear.

"Why did you persuade Llyr to keep silent at his own hearing?"

"Ah." He seemed pleased by the question. "That's perceptive of you. Because I wanted to see if you would defend him, and what the others would do if you did."

She frowned. "Why?"

"I am the High King's counselor. What happens in his domain is my concern. Not only the outcome of council meetings, but the small doings of every day. It is my task to know what his people think; what they do; what they want, expect, and fear. The King can't be everywhere at once. I am his eyes and ears away from court."

It was too long an answer. Instinctively, Guinevere knew he was hiding something.

"I know nothing about those things. What can I tell you that others can't?"

Merlin paused. "You can tell me something about yourself."

"Why not just ask me?"

Something flickered behind the black eyes, something sharp and dangerous. "Because, princess, it is something that you do not yet know."

She sank back against the filly's side, trembling. Zephyr rolled an eye, but stood still.

"Is it necessary?" She was thinking of Sir Bedwyr's dream, the warrior's dream, and of Stannic's silver coin. "For the Kingdom?"

Merlin spoke gently. "I regret the necessity, princess."

She drew one deep breath and then another. *Be yourself.* She put prophecies and kingdoms and wizards out of her mind and concentrated merely on the present. The filly shifted, forcing her upright.

"Very well. What must I do?"

The enchanter's relief was visible. "Look at me," he said.

This time, it was easy. There was no demand, no arrogance, and no fear, only warmth, care, and a cat's-paw touch of tenderness.

"Thank you," he murmured at length, and made her a little bow.

She shook herself awake to find that she had learned something about *him*. "Prince Merlin, you are disappointed."

He smiled faintly. "It is not your doing. You cannot change your fate, my dear, and neither can I. Go on your way in peace."

But that was not enough. She could not let him leave with the burning question still unanswered.

"My lord Merlin!"

He turned back. "Yes?"

"Is it true I will betray? Will it . . . matter very much?"

"To some it will; to others not." He smiled sadly. "*Betrayal* is perhaps too harsh a word. Glory is less bright when shared among a crowd."

She did not understand him, but she saw all too well his eagerness to be gone. He was already turning away for the second time.

"You—you do not hate me for it?"

He paused and shook his head. "Glory and greatness are built on love. I would not avert what is coming, even if I could. What will be, will be. Let it be so."

He turned and vanished into the forest.

She pressed her face into the filly's mane. She could not begin to guess what he meant. Betrayal *is too harsh a word.* What other word could there be? If she was always going to be faithful, why hadn't he said so?

"Lady Guinevere!"

She whirled, startling Zephyr. But it was only Sir Bedwyr, come to say good-bye. "Good morning, Sir Bedwyr."

"Good morning, Guinevere. They told me I'd find you in the horse lines. You'd best hurry if you want anything to eat. They've almost finished breakfast."

She realized with a start that the sun was up and shining, the grass was nearly dry, and the wagons were all but loaded. Where had the morning gone? A few moments ago, it was not yet dawn.

"I—I didn't know it was so late."

"I came to thank you for your help, your inestimable and valuable help, in defending Llyr. And in keeping Morgan's name out of it. I won't forget it. If your aunt ever brings you and your cousin to court, you'll have a friend in me, I promise you."

She flushed. After her conversations with Llyr and Merlin, talking to Sir Bedwyr was a breath of spring air. "Thank you, Sir Bedwyr."

"The marriage to Urien is going forward as planned, I'm pleased to say."

"Did Morgan threaten to call it off?" The question was out of her mouth before she had time to stop it. It was sheer effrontery to ask, but Sir Bedwyr laughed.

"Of course. How else does a woman wield power but through the men who need her? She'll find her match in Urien, I expect. He's not likely to put up with handling such as that." He grinned. "He won't have to."

Guinevere smiled. "I begin to feel sorry for her."

"Don't. She'll lie in the bed she makes, as we all do. Speaking of marriage, I hear that your cousin is betrothed to Trevor of Powys."

"Yes."

"The news surprised me. You were the one who was always with him. No hard feelings?"

"None at all."

Sir Bedwyr smiled. "I'm glad to hear it. He's a bright lad. He spent half the night talking to Bran around the bonfire. Apparently, he's organizing a network of communication with the Old Ones. No one knows how the clans get and distribute news so fast, but they always seem to know what's going on. Trevor plans to put Powys in the middle of all that." He glanced at her quickly. "He befriended the Old Ones in Powys as a boy. That's why I thought . . . Well, he's a clever lad. I told him to come see Arthur as soon as he can ride. Kings live on information. There's a place for him at court."

"That must have pleased him very much."

Sir Bedwyr frowned as he gave the filly a farewell pat. "You've a good horse here. It's odd, but she looks like one of

Arthur's. I didn't know King Pellinore bred such stock in Gwynedd."

Guinevere explained that Zephyr had been bred in the High King's stables, but that King Arthur had given her to King Pellinore last spring. King Pellinore, in turn, had given the filly to her.

Sir Bedwyr looked amazed. "That's quite a gift. As a rule, Lancelot doesn't allow the mares to go. I'd have loved to see his face when he learned Arthur gave this one away!"

"Who?" Guinevere asked. "Is that the knight who trained her? What did you say his name was?"

"Sir Lancelot of Lanascol. It's a kingdom in Less Britain. He's the heir."

"And King Arthur's master of horse?"

"Aye, and such a one with horseflesh you never saw."

"Oh, Sir Bedwyr, would you do me a kindness?"

"Anything within my power, lady, after all you've done for me."

"Would you thank Sir Lancelot for me? For the filly? I have wanted so long to know who taught her such beautiful manners. She's so quick and easy to sit, I knew she'd been handled by a master. Will you thank him for me?"

"With pleasure," said Sir Bedwyr with a smile. "Perhaps one day you can ride her to court yourself and show her to him."

She took his arm as they started back to camp.

"Sir Lancelot of Lanascol," she repeated. "Why, it sounds like singing."

CHAPTER THIRTY-EIGHT

Snowfall

On a snowy evening a week after Christmas, Guinevere stood alone by the western parapet of King Pellinore's castle, gazing out toward the black, invisible sea. It was a still night, still enough to hear the soft hiss of falling snowflakes, still enough to slow the swift beating of her heart.

What was it Llyr had told her Merlin the Enchanter had foreseen? Half against her will, she dredged up the words: *Woe betide the dragon in his lair, the mage in his conceit, and the innocent in his womb. The dark time comes.* He had been right. The dark time had come. A courier had arrived that very evening with the news.

After Princess Morgan's wedding to Urien of Rheged, Merlin the Enchanter had vanished. At first, no one worried, for Merlin had a reputation for disappearing. This time he did not come back. Both Urien and Arthur sent troops to search for him, and in the end joined the search themselves, but no sign of him was found. Desperate with anxiety for the man who had been more than a father to him, King Arthur had only been called away by a more dire emergency at home. His young wife, pregnant with his heir, had begun to bleed.

For three long weeks, the courier said, the King had sat at her bedside and watched in a passion of helplessness her agonizing struggle for life. When the physicians could not stop the bleeding, he had thrown wide the doors of Caerleon to any seer, witch, or herbalist who volunteered to try. All had failed. On Christmas Day, Arthur's nineteenth birthday, the young Queen died in her husband's arms. Their tiny son died with her.

Arthur shut himself away. He would see no one. He fasted; he prayed; he mourned; he grew cantankerous in grief. He allowed no one to console him. If Merlin had been there, the courier said, he would have known how to deal with the King, but Merlin was gone. Arthur would let no one near him, not even his closest friends. The King was utterly alone for the first time in his life. No one knew what would come of it.

Standing silent in the snow, Guinevere recalled the prophecy of Morgan's that had terrified her so when she thought it referred to Queen Alyse: *The Queen shall die of what she carries in her.* Now, alas, its meaning was all too clear. She grieved for the young girl who had given her life for the King's heir, and she wished with all her heart that Elaine and Queen Alyse could share her grief.

Guinevere shivered. She had come up here into the dark,

into the silence, to escape the secret celebration taking place below. Elaine's betrothal to Trevor of Powys had come to an end with the courier's news. Ambition had revived in both mother and daughter the instant they learned of the young Queen's death. Never mind that there would be consequences to breaking the betrothal. Never mind that Powys might never be an ally. Never mind that King Arthur was sunk in grief and in no mind to marry again. He was unwed. To them, that was all that mattered.

Their joy had sickened her, and she had come up here to escape it. Here, in silence, she could grieve for the King in his tortured isolation. She could grieve for the unknown fate of Merlin the Enchanter, who had dealt fairly with her in the end. But most of all, she grieved for the girl who had died of her child, as Guinevere's own mother had died of hers.

She gazed out at the veil of snow that blurred her view and wondered about the future. All her life she had been used to living in a safe and stable land. Horror stories of Saxon landings and people running for their lives into the hills, abandoning their babes, their sick, their slow—these were tales of the past, like stories of faeries and shape-shifters. She had become used to peace. She barely remembered anything else.

Now, for the first time, the future of the Britons seemed less certain. Not that Saxons were likely to land on their own shores any time soon, but they landed often enough in the south and east to keep the King fighting upwards of three campaigns a year. She could not imagine what it must take to maintain such a fierce pursuit. It was easier to imagine what might happen if the pursuit should fail. Sir Bedwyr had hinted that all their fortunes might depend on the marriage of Arthur's sister. If the alliance of kingdoms was so fragile, what would happen to it if Arthur fell in battle? Or ceased to win? Or lost his closest advisor? His wife? His child? The Saxons were coming in floods. The Saxon tide, they called it. If King Arthur faltered, the future might be very different from the peaceful past she had known.

She had wondered about this often in the last two months. Things had been different since she'd come home. She had not been able to slip back into the routines of daily life with the same sense of comfort as before. Something had changed, inside and outside.

That afternoon, she had gone alone to Queen Alyse's chamber to look at her image in the mirror of polished bronze. In the gray gloom of a room shuttered tight against the wind, a trio of flickering candles had provided the only light. Even so, her image had startled her. She had not recognized herself. Ten months ago, the last time she had been there— dragged by Elaine—she had been twelve years old. Now she was nearing fourteen. She told herself that change was to be expected.

But the change went deeper than physical transformation. She longed for different company. She missed her conversations with Trevor, Queen Esdora, and Sir Bedwyr. They had treated her like one of them. They had listened to her. They had wanted her opinion. They had made her feel adult. Here at home she was the queen's ward again, and unquestioning obedience was her foremost duty. As difficult as it was to be back in this isolated corner of Wales with little news of the outside world, it was more difficult by far to be without companionship of mind.

Guinevere pulled the hood of her cloak tighter around her face. A little wind had sprung up, flinging the snowflakes sideways as they fell. It was time to go in, but still she lingered. She felt her future close upon her but unseen, like the sea behind the blowing veil of snow. She was going to have to learn to come to terms with that young woman in the mirror, and that was going to take a deal of courage. For the face she had seen emerging in the shimmering surface of the bronze would soon be one people would not forget.

How she was to live with beauty, she did not yet know. It was part of the prophecy, but like the rest of the prophecy, it was too overwhelming to take in all at once. She would follow Llyr's advice and face it a little every day—as the High King in his solitude faced the loss of his wife and child, and as Merlin the Enchanter, if he lived, faced whatever malevolent fate had come upon him.

Day by day, step by step, life would go forward. Eventually, the veil would lift, the cold would yield to the sun's warmth, and the world would be reborn. This dark time would pass.

As she turned away from the parapet and headed for the stairs, she spared a thought for Merlin the Enchanter. What would come, would come, he had told her as he left her. And when it came, she would accept it. She had outgrown girlhood. She was ready for something else.

Let it be so.

A Note to Readers

This is the story of the girl who grew up to be King Arthur's queen. It is important to remember that this book is a work of fiction. If King Arthur existed—and this is still a matter of debate among scholars—he lived in late-fifth-century to early-sixth-century Britain (somewhere between 485 and 526 CE), not in the Middle Ages. This is the beginning of the Dark Ages, so called because we know relatively little about them. There is only one contemporaneous account of Arthur's time, as far as we know, and it does not mention him.

If Arthur lived, he lived around a hundred years after the last Roman legions pulled out of Britain, leaving the Britons to defend themselves against the invading Saxons, Picts (from Scotland), and Scots (from Ireland). Legend holds that for a short time, the invaders were held at bay by a strong war leader who united the Britons and gave them perhaps two or three decades of peace. He was called Pendragon, or "High King." Arthur's parentage, marriages, offspring, friends, and fortresses are not matters of fact but of legend.

Archaeologists have discovered that there was a brisk trade between Roman Britain and the Mediterranean, which continued even after the Romans left. I have therefore assumed that any objects used in a Roman household might have been used in a Briton one as well.

Names of characters are drawn from historical tradition (Arthur, Guinevere, Merlin, etc.), other authors of the Arthurian legend (from Sir Thomas Malory to Mary Stewart), Ronan Coghlan's excellent *Encyclopaedia of Arthurian Legends*, and my own imagination. The genealogy of "Descendants of Magnus Maximus" is entirely invented.

I am not a speaker of Welsh or Gaelic and can give you only one clue to the pronunciation of the names and place-names in the book. I am indebted to Mary Stewart (author of *The Crystal Cave*, *The Hollow Hills*, *The Last Enchantment*, and *The Wicked Day*) for the advice that the *dd* in

Gwynedd and *Gwarthgydd* is pronounced like the *th* in *them* (not like the *th* in *breath*).

Whether you are new to the Arthurian legend or an established fan, I hope you enjoy this journey into the days of King Arthur.

Acknowledgments

This is my chance to thank publicly all the people who have helped me with this book. For their patience, tolerance, and emotional support throughout, I thank my husband, Bruce; my sister, Meg; my daughters, Elizabeth, Katie, and Caroline; my friends Marian Borden, Joellen Finnie, Margie Cohen, Sheri Gipson, and Kate Delaney. They have kept me connected to the outside world while I've been living in the fifth century.

Special thanks are due to Karen Kramer, friend, writer, and teacher, for keeping me sane during periods of intense pressure, and to Deborah Hogan, friend and professional editor, for giving me invaluable feedback when *Guinevere's Gamble* was in its embryonic stages.

The transition from embryo to term was a collaborative effort. I am indebted to my excellent editors at Alfred A. Knopf, Michelle Frey and Michele Burke, for taking such care of the story and working so hard to get it right. Their critiques were precise and fair, their courtesy unfailing, and their dedication inspiring. I am extremely grateful to have such talented editors.

My thanks to the entire production staff for creating such a beautiful book. Tristan Elwell's gorgeous cover is outstanding. When I was a teen, I'd have bought any book with this cover, no matter what was inside. Thanks also to Stephanie Moss for the graceful book design. In the hands of these artists, book, cover, and story become a seamless whole.

Thanks also to Jean Naggar and her excellent team at the Jean V. Naggar Literary Agency for their support, their attention to detail, and their help with the particulars of publishing that tend to slip beneath my radar. Without them, this book would not exist.

I'd also like to thank my readers for taking an interest in Guinevere and caring what happens to her, for e-mailing me their questions and opinions, and for posting comments on the Internet. Thank you all.